Things We Never Said

A Novel by

Nick Alexander

BIGfib

Nick Alexander

Nick Alexander was born in 1964 in the UK. He has travelled widely and has lived and worked both in the UK, the USA and France where he resides today. *Things We Never Said* is his 14th fictional work. His 2015 novel, *The Other Son*, was named by Amazon as one of the best fiction titles of the year; *The Photographer's Wife* published in 2014 was a number 1 hit in both the UK and France, while *The Half-Life of Hannah* is the 4th bestselling independently published Kindle title of all time. Nick's novels have been translated into French, German, Italian, Spanish, Norwegian, Turkish and Croatian. Nick lives in the southern French Alps with his partner, three friendly cats (plus one mean one), and a few trout.

Acknowledgements

Thanks to Fay Weldon for encouraging me when it most counted. Thanks to James for sharing the anecdote which inspired me to write this novel. Thanks to Allan and Sue for their proofing skills and to Rosemary and Lolo for being the most important people on my planet. Thanks to Karen, Jenny, Tina, Diana, Annie, and everyone else who gave me feedback on this novel. It wouldn't have happened without you. Thanks to Apple for making reliable work tools and to Amazon for turning the writing of novels back into something one can actually earn a living from.

Snapshot #24

120 format, black and white. Two children are playing in a sandpit with buckets and spades. The little boy, in a woolly jumper and jeans, is staring at the camera and smiling broadly. The little girl, wearing dungarees and a sweatshirt, has her face obscured by a mop of unruly hair which has fallen forwards as she plays.

6

Prologue

The drive from the funeral parlour to the house takes place in silence. Beside Sean, April, his daughter, stares stoney-faced from the side window. They both cried abundantly during the service but, right now, are feeling more numbed than anything else. Both are thinking about the fact that they should probably say something to comfort or reassure the other but, as none of the normal formulas for filling silences work here – there's no point, for example, in asking if the other is OK when they're clearly not – they continue their journey in silence. The risk of provoking fresh floods of tears is just too high, at least until the journey is over.

On reaching the house, Maggie, one of their most faithful family friends, opens the front door. She squeezes Sean's shoulder and silently hugs April who, bracing herself against further tears, accepts the hug more rigidly than she intended.

"The food's in the lounge," she says. "And Perry's making drinks in the kitchen."

"Thanks, Mags," Sean says. "You're a star for doing all of this."

As Maggie retreats into the house, Sean removes his overcoat and hangs it on a hook in the hallway.

He hesitates between the lounge, where he can hear somewhat incongruous laughter, or the kitchen, where a stiff drink will come at the hefty cost of being forced to talk to his brother.

"Dad!" April prompts, applying gentle pressure on his elbow. "You're blocking the hallway. Let's go get a drink."

"Sure. Yes. Sorry," Sean says, moving reluctantly towards the kitchen.

"Hey," Sean's brother says, looking up as he enters. "How are you holding up?"

"Um, OK, Perry," Sean replies. "Can you make me one of those?"

Perry glances at the bottle of Bombay Sapphire in his hand. "A G & T?" he asks.

Sean nods. "With plenty of G."

"Coming up," Perry says, already starting to unscrew the lid.

"Me too, Uncle Perry," April says. "If that's OK?"

"Sure, it's like a production line, here," Perry says. To fill the silence that ensues as he mixes the drinks, he adds, "It was a nice service."

Really? Sean thinks. *Do I really have to do this?* "Yeah," he replies. "It was."

Someone squeezes Sean's elbow and, thinking that he's chosen the wrong place to stand again, he starts to apologise.

But it's just Maggie trying to comfort him. "Are you OK?" she asks, gently. "I mean, considering the circumstances, obviously. Are you as OK as can be expected?"

Sean takes a deep breath and nods. "I'm exactly as OK as can be expected," he says. "I just need a stiff drink, but Perry has that under control."

Just as he says this, Perry holds out his glass of gin and tonic. The ice cubes tinkle against the glass and Sean's mind unexpectedly flashes back to a different glass of gin and tonic held by his late wife's petite hands in the Grecian sunlight. He shakes his head as if to dislodge the memory and braces

8

himself, because, yes, there are no doubt thousands of these memories yet to come.

"How's Mum?" he asks Perry. "Have you been out there to see her recently?"

His brother nods and shrugs simultaneously. "Most weekends," he says. "And you know... She's pretty much the same. She doesn't know her arse from her elbow most of the time."

"Right," Sean says. "Of course."

"She'd still like to see you, though," Perry says.

Sean restrains a snort. His mother has never shown much sign of wanting to see him, and dementia has done little to improve the situation.

Armed with drinks, Sean and April move through to the lounge where family friends are telling each other amusing stories about Catherine.

April leans in against her father's side and rests her head on his shoulder. "I'm not sure if I can do this, Dad," she murmurs.

"Do what?" Sean asks.

"All of this *do you remember when* stuff. It just makes me feel like punching someone."

Sean smiles sadly and lays one arm across her shoulders. "You don't have to do anything, you know. You can go for a walk with that boyfriend of yours. You can go to bed. Do whatever feels easiest for you. They'll all be gone soon enough, and you and I can be as miserable as sin together. How does that sound?"

"That sounds great," April says. "OK, here goes." Then, visibly steeling herself, she straightens and launches herself towards the group. "Hi," she says. "How are you?"

"Oh, hello!" a friend of her mother's says. "I was just telling everyone about your mum's poor hydrangeas."

By four, everyone has left.

Sean removes his tie and throws himself onto the sofa. He's had four gin and tonics and is feeling fairly wobbly, but it's not helping as much as he had hoped.

"Well, thank God that's over," April says, taking the armchair opposite and lifting a sandwich from the small plate on her knees.

"I know," Sean agrees.

"Have you eaten anything?" April asks. "There are loads of sandwiches left. Mags thought she was catering for a football team, I think."

Sean wrinkles his nose. "Not hungry," he says, then, "How long did you say you were staying?" He's wondering whether it would be easier to be alone with his pain right now, or whether the empty house will be quite simply unbearable. For the moment, he feels so exhausted, so dead inside, that it doesn't seem to matter one way or another.

"Until tomorrow afternoon, I expect," April says. "If that's OK."

"Of course," Sean replies, turning to look out at the sunlit street.

"Could we watch a film or something?" April asks.

"A film?" Sean asks, turning back to face her.

April nods. "I don't..." she says, her voice wobbling as her eyes begin to tear. "I don't know quite what to do with myself. A film might help. Maybe."

Sean blinks slowly. "Sure," he says. "Go for it. The remote's um..."

He fidgets uncomfortably, then reaches below his thigh and retrieves not the Sky remote, but an iPhone. He sighs deeply and frowns at it, then places it on the coffee table.

"Her phone," April says.

Sean nods.

"God."

"I'm not really sure what to do with it," Sean says.

"No," April says. "Just, maybe, stick it in a drawer or something?"

Sean nods. "Yeah," he says. "Yeah, that's probably best."

April finds the remote control down the side of her own armchair and clicks on the television. She starts to surf the list of available films, then pauses. "Can I ask you something?" she says.

Sean nods. "Of course, sweetheart. Anything."

"I don't want to upset you."

"It's OK. I think I'm at one-hundred percent, anyway. I don't think I can feel more upset. What is it?"

"It's just, you know, that last day. When Mum said we'd be hearing from her shortly?"

Sean smiles sadly. "Yeah. She sounded like she was making a dental appointment or something. She was off her face on morphine, sweetie. That's all it was."

April nods. "Mum didn't..." she shakes her head gently. "She didn't, you know, *believe* in anything, did she?"

"What, you mean like an afterlife?"

April shrugs. "Anything, really."

Sean shakes his head. "No, sweetie. You know she didn't."

"That's what I thought."

"That doesn't stop you believing whatever you want, though."

"No," April says. "I know. Only I don't either, really." She glances around the room as if perhaps searching for some manifestation of her mother's spirit. "I wish I did, really. It would be nice to know she was... you know... living on. Somewhere else."

Sean chews his lip and screws up his eyes against a fresh bout of tears.

He taps his chest with his fingertips. "In here, sweetheart," he says. "She's in here."

"Yeah," April says, sniffing and dabbing at her eyes before turning her attention back to the TV screen. "So, a film, eh?"

"Nothing soppy, though, OK?"

"No," April says. "No, I know."

Unable to choose anything that might be too emotional, yet not wanting to watch either an action film or a horror movie, April ends up choosing a biopic about the life of Che Guevara, but with her mind wanting only to think about her mother, she finds herself totally unable to concentrate on the film.

Sean, for his part, falls asleep quickly. Some hours later, when he wakes up, the television has been switched off and the room is empty. He sits for a few seconds, half asleep still, and then, just as he begins to wonder where Catherine is, he remembers. He gasps and sits bolt upright.

• • •

Sean sits at the kitchen table and cups the steaming mug of tea in his hands. He glances at the kitchen sink – it's piled high with washing up – then shifts his focal point to the window and finally to the garden beyond.

It's a sunny spring day and he should probably get washed and dressed and get out there. It might make him feel a little better. Or at least, a little less bad.

But only two days have passed since the funeral and this is his first day alone, so this is allowed, isn't it? He's back to work on Monday, so surely he's entitled to spend the weekend staring into the middle distance, to spend the next forty-eight hours feeling utterly, utterly wretched if he wants to.

He looks at the rose bush, blowing in the wind. He hears Catherine's voice saying, *"That'll need pruning as soon as this frost is over."*

"But I don't know how to prune a rose bush," he murmurs, as if perhaps Catherine might hear him. It crosses his mind that there are probably thousands of things he doesn't know how to do – things he never even realised that Catherine did. He starts to make a mental list but then, realising that it's just another way of describing her, another route to thinking about the loss, he stops himself. It's just too painful.

He's still sitting, the mug on the table long since cold, when a knock on the lounge window makes him jump.

He twists in his seat and through the arch between the kitchen and the lounge, sees Maggie peering in, her face framed by cupped hands. He exhales heavily and levers himself from the chair and slopes across the room in the direction of the front door. Cold air bursts into the house as he pulls it open. "I'm not properly up yet," he tells Maggie, flatly.

She scans his rumpled clothes, then peers into his eyes in search of... in search of what? Something, anything, perhaps. He sees her see that there's nothing there. He sees her note the emptiness, and the fact of her observing it makes it become real, makes it become a thing he's aware of.

"I brought you sushi," she says briskly as she raises the pink paper bag held in her left hand. Under her right arm she's holding a box wrapped in brown paper. "I'll bet you've not eaten anything and I know how you love sushi."

Sean nods and reaches for the bag. "Cheers," he says.

"It's from the place on Mill Road. They're the best, I reckon. May I come in?"

"Er... do you have to?" Sean asks, wincing awkwardly. "It's just... as I was saying... I'm not really up yet."

"It's only for a minute," Maggie says, stepping forward, and in so doing, forcing Sean to move to one side. "Just long enough to check that you're OK."

"OK..." Sean repeats, quietly. He's not sure what that even means anymore.

He rolls his eyes at the now-empty doorstep, sighs deeply and then turns to follow Maggie into the house.

"The place looks like a tip, Mags," he calls out, peering inside the bag at the plastic tray of sushi as he follows her. "I want to be quiet at the moment, that's all."

When he reaches the kitchen, he finds that Maggie has removed her coat. She's already stacking the dishwasher. "... and just leave the dishwasher door open if that helps," she's saying. "That way you'll automatically dump your plates and stuff in the dishwasher rather than the sink. And once it's full all you have to do is close it and switch it on. I'll even put a dishwasher tab in so that it's all ready for you. How does that sound?"

"I do know how to stack the dishwasher," Sean says through another sigh. "I'm just... you know..."

"Look, I know you must be feeling awful. I can't even imagine how awful you must be feeling, to be honest," Maggie says. "But if you let everything go to pot, well, it won't help."

"Maggie," Sean pleads.

Maggie pauses and straightens, a dirty mug in one hand. "I know. You want me to leave. I know that. I'm not stupid."

Sean nods gently. "This is very kind of you," he says, "but yes. I just want to be on my own right now."

Maggie presses her free hand to her hip and twists her mouth sideways. "I'll do a deal with you," she says, gesticulating with the mug. "You go have a shower and change. And in the time it takes you to do that, I'll tidy up a little bit down here."

"But Mags, I..."

"By the time you've finished, I'll be gone. I promise."

Sean nods and swallows with difficulty. Her kindness makes him want to cry but he reckons he has cried enough these last few days. "OK," he says, turning to leave. "OK. Whatever."

He walks to the base of the stairs then pauses and looks back. "Thanks Mags," he says, his voice croaky. "I um... I do appreciate it, you know."

Maggie, who has just pulled on Catherine's rubber Marigolds says, "I know. Now go wash yourself. Because that's the bit I *can't* do and frankly you're a bit smelly."

By the time Sean has showered, shaved and dressed in fresh jeans and a sweatshirt, Maggie, true to her word, has gone.

The kitchen surfaces are clean, the room smells of bleach, the dishwasher is chugging away and the dining table, previously covered in a seemingly insurmountable mixture of cups, wrappers, unopened post and random computer cables, is now clear. Only a mug of fresh tea and the wrapped box remain. The box has been carefully set in the exact middle of the table. Sean can imagine Maggie, her head tipped to one side, adjusting it until it's perfectly centred.

Though grateful for the gift, whatever it turns out to be, he finds himself unable to summon the energy required to

15

investigate the box's contents. Or perhaps, more precisely, he finds himself unable to risk the energy that might be required if Maggie's gift turns out to be touching or moving or emotional in any way. He feels too fragile to take that risk.

He reaches for the fresh mug of tea, stares at the carefully wrapped box for one second longer and then moves instead to the lounge, where he hurls himself lengthways onto the sofa. As he reaches for the remote, he notes that Maggie has hoovered in here, too.

Jeremy Kyle's face fills the TV screen. "So how could you *not* know that your lover was your brother?" Kyle asks, smug, mocking laughter in his voice. "Please. Do tell us."

• • •

The next morning, Sean has barely reached the kitchen when the landline rings. He switches on the kettle, turns the heating thermostat up a notch (it's cold and raining outside) and swipes the phone from its base. "April - Mobile" the screen says.

"Hi honey," Sean answers. "I'm barely up here."

"Mmm, same here," April replies, the sound of a warm bed somehow present in her voice. "I'm not up at all, actually."

"It's Sunday. It's allowed."

"So they tell me. How are you holding up, Dad?"

"Well, I'm still here," Sean says. "And you?"

"The same, really. I keep bursting into tears, but I suppose that's normal."

"Yes. Yes, that's totally normal."

"Do you want me to drive back up?" April asks. "I'm free all day. I could be there in an hour."

"There's no need," Sean replies. "I'm... you know... I'm just slouching around watching rubbish television really."

"It's hard," April says. "I feel like I should have been readier – is that a word? Readier?"

"I think it is."

"Anyway, I feel like I should have been readier, more ready, or whatever. I mean, we knew, didn't we? But it's still... I don't know. It's hard to get my head around it."

"It's a shock, isn't it? But I think that's normal. It's a big thing. You only lose your m–" Sean has to clear his throat before continuing. "It's a once in a lifetime thing, thank God."

"..."

"April?"

Sean hears his daughter blow her nose at the other end of the line. "I just miss her so much," she finally says, her voice wobbling. "But even that doesn't make any sense. I mean, it's not like I even saw her that often. I wish I'd come up more, Dad. I wish I hadn't let work get in the way so much. But even though I knew... I... I don't know. I sort of didn't believe it. I couldn't really imagine that she would be..." April starts to sob freely.

"It's all right, honey," Sean says gently, fighting back unwelcome tears himself.

"I didn't imagine that she'd be, you know, *gone*..." April says, through tears. "That doesn't make any sense, does it? But I didn't realise how... *final* it would all feel, I suppose."

"Things don't get much more final than this," Sean says, his own voice trembling.

"I know. But I didn't believe it in a way. I do wish I'd come up more, though. God."

"It's fine, sweetheart. Really it is. She wasn't up to talking much towards the end. You know that. And she wanted you to get on with *your* life. She was *glad* you were getting on with your life. She was really proud of you."

"I know," April says. "It's just... you know."

"I know," Sean says, kindly. "But there's no need to feel guilty."

"So, are you eating OK, Dad? Are you looking after yourself?"

"Uh-huh. There are still sandwiches left over," Sean says. He thinks of the sushi box and looks around the room, then remembers that he put it in the refrigerator. "And Maggie has been dropping food parcels in," he adds. It's an exaggeration, but at least it will reassure his daughter. Then again, perhaps it's true. Perhaps the box on the table is food as well. He reaches out and runs one finger across the rough brown string looped around the box.

"Oh, that's good. Good old Maggie," his daughter says.

"And you?"

"I'm not hungry to be honest," April admits. "But that's no bad thing. I've been wanting to drop a few pounds for ages. So... golden opportunity I suppose."

"Well, don't lose too much. You're skinny already."

"I'm *not*."

"No, well... You girls never think you're skinny enough. But you have to eat something. You know that, right?"

"I'm living on cornflakes at the moment. I can't stomach anything else. But there's, you know, loads of takeaways and stuff around the corner. If my appetite does suddenly return, I've only got to nip out."

Sean, who has been absentmindedly fiddling with the string on the package, now slides the box towards him. It's not as heavy as he expected. Perhaps not food, then.

"Are you *sure* you don't want me to come back up?" April asks.

"I'm sure," Sean says. "You just rest and eat something and look after yourself. Are you back at work tomorrow?" Without thinking about it, he has pulled the end of the knot holding the packaging together. The crisp folds of brown paper are opening slowly, like the petals of a flower.

"I am," April says. "Three days. That's all you get for... for this sort of thing. I mean, I could probably take some more holiday and stuff, but I'm kind of wondering if work isn't the best place to be. That doesn't sound callous, does it?"

"Not at all," Sean says. "I've been thinking pretty much the same thing. Now Monday's almost here though, I'm having second thoughts. But I'll just see how I feel in the morning, I expect. No one will mind if I don't go in. No one will care either way."

"And you're *sure* you're OK?" April asks, yet again.

"I am. I'm fine," Sean says, thinking that how he is right now is a whole new, most unpleasant definition of 'fine'. "And Mags brought me some sushi, like I said."

"You can't live on a bit of sushi, Dad."

"And other stuff too. A whole box of stuff. Really, don't worry."

"Right, OK then," April says. "Well, I think I might try to sleep some more. Sleep's the least horrible place to be at the moment. I'm sleeping *loads*. It's just the waking up bit that I hate."

"When you suddenly remember?" Sean asks.

"Yeah. There's this brief window, like, just a few seconds, yeah? And then I remember."

"It's horrible. I get that too."

19

"I'm seeing someone tomorrow lunchtime, actually. A counsellor or something. My friend Sinead saw her when her brother died. Sinead said she was good, so I thought, why not? I mean, it can't do any harm, can it?"

"No, you're right, it can't. That's good. If you feel you need it, that's good."

"Have *you* thought about seeing someone?"

"Oh, I'm not really the seeing-someone type," Sean says. "You know that. I think I'm OK though, considering. But let me know how it goes."

April yawns loudly, then says, "Sure."

"You go back to sleep, sweetheart."

"OK, talk later, Big Daddy."

"Sure thing, Little Daughter."

Once the phone call has ended, Sean stands and crosses to the refrigerator where he retrieves – and sniffs at – a bottle of milk. This he places on the kitchen table along with the pack of muesli and a bowl and tablespoon plucked from the dishwasher.

He's been feeling nauseous ever since Catherine died. He supposes that he, too, should probably try to eat something.

He pours the muesli, adds milk, and raises a spoonful to his lips. He chews unenthusiastically, then forces himself to swallow, before pulling a face and pushing the bowl to one side. No. It's still too soon for food.

He pulls the box towards him and peels back the wrapping paper revealing a baby-blue shoebox. At the sight of the lid, he inhales sharply.

Across the top of the box, someone has written, *All about us*. The handwriting looks a lot like Catherine's own but, in capitals and written in chunky marker, it's hard to be certain.

He runs his finger across the lettering as he thinks about this, then chews his bottom lip as he removes the lid from the box, revealing one small package and a neat wad of white envelopes stacked end-up, like index cards.

His hand shaking, he lifts one from the pile and inspects it, then another, and sees that they are numbered and in order. Each envelope seems to contain a small object, the size of a box of matches.

He spins the box around so that the numbers are facing him and pulls the first envelope from the box. It reads: *Week Two.* He hunts for *Week One* and then finally lifts the small parcel from the box. The inscription says, *Start here. Open me first.*

Written in ballpoint pen, the handwriting is clearly identifiable as Catherine's messy scrawl.

He slowly rips the paper from the package revealing a small Olympus Dictaphone and a single Polaroid photo. "Oh, God," Sean murmurs.

He picks up the dictaphone and moves his finger towards the play button, but then puts it back down and studies the photo instead.

Snapshot #1

Polaroid, colour. A woman lies in a hospital bed. A man is crouched beside her, his head laid gently on her shoulder. The woman is wearing men's striped pyjamas and from the buttoned chest sprouts a cluster of cables which run across her free shoulder to a monitoring device. Despite the oxygen mask, which covers her mouth, one can see from the shape of her eyes that she's somehow managing to smile.

Cassette #1

Hello Sean.

Well, this is spooky, isn't it? The voice of your late wife. "Late Wife" – you hadn't thought about that before, had you? Well yes, having been absolutely obsessed with being on time my whole life, I finally get to be "late."

I'm recording this on Friday night. I started off writing you letters but I kept having to bin them – you know how insecure I've always felt about my dodgy spelling – and one of the nurses came up with this idea. I'm sure April would tell me I can do it on my iPhone or something, but I'm far more comfortable with these little cassette things, even if they do seem to cost a fortune. Seven quid each, apparently! Can you believe it?

Anyway, this system has seemed to work better for me, so it's probably worth it. Plus, you get to hear my lovely voice instead of trying to read my spidery handwriting and that's got to be a blessing.

Have you looked at the photo yet? It's the one that April took with that new Polaroid of hers. Isn't it funny that something as old-hat as a Polaroid camera should become fashionable again? I think it must be because people are fed up with looking at screens.

You have both just left the hospital and they have given me one of those horrible adrenalin pills to get my blood pressure back up, so I'm galloping like Patti Smith's *Horses*.

I've been putting off recording this last tape because, well, it's my goodbye message, I suppose.

That's an idea that neither of you have been able to get your minds around, I know. Just this evening, you said, "Oh, you'll outlive us all," which, considering the state I'm in, is pretty much a dictionary definition of being in denial. But the truth is, I'm pretty sure you'll be listening to this before the end of the month.

The shadows – have I told you about the shadows? I think I did, but I might have dreamt it. I have been having the strangest dreams... Anyway, there are shadows when I dream, shadows like dark forests crowding in on the path. And the path is lit by an ever weaker beam. It's as if my torch battery is running out, and the shadows at the edges have been becoming deeper and darker and scarier for some time now.

The doctor has said repeatedly that this is just an effect of the morphine pump, but I'm convinced that the shadows are death crowding in on me.

Hum, the nurse interrupted me there, so I had to stop and start again. It's amazing that it hasn't happened more often really.

Anyway, where was I? The shadows. As I was saying, they've been crowding in on me.

But recently, these last few days, I've ceased to be afraid of them. I've started to see the shadows as a calm restful place out of the sun, soft grass off the beaten track to lie back in. I'm starting to want to lay down my torch and ramble off into the undergrowth. There's so much pain on the path, that's the thing.

I haven't told you much about the pain, I don't think, and I don't intend to now. But know that there is pain. So. Much. Pain. Will you forgive me for not hanging on? Will you understand that the cost to me of staying has got to be too high? It's the only reason I'm mentioning the pain now – so that you understand that I would have stayed if I could. But it's no longer possible, darling. I'm sorry.

So, the packages. There are twenty-eight more of them (I've been recording them for months, a real labour of love) and they are already packaged and sealed in that little cabinet beside my bed, here at the hospital. If all goes to plan, Maggie should deliver them to you once I have wandered off into the forest.

The idea came to me when you brought that box of photos in. As we were going through them we came across a picture of me looking peculiar on Margate jetty. Do you remember the one? And you said, "Gosh. Look at your face! I wonder what you were thinking about?"

Well, the thing was that you had already said that. You had said almost exactly those words when we got the batch of photos back from the developers in '94. "Gosh. Look at your face. I wonder what you were thinking about?" And a little later, when I denied that I'd been thinking about anything in particular, you said, "No one really knows anyone. That's amazing, isn't it? We share everything, but we all have our secret gardens too. We all have fantasies and fears and fetishes. We all have secrets about ourselves we don't want to share."

I asked you what your fantasies were, what fetishes you had, and you replied, "Oh, I mean most people. Not me. I'm pretty boring that way. And you know I tell you everything."

But I knew that it wasn't true. And I knew that even to *you*, there were things I'd never be able to say. So you were right. To spend your entire life with someone and still not know them is pretty strange.

The other thing that set me thinking was a conversation we had when Mum died. I was talking about what a wonderful person she was and you said, "Well, the dead make so few mistakes." You'd had a few beers, so you had a bit of an excuse, but I felt that you were sullying her name (I was very over-sensitive about her at the time) so we had an argument about it. But you were right about that too. When people die, we choose to forget the arguments. We wipe out the slights and the injustices. We turn our dead into saints and that clearly doesn't make the grieving process any easier.

So, I've been worrying about your memory playing tricks on you. I've been worrying about you canonising me! Because when I die, which is pretty soon I reckon, I want you to move on with your life. I want you to make a fresh start for yourself. I want you to meet someone new and have drunken arguments and holidays in the sun with her. I want you to make that horrible carrot soup of yours even if it's just so that you get a second opinion on it, so that you realise that it wasn't me being overly critical after all.

Oh, I can hear you protesting as if you were here, sitting next to me. I can hear you saying that it's never going to happen, that ours was a once in a lifetime thing. But I hope that you're wrong. I pray that you're wrong.

And these messages, well, they're everything about me that you know, that I don't want you to forget. And they're everything about me that you never knew, as well. And I'm hoping that with it recorded, it will stop you from turning me into some kind of angel. It will stop me being remembered as some ridiculous Stepford Wife in whose footsteps no one could ever follow. Because, God knows, I've got my faults. And this is my way of reminding you of them.

Now the next bit is going to mean that you'll call me a control freak, but that's OK, because you're right. I am. That's just one of my many faults.

The packages are numbered two to twenty-nine (this is number one) and I really want you to open them in order and I really want you to open them at the rate of one a week.

These weeks are going to be so hard for you. I know that, and it's one of my life's great regrets that I can't be there to help you, to look after you at this difficult time, as they say. So this is my way of being there for you. One message a week. No cheating. Trust me, please.

The pain is back now, so I'm going to have to press that little grey morphine button. Which means that I've reached the hardest part of all. I have to say goodbye and I really don't know how to do that. It's so final.

Your mother would say there's an afterlife, but she'd probably also have me booked on the first train to hell, so that's no real comfort to me.

As you know, I'm no great believer in the afterlife and that's OK with me. I've been. I've seen. I've partied. I've loved. As long as the coming nothingness is pain-free, I'm ready to go there.

I want you to know that it's been great. It's been brilliant. It's been amazing. It's been better than anything I ever imagined for myself and that's all thanks to you.

As far as I'm concerned, there's only one thing luckier than getting to spend your life with someone who loves you and that's getting to spend your life with someone who loves you whose name is Sean Patrick.

I love you with all my heart, Mr Patrick. I love you so much that my heart is breaking at the thought of having to leave you. But the path is so painful, darling. And the shadows look so inviting.

So listen to the tapes, one a week. Take time to look at the photos, to remember what we had at each step of the way. Take time to cry over the good things we had. Take time to shout at me for the things I never told you at the time. And when it's done, put the box away and get on with your life.

Tell April how much I love her. Tell her how proud I am of her. Don't ever let her doubt either of those things for a single second. Tell her over and over and over – she'll need it.

God that hurts, perhaps more than all the rest put together: the fact that I won't be there to say the things she needs to hear. That I won't be there to tell you I love you anymore.

Because I do. I love you. Forever.

Hi there again. I've just played this back and it doesn't even begin to express how I feel. There simply aren't big enough words in the dictionary. Or perhaps there are and I just don't know them. So I'm going to end by sending you a big sloppy kiss and a virtual love-heart which you'll just have to imagine I'm drawing in the air as I speak. Gosh, that made me think of those love heart sweets you used to buy me. I have the sherbety taste in my mouth, right now, even as the morphine is rising up in me like a deep, dark, soft, hot toddy. Isn't memory strange?

Snapshot #2

Photo booth format, black and white. A teenage girl with bleached, shaggy, layered locks and a back-combed fringe is squashed into the frame beside a thin-faced young man with smooth dark hair which almost entirely obscures his right eye. The couple appear to have collapsed into a fit of giggles.

Sean sits and stares at the photo. It is five o'clock on Sunday morning and he has just abandoned his attempts at sleeping, pulled on a dressing gown and come down to the kitchen. Beyond the window, the garden is dark and cold.

Sean feels shattered. His first few days at work have groaned by. He has found himself totally unable to concentrate on his work and has had to mentally prod himself tens of times every hour to think about the balconies he was supposed to be designing rather than the images constantly springing up in his mind: Catherine gasping for air. Catherine pressing the morphine button. Catherine in pain. Catherine's body, no longer in pain but no longer Catherine at all. On Wednesday, though, something blessed had happened. Just for an hour, he had managed to lose himself in his work. Just for one hour, he had managed to forget everything and think instead about the tensile strength of reinforced concrete, about the shock resistance of sandwiched glass and chrome plated brackets. On Thursday, he had managed it twice. And by Friday, he was dreading the weekend, dreading a rainy Saturday in front of the television. A rainy Saturday in that oh-so-empty house. So he had brought work home with him. He had managed to survive Saturday by pretending, simply, that it was Friday all over again.

Now, it's Sunday morning and Sean is surprised that he managed to sleep at all. This second message has been playing on his mind all week – so much, in fact, that he has handled the envelope repeatedly before relenting and returning it to the box. Yesterday evening he even started to peel back the flap. But he can't help but wonder if Catherine isn't somewhere watching him. He couldn't stand the idea of being a disappointment to her.

The photo is from the summer of 1982, the day that they met. He and three college friends, Tracey, Theresa and Glen, had travelled to Margate for the weekend. Tracey had invited them to visit during the summer holidays. Her mother ran a slowly disintegrating guesthouse in down-at-heel Cliftonville and was letting them all stay free of charge in exchange for their help with wallpapering one of the bedrooms.

Catherine was the prettiest girl that Sean had ever seen. He isn't quite sure what it was that first caught his eye, perhaps her lion's mane of hair, or maybe her makeup, which was bold, verging on punk. Looking at the photo now, it's surprisingly hard to see what the all-consuming attraction had been. Her hair had been a mock-Bonnie-Tyler mess. Her earrings had been huge, vulgar hoops. He remembers a twinkle in her eyes, though. They had always somehow looked as though they were smiling, as if, perhaps, she was in on some private joke.

Whatever it was, he had glanced across and spotted her filing her nails while manning the turnstile to the hall of mirrors. He had turned back to Glen, who'd been spouting forth about something (most likely the Falklands war, which he opposed with a vengeance), but then something had made

Sean turn to look again and the girl had glanced up and winked at him. She'd pointed towards the interior with her nail file and said, "Go on. You know you want to. It's only 10p."

So Sean had dragged the others, in varying states of willingness, into the maze of mirrors and they had stumbled around laughing at their reflections. Glen had complained continuously how "naff" it all was. But even Glen had laughed at the "alien head" mirror.

Sean had made sure he was the first to reach the exit.

"That was quick," the girl had said. "I hope you don't want your money back." Slapping the top of the turnstile with one hand, she'd added, "This thing's got a counter in it, so there's not a lot I can do."

"No," Sean replied. "No. I just..." He could feel himself blushing.

"You wanted to invite me out for a drink or something?" the girl asked, grinning cheekily. "Is that it?"

"No, I..." Sean spluttered.

She had pouted with exaggerated sadness and Sean remembers noticing her lips. They were plump and shiny. She had applied two different shades of lipstick, both pink and purple. "Oh, well..." she had said.

"I mean, yes, then," Sean said bravely. He was imagining kissing those multicoloured lips.

Her mouth then slipped into the broadest of grins. "I don't get off till nine," she said.

"Um. OK."

"But I get twenty minutes for lunch. At twelve-thirty. We could go get a hot dog or something if you want."

At that moment, Glen, Theresa and Tracey had lurched from the maze. "Well that was shite," Glen was saying.

33

"Oh, it was OK," Theresa insisted. Theresa believed in seeing the positives in everything. She studied the girl's face for a moment, then checked out Sean's expression and frowned before addressing her. "Hello. So who are you, then?"

"Me? I'm Catherine."

"I'm Theresa. Pleased to meet you. And this is Glen, Tracey. Oh, and Sean, who you *seem* to have met already."

Sean hadn't had the nerve to return for their lunch date. He had fully *intended* to have the nerve: he had even managed to ditch his friends on the other side of the funfair before speeding back to the hall of mirrors. But when he got there, his courage had failed him. Sean had never considered himself attractive, that was the thing. His mother had spent most of his childhood telling him that his face was as long as a "rainy Sunday" which probably hadn't helped. So why, he had wondered, would Catherine possibly be interested in him?

Instead of walking up to her and inviting her for lunch, he had lingered, instead, outside the postcard shop opposite, praying that Catherine would notice him there.

He had gone inside to pay for the cards he had chosen – tacky images of people in kiss-me-quick hats on Margate seafront – and by the time he came back outside, she'd been replaced by a tall, skinny lad whose acne was even worse than Sean's. Feeling panicked and remembering her mentioning hot dogs, he had jogged to a nearby stand he had spotted. And there, at the front of the queue, had been Catherine.

"Oh, you made it then," she had said, on spotting him. "So come on," she had added, slapping her thigh, inciting him to jump the queue. And he had felt as if he had known her forever.

Cassette #2

Hello gorgeous, it's me.

This is my first ever recording and this is my third attempt. I keep erasing them and re-doing them. I had the machine too close and then too far away so you couldn't hear a thing. Like most people, I hate the sound of my voice, too. So it's very tempting to hit that erase button and start again, but if I keep doing that, I'll never get these done. Hopefully I'll get the hang of it in the end.

So, I've been sitting looking at this photo trying to remember what it was that first attracted me to you. That will sound wrong, I know. It sounds as if I can't believe that I *was* attracted to you and that's not what I'm trying to say at all.

When I look at this photo, I see a chavvy Margate lass with a Chewbacca hairstyle and a skinny, spotty boy with a fringe. But I *did* like you. I liked you instantly. And when I try really hard, when I close my eyes and try to remember, the two things that keep coming back to me are how shy you were and how familiar you seemed. Of course, we came up with a reason for that strange sense of familiarity much later on, but at the time it seemed magical.

But your shyness was very attractive to me. I remember, for instance, how when I winked at you, you averted your gaze. And the more I think about it, the more I come to the conclusion that you were simply the first shy boy I had ever met.

That will sound strange, I expect, but there weren't any shy boys at my school. They were all too busy being tough and jack-the-lad, even when it was just pretence.

I remember asking you how you liked your hot dog and you saying that you didn't know, and then blushing when I laughed at the fact that you'd never had a hot dog before.

I thought that was so sweet! Not that you'd never had a hot dog before but the fact that you were *embarrassed* about never having had one. You actually apologised.

Your voice was really soft, too. That was partly your West Country accent, I suppose, but I loved how quietly you spoke. Half the time I wasn't sure if I'd heard you correctly.

I remember that tic you had, where you tipped your head all the time to get your fringe out of your eyes, and I remember that your eyelashes seemed huge.

You've still got long eyelashes, of course, but your face got wider and more rugged as you grew into manhood, and the lashes somehow got lost in the whole. But when you were twenty, they seemed huge. I remember wanting to kiss your eyes. I don't think I ever told you that. Isn't that funny?

So, you jumped the queue and we got our hot dogs. You smothered yours in mustard and then raved about how good they were, which was funny and sort of cute, as well.

You asked me about my job and I told you it was just for the summer, and you asked me if I had a boyfriend and then stared at your feet when I said "no". You talked about me. You wanted to know all the silly, boring details about my life in Margate. You wanted to know what pub I went to and if I lived with my parents. And that was new to me, as well. Boys generally seemed to spend all their time telling girls about themselves in my experience. But you, you wanted to know all about little old me!

We walked past a photo booth and you said you needed a picture for your student railcard or something and I ducked in halfway through to join you. The first two were of you looking all serious and the third one was blurry, but this one came out. I can't believe how young we look. And I can't believe our hair! Still, it was 1982. Bucks Fizz were in the charts so, clearly, no one knew what bad taste meant.

When we got back to the mirrors, I asked you about you, and you said you were at college, that you were studying to be an architect, and I remember being really shocked. I remember not quite grasping it. I think I must have said something daft like, "What, you're going to build houses and stuff?"

The people I knew worked in Dreamland or Tesco's. Mum's boyfriends tended to be bricklayers or car mechanics or, more often than not, on the dole.

So your being at college, your intention to design actual houses, seemed incredible to me. You were like no one I had ever met.

You spoke softly, you blushed, you were learning to design buildings, and you wanted to talk about me! And I thought, *Oh God. This is the one I want!*

That might sound... what's the word? Mercenary? But it wasn't like that at all. I felt, almost instantly, as if I'd known you forever. And I felt, suddenly, as if I'd been a square peg in a round hole all my life.

You had this whole different way of talking and listening and *existing,* and it was as if you'd opened a door I had never noticed before and I peeped through it and suddenly realised that I'd spent the first eighteen years of my life in the wrong room.

So by the time your friends came by and swept you up with them, I knew. You were everything I wanted.

Actually, it was more, even, than that. You were everything I had *ever* wanted. I just hadn't known it until then.

As you went off with your friends, I got all tongue tied. I watched you leaving and felt a sensation of utter panic. And as you turned the corner, I realised that I might never see you again. I imagined myself twenty years down the line still thinking about you, still regretting. So I abandoned my turnstile and I ran after you.

I caught up with you in front of the skating rink. *Skate on plastic, it's fantastic.* Do you remember the plastic ice rink?

I grabbed your arm. "Sorry," I panted, "but are you coming back later?"

"Um, if you want me to," you said, blinking madly and blushing again. "At nine, right?"

Your friend Glen made a stupid "Ooooh," noise and you told him to "shut it".

"Yes, nine," I said. "I'll meet you there, by the exit. OK?"

Then, ignoring Glen, who was still being an idiot, I asked you to promise you'd be there. And you did. And you were. And I was so relieved that I kissed you.

• • •

It's Wednesday evening and Sean is in the process of unloading shopping from the car when Maggie's little Fiat pulls up.

He carries the shopping bags he's holding to the front step, then returns to greet her.

"Hello," he says, as she steps from her car. It's baby blue with leopard-print trim. Sean always thinks it looks more like a handbag than a car and had been mortified the one time he had been forced, by circumstances, to borrow it. "Have you come to check up on me?"

"Well, if you won't return my calls..." Maggie says, closing the car door behind her.

"Sorry," Sean says, leaning in for a peck on the cheek. "But I've been ever so busy. We've got tons of work on at the moment."

"Really?"

Sean nods vaguely. "Plus, if truth be told, I've not been feeling that sociable. You know..."

"Of course," Maggie says, joining him at the rear of his Astra. "Let me help you with that."

"I'm nearly done," Sean says. He lifts a final insulated carrier bag from the rear of the car and slams the hatch.

When they reach the doorstep, Maggie lifts one of the bags, and as they enter the house, she peers inside at the contents. "Wow," she says, mockingly. "It's a ready meal bonanza. That's not like you." Within their circle of friends, Sean is famed for his cooking, specifically his authentic Kerala curries.

"I'm failing to get motivated to cook at the moment," Sean says. "At least it's better than sandwiches."

"I'm just glad you're eating," Maggie says. "You're looking skinny."

"I know." Sean shrugs and forces a weak smile. "I had to make a new hole in my belt. My trousers kept falling down. But I'm eating better now."

"So how is it going?" Maggie asks, lifting the bag onto the kitchen counter.

"It?" Sean repeats.

"I mean, how are you coping?"

Sean shrugs again. "I'm OK, I suppose," he says, opening the freezer and beginning to stack the newly-bought packages. "I've got lots of work on, like I said. So that's good."

"Yes," Maggie says, scanning the room. "Yes, I'm sure."

"Are you looking for something?"

"Oh, no. Just, you know, the box I left."

"Catherine's box?"

Maggie nods and looks into Sean's eyes. "I take it you opened it?"

"Yes. Did she tell you what was in it?"

Maggie shakes her head. "Not really. I'm assuming it was photos. Was it photos?"

"Yeah," Sean says. "Yeah, that's pretty much it."

"Do I get to see them?" Maggie asks. "Over a cup of tea, maybe?"

Sean frowns and smiles at the same time. "Er, no, Mags. You don't."

"Oh, fair enough," Maggie says. "Sorry. Am I being insensitive? It's just without knowing exactly what..."

"It's not just photos," Sean says. "There are messages too. On those little dictaphone tapes. Quite personal. Well, *very* personal really. I'm supposed to open one a week."

"Oh," Maggie says. "One a week, eh? That's very organised."

"Well, Catherine is... *was*... very organised," Sean says, wincing at the pain of having made the is/was mistake yet again. It's still happening regularly.

"Yes, yes, she was," Maggie agrees, reaching for her car keys.

She looks so uncomfortable that Sean suddenly wants to help her out. "I alternate between wanting to open them all at once and never wanting to open any of them, to be honest," he says, feeling that sharing this intimate detail will in some way ease Maggie's discomfort. "But so far, in the absence of a better idea, I'm just sticking to orders. One a week."

"Right," Maggie says.

"It's hard, though."

"I'm sure."

"How's Dave?" Sean asks. "You don't seem to mention him much at the moment."

"Oh, you know," Maggie says. "Dave's Dave."

"Meaning?"

"Messy. Disorganised. Confusing. Distracted."

"Things are no better, then?"

"Do things get any better at our age?" Maggie asks, through a sigh. "Does anything change?"

"I don't know," Sean says, thoughtfully. "Things can certainly get worse, so..." He scratches his head.

"Yes," Maggie says, looking uncomfortable again. "Sorry, here's you with... with all of this to deal with and I'm the one complaining. I'm sorry. I don't seem to be very good at this."

"It's fine, Maggie," Sean says. "You're fine. Really."

"It's just that I don't know how to... I don't know. I mean, you don't want to talk about... all of that... And that's understandable. Of course, it is. But everything we normally would talk about... sounds silly. Unimportant. Compared with... your stuff. Do you know what I mean?"

Sean blinks slowly. "A dead wife trumps everything, I guess."

"Yes," Maggie says. "I'm sorry. I should go."

"You don't want that cup of tea?"

"No. I should just..." she gestures towards the hallway. "I just wanted to check that you're OK."

"Well, your concern is appreciated."

"Thanks. And you're doing very well."

"Am I?"

"You are. So, just, you know... keep it up."

"Thanks. I'll do my best."

"So, what's for dinner tonight?" Maggie asks, nodding at the freezer.

"This," Sean says, lifting a still frozen Chicken Tikka Masala box from the countertop. "They're quite edible, actually."

"Good," Maggie says, stepping towards him and leaning in for another peck on the cheek. "Bye sweetie."

"Oh, Mags?" Sean says as she turns away.

Maggie pauses, her hand on the doorjamb and glances back. "Yes?" she asks. She sounds almost hopeful.

"Don't tell April, yeah? About the messages."

"Oh. No," Maggie says. "No, of course not."

"It's not that... it's not, like, a secret or anything..." Sean stumbles. "I just want to listen to them all first. Before I tell her."

"Of course," Maggie says. "And you know me. I won't say a word."

Snapshot #3

110 format, colour, faded. Slightly out of focus. A woman in a pinafore, wearing oversized, lightly tinted glasses, is raising a stemmed glass and smiling broadly. Behind her can be seen a number of yellow Formica wall cabinets and a white electric cooker.

Sean's childhood had been pretty loveless, but he had never been aware of the fact until he met Catherine's mother.

Sean's father was a retired RAF officer with a gammy leg, his mother a non-tactile woman whose moods were even less predictable than the British weather.

His frigid childhood had seemed entirely normal to him, as had his father's heavy-handed discipline and his mother's almost constant criticism. And being sent, like his brother before him, to boarding school, had seemed no less than inevitable.

Similarly, his exposure to those to whom his father referred as "the working classes" had been limited almost entirely to what could be seen on television. So he had grown up with his parents' prejudices reinforced by occasional glimpses of *Coronation Street* and Alf Garnett. It all looked pretty sordid, to be honest.

At college, he'd met people from all over, and his perception had started to change. But what he still hadn't imagined, until the day he went to Catherine's house, was, when etiquette and social expectation were cast aside, how relaxed a household could feel. How welcoming. How fun. How loving.

And as he had sat, feeling "gob-smacked", eating chips on Wendy's tatty sofa, he had understood for the first time ever that being born a Patrick (something his mother constantly insisted was akin to winning life's great lottery) had its downsides as well.

Cassette #3

Hello Sean.

So here, as you can see, is one of the few remaining photos of Mum.

She's almost certainly waiting for a batch of those McCain oven chips to be ready. They had only just been invented, as far as I recall, or perhaps we had only just discovered them, but either way, Mum was conducting her own clinical trial to see what would happen if you fed your kids nothing but oven chips and brown sauce. The answer, surprisingly, was "nothing out of the ordinary". The human body is surprisingly resilient. Then again, look at me now. Could all of this perhaps be the result of all those chips way back when?

I was so ashamed about taking you to our house, because I could tell that you were posh.

You had that lovely West Country accent, but you spoke differently from anyone I knew. Back then, I would have said you "spoke different" of course.

Mum used to call you Sean Leadbetter, after Margo and Jerry in *The Good Life*. I don't think you ever knew that.

So yes, I was terrified. But you begged me to show you where I lived and as we only had that weekend, I took the risk. And amazingly, you loved it there.

It wasn't till I got to see a photo of where your parents lived that I realised just how much of a shock our council estate must have been.

We had that old sofa plonked in the middle of the front garden and when we got there, Mum was sitting on it, still in her dressing gown, smoking.

Indoors, that horrible Dennis Shelley, her boyfriend-of-the-moment, was watching telly in his underpants.

But Mum gave you a hug and asked if you were hungry, and when you said "Yes," she told you to stick some chips in the oven. That was another thing you didn't know existed: oven chips.

So we sat and ate chips and drank cans of Stella in front of the telly and then I took you upstairs. I remember you were shocked that I was allowed upstairs with a boy and I remember wondering what sort of rules posh families had to operate by, because Mum had never stopped me doing anything, really.

You laughed at my ABBA poster and I introduced you to Barnie, my teddy bear. I put the radio on and we sat side by side in that tiny room – I was just gagging for you to kiss me.

Eventually, I realised that you weren't going to do it and I worked out that was probably because of some other posh rule I didn't know about. And so I grabbed you and *snogged the face off of you* – as we used to say, back then. You didn't, you'll remember, resist.

Now, I know you probably remember all of this, but it does me good to remind myself of it. It cheers me up to record it for infinity. That's not the word, is it? *Infinity*. Definitely not right. Ugh. Sometimes words just vanish and no amount of hunting can track them down. Oh, I know: prosperity. That's what I meant. No, posterity! Record it for all *posterity*.

Anyway, once you'd left, Mum said, "Well he's a bit *la-di-da*, isn't he?"

I told her that you weren't *la-di-da* at all.

"Well I hope you didn't shag him," Mum said.

I told her that of course I hadn't.

"Good," she said. "Because boys like that want a bit of rough for the weekend. But he'll end up marrying some posh bird from London. You mark my words."

I suppose she was telling me that I was a "bit of rough", but I didn't even think about it at the time. I just worried in case she was right.

• • •

Sean pours the chips into the grill pan, studies the instructions on the packet and then slides it into the oven and sets the timer. He has been craving chips and brown sauce all week, ever since he played last Sunday's message. But yesterday, Saturday, was the first opportunity he's had to actually go to buy some and, as April has been visiting, he's been busy all day.

He was tempted, twice, to mention the messages to her. She's missing her mother horribly and the messages might help comfort her, in the same way that their regular, drip, drip into his life is comforting *him*. But if he lets April know about the messages now, she'll want to know the contents of *every* message, *every* Sunday. And until he knows what they contain, he can't possibly know if that's a good idea. For the moment, he feels that by keeping them from her he's protecting her, even if he's not sure yet exactly what he's protecting her from.

So the box has remained stashed beneath the stairs and they have spent the day wandering around Cambridge. They have walked along the Cam and eaten a pub lunch at The Fort St George. They have done their best to comfort each other, but in truth Sean feels more alone with April present than he does without her, her grief seemingly compounding his own.

Now that she has returned to London, Sean's finally able to cook his oven chips, he's finally free to open his box.

He retrieves envelope number three and props it against the edge of the box. He puts out a plate, salt, vinegar and the unopened bottle of brown sauce and sets about making himself a cup of tea.

Twenty minutes later, he tips the chips onto the plate and sits down.

"This is your fault, Cathy," he murmurs, addressing the box as he raises the first chip to his lips.

It's much too hot to eat for the moment, so he puts it back down and reaches for the cassette instead. He removes last week's tape from the machine and clips in the new one. He's been waiting for this all day. He's been waiting for this all week. He flips over the photo.

Snapshot #4

35mm format, colour. The photo is crumpled and scuffed. A man with long hair is slouched on an ugly leather sofa. He is smoking a joint. Behind him is a shelf stacked with records and a turntable with a tinted plastic lid, beside which is an enormous loudspeaker. The grille has been removed to reveal the round black cones of the drivers.

Wow! Alistair! Sean thinks.

Alistair had been the first person Sean ever shared a house with once he moved out of halls of residence at the end of the first year. He'd been a heavy dope smoker and had been kicked off his art course at the end of the second year but had been rich enough to stay on and continue making his art – a series of horrific splatter paintings – in the attic.

Sean hasn't thought about Alistair for years. He wonders what he's up to now. Sean bets he's not an artist anymore. He reckons that he most likely caved in to his father's wishes at some point. He probably ended up in banking or something.

Initially, they had bonded for the simple reason that they were both from upper class families, yet had both, each for his own reasons, ended up at Wolverhampton Poly.

Alistair was there because he knew it would upset his parents. Sean, on the other hand, had forgotten to post his uni applications. They had sat, stamped and addressed and ready to go, in the glove compartment of his father's car for months and by the time they were found it was too late for Cambridge and too late for Oxford and too late, in fact, for any major university. He had gone onto the reserve list and when a place had come free at Wolves he had jumped at it. They had a decent architecture course, after all. And the far less appealing alternative was staying at home for a year.

Sean remembers being mortified about the state of their shared house. Alistair had found the house and Alistair had stumped up the hefty security deposit as well. But that's where his implication had ended. He had certainly never done his share of the housework and this, particularly the piled-high washing up, had been a constant source of discord between them.

Sean had spent three hours cleaning, the morning Catherine arrived, but the place still looked like it had been turned over by the SAS by the time they got home. Sean wouldn't have blamed her if she had turned around and walked back out, but she had pretended, he remembers, to love it.

Cassette #4

Hi Sean.

So look at this! A photo of the house you were living in. A photo of Alistair, too.

We had only spent two days together, our weekend in Margate, mostly mucking around with your college friends, occasionally stealing kisses beneath the sun deck, but on Monday you had to go back. Your train ticket was already booked and you couldn't afford, you said, to change it. At first, I thought that you'd just had enough of me. I thought you were using the ticket to escape. But then you admitted to working part time in a corner shop and I realised you'd just been too embarrassed to tell me.

Looking back on it, I'm surprised that you ended up at Poly. I would have thought that someone with your background and education would have gone straight to Oxford or Cambridge. I'm sure you must have explained to me way-back-when how that came about, but I must have forgotten. Maybe your A level results weren't up to scratch? That sounds familiar, so I expect that's it.

Still, back then, the word Wolverhampton meant nothing to me. I was as excited at the idea of going there as I would have been if you'd invited me to Paris or New York. I'd never been anywhere much. Well, I'd been to London a couple of times but only on school trips to the Science Museum and the like. I think I went once with Mum to the January sales as well, but I was really little. The only bit I remember is that we took a black cab to get to the station because we were late. I thought that was really exciting.

As far as I was concerned, Wolverhampton was quite exotic.

Mum was outraged. "Why the buggery do you want to go there?" she asked.

"It's that Sean fella," Stinky Dennis chipped in. "Fancies 'im, don't she."

Train tickets were expensive and complicated (you had to travel across London on the Underground in those days), so I bought a ticket on a National Express coach. I can't remember how long the journey took, but I do know it seemed like a very, very long way.

As the bus drove into Wolverhampton, I felt a bit disappointed, to be honest. I never told you that, but it was a grey day and drizzling and the outskirts of the town were these desolate industrial wastelands back then. I remember seeing half-demolished factories. I think industry in the Black Country just sort of died around there during the Thatcher years.

Anyway, even coming from Margate, everything looked a bit poor and grey and dusty.

You met me at the bus station and took me to a wine bar, Kipps I think it was called, but I might have got that wrong. It was dark and cavernous and the tables were sticky.

Once we'd had a drink and shared a plate of cheesy chips, we walked across town to your house. You carried my bag for me and talked all the time in that gentle, thoughtful way of yours. You told me about a party you'd been to at the weekend and about a band who were coming to play at the student union. I can't remember who it was anymore, but I know I'd never heard of them and as we walked through this scary underpass that went beneath a big roundabout, you sang their hit song to me. You were convinced that I should know it, but I didn't. I'd spent too much time singing along to ABBA and Buck's Fizz to know groups like that.

I think that's the moment I fell in love with you. Oh, I was already fascinated by you, but when you sang to me, I fell in love properly. You've always had a lovely voice, but when you sang, it used to make my heart go all fluttery and you used to sing a lot. I wonder when that stopped and why? I suppose it's just something that happens when you get older.

When we got to the house, music was blaring out. It's funny that I remember this, but I do: Alistair was playing The Pretenders. It was that album with Chrissie Hynde on the cover wearing a red leather jacket. The song that was playing as you opened the front door was *Kid*.

I'd heard it on the radio, but I'd never really *listened* to The Pretenders before and I'd certainly never heard them on a proper hi-fi like the one Alistair had.

That memory, walking into that messy lounge, seeing Alistair blowing smoke rings into the air; it's as fresh as if it happened just yesterday.

You asked him to turn the music down – you had to shout to be heard – and Alistair asked, "Why?"

He had no intention of turning it down so, to avoid an argument, I told you it was fine. I said that I liked it and, in a way, I did.

That weekend was so... dense... I suppose you'd say, in new experiences. Alistair played me The Pretenders and Patti Smith and Yazoo. I smoked my first joint and threw up discreetly in that horrible mouldy downstairs toilet. I met more interesting people in those three days that I'd meet in Margate in a year. But the things I remember the most are the conversations you all used to have.

I suppose, looking back on it, that you students were all a bit up yourselves really, but at the time, sitting up until four in the morning talking about whether God existed or not was a revelation to me. You'll think I'm overstating it, but the conversations I'd had back home rarely got much further than whether or not Tracey Furlong was up the duff and who the father might be.

It was hard at first because I realised that I didn't fit in. I wasn't used to these kinds of conversations and had nothing, really, to contribute. So I just sat quietly, soaking it all up.

Your friend Theresa declared that I was a listener. "Anyone can talk," she said, "but the cleverest people spend their time listening." And that really pleased me. It provided me with an identity, a sort of camouflage, so that I could sit and listen to you all and not get noticed and not be judged for not saying anything. But the more that I sat and listened, the more that I realised that I didn't fit in at home, either. It was a real shock when I got back, to suddenly feel so out of it, to suddenly feel such disdain for all the boring chit-chat around me.

On the Sunday evening, you took me to the student bar and we danced. The music was strange stuff that they never played in discos in Margate. It was all Lloyd Cole and The Smiths and The Cure, and I had to look around me at the other girls to work out how to dance to it. They didn't really dance at all, actually. They just sort of moved their arms back and forth and shuffled their feet a bit. Margate dancing was *Saturday Night Fever* by comparison.

Predictably, by the time we left we were drunk. You were so drunk, you lay down in the middle of the ring road and I yanked on your arms to get you to get up again, but instead you pulled me down on top of you and we snogged, there in the middle of the traffic island.

The next morning we did the deed for the first time and even that was different from everything that had gone before.

I'd slept with five boys before you (another thing you never knew) but they'd all wanted just one thing: to get their rocks off as soon as possible. But as always, you made it about me instead. By the time you'd finished, I'd come – I'd actually come! Oh, I'd managed that before on my own, but no one I had slept with had ever bothered before. I remember thinking on the bus back home that you were definitely what Mum would call "a keeper".

• • •

Another week scrapes by. If he tries really hard, Sean can just about manage to feel a little pride in the fact that he's surviving, that he's still functioning: he's doing his washing, his ironing; he's making it to work each day. For the moment, there's not much more he can do. It reminds him of that Tom Hanks film, where Tom just sits waiting to see what the tide will bring each day.

He feels like he's in stasis, waiting for Catherine to return. That idea, that she isn't going to return, is one of the hardest to get his head around and he's surprised, even though he knows that it's ridiculous, every time he gets home and rediscovers that she's not there.

On Monday, he barely manages to work at all. He sits, instead, staring at his computer screen, his mind lost in the 1980s.

The recordings are reminding him how it felt to be young: how exciting, how fun, how nerve-wracking everything was back then. He had somehow forgotten that all of those memories were his own, that these were all things he had lived through, not simply stories he had read.

On Wednesday evening, he bursts into tears while driving home and has to pull over into a lay-by until he can see properly again. He sits with his hands on the steering wheel and searches for the origin of this particular batch of tears. It's not until he glances over at the grassy traffic island that he realises that he had been remembering kissing Catherine in the middle of the ring road.

Once again, it's hard to believe that was he and he wonders about this sense of lost continuity between the young man that he once was and this man in a grey jacket in an Astra, crying at the side of the road. He wonders why his memories feel like a story from a film or a book he once read. Why is it so hard to feel the connection between that drinking, kissing, shagging, singing Sean and this one?

He feels, perhaps, closer to the Sean he was *before* he met Catherine and that, after all, isn't so illogical. Those old, adolescent sensations of feeling scared and alone, of not being able to imagine the future, are returning.

In an attempt at trying to work out who he is now that she's gone, he's lapsing into old ways, in some cases, very old ways. It's as if he perhaps needs to remember that he changed when he met Catherine, that he did exist before he met her

So he's buying oven chips and he's drinking cans of beer. He's smoking the occasional cigarette (after a twenty year break) and on weekends, he's slobbing around in a track suit until lunchtime.

On Friday evening, he leaves work early and swings by a hi-fi store on Hills Road.

He has been thinking about what Catherine said, that he has stopped singing. He's been trying to work out when and why that happened and has realised that he's even stopped *listening* to music.

As far as he can work out, this musical hiatus seems to have sneaked up on him in the mid-2000s, which would make sense because that is when he converted all of his CDs into MP3 files and stacked them in the loft with his records. It's perhaps no surprise that the moment he stopped listening to albums is the moment they quite literally dematerialised.

And now, it is Sunday morning and he has just finished wiring the new turntable into the TV's surround sound speakers. He doesn't even have a proper amplifier anymore.

He opens the trap to the attic and lowers the step-ladder. He rummages around until he finds the box of vinyl.

He looks through the records, one by one, each album cover provoking a flood of memories. He finally selects Pink Floyd's *Animals*, and the record is so dirty that he has to wash it under the tap before he dares to play it.

He lowers the needle onto the groove and settles on the sofa with envelope number four in one hand and a Marlboro Light in the other. He'll listen to the first side and then he'll play Catherine's message.

Snapshot #5

Kodak disc format, colour. A faded, low quality, grainy image. A very young woman with a frizzy perm stands on Margate seafront. A man in Doc Martin's, bleacher jeans and a green US military bomber jacket is standing beside her with his arm around her shoulders. He's raising one finger at the person taking the photo, half smiling, half sneering. Behind the couple, in better focus than the couple themselves, are the rusted remains of Margate Pier.

As he listens to Pink Floyd, Sean studies the photo, but his mind remains a blank. Catherine looks very young to him and he's not sure he ever saw her with a perm. He has no recollection of the photo being taken and no idea who the skinhead is either. In the end, curiosity gets the better of him so he gets up, lifts the needle from the record and presses play on the dictaphone instead.

Cassette #5

Hi Sean.

It's me again. So, today you get to meet Phil.

As I explained in my first tape, the aim of all of this is not in any way to sanctify your memories of me but to create a realistic record of who I really was, warts and all. Hopefully that will make it easier for you to let go, to move on, as they say. But that means that not all of this is going to be pleasant, so if you need a drink before listening to the rest of this one, be my guest.

This is Phil. You actually met him once, though I doubt very much you'll remember it. We were walking along the seafront on our way to pick April up from Mum's – she was about three, I think. And a guy on a motorbike pulled up to say hello to me. I told him that you were my husband and without saying another word he roared off, so I don't think you even saw his face. As I recall, you asked me who he was and I replied that he was "just a schoolfriend". But that was a lie, so I'm sorry about that.

The truth is that I was going out with Phil until I met you. I'd actually come from Phil's flat, from Phil's bed, that morning I met you in Dreamland.

Now this may sound horrible and cruel, but from the second I met you, he was nothing to me.

Phil was a drunk. He was a waster who lived on benefits he shouldn't really have been getting and the sale of "knock-off" gear that an acquaintance of his somehow came by. Things fell off the backs of lorries a lot, back then, in Margate.

I'd love to be able to list all the reasons I was going out with Phil but I don't really have a clue. I'd love to be able to tell you he had his good points, but I don't think he really did.

He was, like I say, a heavy drinker, a heavy smoker and a petty thief. The sex was OK, I suppose, though only, really, because I didn't have anything to compare it to. But it was very rough and ready and at the time I liked that, or at least I thought I did. Compared to Phil, you were so unbelievably wonderful in every way that it's really difficult for me to justify, even to myself, that I was with him, except perhaps to

60

say that he was like a younger version of every guy Mum ever dated. So in a way, it was all I knew.

I only ever saw Phil once after you left that Monday. I spent one evening with him, just to be sure. We ate fish and chips together, then had "goodbye" sex, after which I provoked, as far as I can remember, an argument. And then I stormed out, feeling all smug and pleased with myself.

I was only eighteen. Please forgive me.

• • •

Sean spends the week feeling jealous. He's fully aware that it's absurd to be feeling jealous of one's late wife's ex-boyfriend from thirty-five years ago, but he can't help himself. It's just as well that Catherine didn't provide Phil's surname, Sean reckons, because otherwise he might have been tempted to hunt him down.

On Thursday lunchtime, Sean accepts an invitation to a pub lunch with three colleagues from Nicholson-Wallace and it's the first social interaction he has had since Catherine died where the major subject of conversation *isn't* how he's coping. This is a sublime relief and for one precious hour, he's almost able to forget that his life outside these walls has stopped.

They are just finishing their drinks when Jenny, the company secretary, asks him what he has got planned for the weekend.

"Um, nothing really," Sean replies.

Jenny stares at him, nods gently and smiles understandingly. A wave of sadness sweeps over Sean. *Nothing planned, ever again*, he thinks, dramatically.

"Um, why don't you come out with Mike and me, then?" Jenny asks. "We're going to that place out in Bourn for a curry. It's supposed to be amazing."

Sean starts to feel embarrassed. He can see what Jenny's doing. He can picture how Jenny sees him. Because though Sean and Catherine have eaten with Jenny and Mike before, without Catherine it becomes a whole different thing – it becomes an act of kindness towards him, an act of sacrifice. Just imagining it makes him squirm.

"Um, thanks," Sean says. "But not this weekend. I've... some... um, things to do at the house. But thanks. Now, I really do need to get back and finish off these bloody balconies."

Jenny nods gently and flashes a knowing look at Steve and Jim.

"You should go," Jim says. "It'll do you good to get out."

"Yes," Steve says. "I think so too."

"Not this time," Sean says, standing so fast he almost knocks his chair over. "See you back at the office, then."

"Stupid!" Sean admonishes himself as he crosses the car park. "What's so difficult about a bloody curry with Jenny and Mike?"

But despite his attempts at convincing himself, the vision of him sitting opposite concerned Jenny and matey Mike remains tooth-achingly uncomfortable.

So, no, he won't be going to dinner with Jenny and Mike, or with any of the other couples they know. He'll be drinking his cans of beer alone. He'll be listening to his old records, alone. And he'll be waiting for Sunday to arrive so that he can open the next damned envelope.

Snapshot #6

Computer printout from Google Street View. The image, in the middle of a large empty sheet of A4 paper, shows a pub called the Dog and Doublet.

Cassette #6

Hi Sean.

I don't think we ever took a photo of us in Kipps wine bar, so I asked Maggie to help me out. Unfortunately, this is all she could come up with.

Don't worry, by the way. Maggie doesn't know anything about what's in these tapes. What you tell and to whom and when you do it is entirely up to you. If you do have a need to share any of this, feel free. I won't, being dead, object.

So, The Dog and Doublet is what they're calling Kipps wine bar these days, or so I'm told. I'm pretty sure they changed the façade too, because I don't remember it looking like that at all. I hope it's the right place. I secretly suspect that Maggie got this wrong.

Anyway, it's important because it's supposed to be Kipps, and Kipps is where we spent some of the best nights I've ever had. And because Kipps is where I told you I was pregnant.

I'd spent three weeks arguing with Mum – she wanted me to have an abortion and she had finally (almost) worn me down. She had very nearly convinced me that it was the only sensible option. I was only eighteen, after all. I was too young to have a baby. I had my whole life ahead of me and blah blah blah.

But as far as I was concerned, the main reason was that I didn't know who the father was.

Even though I never told you that, I suspect it doesn't come as a complete shock to you. I reckon you must have worked that out.

So that night, we went to Kipps and we got our drinks. I needed some Dutch courage in order to say what I had to say. I was terrified that you would dump me on the spot. I was imagining sleeping on the bench in the bus shelter and going home the very next morning. I could hardly breathe, I was so scared.

You could sense that something was up and you asked me what was wrong. By that point I had a couple of pints of Tennent's inside me, so I blurted it out. "I'm pregnant," I said.

I was going to tell you that it might be Phil's, I honestly was. It was the very next thing that I was going to say. But I didn't get any further than, "but the thing is…"

Your face slipped into this enormous grin. It wasn't what I had been expecting at all.

"What?" I asked. I thought you were maybe about to laugh in my face.

"I don't know," you said. "That's just amazing. That's brilliant!"

And so I couldn't bring myself to tell you, there and then. I promised myself I'd tell you the next morning, or at the very least before I left.

I asked you, instead, if you thought that I should keep it. I thought you might ask why not, in which case I could explain that things weren't as simple as they seemed.

But you said, "Of course! Of course you should keep it! We're going to have a baby!" And then you leaned over the table to kiss me and knocked your pint over.

I was soaked, but we stayed and I spent the evening putting up objections. Where would I live? What would I live on? And you just got drunker and drunker and happier and happier. "I don't care," you kept saying. "I don't care about any of that. We'll sort it."

I woke up late the next morning with a terrible hangover. I lay in bed for ages thinking about how I was going to announce my bad news.

But when I came downstairs, you, Alistair and Theresa, who had just moved in, were having one of what you called your "house meetings".

It had all been decided, you announced. I could stay. We would live together. Alistair and Theresa agreed. "It'll be like a commune," Alistair commented. Theresa was looking forward to babysitting, she said.

It was the most exciting thing that had ever happened to me, so I didn't say a word.

I phoned Mum from that call box at the end of the road and told her the news. I told her that I wasn't coming to my appointment at the abortion clinic and then I told her I wasn't coming home at all.

She went all weird and shrieky on me then, and in the end I had to hang up on her.

I don't think she ever forgave me for that, or not until she met April at any rate.

I'm sure this was hard to hear, my darling. So I apologise again for that. But brace yourself, for there are, I'm afraid, a few more shockers to come.

• • •

The following Saturday, Sean decides to phone Maggie. She has left three messages on his voicemail in the last forty eight hours and he's pretty certain that if he doesn't speak to her soon she'll appear on the doorstep.

As the house is a mess and the freezer is empty again and because he finds himself unable to sum up the energy to fix either, he really doesn't want her checking up on him right now.

The truth of the matter is that he's been feeling sadder than usual since last Sunday's tape, perhaps even what people call *depressed*.

He has only once or twice had doubts about April's lineage in the past and nowadays, having parented her since she was born, all logic tells him that it's immaterial. He loves her, that's all. He has always loved her and nothing anyone could ever say is going to change that. And yet, and yet... was it not more comfortable feeling certain that he was her biological parent? Because even though he had doubts from time to time, in the end, this is what he had decided to believe, for the simple reason that believing anything else was unbearable.

But now, unless he does a DNA test, he'll never know. And what possible point could there be in taking a DNA test at this point? What possible advantage could there be in knowing, other than avoiding this, other than avoiding ever having to think about it again.

So he's angry at Catherine, too. Not for what she might or might not have done when she was eighteen but perhaps for not telling him at the time and definitely for deciding to tell him now. It strikes him as cowardly, actually. Yes, waiting until she's not even there to hear how he feels about it is cowardly.

"Ah," Maggie says, when he finally makes the call. "He lives!"

"Yep," Sean says, pretending to be upbeat. "He lives! How are you?"

"Oh, you know," Maggie says.

"Not really. That's why I'm asking."

"Oh, we've been trying to choose where to go on holiday this summer," Maggie says. "But it seems we can even argue about that."

Thinking that the more they talk about Maggie and Dave, the less he'll have to talk about himself, Sean asks, "So what are the options?"

"Well, I want to go to Portugal."

"Ooh, nice," Sean says. "I can't see why anyone would argue with that."

"Well, thank you! Maybe I should just go with you."

"So what's Dave's objection?" Sean asks, ignoring that comment.

"Oh, Dave says the sea's too cold. On account of it being the Atlantic or something. He says it'll be boiling hot on the beach but we won't be able to dip a toe in the sea without having a heart attack."

"Ah," Sean says. "Well, there might be a little truth in that. This is for when?"

"June or July."

"Then yeah... the sea could be pretty chilly."

"Damn you both," Maggie says. "It's cheap as chips. And the hotel's gorgeous. And there's a bloody pool anyway. And I don't want to spend a thousand pounds going to Bali."

"Oh, that's an altogether different proposition," Sean comments.

"Tell me about it."

"Very nice! Bali's stunning, so I hear."

"Yes. But it's a day to get there and a day to get back and it's way over my budget."

"Maybe you could settle for somewhere halfway?" Sean offers.

"Maybe," Maggie says, doubtfully. "Where would that be? I'm rubbish at geography."

"Um, Israel, I reckon," Sean says. "Or Saudi Arabia. Dubai maybe?"

"Oh, faaabulous," Maggie says, sarcastically. "I'll get my burka dry cleaned."

"Israel's quite trendy at the moment," Sean says, "surprising as that may seem. A couple of people from the office have been there recently. And no burka necessary."

"You know I spent all winter collecting for the poor Palestinians, right?" Maggie says.

"Ah, of course. Sorry, forgot. Egypt then? That's a bit closer than halfway. Or Greece. Or Turkey."

"Actually, Turkey might do it. That's gotta be fairly cheap, right? I don't think I'll ever be going to Greece again. Not after last time."

"Ah, no. Sorry. I forgot about our Grecian extravaganza."

"I didn't. Would Turkey have warmer water, then?"

"Than Portugal? Oh, definitely. It's the Med, isn't it."

"Great, well, if Monsieur deigns to calm down, I'll suggest it. Unless *you* want to go with me? To Portugal? What do you think?"

"I... think that wouldn't do your relationship with Dave much good," Sean says.

Maggie sighs. "No, you're probably right. So how are you, honey?"

"I'm OK."

"We don't seem to be seeing much of you."

"No?"

"No. Are you still not feeling... you know... up to being sociable?"

"I guess I'm not really. No."

"Well, I'll give you a few more weeks, but then we'll come round and kidnap you for a night out if need be. We can't have you sitting at home for the rest of your life."

Sean pulls a face at the phone. "I'm not sitting at home. I'm at work all day every day, Mags. But I'll, um, let you know when I feel up to being kidnapped, OK?"

"Have you finished that box, yet?"

"Catherine's recordings?"

"Yeah."

"No, they're one a week. I told you," Sean says.

"Oh, yes. Of course. How many were there again?"

"Twenty-nine."

"Twenty-nine weeks? Gosh, that's..."

"Almost seven months. Yes."

"I hope they're nice, Sean. I mean, I hope they're doing you good. Because I do worry if that's really healthy for someone in your position."

Forgetting momentarily that he's on the phone and that Maggie can't see him, Sean shrugs. "I don't know really," he says. "Some are a bit... Actually, I'm sorry Mags, but I don't think I want to talk about them at the moment."

"Of course. I can understand that," Maggie replies. "But just remember that... Look, this is difficult to say, but she's gone, Sean."

"I know that."

"I just mean that it's your life. So open them as fast or as slowly as *you* need to. Do whatever's best for *you*."

"Right," Sean says, feeling vaguely irked – he feels as if Maggie might be dissing his dead wife and that's not really OK. "Um, there's someone at the door, Mags," Sean lies. "The postman, I think. So I'll have to go, OK?"

"OK, honey. Look after yourself. And remember we all love you, OK?"

"Thanks," Sean says. "Bye Mags."

He hangs up the phone and then blows noisily through pursed lips. "Well, that's that done," he mutters.

He makes himself a cup of coffee and sits and stares at the box of envelopes. He thinks about what Maggie said and allows himself to wonder if it *is* healthy.

Because she's right, of course. Catherine isn't here. And only he can decide what works best for him.

The thing is that he *can't* decide what works best for him. Because though there's a certain appeal to bingeing on the tapes, to getting it all over with, the image of him sitting with that pile of opened envelopes, the idea that there would be no more to look forward to and no more surprises to be afraid of, is terrifying to him.

In a way, of course, the tapes are keeping Catherine alive. As long as she remains unpredictable, as long as he doesn't know what she's going to say next, it's as if she hasn't, entirely, ceased to exist.

For want of a better idea, he decides that, for now, he'll stick to the plan.

Snapshot #7

35 mm format, colour. A young woman stands behind the counter of a local store. Her face is framed by the numerous products crowding the counter – a rack of multicoloured chewing gum packets to the right and another containing lollipops and bars of chocolate on the left. Behind her, a refrigerated cabinet is stacked high with cans of beer and beside this a rack of cigarette packets can be clearly seen.

Sean peers into the photo and can actually remember the smell of the place: musky and spicy. For this is the corner shop where he once worked, his first ever part-time job. And it's also where Catherine, who is manning the counter in the photo, worked once he had returned to college. In the photo, she looks young and excited, and beautiful.

It's a stunning photo, but Sean has no recollection of it being taken, nor, in fact, of ever having seen it before. He scans the products in the store and remembers the taste of Tennent's Extra and the sensation of Toffee Treets melting in the mouth.

Cassette #7

Hello Sean.

I'm not feeling so well, today, so this is my third attempt at recording a message. Hopefully this time I'll make it through.

So here we have the "Paki Shop". Of course no one says that anymore, thank God.

It's quite shocking to realise how naturally we used to say that. "I'm just popping to the Paki shop." Horrific, isn't it?

I even heard Bilal, the owner's son, call it that once, but then I suppose that's probably OK. I guess it's like the gays reclaiming the word "queer", or the blacks calling each other "nigger".

The shop is the reason you had to return to Wolverhampton that first weekend we met, only you were too embarrassed to tell me. How silly, eh? As if I of all people would judge you badly for something like that. But then, I suppose, you didn't know me yet.

Your parents had cut you off and refused to pay their contribution to your student grant, as I recall, so you were earning a bit of money when and wherever you could. You also did envelope stuffing and newspaper delivery. But back to Salman's Mini Mart, because that's the bit of history I want to tell you today. I want to tell you why I loved Theresa so much.

When your courses started again in September, *I* got the job instead. Do you remember how ecstatic I was to be working there? You had all agreed to let me live rent-free but I was so proud to be able to earn a little money and occasionally supply you all with dinner.

Salman was never anything but lovely to me. Do you remember how he used to give me all the stuff that was past its sell-by date? I used to feed the whole house with dodgy tuna sandwiches, out of date individual trifles and boxes of chocolates that had bloomed because of the summer heat. But it wasn't all roses.

Did you see what I did there?

Anyway, Bilal, Salman's eldest, was revolting. He used to push past me when I was behind the counter. He could always find an excuse to squeeze his way behind me when I was serving someone and couldn't say anything. I used to feel him pressing his hard-on against my arse as he reached up for the batteries or lighters that were on that shelf above the counter. And after a couple of weeks, he started talking dirty to me as well. He used to ask me for blow jobs. "How much?" he used to ask, over and over again. "How much for a blow job in the store room? A fiver? A tenner?"

Now, I understood that he had grown up in Pakistan and everything and I realised that he was struggling to understand that a woman in makeup and a skirt wasn't necessarily a prostitute, so I did my best to just ignore him. "More than you can afford," I used to say, thinking that taking the mickey out of him might help keep him at bay.

But it just got worse and worse and I started to become afraid that he'd actually try something on with me, especially when I was working evenings and it was dark.

These days, I would have recorded him on my phone or something and sued the arse off him for sexual harassment, but these were the eighties and this was Wolverhampton. And we needed that money so badly...

I nearly told you about it a couple of times, but I was scared that you'd kill him and end up in prison. Really. I really thought that might happen.

In the end, I told Theresa and she was simply amazing.

I came home one afternoon and she was the only person in the house. Alistair was off scoring dope somewhere, I expect, and you were still at college.

Theresa asked me, jokingly, how it was going with Bilal. She thought that he was cute, which, purely in aesthetic terms,

75

I suppose he was. He was neatly groomed and smooth skinned and muscular; he had olive skin and that amazingly shiny jet-black hair. But it was the wrong question at the wrong time. I'd been having my first bouts of morning sickness and I'd been feeling tired and irritable even before I had spent the day being hassled by Bilal. So the minute she asked me the question, I burst into tears.

Theresa was furious. She let me cry myself out and then she marched me back to the store.

Now Theresa, as you'll remember, was a pretty full-on feminist. She spent all her free time blockading Cruise missile convoys with the women at Greenham Common and she certainly wasn't afraid of Bilal.

"I want to talk to you," she said, once we had entered the store. There were three or four people queuing to pay, but she didn't give a damn. "I want to know why you're harassing my friend here."

"I don't harass no one," Bilal said, continuing to serve the next customer.

"Yes you did!" Theresa shouted. "You've been rubbing your erect penis against her arse and trying to force her to give you oral gratification." She sounded like a lawyer in a television programme cross-examining someone.

The people in the shop were all mortified. So was I. A woman with a child muttered something disapproving and bustled her kid out of the store.

"My friend, your employee, is married!" Theresa said, which was a lie at the time. "And she's also pregnant!"

Bilal was speechless. He didn't know where to look, so he just kept on serving people.

"Now if I ever hear you've said *anything* inappropriate to her *ever* again, you'll regret it because, one, I will tell her
76

husband – and he's a big man with a nasty temper – and two, I'll have fifty women from the S.U. outside your store with banners and placards and we'll demonstrate until every newspaper covers it and everyone in the community knows what a pervert you are. And three, I'll call the police and get you arrested. I'm a law student, by the way, so I do know how to do that."

Oh, you should have seen her, Sean, she was shaking all that hennaed hair of hers around. She was on *fire,* and I remember thinking that she'd be some great human rights lawyer one day, which of course, she turned out to be.

The shop had emptied by now and Bilal didn't know what to say or what to do, so he just stared at his feet.

"Is that clear?" Theresa asked him. When he didn't reply, she shouted it. "IS THAT CLEAR, Bilal?"

"Yes," Bilal mumbled.

"Come on," she said, taking my hand. "We're done here."

As we reached the door, Bilal mumbled, "Fucking lesbians," so Theresa spun back to look at him. "What did you say?" she asked.

"Nothing," Bilal said.

"That's what I thought," she said. "Well, I am a lesbian and you'd do well to be afraid because we lesbians are a sisterhood and we're mad, bad and dangerous to know. Oh, and Bilal. Don't even think about sacking her over this, OK? Because the laws on undeclared workers are extremely severe and you'll end up in jail. And all those beefy men in prison would certainly know what to do with a pretty boy like yourself. Your arse wouldn't know what'd hit it."

As we walked home, she put her arm around me. I was still shaking.

"Is that true?" I asked, eventually.

"What, me being lesbian? Not really. I prefer to remain undefined," she said. "I don't like to submit to other people's sexual stereotypes."

"No, I meant about going to prison?"

"Oh. I've no idea to be honest," Theresa said. "We haven't done employment law yet. It put the wind up him though."

I never had a problem with Bilal again. In fact, from that day on, he was always extra-nice to me. And God, I loved Theresa after that.

• • •

It's just after eleven in the morning when Sean pulls up outside The Cedars care home. He levers himself from the driving seat and places his hands behind his head as he stretches after the long drive.

It's a beautiful May morning – the first time this year that it has actually felt like summer – and as he looks up into the deep blue sky and notices the tweeting of the birds in the tree above him, his spirits momentarily lift.

He scans the car park for April's Mini and on spotting it – lazily parked diagonally across one of the visitor's bays – he pulls his coat from the car and heads indoors.

April, who is sitting in the lobby, fiddling with her smartphone, glances up as he enters, returns her gaze to her phone for a fraction of a second and then, once his presence registers, looks up anew. "Oh! Hi Dad!" she says, dumping her phone in her handbag and jumping up.

Sean crosses the lobby to meet her and pecks her on the cheek. "You found it OK, then?"

April nods. "The GPS did," she says.

"You haven't been waiting too long, have you?" he asks.

April shakes her head. "Ten minutes, max. The traffic was easy, that's all. I should really have just gone in, but..." By way of explanation, she shrugs.

"It's scary," Sean says. "You know you don't have to come at all. I know how upsetting she can be."

"I'd feel bad if I *never* came," April says. "And I'm overdue. I haven't been once since she changed homes. Plus, like I said on the phone, I'm on my way to Cardiff."

"Cardiff, eh?" Sean says, as they cross the lobby to the reception desk. "The lives of the rich and famous, eh?"

"It's where Simon's living now," April explains. Simon is her oldest, most faithful friend from her student years and Sean has met him on a number of occasions.

"And how is Simon these days?" he asks.

"He's good. Writing for the Beeb, these days. And still dating Gavin."

"That's good," Sean says.

"Hello? Can I help you?"

Sean turns to face the receptionist. "Hi, yes," he says. "Sean Patrick. Here to see Cynthia Patrick, my mother. This is my daughter, April."

The receptionist checks her computer screen, then gives Sean's driving licence a cursory glance before handing it back.

"Room twenty-three," she says, then, glancing at the clock, she adds, "She should be in her room at the moment. You know the way, right?"

Sean nods. "I do, indeed," he says.

She buzzes them through the glass security door, and they walk past the empty dining room and on through the open-plan lounge area. It's a large, airy space, elegantly furnished with blue wing-back armchairs and comfortable blue velour sofas. Large French windows look out onto a pretty garden

79

area. A dozen elderly residents are dotted around the room in various states of wakefulness.

"It's not bad here," April says. "It's definitely better than the old place, anyway."

"Well, it needs to be," Sean says. "It's costing a bloody fortune."

When they get to room twenty-three the door is slightly ajar. "Ready?" Sean asks, his hand raised in preparation to knock.

April takes a deep breath and smiles tightly. "Go for it," she says.

Sean raps with his knuckles and eases the door open. "Hello?" he asks, gently pushing at it until they can step inside.

The room is clean and pretty if minimally furnished. It has a blue carpet and matching blue bedspread and curtains. It contains an unmade double bed, a chest of drawers, a small desk with a chair and another blue wing-back armchair. The interior designer at The Cedars clearly has a favourite colour.

Sean's mother is sitting in the armchair. She's staring into the middle distance and working her mouth.

"Hello?" Sean says again more loudly as he steps into her line of vision. "Hello, Mum? Look who I've brought to see you!"

Cynthia turns her head only slightly. Her eyes flick towards April and then back again to face Sean.

"Hi Gran," April says, wiggling her fingers and looking doubtful.

Cynthia wrinkles her brow.

At that moment a pretty black nurse appears in the doorway. "Oh, hello!" she says with fake-sounding enthusiasm. "Got visitors have we?" Her accent is an unusual combination of Caribbean and West Country.

She enters the room and crosses to Cynthia's side, then gently reaches out and tucks a stray wisp of grey hair behind Cynthia's ear, before turning to face Sean and April. "It's good that you've come see her. You's her son, yes?"

Sean nods. "Yes, and this is my daughter."

"Of course," the nurse says. "Yes, it's good of you to come, only..." She blinks slowly and shakes her head almost imperceptibly.

"Not a good day for it?" Sean asks.

The nurse shrugs. "You know how it is," she says. "It be coming and going. There's no harm you sitting with her. She'll probably like that. But I wouldn't be hoping for much more this morning."

Sean nods. "Fair enough," he says.

"Can I get you a tea, maybe? Or a coffee?"

"Tea would be nice," Sean says.

"Yes, tea would be great," April agrees.

"OK. I'll, um, just fetch those for you. I'll be getting you a chair too," she tells April.

"Oh, I'm fine," April replies. "I'll just sit on the bed if that's OK?"

"So, how are you, Mum?" Sean asks as he pulls the chair from the desk and sets it opposite his mother.

Cynthia grinds her teeth noisily and continues to frown at him as if, from wherever she currently thinks she is, Sean's presence presents her with some unsolvable riddle.

"I'm Sean. Your son."

Cynthia frowns more deeply. "Sean?" she repeats.

Sean reaches out for her boney hand and places it between his own. "Yes. Sean. Your youngest son."

"Sean?" Cynthia says again.

"Yes, Mum. Sean. That's right."

"Hello, Sean," his mother says, flatly.

"Hello, Mum," he replies, patting her hand gently with his own and then casting a discreet grimace at his daughter.

"Do you know who *I* am?" April asks, her own brow beginning to furrow.

Cynthia wrinkles her nose and nods vaguely in April's direction.

"April's asking if you remember her," Sean says. "You remember April, don't you?"

Cynthia shakes her head. "I don't like her," she mumbles. "I never liked her. I don't know why you brought her here."

"Mum!" Sean says. "That's *April*. It's not..."

But April, whose mouth has dropped, is already standing, already heading for the door. "I'll see you outside," she croaks. "Take your time."

Sean catches up with April at the security door, where she is trapped waiting for the receptionist to notice her presence and buzz her out. "Hey," he says, catching her by the elbow. "Honey..."

"Oh... no..." April protests. "No, go back. I didn't mean... Go back and take your time." Her eyes, Sean notices, are glistening.

"She doesn't mean that, you know," Sean says. "She thinks you're Catherine, that's all."

"Really?"

The door buzzes to signal that they can push it open, but April raises her hand and makes a *gimme five* gesture to the receptionist, so she locks it again.

"Yes," Sean says, reaching out to stroke his daughter's back. "She never liked your mother much. And the only memories she has these days are from way back. She thinks you're Catherine. And she thinks this is nineteen-eighty-something."

April sighs and nods. She swipes at one eye with the back of her index finger. "That's still... I don't know..."

"Unpleasant?" Sean offers. "Hard to bear?"

"Well, yes."

Sean nods. "You're right. It is. But her brain's frazzled and her filter's gone haywire. It was never very good, to be honest – the filter. But now it's completely packed up, so she just says the first thing she can think of whether it makes any sense or not. Try not to take it to heart."

"Does she even know about Mum... you know...?"

"Does she know about her dying?" Sean asks.

April nods.

Sean shakes his head gently. "No," he says, looking pained. "No. I didn't tell her. There's no point, really. She doesn't... you know... *retain* anything. Even if she did understand, it would only be fleeting. And she'd probably just say she was glad or something. There's really no point."

April nods and reaches out to squeeze her father's arm. "You're too nice to her, Dad."

"Hum," Sean says. "I've heard that before."

"From Mum?"

Sean nods and bites his bottom lip.

"So, are you going back in there?" April asks.

"I have to, really," Sean says. "I mean, there's not much point, but now I've driven all this way..."

"I'll come back in if you want me to."

Sean shakes his head. "No," he says. "I think it's easier without you, to be honest. You just relax or go for a walk or whatever. And then..." He glances at his watch before continuing. "At, say, twelve thirty, we can go for lunch. There's a nice pub down the road. How does that sound?"

"OK," April says. "I'm sorry Dad, really I am. But the truth is that she does my head in."

Sean laughs sourly and as he turns and starts to head back towards room twenty-three, he says, "Don't worry, honey. She does my head in too."

· · ·

As they enter the Langford Poacher, April pulls a face. "God," she says, "it looks more like an old people's home in here than back there."

"Really?" Sean asks, looking around. "I quite like it. Well, the food's good, anyway. And they're friendly."

"Sorry," April says. "I suppose it's just the carpet, really."

"Hum," Sean says, looking down at his feet. "Yes, I see what you mean. It is a bit 1970s."

Once they have ordered food and carried their drinks to a table, April asks, "So? How was it?"

Sean shrugs. "You saw how she was, today. I just sat and read the newspaper to her, really. I'm not even sure if she understood who I am. But you know... These things have to be done. Sometimes she has good days and she's almost like normal. But you just can't tell."

"What about Perry? Does he still come regularly?"

Sean nods. "Mum always got on better with Perry than with me. I don't think she's quite such hard work when he comes. But yeah. He comes every weekend, I think."

"So she must recognise you. I mean, if she treats you differently."

"On some level, she does, I suppose," Sean says, sipping at his pint of IPA. "Though I don't think she's really *conscious* of who I am. Not on days like today, anyway. It's more as if my presence brings out a habit of behaviour, you know? She's always been grumpy towards me, so she still is, but it's just a habit really. It's the same with Perry. She was always nicer to him so, out of habit, she still behaves the same way, automatically."

"I still think it's weird," April says, "to like one of your kids more than the other."

"Ha," Sean says. "It's more common than you'd imagine. You're just lucky you were an only child. You got *smothered* in love."

April pulls a face. She's pretending to be unconvinced. "Will you go and see him afterwards?" she asks.

"Perry?"

April nods.

"Oh, no," Sean says. "No, I saw him at the funeral. Once a year's enough."

"You're right," April says. "I am lucky to be an only child."

"Anyway, the Patricks are a depressing bunch," Sean says. "Tell me about you."

"I'm a Patrick," April protests.

"You know what I mean."

"I do. And I'm fine. All things considered, I'm OK."

"How are things with Ronan?"

"Great," April says. "He's working loads at the moment, which is why I'm off to Cardiff on my own. He couldn't afford to take a break right now."

"That's a shame."

"Well, you know how it is. He's self-employed. He has to take the work when it comes. He's doing a whole bunch of stuff for Pfizer at the moment."

"Brochures and what-have-you?"

April nods. "I've been helping a bit in my free time, too. Which is why I'm off to see Simon, to be honest. I don't really want to spend my week's holiday writing copy about anti-depressants."

"No," Sean says. "I can understand that."

"What about you?"

"Work?"

April shrugs. "Work, home, everything. How are you doing?"

"I'm OK, too," Sean says. "I have my ups and downs but I'm basically OK."

"Do you get lonely?" April asks. "I think about you, you know, watching telly on your own, heating up your own meals and all that stuff. It must be really hard after all those years."

"Sometimes it is," Sean admits. "But I just feel sad when I feel sad and lonely when I'm lonely. And I tell myself it's OK to feel fine some days, too. You can over-analyse this stuff."

"That sounds quite wise. I hope Mags and Dave and everyone are looking after you, are they?"

Sean laughs. "Oh, they try. But to be honest, I've not been feeling that sociable. I tried to force myself a couple of times, but in the end I decided to let myself off the hook. I mean, I'm out at work all day. It's not like I'm a hermit or anything. And if I don't want to see anyone at the weekend then I reckon that's up to me. Right?"

"I suppose," April says. "As long as it doesn't go on forever, I suppose that's fine. But you'll need to get up and out there at some point. You realise that, right?"

"Hum," Sean says, vaguely. He'd rather not even try to imagine what getting "up and out there" implies. "Are you still seeing your counsellor guy?"

April laughs and sips at her Coke before replying. "It's a woman. Oh God, I haven't told you about her, have I? She was a bit rubbish, to be honest."

"Yeah?"

"Yeah... She told me all this really obvious stuff that everyone knows. You know, the different stages of grief. Denial, anger, all that stuff. And then she started banging on about crystals."

"Crystals?"

April wrinkles her nose cutely and nods. "Yeah. She said I needed to get myself some Rose Quartz. She said it was the most *compassionate* crystal of all."

"Compassionate, eh?"

"Uh-huh. And you know what I'm like about anything that even remotely smacks of mumbo-jumbo. I suddenly felt like I was paying the most unstable girlfriend I ever had at college for counselling. It's funny really, because half the time the women who become counsellors can't even make a cup of tea without bursting into tears. It's nearly always the emotional wrecks who suddenly want to become counsellors."

Sean laughs. "Yes, I know what you mean, actually. There's definitely some truth in that."

"Oh!" April says, reaching down for her handbag and rummaging inside it. "She actually gave me a bit of compassionate quartz. I've got it here somewhere."

"Yeah?" Sean asks.

"Ha!" April says, producing a small rose coloured stone from the depths of her bag. "Ta-dah!"

"Ooh, my," Sean says mockingly, peering in to study the stone. "That does look like a compassionate bit of rock."

"You can have it," April says, pushing it towards Sean with her fingertip. "I think it's healed me now, so..."

"Well, thanks," Sean says, taking the stone and rolling it between finger and thumb. "I, um, don't know what to say."

"Om, maybe?" April says.

"Om?"

"As in, Ommmmmmm," she says, making meditational O signs with her fingers and thumbs.

"Ah, *Om*... Yes," Sean says.

A waitress appears at their table. "Cod and chips and a Niçoise Salad?" she asks.

"Yep," Sean says, sliding the stone into his trouser pocket. "Yep, that's us."

Snapshot #8

35 mm format, colour. A young couple stand in front of a red brick council building. The woman is wearing a simple white satin dress with translucent lacy sleeves. She has back-brushed her hair to increase its volume and is holding a posy of pink flowers. The man is dressed in a black, wide-lapelled, pinstripe suit, a white shirt and a wide red tie. He's wearing oversized aviator-style glasses and grinning broadly.

Sean studies the photo as he eats his Sunday breakfast of toast and Marmite. He can remember the sensation and the mothball smell of the too-big suit, purchased from the local Oxfam shop.

He looks at his own beaming grin, his wispy beard and his huge NHS prescription glasses. "The eighties..." he mumbles. "Jesus!"

It had been an incredibly stressful day and he had been smiling because that was the moment he realised that they had made it through. They had, despite all of the objections, managed it.

His father had refused to come. Because his mother had made an excuse for him, Catherine had never known this. Cynthia had said that her husband's back was bad. But yes, he had refused, point blank, to come. If Sean wanted to ruin his life, that was up to him, he said. But he was damned if he was going to bear witness to it.

Cynthia had come, though, driven by Perry in his brand new Jaguar. Perry was in real estate and these were the Thatcher years. Perry's double-breasted suit had probably cost more than Sean's entire student grant.

But the truth was that it would have been better if they had all just stayed away. Perry seemed to think that his brotherly duty was to ask Sean repeatedly if he was absolutely certain he *wanted* to get married. And his mother had spent the day looking thin-lipped and inexplicably angry.

Even Catherine's mother had been against the wedding to start with. But being of a more pragmatic nature than Sean's, she had performed an impressive U turn once she realised that it couldn't be stopped. The second her daughter had entered the register office, Wendy had switched from sucking lemons to become their most enthusiastic cheerleader. Once the deed had been done, she had even, somewhat bizarrely, thanked Sean.

"I think this is incredible, what you're doing," she had said. "Thank you so much."

When he had asked Catherine about this a few days later, she had simply laughed. "She's just thankful someone's taken me off her hands," she said. "She never thought anyone would be mad enough."

Cassette #8

Hello Fiancé.

So, the big day! The 27th of November, 1982. I was freezing in that dress, but I didn't have a nice coat I could wear, so I grinned and put up with it. Just look at how young we were!

Looking at this photo now, I can see why Mum was so upset. We *were* too young to get married. And I *was* too young to have a baby. Not that I regret any of it, but lord, can you imagine how we would have felt if April had got pregnant at eighteen? You would have had a hissy-fit.

I found a couple of wedding photos, actually, but as they all also featured your mum and Perry looking as miserable as sin, I chose this one. But do hunt them out and have a look because Theresa and Alistair are in there as well and for some reason it quite cheered me up to see their faces again. I wonder where they are now?

God, the parents were a bit of a nightmare though, weren't they?

Your dad was laid up with sciatica and your mum was furious, I think, because he wasn't there. Well, that was the official version, anyway.

We all knew that the truth was simply that they thought I was too common for you, which is unsurprising in a way. My own mother thought that. God, *I* thought that!

I think your mum thought I was slutty because I'd got pregnant, too. As if that was something I could do on my own!

Anyway, you know when Mum came with me in the taxi? Well, I know how perfect you've always thought she is, but I have to tell you that even she tried to talk me out of getting married until the last possible moment. "Are you *sure* you want to do this?" she kept asking. "You don't have to marry him just because he's got you up the duff." She always had a way with words, my mum. "Look at *me*!" she said. "I had you but didn't *marry* the guy. Even I knew better than that!"

Unlike your mother, who was angry with me, mine thought it was all your fault, of course. "Just because he's been irresponsible," she said. "It's not like we're living in the fifties anymore. It's not like he's never heard of johnnies."

In the end, I couldn't stand it anymore, so I told her about Phil. It was meant to shut her up. I told her that I didn't even know who the father *was*.

She got upset then about what would happen if you found out. "He'll dump you in a second," she told me.

So I lied and said that you knew. I told her that you didn't care. And that did the trick.

By the time that had sunk in, she had completely changed her mind about you; she had decided that you were the bee's knees after all!

The ceremony was a bit lacklustre. This was, after all, Wolverhampton Civic Centre, not Canterbury Cathedral. But we didn't give a damn, did we? We'd made it to the altar, or the registrar's desk at any rate. We were in our little private bubble of happiness and we didn't care about any of them.

Afterwards, we went back to the house for our little party. There were quite a few people, though I can only really remember Theresa and Alistair, oh, and that Welsh girl, Bronwen. That tall, bald guy, Dave, was there too, I think, but then he was always at all the parties. He was always wherever there was free beer. Alistair soon had music blasting out and everyone got drunk except your mother, but even she didn't get me down for long.

She complained about the state of the house, I remember, and she was upset that there wasn't a wedding cake, too. She moaned about the cigarette smoke and the loud music, but we just partied on regardless, dancing around her and Perry looking outraged together in the corner of the room.

At one point, I went over to try to get her involved. I was tipsy (we didn't worry about drinking when pregnant back then and, thank God, April turned out just fine).

My mum was drunk on Alistair's home-brew and stoned on Alistair's joints, too. She was dancing around like a Dervish to Dexys Midnight Runners and I felt sorry for your poor Mum looking so out-of-it in the corner, watching us all dancing. I suddenly wanted us all to be friends.

So I grooved up to her and said something like, "Come on Cynthia, let your hair down a bit. You might as well."

Now, I've never told you this because I knew it would upset you, but you've probably always wondered why we got off to such a bad start. Well, your mum didn't want to be friends, that's the thing. She said, "How dare you call me that. It's Mrs Patrick to you."

"Oh," I said, thinking that this must be another one of those posh rules I knew so little about.

"And don't think I don't know what you are," she said. Her voice was quite unpleasant. It was a sort of snarl, really. "I wasn't born yesterday. I know *exactly* what you are."

Theresa, who was watching all of this, swooped in to save me again. She yanked me back to the middle of the room where everyone was whooping and dancing to *Come On Eileen*. She leaned into my ear and said, "Don't worry about her. She's so uptight, she doesn't even know what letting her hair down means."

I glanced over at your mum – I was on the verge of tears – and she said something to Perry and pointed at me and Perry laughed.

Mum, who was dancing beside me, had noticed something was up. She leant in between Theresa and me and said, really loudly, "She probably hasn't had a shag since Sean was conceived. That's her trouble. She just needs a good bonk."

All three of us fell about laughing.

I'm sorry, Sean, because that was a bit rude, really, wasn't it? But it was better than me crying all over everyone, I suppose. And we were, after all, very drunk by then.

Anyway, that's when I realised that your mum and I were never going to be mates. I found that out on my wedding day.

• • •

It is Sunday morning and Sean is at work.

He's alone in the vast open-plan offices of Nicholson-Wallace and is enjoying the eerie silence of the place. Despite it being nearly eleven o'clock, it's almost dark outside and his desk lamp casts a warm glow across his workspace.

Sean's behind schedule on a retirement home he's supposed to be working on. He's been putting it off, he has just realised, because it reminds him of his mother, and being reminded of his mother makes him feel very angry at the moment.

Actually, thinking about his parents has almost always made him feel angry, but since last week's tape, that feeling has become even more acute than normal.

He has always known that neither of his parents approved of his marriage to Catherine, but he always saw it as little more than part and parcel of their generalised disapproval of everything he did.

But he hadn't known that his mother had actually had words with Catherine. He never knew that she had been rude to her, and on their wedding day to boot.

As he clicks on the corner of a window and resizes it to fit the proportions of the wall, a rattling sound startles him and

94

he looks up to see that it has started to rain heavily. The wind is blowing the rain against the eastern windows with gusto.

The rain on the windows is actually a blessing in disguise, because Sean realises that he has forgotten an essential part of the brief for this job, namely that the windows must be cleanable from the inside, without ladders or any form of external access. He'll just have to change the hinge mechanism so that they can flip over 180 degrees for cleaning purposes. He really needs to stop thinking about Catherine and his mother. He really needs to concentrate.

In a way he blamed Catherine a little for their fraught relationship, he realises. Oh, he blamed his mother more, but if he's honest with himself, it was only because it was easier for him that way. It was Catherine he lived with, not his mother, after all.

He tries to think back to all the times he and Catherine had discussed his parents. Though he can't remember actually having reproached her in any way, there were times, he reckons, when he could perhaps have been a little more understanding. He could have apologised more often for his parents' behaviour.

The last tape message made him angry, specifically because he had wasted the entire Saturday visiting Cynthia in The Cedars. The message had made him wish he hadn't bothered. It had made him want to never bother again.

But this familiar feeling puts him in conflict with himself. It pits the Sean who wants to be loyal to his dead wife against the Sean who feels obligated towards his parents no matter what they might have said or done. Lordy, those blood ties run deep.

It's just before three when Sean gets home and though the sky is still threatening, the rain has now stopped.

On the doorstep, he finds a family sized apple crumble. It's wrapped in a plastic bag which also contains a Post-It note from Maggie.

"Came to see you but you're out! Which is a good thing! Eat this! Love Mags. xxx"

Sean lets himself into the house and peers into the empty refrigerator before heating up half of the apple crumble in the microwave. He had been intending to order a pizza but he finds himself suddenly too hungry to wait.

While he waits for the microwave to go "ping", he pulls the box from the cupboard and retrieves the next envelope.

Snapshot #9

Polaroid, colour. Faded. An exhausted, shiny-faced woman holds a swaddled baby in her arms. The baby's face is almost as pink and blotchy as the mother's.

"Huh," Sean says, fondly. He reaches out and runs the tip of his finger over April's tiny head as if, perhaps, he might feel again the warmth of her newborn skin.

He had been desperate to touch her, that was the thing. It had felt as if only touching her skin would make this moment real.

The labour had been difficult. Actually, he hadn't known at the time whether this labour was more or less difficult than your "average" labour, but certainly no one could, or ever did, describe Catherine's labour as "easy".

She had screamed and screamed for hours. She had screamed blue bloody murder. She had begged him to make it stop, as if such a thing was somehow in his power. Was this not his fault, after all? She had cried that it was a mistake, that her mother was right, that she wasn't ready for this, that she'd *never* be ready for this.

All of this, the nurses assured him, was "normal".

Eventually the screaming had stopped and his fear that Catherine was dying had been replaced by fear that something was wrong with the baby. Because this baby looked like no baby he had ever seen on television. This baby, covered in blood and blotches, looked like a baby from a horror film.

The nurses told him that this too was normal, but he hadn't been convinced.

But as soon as she had cried, everything had changed and he had switched from being scared to being desperate to touch her, just to confirm to himself that she was real. She looked so much like a tiny, plastic dolly, albeit a tiny, plastic *Halloween* dolly.

When he did get to hold her, a strange sense of pride had washed over him and the concept of "unconditional love", which he had recently discussed with Alistair, suddenly made sense. He understood only now, how you could love someone, how you could be *proud* of someone, simply because they *were,* simply because they existed. He had vowed, then, never to be like his own parents whose love had always seemed entirely conditional on recent performance. He had promised himself that he would never allow himself to forget this feeling no matter who April became, no matter what she ended up doing, no matter what her life choices turned out to be.

Alternating in waves with that sense of pride was fear. Because being a father felt like a whole different thing. It felt vast and terrifying. And in those moments of fear, everything his parents had said, everything Perry had said, seemed true. Because no, he *wasn't* sure about this. And no, he wasn't ready for this at all.

A nurse had taken April from his arms and handed her back to Catherine then, and this had prompted Catherine to start crying. Her emotions would be all over the place for weeks to come, but they didn't know that yet.

As Catherine wept, her tears falling on baby April's face, Sean had momentarily returned to his initial fears that something wasn't right with the baby. Catherine had now, he thought, spotted it too. It was the only explanation he could come up with for her looking and sounding so heartbroken.

He had tried to comfort her then but she had laughed maniacally through her tears, insisting that she was fine.

Even this, the nurse said, was normal. Nurses, it seemed, had different definitions for words like "normal".

"Go get yourself a hot chocolate from the machine at the end of the corridor," she had told him. "Give us a chance to clean things up here, eh?"

So Sean had done just that.

On his return, he had peered through the window and seen the baby suckling on her sleeping mother's breast, and in that moment yet another sensation had washed over him, a feeling so powerful that he can remember it vividly today, and as, looking at the photo, he does so, the hairs on the back of his neck bristle.

He had felt himself disappear, that was the sensation. It was as if he had stepped outside himself and could see his life from an entirely different perspective.

For his whole life, up until that point, had been about him. His only priority had been to work out what *he* wanted, what *he* was going to do to make *himself* happy.

Sure, there had been moments, many moments even, during which he had acted to make those around him happy. No one had ever accused Sean of being selfish.

But even those moments of supposed selflessness had, he suddenly saw, been motivated because doing whatever he was doing for whoever it was made *him* feel happy.

At the moment he looked through that window, however, everything changed, and something, his ego perhaps, momentarily vanished. The only thing that mattered henceforth was April, protecting April, providing for April;

making sure April was happy and healthy and loved. The sensation of selflessness, of total devotion to another, come what may, was like nothing he had ever sensed before.

It hadn't lasted, of course, but that was no small mercy, because who could survive with such intensity of emotion?

But the sensation had returned from time to time, whenever April was ill, or twice when she went missing, and a few times when she ran towards traffic, or rolled out of a taxi in high heels, drunk, in her late teens. And in those moments he had remembered that she was the only thing that mattered, that protecting this child was his only reason for being on this planet.

Cassette #9

Hi Sean.

April has just been to visit me – she has literally just left – which is why I dug this photo out. She told me that Ronan wants to have a baby! Has she told you that yet? If not, don't say a word! I'm probably not supposed to tell.

She's such an amazing girl. I'm sure she must have her down moments, but she certainly doesn't force them on anyone else. She's always "up", always buzzing around at full tilt.

The idea of her having children is a strange one for me, because I sort of believed that she would never get around to it. I don't know why I thought that, but I did. Anyway, she's certainly considering it now, so you may end up a granddad yet.

If it does happen, please don't get all weepy about my missing out on it all. I can honestly tell you that I have *never* longed for grandchildren. Bringing up one child was hard enough, but looking after other people's children has always struck me as a special kind of hell.

Looking at the photo, the first thing I remembered was how worried you were that she might be born on April the 1st! Do you remember? You were totally obsessed about her being called an April fool by everyone. You even asked me if I could "hang on" if she did want to come out on April the 1st. I think that you believed I just had to keep my knees together and she'd stay in there.

In the end she came, or rather was yanked out, at ten minutes to midnight and so was saved the ignominy of being an April fool.

Do you know, I can't for the life of me remember how she came to be called April! Isn't that the strangest thing? I think all these drugs they give me are messing with my brain.

I have some vague recollection that I was disappointed she'd been born in March as I wanted to call her April and you said, "Let's do it anyway". So perhaps it was as simple as that.

Giving birth was the hardest thing I have ever had to do. It was far harder than all this chemotherapy lark and this is, let's face it, pretty bad. But giving birth was so painful, Sean. There are no words sufficient to describe that level of pain. I would guess, though, that if hitting your funny bone is a three and shutting your finger in the door is, say, a five; if having your leg sawn off without anaesthetic would be a ten, then giving birth must be a fifteen. At least. People say you forget how bad it was but that's rubbish – it's just a lie people tell mothers-to-be to make them a little less scared. But they *should* be scared. It really is that bad.

I had been led to believe that I could ask for an epidural at any point, but when I finally caved in, by the time I finally thought, *oh, fuck this all-natural lark,* there were no anaesthetists available. They were dealing with a pile-up on the M6 or something and were up to their tits in mangled bodies (the nurses' words, not mine). What a nightmare!

So it was awful. Eight hours, as I recall, including two hours of screaming, horrendous, *Friday the 13th* horror-film pain.

By the time April appeared, she had put me through so much that I hated her. I know you're supposed to feel some instant, incredible bond with your offspring, but I didn't, I hated her.

I kept that to myself, though, I think, and over a few days it passed and was replaced by a terrifying kind of love that changed my entire world vision so that everything I could see, think, or imagine came to represent nothing more, nothing less, than a series of dangers to April.

I became terrified of cars and steps and injections and coughs. I became terrified of kettles and boiling saucepans and dogs and cats and nuclear accidents and just about anything else I could think of that might possibly somehow harm our child.

Human babies are so pathetic, that's the thing. I mean, I've seen wildlife documentaries and caribou foals, or whatever they're called, pop out ready to run away from lions. They can literally sprint about a minute after being born.

Whereas April... she was just this warm lump to be looked after, a dribbling, almost blind, hungry, screaming little bundle of needs, hoping to be protected by me from all of the dangers and all of the evil in the world. It felt absolutely terrifying.

To say that my emotions were all mixed up would be an understatement. I hated her for hurting me, for scaring me, for depending on me, and yet I loved her for... I don't know. Just for existing, I suppose.

But if I'm honest, the overriding emotion those first days was definitely terror – terror that something would happen to her, terror that, for no reason, she would suddenly stop breathing. She just seemed so *fragile*. At times I couldn't imagine how she could possibly make it through the next twenty-four hours. Even when April slept, *I* couldn't, because I had to watch her breathing.

I think the midwives and antenatal teachers are more honest about all of this, these days, but back then no one ever told me that I might feel upset, or scared, or depressed. You were just supposed to get on with it all. And no matter how weepy and grumpy and unreasonable I may have been (and I know that the answer to that is "very"), know that I did my best to keep it all under control. Inside me things were *even worse* than they looked on the outside if you can imagine such a thing. Thank God you were there.

At least one good thing came out of it all, though. Well, two, including April, obviously. All that fear taught me that I'd been right about you. Because you, my darling, were perfect. I think you must have been almost as scared as I was, but you remained calm and collected, you were reassuring and helpful and devoted at every step.

People kept saying how much she looked like me and that, I recall, really upset me. I so wanted someone to tell you that she looked like you.

But even that didn't seem to faze you. You just plodded on through, learning to change nappies and give a bottle, and somehow managing to put up with my crazy moods even as you cycled in and out to your courses at the Poly. What with the studies and the homework and the part-time jobs, it's amazing, looking back, how you managed to still be such a perfect dad. But you did. You were a keeper all right!

• • •

It rains solidly for three days. It rains so hard and the sky is so dark, that it doesn't look like May at all. January would be more like it. January in Iceland, perhaps.

Surprisingly, Sean doesn't mind. Sunshine makes him feel guilty, as if sitting indoors feeling miserable is perhaps more acceptable during a downpour.

Yet on Thursday morning, when Sean wakes up to blue skies and a miraculously warm breeze, his spirits unexpectedly lift.

As he drives to work, the window open and the radio on, he feels better, he admits to himself, than he has in months. He even allows himself to sing along a little to an old Steely Dan song on the radio.

He works enthusiastically all day. The windows and doors are finished on the retirement home, and he's now landscaping the gardens – in a virtual way, of course. When a blackbird settles outside his office window and starts to chirp with gusto, he can almost convince himself that he's there, inside his drawing, doing it with a shovel. He wonders if, just maybe, his grief is waning. He wonders if his fog of depression might not be lifting.

Superstitiously, he fears that even allowing himself to ask that question puts his good mood at risk. It's as if hope is a ghost in the corner of his vision, a ghost he knows will vanish if he turns to look at it straight on. So he does his best not to wonder how long this will last and hums the Steely Dan song in his head like a mantra, and concentrates himself fully on the task at hand. Incredibly, the mood lasts all day.

His arrival at the house that evening feels dangerous and he hesitates, his key in the lock, as he imagines the cool, dark, silent interior. And then, feeling spooked, he withdraws the key and walks down to the river instead.

It's a gorgeous evening and half of Cambridge seems to have had the same idea. The cycle paths are congested with parents on pushbikes and kids on trikes; the beer gardens of the pubs are packed solid with laughing, drinking students. Goodwill seems to float in the air, there for the taking.

On his way home, Sean sits outside the Fort St George and eats a burger and chips – anything to put off his arrival at the house. Even this, eating alone, does not dent Sean's day. An old, raggedy pigeon perches on a fence to his right and tips his head from side to side, so he isn't quite alone after all.

Returning to the house, just as the sun is setting, does provide a significant challenge, but instead of submitting to it he's able this once to analyse it. He considers, for the first time ever, that he may have to move, and imagines himself, almost with pleasure, in a modern, architect-designed, bachelor flat somewhere. Perhaps he should buy a plot of land and design his own house – a long forgotten dream.

On waking the next morning, he lies in bed for a moment before he dares to ask himself the question: has the mood survived a night of dreams? Amazingly, he has woken feeling OK again. Frowning in surprise and silently apologising to Catherine for his good mood, he climbs from the bed, nods with relief, and descends to the lounge where he puts an old Simple Minds album – *New Gold Dream* – on the new turntable before heading through to the kitchen to make breakfast.

He very nearly makes it all the way to the weekend without being tripped up. But at ten to five on Friday afternoon, as he is closing documents on his computer, the company secretary sidles up and leans on the top of his alcove.

"Hi Sean," she says. "How *are* you?"

Sean scratches his head. He's tempted, he's not sure why, to lie. But after a brief internal argument with himself, he says, "I'm fine, actually. I'm good."

"Oh!" Jenny says. Does her surprise indicate reproach or is Sean being paranoid? Perhaps his first instinct to lie was the right one. Perhaps he's not *allowed* to feel this good just yet.

"Oh," Jenny says, a second time. "Well, that's good. That's *great*, Sean."

"Thanks," Sean says, frowning. "Sorry, but did you want something specific? Because I was about to head off."

"Oh?" Jenny says, glancing at her watch. "You're usually such a night owl. Still, I suppose it is such a lovely weekend."

"Yes."

"It can wait till Monday," Jenny says. "Not much longer, but it can wait till then."

"What can?" Sean asks.

"Oh, nothing important," Jenny says. "Just holidays. I need to slot your dates into the rota. Everyone else has done theirs. You're the last one."

"Right," Sean says, trying not to think about the implications of this, trying desperately not to realise that this simple, stupid question has the power to demolish his upswing. "I'll, um, give you the dates on Monday," he says, forcing a smile.

"Great," Jenny says. "Um, well, have a good weekend."

"I'll try," Sean says.

"And, erm, Sean," Jenny adds as she leaves. "It's good to see you doing so well."

By the time the spinning wheel has vanished and Sean's computer screen has gone blank, he's no longer doing well. He's wondering, instead, how to survive this weekend, how to make it through to Monday now that the subject of the next twelve months' holidays has been launched, like a Cruise missile, at his oh-so-fragile cheer.

Because what, after all, could be more depressing than trying to work out when he wants to take five weeks of holiday? Five weeks to be spent alone. What could possibly be worse than deciding what he should do and where he should go. Is there even any possible destination that would not make him feel ten times more scared and one hundred times more vulnerable than he does right now?

Snapshot #10

110 mm format, colour. A group of young people are posing for a photograph. The front row is made up of children holding handwritten placards. One of these reads, "When I grow up I would like to join the coal line, not the dole line." The second row is made up of students, some of whom are holding Socialist Workers Party placards saying, "Victory to the miners." Behind the group can be seen a row of middle aged miners' wives with their own larger banner stretched between flagpoles. It reads, "BLYTH MINERS WIVES. Thatcher snatched our milk, now she wants our daily bread."

Sean peers in at the photograph until he spots Catherine's and Theresa's grinning faces.

The trip had been organised by the Miners' Support Committee of the students' union. They had booked a coach to take people to the Orgreave picket line, and Theresa, a willing militant for almost any cause, had roped Catherine into going with her, much against Sean's wishes.

Though Sean had been terrified that the demonstration would turn violent, he had been unable to talk sense into Catherine, and as Theresa was their usual fall-back babysitter it had fallen to him to stay behind with fifteen-month-old April. The result was that he wasn't even able to go along to make sure Catherine stayed out of trouble.

It was, he remembers, the first time that he had been left alone with April for more than a few hours, but Catherine had insisted that he'd be "just fine". He'd been terrified that something would go wrong and he wouldn't know how to deal with it. But he had been flattered, too, by her confidence in his parenting abilities and determined to prove her right.

In a last ditch attempt at getting her to change her mind, he had walked with her into town through the deserted early morning streets, little April sleeping in the pushchair. Theresa had stayed at a friend's house for the night and would meet them there.

He can remember the huddled mass of students waiting in a fug of early morning cigarette smoke, their rolled up banners at their sides. And he *had* managed to convince Catherine not to go, albeit momentarily.

Theresa had turned up carrying a bunch of Socialist Workers Party placards, which she had spent the evening stapling to wooden sticks. "She's coming," Theresa had insisted, when Sean had told her the news. "I don't know what kind of patriarchal society you think you're living in, Sean, but the days when husbands could decide that their wives should stay at home is long gone, honey. It's her sisterly duty to come and she's coming, aren't you, Catherine?"

Catherine, torn between her husband and her friend, had looked hesitant.

"Plus, it'll be fun," Theresa continued. "You've hardly been anywhere since April was born. It'll do you good to get out and about."

This, apparently, had clinched it, because Catherine had wrinkled her nose and nodded. "She's right, you know. I think I need this."

"It'll be dangerous, though," Sean had protested. "You've seen what's happening on the telly. It's really rough out there."

"You think I won't look after her?" Theresa had asked, feigning offence.

"No, I..."

"Well then," she said. The subject, it seemed, was now closed.

Sean had spent the day watching the television, partly terrified he might catch a glimpse of his wife being whacked with a truncheon, partly hopeful he'd spot Catherine and be able to say, "Look, April, that's Mummy on the screen."

But despite the hundreds of support buses Sean knew were travelling from all over the country, there was remarkably little coverage. The news, instead, was full of upcoming elections to the European Parliament, a subject that the media had never shown any interest in before, or, for that matter, since, but which they had, that day, inexplicably preferred to the massive pro-miner demonstrations around the country.

Cassette #10

Hello Sean.

I bet this photo gives you the willies, doesn't it? Do you remember how scared you were I'd get run over by a horse?

I felt terrible for leaving you behind and though I pretended otherwise, I worried about April all day. But looking back, I think it was the right thing to do, both in political terms and personally.

I grew up a bit that day, that's the thing. Talking to all those struggling miners' wives and singing protest songs on the bus and getting angry, really angry, about the injustice of it all, changed me, or at least started a process of change. It really did.

I was still so young, that's the thing. I had lived so little. I honestly think that I was still working out who I was meant to be, back then. I had never been on any kind of demonstration before and it was, to my surprise, the most exciting thing I had ever done.

As an aside, thinking back on it all, I do worry about the kids today, don't you? I mean, we were hardly communist radicals, were we? But we still knew right from wrong. We still knew when to stand up and say, "No!" We knew when to protest and shout and lie down in the road. April's generation, and younger kids even more so, all just seem so passive to me.

Whether it's the NHS or the rich not paying their taxes, or this stupid Brexit business, there are plenty of things to be furious about, but I don't think many of them even consider getting off their arses to vote, let alone demonstrate. I've talked to April about this and she's all, "Oh, what's the point?" which seems to be the overriding belief of our time. She seems to think that clicking on some Facebook petition is about as radical as it gets. So, I do worry that we've somehow produced a generation of ostriches.

And I don't just mean that they bury their heads in the sand and let the politicians get away with murder these days, either. I mean that April's generation is missing out on all of that fun, as well. Because, yes, we believed in the causes and, yes, we were genuinely angry about entire mining communities being left without a livelihood. But God, we had fun fighting it, didn't we?

To start with, on the bus going down that morning, everyone was sleepy. It was a very early start and they were students, after all.

But as we got nearer to Orgreave, we began to see the rows of police vans lined up, and the atmosphere became electric. I have never seen so many police, Sean. They were like an army.

The people we met that day were amazing. I remember getting involved in a big argument with a guy from the NUM who was worried about what he called "lassies" getting involved in the picket line. He and this friend of his, who had the biggest moustache I had ever seen, argued with Theresa and a friend of hers for half an hour about whether we should be there at all. But in the end, he understood that it was important for us to be there, and we understood that, like yourself, he was genuinely scared for our safety. The truncheon wielding police, he pointed out, weren't women. They were very heavily armoured, surprisingly angry policemen.

In the end we split up. The lads went off with the pickets and we joined the miners' wives and their kids to demonstrate on the sidelines.

It was a brilliant experience talking to them. They were so involved, so aware of the way the story was being manipulated by the media. They were so grateful that we were there, that someone who wasn't a miner or a miner's wife could actually be bothered enough to go to fight alongside them. A couple of the women were so moved that they cried all over us. I had never really done anything for anyone before and to feel that gratitude, that bond, was lovely.

About eleven o'clock the so-called "scabs" arrived for the shift change, and the police began to force their way through the picket line. I was relieved, if the truth be told, to be on the sidelines.

We shouted and screamed and waved our banners. I was completely hoarse by the time I got back to the bus.

I think a couple of people got bonked with a truncheon that day, and one guy got tripped up by a policeman and cut his ear open. But that's about all that happened as far as I could tell. Things really weren't that bad.

The real violence happened the following Monday, as I recall. They waited until the weekend was over, knowing that all the non-miners would be back at work, that all the stroppy students would be in lessons. You, Theresa and I watched it all on television together on Monday night. It was horrific, even to watch, and I think that it was only then, only when I saw the images of police on horseback riding into the crowds and beating people over the head with their batons, men and women alike, that I finally understood what you had been so afraid of.

I cried as we watched it and I cried about it for days afterwards. I cried, too, when the NUM finally caved in, because I knew that all of those lovely people I had met had no hope left at all.

Despite all of our demonstrations and all of those pamphlets we gave out in the Wulfrun Centre, we failed, I suppose. Thatcher won, the mines closed, exactly as Arthur Scargill had said they would, and nothing was done to help any of the people left behind. Perhaps *that's* why no one bothers to demonstrate anymore, because it turned out that no one cared how many people demonstrated. Perhaps that's the day we were *all* beaten.

Still, it was a life changing experience for me, like I say. I felt part of the strike and part, even though I wasn't, of the students' union. I felt part of Theresa's so-called sisterhood, too.

114

Oh, here's a juicy story you've never been told. I just this second remembered.

So, on the way back, I fell asleep with my head on Theresa's shoulder. When I woke up she was caressing my hair and do you know what she asked me? She wanted to know if I had ever made love with a woman. When I said that I hadn't, she asked me if I'd like to try. Can you imagine how embarrassed I was? This was in the middle of a crowded bus, after all. I had only just turned twenty.

I said "no" of course. I was way too prudish to ever discuss such a thing, and I can honestly say that I have never been tempted since.

But I was quite in love with Theresa that day, and in that moment, though I said, "no", it wasn't the whole truth. In that specific instant, I would actually quite have liked to say yes. Just to try it, so to speak. I bet you're shocked now, aren't you?

Anyway, when we got back to Wolverhampton, you and April were there, waiting for me, and I was so tired and so happy to see you both that I cried.

As far as any lesbian tendencies were concerned, that, as they say, was the end of that.

• • •

On Monday, Sean chooses his holiday dates. He books three weeks in January and two in March. He has no idea exactly why he chooses the dates he does, other than the fact that it means he doesn't have to think about holidays for the longest possible time. "You're sure you don't want Christmas week?" the secretary asks. "Because I think you'll be the only one here."

115

"Yes," Sean says, trying to block even the thought of what a week's holiday, alone, at Christmas, might feel like. "Yes, I'm sure."

On Thursday evening, April phones him.

"Hi Dad," she says. "Ronan and I were thinking of coming up for the weekend. The weather's going to be fabulous, apparently. What do you think?"

"Sure," Sean says. "Why not? I was going to go and visit Mum, but there's no reason that can't wait. I'll just tell Perry."

"We can postpone it for a week if you want," April says, "but there's a massive anti-Brexit demo happening in Central London, so it's going to be a nightmare around here. We thought we might as well."

"Can't you hang out at Ronan's place?"

"Nah, it's rented. You know he rents it on Airbnb sometimes? Well, it's booked for that weekend. And round here is going to be madness. The demo's starting in Hyde Park, I think."

"Oh," Sean says, thinking back to Catherine's last tape. "And you don't want to go to that?"

"The demo? Me?" April says, sounding shocked. "No."

"Why not?"

"When did you ever see me at a demo, Dad?"

"You spend enough time complaining about Brexit," Sean says.

"Well, of course. It's stupid. But there's no stopping it now. You know that."

"Yes," Sean says. "Yes, I think I do."

"So are we on?" April asks. "For the weekend."

"Sure," Sean says. "I'll see you then. When are you coming?"

"Friday night. To avoid all the hassle."

116

Once the call is over, Sean lays his phone on the table and pushes it around with one finger like a toy car as he runs the conversation and the contents of Catherine's tape through his mind. Because, yes, he can see, in a way, how that day changed Catherine. She had been a poorly educated girl from a council estate when he met her. She had been bright as a button, that's for sure, but she had never asserted herself in any of the discussions that happened at college until that day. But after the demonstration she had known what she thought, at least about that one subject. And she hadn't been afraid to take on anyone who disagreed with her.

"You've changed your mind?" April asks, the second she picks up the phone.

"No. Well... sort of," Sean splutters. "Look, how would it be if I came down instead?"

"But I told you. Central London's going to be..."

"How would it be if I came down and we went to the demo together."

"Really?" April asks. "Why?"

"To express our disagreement, maybe?" Sean offers.

"There was a vote, Dad. We expressed our disagreement then. And we got outvoted."

"Maybe that's not enough," Sean says.

"You're freaking me out a bit, now."

"Have you ever been to a demonstration?"

"I don't see what that's got to do with anything."

"No," Sean says. "But have you?"

"Well, no. Have you?"

"Yes," Sean says. "Lots."

"Really? For what? I mean, which demos? In aid of what?"

"Lots of things. With your mother. I'll tell you tomorrow. And on Saturday – it's on Saturday, right?"

"Yes. But..."

"On Saturday, we can go. Together."

"Hold on, Dad. Ronan's just got in."

April's voice becomes muffled, but despite the fact that Sean can't quite make out her words, he can tell, from the tone, that she's explaining his proposed change of plans to Ronan and not sounding happy about it.

"Is this to do with Mum?" she asks, when she returns. "Is it some sort of post-Mum midlife crisis?"

"No," Sean says. "Look, if you're really against it, then forget it."

"I don't *mind*," April says. "Not really. And Ronan actually thinks it'll be fun."

"It will."

"But it just sounds strange. It doesn't sound like you."

"Hum," Sean says. "Well, maybe you don't know me quite as well as you think you do. Maybe we never know anyone quite as well as we think we do."

"You are weird at the moment, you know. But look, I'll check with the others," April says. "Because there's only the one sofa. And if anyone else has people staying it won't be possible."

"Of course."

"But I think it's probably OK. Matt may even be away that weekend, so you might be able to have his room."

"Sure," Sean says. "Well, let me know."

• • •

As parking near April's place is impossible, Sean travels to London by train.

By the time he has negotiated the underground and made his way to her shared apartment it's almost eight p.m.

Matt, as predicted, is away for the weekend, so April shows Sean to his room.

The flat, in Hyde Park Gardens, is beautiful if tatty, and from Matt's rear windows Sean can even glimpse, through a gap in the houses on Bayswater Road, Hyde Park itself. He dumps his bag on Matt's Swedish office chair and crosses to the window, looks out, then turns back to scan the room.

Matt, who is a successful graphic designer, is young and funky, and it shows. The room is youthful and colourful. There's an *Aladdin Sane* Bowie poster on the wall and a large collection of vinyl. Matt has twin DJ decks permanently installed and bookshelves stuffed with art books.

Sean walks around the room. He runs his fingers across the spines of Matt's records and then peeps, nosily, into a wardrobe. The room makes him feel young again, even as it makes him nostalgic for his own lost youth. God, how he'd love the chance to live the whole thing again!

"You all right in there?" April asks, peering through the open door.

"Yeah," Sean says. "I'm just looking around. This is such a cool room."

"Matt's life's work," April says.

"The room?" Sean asks.

April takes a step into the room and expounds, "No. Being cool, I meant."

Sean detects a note of bitterness in her voice and remembers that at the beginning, before she met Ronan, his daughter had, Catherine said, had a thing for Matt.

"Weren't you a bit in love with him at the beginning?" Sean asks.

"God, Mum tells you... told you... everything," April says, faking outrage. "And I wasn't *in love* with him. I just..." She shrugs coyly. "I had a crush, that's all. He's pretty good looking. But he knows it, if you know what I mean."

"Right," Sean says.

"Waaay too busy being cool," April explains.

"Yes. I know the type."

The doorbell rings, so April turns to head to the front door. "Great," she says. "I'm starving."

When Sean gets to the kitchen, Ronan is already unpacking a series of metal trays from a carrier bag. "Hey, Sean," he says.

Sean slaps him gently on the back then squeezes his shoulder. "Hi Ronan," he says. "You brought food. I was intending to take you both out somewhere."

"You can do that tomorrow," April says, peeling back the cardboard lid of one of the containers and peering at the contents, then dipping a finger in and sucking it. "We thought this would be nice," she explains. "Just the three of us."

"No Aisha, either?" Ronan asks, his Irish lilt making the word *Aisha* run into the following word *either* to form one long list of vowels.

"No. She's out with friends," April tells him. "... said she was going clubbing afterwards, I think."

Together, they divvy out the curries before moving to the fold-out table in the lounge.

"This is such a nice flat," Sean says, looking around. "It reminds me of being a student."

April laughs. "Only, we're not students, are we? We're thirty-something professionals. But no one can afford a flat anymore in London."

"Sure," Sean says. "But I still think it's kind of fun. How much do you pay again?"

120

"A thousand a month," April says.

"Each? Wow."

"Yes. It's going up to £1200 a month in June, too."

"Only..." Ronan starts. But April shoots him a glare, effectively silencing him.

"Only what?" Sean asks.

"Only nothing. So, how have you been, Dad?"

"Yeah," Ronan says, forking mushroom Biryani to his mouth. "How *have* you been?"

April, who isn't drinking, waits until the second bottle of Chardonnay has been opened before she dares to say what's on her mind.

"So Dad," she says. "Ronan and I... um... we have something to tell you."

Sean sips at his wine and nods encouragingly. "Go on?"

April glances at Ronan. "Shall I, or...?" she asks.

Ronan shrugs. "Whatever you want. It's up to you."

"Right," April says, taking a deep breath. "So, we want to move in together. We've found a great little flat in South Hampstead that we can just about afford. It's small..."

"But lovely," Ronan interjects.

"It is," April agrees. "And it has a little box room Ronan can use as an office."

"You know that I work from home most of the time, right?" Ronan asks.

Sean nods. "Sounds good," he says, wrinkling his brow and smiling simultaneously because he senses that there's more to come. "But won't you miss this place? I thought you liked sharing with Matt and Aisha."

"God, no," April says. "No, I'm sick to death of sharing."

"Aisha steals her makeup," Ronan says, raising his eyebrows. "And Matt won't do any housework."

121

"Ah," Sean says. "The joys of sharing. I remember it well."

"We just want a place of our own," April says. "You get to a certain age and you just want to be on your own, you know?"

Sean nods knowingly. "And then you get to a certain age and the worst thing you can imagine is being on your own."

April bites her bottom lip. "Sorry, I'm being insensitive," she says. "I need a padlock on my mouth or something. I always have done."

"Not at all, sweetheart," Sean says. "I'm just being silly because I'm jealous of your setup here. I want to live in Matt's cool room and mix records at parties, I think."

"You could move into April's room," Ronan offers, jokingly. "It'll be free soon."

"The commute might be a bit of a drag," Sean says. "To Cambridge, I mean."

"Anyway," April says, sounding frustrated by all the small-talk. "There's another reason we need to move."

"There is?"

She glances at Ronan and reaches for his wrist before turning back to face Sean. "I'm pregnant," she says. "So we really need to sort out our own place before that happens."

"God!" Sean says. "You're *pregnant*?"

Despite the fact that he thought he had sounded pretty convincing, April pulls a face. "You knew. Did Mum tell you that we were trying?"

"No," Sean says. He looks at Ronan and, despite himself, wonders if the baby is Ronan's. And then he looks at April and wonders, then forcefully decides, that she *is* his daughter. "Nope," he says. "She really didn't say a word."

"Huh," April says. She's clearly unconvinced.

"She didn't," Sean insists, even though he's not sure why he's lying. Perhaps because Catherine has told him not in person but on the tapes. And April doesn't know about the tapes, yet, does she? "But it's not a new concept, you know?" Sean continues. "Boy meets girl. Girl gets pregnant... Plus, I noticed that you're not drinking."

"Ah," April says. "Yes, I suppose with my track record that is a bit of a giveaway. Anyway, you can understand now why we need our own place."

"You know we had *you* in a shared student house for your first two years," Sean reminds her.

"Yes. But like I said. I'm not a student."

"No. That's true. I wasn't saying..."

"The thing is," April interrupts. "We need your help."

"OK. Fire away."

"They need a guarantor. For the rent. It's two thousand two hundred a month."

"It's only because I'm self-employed," Ronan tells him. "I mean, we can pay it. But we need to convince *them* of that."

"Of course," Sean says. "No problem."

"Really?" April asks.

"Of course. Why would I say no?"

April's features slip into a cute frown. She leans in and pecks her father on the cheek. "Oh, thanks Big Daddy," she says. "You're the best, you are."

"You're welcome, Little Daughter."

"I would ask my dad," Ronan says. "But..."

Sean raises one hand, interrupting him. "It's not a problem," he says. "Really." His voice sounded slightly broken, and he realises that he's unexpectedly on the verge of tears. "Sorry, um... need the loo," he says, stumbling from the table before they can notice.

In the bathroom, he closes and locks the door, then sits on the closed toilet seat and rubs his brow. He swallows with difficulty. Because, yes, despite having prepared himself for this moment, he's upset. Catherine's absence, at this specific moment in his life, feels devastating.

After a minute or so, he stands and looks into the mirror, at his own, glistening eyes.

He hears Catherine's voice saying, "I never wanted grandchildren. Other people's kids have always seemed a special kind of hell." He hadn't realised it before, but he now knows that it was a lie designed to make him feel better. Because of course nothing, quite simply *nothing*, would have made Catherine happier than meeting her daughter's first child.

When Sean gets back from the bathroom, April and Ronan are smiling at him and looking expectant. There's a vaguely fake air to their expressions from which Sean deduces that they've been discussing something contentious in his absence.

"So, there's one more thing," April says, as Sean resumes eating. "We don't... We don't think we want to get married."

"OK," Sean says, slowly. "Why not?"

April screws up her nose. "We just don't really believe in it. Neither of us do."

"That's fair enough. It's entirely up to you two, I would think. As long as you agree."

"We basically do," April says. "You don't mind, then?"

"Do I mind not having to pay for your huge, white wedding?" Sean asks. "Uh... let me see..."

"And you're not shocked?"

Sean laughs.

"Do you think... ? How do you think... ?" April stammers.

"What would Mum have said?" Sean prompts.

"Yeah." April nods. "She wouldn't have minded, would she?"

124

"I doubt it," Sean says. "But I really couldn't say."

"I don't think she would have minded," April says, clearly trying to convince herself. "I honestly don't."

"It's immaterial," Sean says with a sad shake of his head. "She's not here, sweetheart."

During the train journey back to Cambridge, Sean tries but fails to sleep.

To say that he had not slept well in Matt's bed would be an understatement. The streetlamp outside had shone directly on his face (there were no curtains) and Matt's lumpy, sagging mattress was quite simply the worst Sean has ever known. Matt needs, Sean thinks, to spend a little more on his bedding and a little less on records. He berates himself for being an old fogey as soon as he thinks this, but the fact remains that it's true. The bed really had been awful.

By Saturday morning, Sean's back had been stiff, and by Sunday, he had been thinking that he would have to book an appointment with an osteopath just to get his vertebrae yanked back into line.

But despite his lack of sleep and despite the gentle motion of the train, Sean's unable to doze. His mind, instead, is running over April's declarations, and the experience of the anti-Brexit demonstration. Because, yes, the demonstration had been a disappointment.

They had joined the straggling line of protesters just as they were leaving Hyde Park but within an hour they had abandoned the procession to duck into a branch of Pizza Hut instead.

"I feel like a real traitor," Sean had said, once they were seated. The last stragglers were still walking past the window.

"Now you know why my generation doesn't go to demos," April said. "It's just too depressing."

"Surely it's depressing *because* no one goes, not the other way around?"

"I think it's like a vicious circle of apathy," Ronan suggested.

"Plus, it doesn't change anything, Dad," April said. "Do you remember all the people who protested against the Iraq war? There were millions of them. But it didn't change a *thing*. That's how they've turned us into such an apathetic nation. By never listening. By not giving a damn what people think."

Thinking back to Catherine's similar analysis of the miners' strike, Sean could only concur.

"But to concentrate on the serious stuff," Ronan had said. "What kind of pizza are you having?"

Once home, Sean is finally able to catch up on his missing sleep. He lies down on the sofa and it's only when he wakes up to darkness that he remembers he still hasn't opened this weekend's package. He glances at the broadband box and sees that it's almost seven-thirty. He'll make dinner and then he'll open the next envelope and he'll spend the evening with Catherine. It will be almost like not eating alone, he thinks.

Snapshot #11

35 mm format, black and white. Young people are dancing in the middle of a lounge. On the settee, which has been pushed to the far side of the room, can be seen three young men. They are grinning and holding bottles of beer. Draped across their knees is a young woman with long hair whose face is too blurred by movement to be identifiable.

Sean recognises two of the men on the sofa immediately. The man on the left was Andy. He looked so much like Sean that people had called them "the twins".

The man on the right they had nicknamed Dave the Rave to distinguish him from Dave the Shave (who was beardless) and Original Dave (who had simply got there first). Dave the Rave never missed a party and had been the first person Sean ever saw performing the *big box, little box, cardboard box* dance. The guy in the middle, Sean never knew, but he seems to remember that he had been a friend of a friend who had turned up with the stunning Swedish exchange student in a mini-skirt. Sean can still picture the girlfriend vividly. And in his memory, she is still one of the most beautiful women he has ever seen.

"Who the hell is she?" Sean had asked Andy, on laying eyes upon her.

"She's hot, huh?" Andy had said. "Her name's Leah, I think."

"*Princess* Leah?"

"*Exactly.*"

"She's *smoking* hot," Sean had mumbled.

"Hum," Andy had said, laughing. "You regretting that wedding, mate? Already?"

Troubled by Andy's comment as well as his own inability to drag his eyes from Princess Leah, Sean had gone in search of Catherine, who had vanished.

He had found her in the back garden, vomiting into a dustbin. Half walking, half carrying her home had saved him from his indisputable attraction to Princess Leah of Sweden.

It had been one of those moments when he had imagined that it might just be worth risking everything for a fling, for a simple moment with someone that beautiful. He had realised that physical attraction could be so powerful that one could become stupid enough to throw everything important down the drain. He had never, thank God, bumped into her again.

Cassette #11

Hello Sean.

It's eleven o'clock on Friday morning and I've just seen the oncologist. He gave me the results of yesterday's CAT scan and the results aren't great, I'm afraid. I'm a bit in shock, I think, and trying to take my mind off it by doing another one of these tapes.

That crazily expensive drug I've been on, the gem-city-din or whatever it's called, the one which has been making me so ill that I can't walk, hasn't been working at all, it turns out. The doc wants to schedule a meeting with both of us to discuss what he called "remaining options" but to be honest, I'm not hopeful. I don't think that any of the remaining options are going to be much fun.

The good news is that they stopped giving me that rubbish immediately, so I should be able to come home for the weekend. I think that I'll leave it until Monday morning to tell you the bad news. I'll have to make something up, I suppose. I'm desperate for a normal weekend with you, that's the thing. I'm desperate for a weekend where we can talk about something other than my desire to vomit or the survival rates of different types of cancers.

Anyway, I had a little cry after he told me, but I'm all right again now. I'm ready to talk about the next photo. This little project is really helping me get through all of this.

It's funny, because I realised that these tapes are turning into a whole different thing.

At the beginning, I just wanted to tell you some things you didn't know about me, I just wanted to share some secrets. But it's becoming more like the complete story of us. It's becoming more and more like that novel I always said I'd write. Perhaps you can get it typed up and publish it one day. Anyway, I hope you're not bored yet. You were, after all, there for most of this.

I had thought there would be more photos like this one. There were so many parties, after all. But I suppose we were too busy getting drunk to take pictures.

I think the only reason we have a picture of this one is because Theresa was going through her photography phase. She had set up a darkroom in our dusty cellar with an enlarger and everything. This black and white one will definitely be one of hers. I may even have helped develop it.

I don't think her photography thing lasted for more than six months, but it was fun for a while. All of her mates from

129

the photography society used to traipse through the house, and they were all pretty nice people. They all used to fawn over April, I remember. We had lots of black and white photos of her at one stage, but they all seem to have vanished. Perhaps they're in that other box in the loft.

We were the strangest students, weren't we? Especially me, of course, because I wasn't a student at all. We were a married couple with a toddler, and yet you were also a budding architect. And even if I spent my days looking after April, I felt like a student as well. A student of life, perhaps.

I've always thought that at least half of what you learn through being at college is life stuff, rather than the proper stuff you learn in lessons. It's why I was so determined that April should go to college. It was learning how to live in a shared house and arguing until three in the morning about washing up and God and politics, and electricity bills that made us who we ended up being. Learning to love and have friendships and let go of them when people got to the ends of their courses, too. And the incredible thing for me was that I got to participate in all of that by proxy. So despite being basically a chavvy bird from a council estate, I still got to do the whole student thing. I got exposed to feminism and socialism and Buddhism, and a hundred different isms. And I made some really great friends.

And when we weren't putting the world to rights, we were partying. We never needed much of an excuse, did we? A few bottles of home-brew and a record player and we were away. That's me in the photo as I'm sure you realised. I had just smoked my second ever joint, but hadn't thrown up yet.

I'm not sure that you'll remember this, but you found me out in the garden, being sick, and I lied and said I'd just had too much to drink. But it was Alistair's joint that had pushed me over the edge. That's when I decided that joints really weren't for me.

I owned up to you the next morning, and you said you'd tried it too and had also been sick. Neither of us really liked smoking grass, which was probably a blessing. The people who *did* like the stuff were the ones who got kicked off their courses. It isn't, I don't think, the most motivational drug!

I can't remember who was babysitting April that night, but it wasn't us and it wasn't Alistair, and it can't have been Theresa either if she took the photo. I expect it must have been Annie or Steve, or Green Donna. Actually, Donna wasn't green yet, was she? She was still plain old Donna back then. The Green thing came later.

But even before Donna moved in, we never had any shortage of babysitters, did we? Everyone loved April. I don't think many kids out there have had quite so much love thrown at them.

• • •

It is Saturday morning and Sean is busy vacuuming the lounge. Because of the noise of the Dyson, he fails to hear the doorbell and visibly jumps when he turns to face the lounge window. Maggie, beyond the pane, is jumping up and down waving her arms.

Sean kicks the off button on the vacuum cleaner and strides to the front door.

"Finally!" Maggie says. "I've been jumping up and down like a loon out here. Plus, it's freezing."

She kisses Sean on the cheek and steps past him into the hallway.

"It is cold," Sean says, peering out into the crisp, sunny day.

131

"It's air coming down from Iceland or something," Maggie says, stepping into the lounge.

Sean closes the front door and follows her. He's glad of the visit but simultaneously regretful for his vacuuming. It had taken him so long to pluck up the courage that he wonders if he'll ever manage to get motivated again. "A man with a Hoover," Maggie says.

"A Dyson," Sean corrects. "And I've always done the hoovering. Even when Catherine was around, it was always my job."

Maggie stares into his eyes for a moment and smiles vaguely. Sean can sense that she is noticing his newfound ability to mention Catherine without his voice becoming brittle. "Good," she says, then, "I suppose it should be Dysoning, really. Not Hoovering. But it doesn't have the same ring to it, does it?"

"Not really, no," Sean agrees. "Vacuuming, maybe?"

Maggie wrinkles her nose at the suggestion. "So in addition to Hoovering, do you make coffee?"

Sean smiles. "Sure," he says. "Come through."

"So how have you been?" he asks as he plugs in the kettle and pulls the cafetière from the cupboard. "I haven't seen you for weeks."

Maggie shrugs off her coat and hangs it over the back of a chair. "And whose fault would that be?" she asks.

"I wasn't really thinking it was anyone's fault," Sean says.

"I came last weekend, actually," Maggie says. "But you were out."

"I was at April's place," Sean explains. "We went to that Brexit demo."

"Brexit demo?" Maggie repeats.

"Well, anti-Brexit demo."

"I didn't know there was one, to be honest."

"I'm not surprised," Sean says as he spoons ground coffee into the glass jug. "It wasn't huge. And the media pretty much ignored it."

"I think everyone's given up," Maggie says. "But well done for trying."

"I think you're right. That's what it felt like, anyway."

"It's strange," Maggie says. "I mean, they've admitted that the money won't go to the NHS. And they've admitted we aren't getting some fabulous trade deal. And they've said that immigration won't even go down, now, too. It's as if everyone agrees that it's a stupid idea, but everyone accepts that we're going through with it anyway. It's like a horrible toddler who has made a stupid decision but is sticking to it rather than admit the error. It all smacks of cutting off your nose to spite your face more than anything else. Cutting off your continent to spite your face, perhaps."

"That's *exactly* what's happening," Sean says.

"My sister's all for it, you know?" Maggie says.

"Really?"

Maggie nods. "She lives in Ealing. They call it Little Warsaw. Not that I think that's a recent thing. I think the Poles have been in Ealing since the war, but there's no telling Angie that. Anyway, she's all for Brexit if it means the poor Poles will have to bugger off."

"They may *well* all bugger off," Sean says. "But *they* include her doctor and her nurse and probably her plumber, too. I think she'll miss them if they do leave."

"That's what I keep saying," Maggie says. "Anyway. You went to the demo. That surprises me. But in a good way."

"It was just something to do with April, really," Sean says. "She'd never been to a demo before."

133

"Never?"

Sean shakes his head.

"Gosh," Maggie says. "Kids today! And how is lovely April?"

"Um, pregnant," Sean says.

Maggie's eyes widen. "No!"

Sean nods. "She and Ronan are moving to their own place. They're both flat-sharing at the moment, so..."

"Of course. And does this mean there'll be a wedding?" Maggie asks.

"Nope," Sean says. "They don't believe in silly old-fashioned concepts like marriage."

"Do you mind? You sound like you do."

"Do I?" Sean asks. "I don't think so. Maybe. But no, I don't think so."

"Gosh, a baby!" Maggie says. "How exciting."

"Yes, it's quite a shock, really."

"You know, I never saw April as the baby-type," Maggie says. "I don't know why, but I just never really imagined it."

"That's what Catherine said."

A shadow crosses Maggie's features. She sighs gently.

"Don't say it," Sean says.

"No," Maggie says. "It's just... I was only going to say that it's a sh–"

"*Don't* say it," Sean repeats. "Please."

"No," Maggie says. "Of course. Sorry."

Sean presses the plunger and then pours the coffee into two mugs which he places on the kitchen table. "Here," he says. "So, what have you done with Dave this weekend?"

"I buried him under the patio," Maggie says, solemnly.

"That's the first place they'll look."

"Who?"

"The police."

"Ahh. No, he's gone back to his flat for the weekend, actually. Said he needs some 'space'," Maggie says. She uses two fingers to indicate the quote marks around the word *space*.

"Trouble in paradise?" Sean asks.

Maggie laughs sourly. "If this is paradise then give me hell any day of the week."

"That bad, huh?"

"Oh, it's all right, really. It's just so much harder to fit together with someone in your fifties. We get so set in our ways, you know? I mean, when you meet someone in your teens, like you two did, well, you're still growing, aren't you? You automatically adjust so that you fit together. But when you're my age, all the likes and dislikes are set in *stone*. That's the trouble."

"I can imagine it's not easy," Sean says. "But you're clever enough. You'll make it work."

Maggie sighs again, more deeply this time. She looks out at the garden. "So, I'm assuming that if it was you who used to do the hoovering, then the gardening was Catherine's responsibility. Am I right?"

Sean follows her gaze. "Oh. Yes. It's looking bad, huh?"

"You need to at least mow the lawn," Maggie says. "Because soon it'll be too *long* to mow, and then you'll be stuck."

"Yes," Sean says unenthusiastically. "Yeah, I know."

"I could give you a hand. Tomorrow, maybe."

"Tomorrow?" Sean says, frowning. "Isn't it supposed to be raining tomorrow?"

"Nope," Maggie says. "Sunny all day. So, what do you say? I'll bring my secateurs. It'll do me good... take my mind off things."

Sean shrugs. "Sure," he says. "Why not? If you're sure. But tomorrow afternoon, maybe?" He wants to reserve the morning for his next dose of Catherine.

Snapshot #12

35mm format, colour. A pale blonde woman sits on a green bedspread. Beside her is a thin tabby cat, rolling on its back, offering its tummy to be tickled. The light in the room, filtered through curtains, gives to both the woman's face and the cat's fur a distinctly green tinge.

Cassette #12

Hi Sean.

I'm so happy I found this one. A rare photo of Green Donna!

This must have been our final year in Wolverhampton because Theresa had moved out to live in her Buddhist community and Donna had moved in to replace her.

Theresa had asked us to take Donna in because she was depressed and needed what Theresa called a "nice happy house" to live in.

The trouble was that by the time we had swapped Donna for Theresa the house wasn't that happy, was it? Because no matter how chirpy and friendly we all tried to be, none of us could really help Donna with her sadness.

I'd go as far as to say that Donna's sadness ended up winning that round. It oozed out of her room and drifted down the stairs like mist, enveloping us all. Even April went quiet when Donna was around, though, often enough, we took that as a blessing.

The first thing that she did when she moved in was to paint her room green and while she was doing that she slept in the lounge, which irritated us all. Once the paint had dried, I can't recall ever having seen her for any length of time in any of the shared parts of the house again. She was always in her room.

One good thing about Donna was that she got me reading. She started me off with Fay Weldon, which I loved, and then gave me Lynne Reid Banks and Sylvia Plath. She even tried to get me to read Virginia Woolf at one point, but though I could see that the words were lovely, that they had a special kind of rhythm to them, if I'm telling the truth, Woolf was always a bit beyond me.

I used to worry about Donna so much, though. I'd come home from my shift at the shop and you'd be out somewhere with April, and Donna would either be listening to *Dead Can Dance* or *Echo And The Bunnymen*. Other times the house would be in absolute silence so I would creep up to Donna's door and take a deep breath and knock. I was always scared that she wouldn't answer. I was terrified that she had slit her wrists or taken twenty bottles of paracetamol or attached a rope to that beam in her room. But no. She was always there. Always in her room, sitting in that strange green light, reading some book or other for her course, looking utterly, utterly miserable.

Do you remember how funny I was about leaving April with her? Well, I don't think I ever stated clearly why that was. I'm not certain that I was ever even quite sure why myself. But looking back, I reckon that I was afraid that she'd top herself. And I was afraid that she would take April with her when she went.

138

I always thought that something terrible must have happened to Donna before she came to us. I do hope I'm wrong. And I do hope that she sorted herself out eventually.

Before she moved in, Theresa and I went to see her acting in a shopping centre. She was studying humanities and specialising in drama, and as part of her course she had to participate in a play in a public space.

They had organised this *happening* in the Wulfrun Centre, and Theresa took me along so that we could meet.

Now, Donna, believe it or not, was playing the role of a mushroom cloud. There were five people with horror makeup playing the wounded and a girl dressed as a rocket – she was supposed to be a Cruise missile, I think. There was a grim reaper with one of those grass hooks you hold in one hand – I don't think anyone had a scythe available. And Donna, well, she was the mushroom cloud.

Oh, Sean, it was so awful, it was hilarious. You have no idea...

After the Cruise missile had shouted "boom" and the five horror makeup victims had fallen down, Donna, who had a big white sheet over her head, appeared, waving her arms around and whistling. I think the whistling was meant to represent the wind or the fallout or something.

She looked like a five year old pretending to be a ghost. It was so, so bad, Sean. I wish you had been there to see it.

Theresa, who took the whole nuclear disarmament thing very seriously, got angry with me because I got a fit of the giggles and once I started I just couldn't stop. One of the dead people even sat up to tell me to be quiet at one point and in the end I had to leave. I thought I was going to wet myself.

I assumed, based on Donna's performance in the sheet, that she would be great fun to live with, so I told you and Alistair

139

that we should let her move in. But I had got that wrong. Donna wasn't a laugh to live with at all, was she?

The day she moved in, she asked me what I had thought of their play and, because I didn't know what else to say, I told her it had left me speechless.

"I know," she said. "I got so into the part I was weeping under my sheet. All those dead people, you know?"

I almost burst out laughing, Sean, but instead, I managed to say, "Yes, it was very moving." I had tears in my eyes, so I think I got away with it.

I missed Theresa so much once she was gone. I had never imagined that her moving out would be the end to our friendship. I had thought that she was one of my closest friends and assumed it would be that way forever.

But I only ever saw her twice after that and even then it was only because I bumped into her – it was only ever by accident. All she talked about, even then, was how amazing her new housemates were and how wonderful Buddhism was. Not a mention about any of us. Theresa was very self-sufficient, I suppose.

My newfound self-esteem took a bit of a hit over Theresa, I think, but that too, I suppose, was a necessary part of growing up.

You meet people and sometimes they're more important to you than you are to them. Sometimes you just have to give thanks for all the ways knowing them has changed you, and watch them walk away to pastures new.

You know, even now, when I think about Theresa, when I think about how quickly she moved on from one group of friends to another, I can still feel almost tearful about it. I can still feel quite angry, too.

●●●

Maggie's weather forecast turns out to be spot-on. It's a beautiful June Sunday.

After listening to this week's tape, Sean heads down the garden to the shed where he drags the old lawnmower from beneath the other gardening tools. He then hunts for the extension lead for almost an hour.

About a month after Catherine died, Sean had decided to be brave and clear her clothes from the cupboards. Seeing them every morning had been upsetting him, but he had got no further than bagging them up. They had sat in the bedroom for weeks, and then the hallway for a few weeks more, before finally migrating to the cupboard under the stairs. It is under these bin bags of clothes that he finally discovers the extension cable.

He is just finishing a sandwich when Maggie arrives. He's still sucking the crumbs from his teeth as he opens the front door to find her brandishing pruning shears.

"Hi Mags," he says. "You're looking scary."

"I know!" Maggie replies, stepping into the hallway, snipping at the air with her secateurs.

"Have you eaten?" Sean asks. "Because I can make you a sandwich if you want."

"I brunched quite late," Maggie replies. "So, let's just get on with it, eh?" She pauses to look at the pile of bin bags next to the stair cupboard. "Having a clear out?"

Sean sighs and pulls a pained expression. "It's Catherine's stuff," he says. "I bagged it all up ages ago, but I've been struggling to actually get any further than that."

Maggie nods thoughtfully. "Yeah, that's got to be a tough one. I can take them when I go, if you want. There's an Oxfam shop just round the corner from me. If that helps?"

"That would be great, Maggie," Sean says. "Thanks." He leads the way through the kitchen towards the back door. "You're sure you don't want something to eat? Or a drink?"

"Totally sure," Maggie says as she follows Sean into the back yard. She stands with her hands on her hips and surveys the long, thin garden. "So, I'm thinking, you do the mowing while I prune that forsythia. How does that sound?"

"Great," Sean says, then, "Which one's the forsythia?"

Maggie points with the shears. "That bush over there. It had yellow flowers until recently, but they're all gone now, so it's time to prune."

Sean nods. "OK," he says. "I would have started earlier on the lawn. But I couldn't find the extension lead."

"Under the stairs?" Maggie asks.

Sean smiles. "How could you possibly know that?"

"It's just where we keep ours," Maggie says, already starting to snip at the forsythia.

"Right," Sean says. "So! Mowing!"

The grass is too long – much too long – for their feeble electric mower, so Sean has to heave and lift and push to get it to advance down the garden. Even though the lawn occupies a plot of land no larger than the width of the house, by the time Sean has mowed a single strip, he's breaking out in a sweat. He switches the mower off and heads inside to change.

When he returns, in shorts and a vest, Maggie looks up from her pruning and scans him slowly from head to toe. "That's right," she says. "Let those rays in!"

"First time this year," Sean tells her, feeling self-conscious. "I was overheating in jeans."

142

"It's lovely, isn't it?" Maggie says, smiling up at the blue sky. "It's the longest day next week. The first day of summer."

"I always think that's strange," Sean tells her, "that the longest day is the start of summer, rather than the middle of it."

"I just consider myself lucky when we get any summer at all," Maggie says.

By the time the lawn has been mowed, Maggie has pruned three bushes and weeded the flower beds. "That looks much better," she says, as Sean wrestles the mower back into the shed.

"It does," he agrees. "But you were right. I should have mowed it before. I left it too long. The mower ended up ripping it all up."

"It's fine. Tea break?"

"Sure. Tea and cigarette break, actually."

When he returns with the mugs of tea, Maggie has put two fold-out chairs beneath the pear tree at the bottom of the garden. Sean hands her a mug of tea, places his own on the scrappy lawn, and pulls his cigarettes and matches from his pocket.

"I'm surprised you started smoking," Maggie says.

"Yeah," Sean agrees. "I mean, I'm only smoking two a day. But I agree. It's a strange one."

"Particularly..." Maggie says. Then she visibly interrupts herself. "Um, when are the pears ready?" she asks. "What time of year do they ripen?"

"Early September. And were you going to say, particularly because Catherine died of cancer?" Sean asks, blowing a jet of smoke up into the branches of the tree.

"Yes. Sorry. I was being insensitive."

"No, it's fine. And maybe that's why," Sean says. "Catherine never smoked, after all."

"Never?"

"Well, she smoked about ten cigarettes at college, I suppose. But she didn't go near one for thirty years."

"So what's this? Are you getting your own back on the cigarettes that didn't cause Catherine's cancer?" Maggie asks, looking confused.

Sean frowns and studies the end of his cigarette. "No," he says, finally. "No, I think it's a nostalgia thing, to be honest. The tapes she left, they're all about the past. They're all about when I was young and did smoke. And that made me want to smoke again." He takes a drag on his cigarette, then stubs it out in the grass. "But I wouldn't try to analyse that too deeply. I'm pretty sure it doesn't make any sense."

"Perhaps that *does* make sense," Maggie says. "I suppose only you would know. So, how's that going – with the tapes?"

"I'm about halfway through. They're very nostalgic, like I say. I've been finding myself looking up *Echo And The Bunnymen* on YouTube."

"*Echo And The Bunnymen*? Now, what did they sing? I remember the name, but..."

"Um, *The Cutter*," Sean offers. "*The Back Of Love?*"

"Nope," Maggie says. "I think I must have been too mainstream for *Echo And The Bunnymen*. So that's what the letters are? Memories of your college years?"

Sean nods. "Pretty much," he says. "So far, anyway."

"You went up north, didn't you?" Maggie asks.

"The Midlands," Sean corrects her. "Wolverhampton, to be precise."

"That's right. And you and Catherine met there as students?"

Sean laughs. "No," he says. "Do you not know that story?"

"I don't think so. But don't... you know... If it's difficult, then leave it."

"No, it's fine. We met in Dreamland. It's a funfair."

"In Margate? I think I've been there."

"That's the one. And then Catherine came to live with me. At college. But I was the student. Catherine never went to college. She never got past CSEs, and I think she failed half of those."

"Gosh, how amazing," Maggie says. "And I never knew. I mean, she was just so... I don't know. So clever, I suppose. Educated, too. Cultured."

Sean nods. "She was clever all right. I always thought that if we had done an IQ test together, she would have beaten me hands down. And she read so much. She loved to read."

"Yes, she read loads," Maggie says. "And that's what the recordings are all about? Trips down memory lane? I did wonder." She sips at her tea and looks over the edge of the cup inquiringly.

Sean sighs deeply. He's wondering, for the nth time, how much to tell. Because the thing is that there are aspects of the tapes he would quite like to discuss with someone. But like many men his age, he simply doesn't have the kinds of friendships where those subjects are discussable. In fact, since his wife's death, his friends have been steering pretty much clear. "They're not just that," he finally says, thinking simultaneously about the fact that the men he knows don't seem very comfortable with the concept of bereavement. "They're not *just* trips down memory lane. Some of them are quite... *difficult*, I suppose you'd say."

"Difficult," Maggie repeats. "Hum." Her neutral tone expresses that it's entirely up to Sean how much more he wants to tell her, and he's grateful for her discretion.

"Look," Sean says, scratching one ear. "Can I... If I tell you something... something from the tapes... can I be sure that it will stay between us?"

"Of course!" Maggie says. "You know that."

"It's about April," Sean says, after a pause. "Apparently she might not be mine."

Maggie puts her cup down now and frowns deeply at Sean. "Really?" she says.

"Catherine got pregnant pretty quickly when I met her. Well, immediately, really. And April could have been mine. Or she might have been from Catherine's ex, a guy called Phil."

"This was in one of the letters?" Maggie asks, shaking her head. "I mean, on one of the tapes?"

Sean nods. "It was."

"And you didn't know before? God, that's awful."

Sean shrugs. "I wouldn't say that it has never crossed my mind. But I certainly never dwelt on it to any degree."

"Wow, Sean," Maggie says, reaching out and touching his elbow. "That must have been a real shock. You haven't told April, have you?"

Sean shakes his head. "It was a shock in a way. And in another way, it wasn't."

"Why would she say that?" Maggie asks. "I mean, why do that to you?"

"I don't know. I think she just wanted to come clean about everything."

Maggie pulls a face. "Come clean?" she says doubtfully.

Sean frowns. "You don't think?"

"It's not... it's just that... well, it's not true, is it?" Maggie splutters.

"What's not true?"

Maggie half-laughs, half-gasps. "Well, none of it. April's the spitting image of you, isn't she? If she looked any more like you, Sean, she'd *be* you. She's got your eyes, your nose, your everything."

"D'you think?" Sean asks, managing to sound both doubtful and hopeful at the same time.

"Oh, absolutely," Maggie says. "Anyone can see that."

Snapshot #13

35mm format, colour. A thin young man in a blue suit, white shirt and blue striped tie stands before an ornate, covered, neo-gothic bridge. It's a sunny, summer day, and beneath the bridge a number of punts can be seen on the river.

Sean frowns at this image of his younger self. It makes him feel embarrassed.

The suit, brand new from Marks & Spencer, had fitted well enough. But the shirt, which he had borrowed from Alistair, had been too big for him, and his tie, he now sees, had been badly knotted, lopsided and really, rather huge. *It's a wonder I got the job at all*, he thinks.

He had been incredibly nervous, for it was the first job interview he had ever had.

Neither he, nor Catherine, had ever been to Cambridge before and, terrified of being late, they had arrived by train a full three hours early. As it had been a beautiful day, they had wandered around the town centre and then through the colleges while they waited. They had both been stunned by the prosperity of the town and the easy elegance of the people who lived there.

Finally, Sean had installed Catherine in the window seat of a French-style cafe, The Dome, and had gone to his interview with Nicholson-Wallace Architects LTD.

"You'll be great," Catherine had said, straightening his tie. "You'll knock 'em dead."

Cassette #13

Hello Darling.

I've had an enforced break from recording these because I've been back home for a few days and you and April have been keeping a round-the-clock watch on me! But now I'm back in Addenbrooke's and on a new chemo regime which is part of a clinical trial and which, between you and me, feels very much like a last ditch attempt. I'm not getting any side effects, which may be a good thing, or, more likely, probably means that I've ended up being in the sugar-pill half of the cohort. Still, at least I get to carry on with my tapes.

So here's a picture of you looking outrageously skinny and scared in Cambridge, standing in front of the Bridge of Sighs. You know, I used to know why it was called that, but I've forgotten. Like I said before, all these drugs are doing things to my brain.

That was the first time I had ever seen you in a decent suit, I think. Oh, you had worn that striped one on our wedding day, but as far as I can remember it was pretty awful. I was so proud of you that day in Cambridge. I thought you looked so sexy. It's a shame you never once wore it again.

We had left April with Green Donna and Alistair that day, the idea being that Alistair wouldn't let Green Donna commit hara-kiri with April in her arms, and Donna wouldn't let Alistair get her stoned. But I still worried all day. I kept on and on asking you if you thought she'd be all right, and you kept on and on replying that "yes" she'd be fine. Of course, we had no mobile phones back then. There wasn't even a landline in our student house. So there were no updates until we got home.

Cambridge was such a shock to the system. I know that you were surprised by things like the prettiness of the colleges and the crowded cycle paths everywhere, but me? I was gobsmacked. Compared with Margate, compared with post-industrial Wolverhampton, Cambridge seemed outrageous, really.

The streets were spotless, the shops were pretty and full of French cheeses and stripy shirts. A cup of tea was one pound twenty or something, I remember, and we were outraged about it. We were used to paying thirty pence in Wolves.

When we walked around the colleges it all made me feel sick, to tell the truth. And I don't mean that as a euphemism – I mean physically sick, as in queasy.

You kept saying how pretty it all was and, of course, I could only agree. All that grass everywhere, all those flowers and the river and everything... it was lovely. But I saw something else, something that I don't think, coming from your family, you were able to see at all.

I saw privilege. Looking at the students strutting around in shirts and ties and stripy blazers, and thinking about those poor mums I'd met in Orgreave, I saw shocking inequality and outrageous privilege. Because those students looked like they owned the place, and that was for the simple reason that they *did*. The place had been made for the likes of them. I remember wondering what Mum would say if she ever saw Cambridge. Because most people in Margate really didn't know that places like Cambridge even existed, back then. They probably still don't.

You went off clutching that big folder of yours and you were gone for almost two hours, so I wandered in ever-increasing circles around the café you had left me in. I went into a bakery and saw that they had proper French baguettes that cost three times the price of a sliced loaf of Sunblest at Salman's Mini Mart. I saw a shop selling ties that cost more than your suit and pairs of women's shoes that cost one hundred and ninety pounds, and I thought that that we would never be able to afford to live in Cambridge and that, ultimately, it was obscene that *anyone* could afford it.

By the time you got back, I'd decided that not only was Cambridge not for the likes of us, but that I was glad, proud even, not to fit in there. There was something self-satisfied about the place, I thought. Something smug. There were too many men wearing braces and too many women in trouser suits and brogues.

You were beaming, Sean. I can remember your exact expression when you got back. You were beaming and your eyes were all shiny like you were on the verge of crying.

You licked your lips and said, wide eyed, that they had offered you the job, straight off. Just like that. You were to start on the 1st of September, I think. And then you asked me how much I thought you were going to be earning. It took me quite a few guesses before I got the right figure, which I think I remember was seven hundred and fifty pounds a month. Does that sound about right? Whatever it was, it seemed a fortune to us.

We got back to Wolverhampton just after midnight to find April fast asleep in Donna's bed and, even after the day that we had had, neither of us could sleep. You talked until the early

152

hours about being terrified you'd bugger up your degree, because the job offer, of course, was dependant on you getting at least a 2:1. Though I didn't say much, I was terrified too.

I was convinced, back then, that I would never fit in, that I would never be able to open my mouth in Cambridge without people laughing at me. I believed with all my heart that I would never make a single friend here, either. And I thought that I would never be able to walk down King's Parade without feeling queasy.

But you got a first class honours, didn't you? And so we had to move. And I had to get over myself, I suppose, and just get used to life in Cambridge.

Actually, I didn't get used to it at all. That's me being disingenuous. Is that the right word? But no, I didn't get used to it, I came to *love* it here.

That's the funny thing about privilege. When you spend enough time in a town like Cambridge, you come to realise that it's not Cambridge that's wrong, after all. It's everywhere else. You come to realise that *everyone* should get a good education and enough money to buy a baguette and brie if they fancy it. You realise that *all* kids should get the chance to go to a decent school where the teachers are clever and polite, and motivated. You come to think that all towns should have green spaces and cycle paths. And you learn that when you do put human beings in such a pleasant, easy going environment, it brings out the best in them, not the worst. They don't end up being right wing, racist dick-heads who want to protect their privilege, they end up trendy lefties instead. When people don't have to spend every minute of the day worrying how they're going to pay the leccy bill, they end up with enough spare brainpower to worry about the Vietnamese boat people or animal rights or global warming. They end up drinking soya- cappuccinos and wearing vegan shoes.

But I'm getting ahead of myself, aren't I? Because as far as these tapes are concerned, we're not in Cambridge, yet, are we?

We're still just terrified in Wolverhampton: you that you might muck up your degree and miss out on the job, and I that you might succeed and get it and force me to move to snob-land.

I didn't express my fears at the time. I had no vocabulary, back then, for any of this. But as the weeks went by, I became terrified. Really terrified. I was convinced that Cambridge would somehow show me up, that once you saw me there, you'd realise what a mistake you had made. I knew you'd see how the Margate bird stuck out like a sore thumb and you'd suddenly want some posh, clever, educated girl with a name like Camilla and a daddy who'd give you a Bentley for a wedding present.

• • •

As summer arrives, Sean finds himself waking up earlier and earlier, and on Wednesday morning, when he wakes at six, he decides to fit a site visit into his journey to work. It's another beautiful morning: the sky is blue and the air is crisp and fresh.

On reaching the site of his next project – a plot of land where four houses have recently been demolished, a plot of land for which he's designing twelve luxury apartments – he grabs his camera from the car boot and clambers across the remaining rubble.

He stands on the highest point of scrappy grass and looks out at the view. A racing eight and a coxed four are streaking along the river, cutting through the mirror-like surface of the Cam. One of the coxes is shrieking at his team through a megaphone. Sean thinks back to when he used to row, how fit and happy and healthy it used to make him feel. Sure, all that being shrieked at was horrible and, on cold rainy days, it had been hellish. But on days like today, it had been perfect. On days like today it had been the best possible way to start a day.

He takes a deep breath and watches the boats as they vanish around the bend. Yes, the view from the apartments is going to be stunning.

Once he has checked the measurements of the site and taken photographs from every angle, he clambers back down to the street. Attracted by the continuing ripples from the now distant boats, he crosses and leans on the railings. He glances at his watch. It's still only eight, and he suddenly finds himself in no hurry to get to work, no hurry at all. So instead of heading back to the car, he climbs onto the railings where he sits and pulls his cigarettes from his jacket pocket. Hunting for the lighter, he finds the smooth lump of rose quartz that his daughter gave him. He smiles at the memory and slips it back into his pocket.

Below him, a little to the left, a young couple, late twenties, are emerging from their canal boat. They both have fabulously dishevelled bed head hair. Sean watches as the young man sets up a folding table and chairs on the roof and as the woman joins him with a metal pot of coffee and two mugs.

Sean studies the woman, who is a pretty brunette with generous curves, and wishes, suddenly, that he was her twenty-something boyfriend. He wishes *he* lived on a canal boat. He imagines himself spending sexy Sundays in bed as the boat rocks gently.

He feels guilty, as if he's being unfaithful to Catherine, which is silly, of course, for so many reasons. But he feels it all the same.

He wishes above all, he realises, that he was young again. He lights his cigarette and watches geese as they take off and land, their wings whipping the water.

He's feeling restless. Days like this have always made him want to leave.

He once read an article about Aboriginal Australians and how they would get up one morning and head off on walkabout, not returning sometimes for months, and this is exactly how Sean had felt when he was younger, specifically on summer mornings like today. Yes, despite the fact that he loved his wife and daughter and despite the fact that he enjoyed his job, there have always been days when Sean felt an almost biological urge to go walkabout.

He remembers driving to work wondering what would happen if he didn't turn off the ring road – what would happen if he just carried on driving? If he headed south, he could drive to Dover and stick the car on a ferry across the Channel. And then, what? Would he head south to Spain, or east towards Russia? How far would he get before his credit card ran out?

He had resented Catherine on those days. He had (while still loving her) hated her for being the reason he couldn't leave, for being the reason that his life was so adventure-free.

But today, he is free, isn't he? No one is waiting for him, nobody cares what Sean does anymore.

The woman tips her head back and laughs at something the young man has said, and Sean wonders how long it is since he last laughed. She leans in and kisses him, then nervously looks around as if kissing is perhaps a crime.

She smiles at Sean, then winks, and he forces a smile back, then embarrassed, stubs his cigarette out on the underside of the railings and stands. He drops the cigarette butt in a litter bin, then returns to his car.

As he opens the car door, his phone vibrates, so he pulls it from his pocket and checks the screen. It's showing an SMS from Perry saying he can't attend to their mother this weekend and can Sean please go instead? Sean sighs deeply, replies, "Sure. No worries, I'll go Saturday," and slips the phone back into his pocket. *You wanted to drive somewhere,* he thinks.

He climbs into the car, puts on his seatbelt. He starts the engine; he glances one last time towards the couple on the houseboat but they have both vanished inside. He pulls gently away.

When he reaches the roundabout, he heads not south towards Dover but north across the Elizabeth Way, towards work. "Sorry, Catherine," he murmurs. "It wasn't your fault at all."

The reason Sean never left was not, it transpires, because Catherine and April had stopped him leaving, after all. Perhaps there was a little cowardliness about him that made adventure difficult; perhaps there was a certain lack of imagination, an inability to take risk in his genetic makeup, that had kept him here. But mainly, he realises, it was that everything he *really* wanted had been here in Cambridge. His vision is blurring now. He sniffs and wipes away the tears with the back of his hand. Yes, even now that he's free, he doesn't want to leave. Even now, all he wants is another twenty years with Catherine.

Snapshot #14

35mm format, colour. A young man poses for the camera. He is wearing a black gown and a mortar board. He is holding a rolled certificate and blushing deeply.

The results had been published in June, and Sean had received his employment contract at the beginning of July. He and Catherine had spent a final heavenly, lazy month in Wolverhampton celebrating and saying goodbye to everyone, before loading their things into a friend's battered Transit van and heading off to Cambridge where they had rented their first ever flat. It had been small – just one bedroom – and underground; it had been shabbily furnished and surrounded by roads, like living in the middle of a roundabout really, but it had been theirs. It was their first ever private home.

It had been raining when they left Wolverhampton and sunny when they arrived in Cambridge and, despite April's screaming, Sean had taken this as a good omen. But Catherine had been jumpy and strange, which was no doubt why April was so fractious, too. Yes, Catherine had been sad and irritable, and her strange mood had lasted well into September. Sean had hoped that things would improve soon, because coming home from an exhausting day at a new and stressful job only to find a grumpy wife and a screaming child had been seriously starting to test his nerves.

Graduation day had been mid-September, and Sean had not been particularly motivated to attend. He had been at the start of his first ever job and money, time and energy had been tight. He also felt that he had already moved on from Wolverhampton; he felt as if his college years already lived in the distant past. But Catherine, who already seemed desperate to get out of Cambridge, had insisted.

Sean had spent the whole week leading up to it worrying about his parents. He had really hoped that they wouldn't come at all but, just like at the wedding, Perry had driven his mother and, just like at the wedding, they had both sulked all day. Sean's mother had even worn the same dress. It had felt like an unwanted rerun.

Cassette #14

Hi Sean.

I didn't think I'd be able to use this one as we have it framed in the lounge, but apparently we had two copies, so here it is again. My darling baby Sean in the silliest hat that ever existed.

You were so embarrassed about that hat, but I was as proud as I could possibly be. Actually, you weren't just embarrassed about the hat, I don't think you wanted to go to the ceremony at all, but as far as I was concerned, it was non-negotiable.

I was struggling with Cambridge – I hadn't settled at all – and I was gagging to see all our old friends one last time, too. But beyond that, the fact that you had studied for four whole years, the fact that you were now a trained architect, these were amazing achievements as far as I was concerned. These were events that *required* some kind of ceremony.

Perry and your mum came again, which was unfortunate because they, of course, did everything they could to ruin the day.

We stayed in the old house with Alistair and Donna (Donna, being younger, still had her final year to do, and Alistair was still painting those horrible pictures in the loft). So we got to stay up late drinking and listening to music with Alistair while Donna slept with April, and for the first time in my life, I felt nostalgic. For the first time ever, I felt that I had lost something valuable. Even April seemed to agree. She too seemed happier in Donna's arms than in Cambridge.

At the ceremony, we saw Theresa and Bronwen and Angie and just about everyone else. They all had their parents in tow which made them behave differently than usual. Everyone was uptight and on their best behaviour, but no one could have been more uptight than the Patricks.

They turned up together, Perry with one of his girlfriends – I don't even remember her name, there were so many of them – and your mother looking like someone had just slapped her around the face. I don't think sixty seconds passed before Perry upset you. As far as I recall, your mother asked about your new job – she seemed to be trying, for once, to be enthusiastic about something – and then Perry asked you how much you earned, and pulled a face and said that, of course, you were bound not to earn that much with a degree from Wolves Poly. "If you'd gone to Cambridge like you were supposed to, you'd be earning double that," he said.

You pointed out that you were living in Cambridge now, and Perry laughed and said, "Yeah, bro. You always did do everything the wrong way around."

I cried when you were called up onto the stage for your degree certificate. Perry was banging on about how much nicer the ceremonies were at the Oxbridge universities, but I didn't let it get to me. I was so proud of you, I didn't care about anything. And I didn't believe that anything anyone could say could *possibly* get to me that day. I was, as it turned out, wrong about that.

Your mother asked me how April was doing and who was looking after her (she was with Donna and Alistair, again) and I thought, for a moment, that things might improve between us. I imagined that perhaps, having seen that I hadn't stopped you studying and that I hadn't stopped you getting a great job either, she might be ready, finally, to be friends. April had just started talking, so I told her excitedly about that and, again, she was enthusiastic. "They make so much progress at that age," she said.

So I suggested we come and visit them in Dorset with April. I thought that perhaps she was ready to start being a grandmother, finally.

"Oh, Giles would never put up with a baby in the house," she said.

I pointed out that April was almost three.

"The worst age," your mum said.

"Oh well, I just thought it would be nice for you, for all of us," I told her.

"It wouldn't," she said. And then she added, "You know, I haven't changed my mind about you. I know exactly what you are."

Now, these were the exact words she had used on our wedding day, Sean, and I'd often thought about that and I'd often wished I had confronted her about what she meant. I suppose I'd grown up a bit in the meantime, too. I didn't feel so scared of her anymore. So this time, I asked, "So? What am I? Tell me."

"You're a hypergamous little slattern," she said.

Because I had no idea what either of those words meant – though I could tell that *slattern* didn't sound nice – I got her to repeat herself twice.

That amused her, I think – the fact that she could add *ignorant* to her list of adjectives. It made her smile, anyway. It made her smile for the first time that day.

I didn't go to the meal with you all afterwards. I didn't tell you why because I didn't want to ruin your lovely day, so I made my excuses and went back to look after April at Alistair's.

When I got to the house, I asked Alistair what a *hypergamous slattern* was, but he didn't know either, so we borrowed Donna's dictionary and looked the words up. And then Alistair held me while I cried.

While we were waiting for you to come back from your meal, I went to the phone box and called Mum and told her what Cynthia had said. I had to explain what hypergamous meant to her as well, though she knew what a slattern was. Mum said, "Oh, don't listen to her, love. She's a stupid old hag who wouldn't know true love if it came up and slapped her across her ugly, sagging chops." She said that you were lucky to have met someone nice like me, too. She told me that if you hadn't met me you might have ended up with a horrible old witch like your mother. She cheered me up so much that by the time you got home, I was fine.

You were fuming with both of them and happy to have escaped, so that sort of reinforced the deal for me. It enabled me, I think, to convince myself that Mum was right. I wonder. Who *would* you have married if you hadn't married me?

• • •

On Tuesday evening, Sean is driving home from work when April calls him on his mobile. He clicks a button on the steering wheel and her voice springs from the car speakers.

"Hi Dad," she says. "It's me."

"Hello, you," Sean replies. "Are you OK?"

"Fine. I'm sorry, I meant to call yesterday, but I got a puncture on the way home and had to get a tow truck to come out and change the wheel."

"You don't know how to change a wheel?" Sean asks.

"No. Of course I don't."

"Well, you should. It's important. I'll show you the next time you come up."

"Um, thanks Dad, but you're all right," April says, laughter in her voice.

Whatever happened to feminism? Sean wonders, deciding that he *will* teach his daughter how to change a wheel the next time he sees her.

"Anyway, I was too tired by the time I got home," April continues. "Plus, I had a bit of a ding-dong with Ronan."

"Nothing bad I hope?" Sean asks, glancing over his shoulder and then indicating to change lanes.

"Are you in the car?" April asks. "You sound strange."

"I am. I'm driving home. You're on the hands-free thing."

"Oh, OK. And no. Nothing bad. He just said the same thing as you about the puncture, really. Only being Ronan, he went on about it until I got annoyed."

"You should try just agreeing sometimes," Sean tells his daughter. "Especially when people are talking sense."

"Yeah," April says, vaguely. "So, how was Gran? You went on Saturday, didn't you?"

"I did," Sean says, swinging around Mitcham's Corner, past their first ever apartment, hidden behind a high brick wall, then heading right, over the bridge, into town. "She was worse than when you saw her, if that's possible."

"Is that possible?" April asks.

"Yes. Yes, I'm afraid it is. I don't think she even realised that I was there, honey. It felt like a bit of a wasted journey to be honest."

"Oh, Dad," April says, woefully. "I'm so sorry. I mean, on top of everything else... But you'd have felt bad if you hadn't gone."

"Yes, I would have felt bad if I hadn't gone," Sean repeats. "So..."

"So, you didn't tell her? I just wondered what she'd said. If you had told her, I mean."

"About your mother?"

"Yes."

"Like I said before, there wouldn't be any point," Sean says. "I may *never* tell her. Even if she *did* have a good day I don't think there would be much point."

"Because it would just upset her?"

"Because she'd probably just say 'good riddance,'" Sean replies. "You need to stop worrying about the fact that she doesn't know."

"I just think it's weird that you don't want to tell her."

"April, honey, you're not listening to me."

"I *am*, Dad. But she's still family. And we don't have a lot of family left."

"She's my family, unfortunately. But she was never family as far as Catherine was concerned."

"Now, you see, that's weird, too," April says. "I mean, we all know that Mum didn't like her much. But I've only ever heard you defend her, and now, suddenly you agree with Mum."

"Me? Defend her?" Sean repeats, sounding shocked.

"You did. You always tried to... what's the word? *Mitigate*. You always had an excuse for why she didn't buy presents and why she was grumpy, and why she forgot Mum's birthday. There was always a reason, according to you."

"I don't think you'll find that I made excuses for her, as such," Sean protests feebly.

"You *so* did, Dad. So what's changed now? That's what I can't work out. Did something happen when Mum was ill? Did Gran say something horrible about her, or..."

"No," Sean says. "She didn't. But if I did try to find mitigating circumstances, as you say I did, it will just have been to stop things getting even worse between them. They were like cat and dog at the best of times, so I used to try to keep things calm. And it worked, for the most part."

"If you say so," April says doubtfully. "But I still think you should tell her."

"Well, maybe I will, one day."

"If you do, will you tell me what she says?"

"Why do you care, honey?" Sean asks, turning left onto Newmarket Road. "That's what I don't get."

"I don't know," April says. "Because she's still my gran, I suppose. Because maybe I'd still like to believe that she has a heart?"

"Right," Sean says. "Well, if I ever do tell her, I'll let you know. But don't get your hopes up. I think you'll be disappointed." Sean turns into his street and, finding a rare parking space right in front of the house, reverses into it.

"Right. That's me home, April. Do you want me to phone you back once I'm indoors?"

"No," April says. "I need to go and buy some food before Ronan arrives. He's coming over in a bit. We're starting packing tonight."

"But you're not moving for a month, right?"

"No, but you know how I like to get things organised in advance, yeah?"

"I do. You're just like your mother on that one."

"Exactly like Mum," April says. "Are *you* OK, Dad? I didn't even ask. Sorry."

"I'm fine," Sean says. "Go get your shopping. Talk soon."

The phone call over, Sean remains in the car for a moment. He looks out at their lounge window and imagines Catherine pulling the curtains and looking back at him. She'd had a second sense about when he was parking outside and he would often glance at the house and see her peering out, grinning at him.

He thinks about his conversation with April and worries again that he was unfair to his wife. In a way it really *is* true that his attempts at excusing anyone's bad behaviour had been a calming influence on the family. Sean has known families where the slightest of disagreements always mushroomed into the biggest of arguments, whereas in their family, even the most nuclear of disputes had always remained under wraps until eventually they dissipated, seemingly for the simple reason that no one was prepared to stoke the fire.

But he hadn't known that his mother had been so *directly* offensive towards his wife, had he? Why had Catherine never told him? Why had he never asked? Perhaps he hadn't wanted to know. Because what would he have done with that knowledge if he *had* known? Where would that have got him?

167

Snapshot #15

35mm format, colour. A young woman holds a toddler in her arms. She is standing in a shabbily furnished lounge, on a worn green carpet. From the window behind her, weak, cold daylight is filtering into the apartment.

The first memory to surface when Sean looks at the photo is an olfactory one. He remembers the smell of mould which used to hit his nostrils every time he stepped indoors. He can remember the odour of the grubby carpet, too; the distant throb of the almost constant traffic roaring around Mitcham's Corner behind the tall, red brick wall that enclosed their tiny yard.

Following on from these comes, surprisingly, the memory of a taste. The taste of the cheesy, greasy, rather delicious pizzas they used to buy from the kebab shop opposite. And then happiness. Pride. Contentment.

For yes, Sean had felt happy in that apartment. They had their first ever home, just for the three of them. Sure, it was a bit dark and, yes, the carpet smelt pretty terrible. But it was home, and he, Sean, was paying for it, without any help from anyone. And that simple fact had made him feel a whole new kind of pride, something primeval, perhaps. He had become the hunter of the family, bringing home the carcass, in the form of a paycheque, that would feed, clothe and house the whole family.

Cassette #15

Hi Sean,

I'm not feeling very well today, so this may not end up being the longest of tapes. I'm praying that this queasiness indicates that I'm not in the placebo group after all, but to be honest, it's probably just the food here. It is pretty bad.

So, what do you think of this one? Our little flat on Mitcham's Corner.

I had such a bad start in Cambridge, Sean. I'm sure I must have been hell to live with, so I apologise for that if it's the case.

I was scared of the place, really. I was scared I wouldn't fit in and scared I'd show you up. Everyone seemed polite and over-educated and a little too healthy and posh and happy, and I think all of this acted like a mirror to how I saw myself back then, to how I saw my own humble origins.

You, on the other hand, loved the place from the first day. I had never seen you so happy, so energetic, so positive about everything. So I did my best to put on an act. I think I was fairly convincing.

You'd get home from work of an evening and I'd describe the luscious day I had spent with April when the truth was that I'd spent the entire day moping around that mouldy flat.

There were high points, like that Christmas when we went out together and bought our first tree. April was so obsessed by the twinkly lights that we moved her cot so that she could stare at it while falling asleep. But generally speaking, I was miserable.

That first winter, I took April down to see Mum a few times in Margate, I remember. I told you that it was because Mum was single again, that it was Mum who needed me, but in truth it was the other way around.

"Tell 'im," Mum kept saying. "Tell 'im you ain't 'appy. Tell 'im you wanna move." But I couldn't burst your bubble. At least, I couldn't burst it right away.

You were loving your job, you were loving the people you met through it, you were enjoying the projects they had you working on... So I just sort of battened down the hatches and hoped that either things would get better for me, or you'd change your mind and decide to go somewhere else.

It wasn't until the following summer that things changed because it wasn't until then that you felt secure enough in your new job to start socialising with the people there.

I was so scared I'd show you up that I kept making excuses to start with. I had a couple of headaches, I recall. I pretended April had a fever once or twice, too. But eventually I had to cave in.

Maggie, whom you worked with and whom I hadn't yet met, had organised a picnic on the Cam. It was June, I think, or maybe even July.

I had run out of fresh excuses and I think you sort of trapped me by asking if I'd come along or whether I'd be having another headache. I said, "No, of course I'll come, why would you even say that?" I pretended to be a little outraged, I think.

I packed our picnic and threw in the book I was reading as well, reckoning that I'd be able to hide my nose in it and appear all aloof and clever. That was the plan, anyway.

We met at Scudamore's and rented three punts. Maggie came in ours, and she was lovely to me from the minute we met. She spotted the book I was reading – it was Armistead Maupin, I think – and she was reading the same series, so we compared notes. We were both in love with Michael "Mouse".

Everyone was drinking and you and an older guy from work, whose name I've forgotten, punted us along the river. I was surprised how good you were at it. With nothing to do but drink and chat, Maggie and I got quite drunk.

April, who was wearing a little life-jacket they had lent us, trailed her hands in the water while I held on to her feet. We glided past the backs of the colleges and past lots of other punts filled with laughing students and tourists, and eventually ended up in Grantchester where we folded out our blankets and spread out the food. Once we had eaten everything we dozed in the sun.

I can remember the exact moment I changed my mind about Cambridge, and it was there, that day, in Grantchester.

I had my head on your chest – you had fallen asleep with a blade of grass between your teeth – and Maggie was playing with April in the shade of a tree.

Some students who were picnicking nearby had an old gramophone player, one of those wind up ones, and they were playing a really scratched old record of Mood Indigo over and over. I think they only had one record with them.

One of the students, one of those posh ones you see everywhere in Cambridge, in a waistcoat and shiny, proper shoes, came over. He asked us if we wanted some cake. It was someone's birthday and they had this huge birthday cake with them, but they'd eaten too much and were stuffed, he said.

Out of habit, I said "no". But April had heard the magic word "cake" and came running over begging for a piece, so the guy in the waistcoat cut her a bit and then one by one we all caved in. It was lovely cake.

We gave them some of our wine, and you shared your cigarettes and they played the b-side of the record and within half an hour we had moved our blankets together to form one big group.

The students were all quite posh, but they were also shockingly friendly and chatty and open. It was the first glimpse I ever had of what makes Cambridge so special.

When you live in a town like Margate, where so many people are unemployed and no one has any money, you're always, I suppose, a bit suspicious of other people's motives.

But the opposite is true as well, and in a town like Cambridge where, at least back then, everyone had a job and everyone could afford cake and wine, and cigarettes, well, no one worried about sharing stuff, did they? People's first reflex wasn't *what does he want from me?* or *how is this person trying to rip me off?* It was more, sort of, *oh, how nice. Another person in the world.*

I didn't grasp all of this that day, I don't think. But slightly drunk, on a blanket, on the grass, I did feel unexpectedly relaxed and unthreatened by anyone or anything.

It still felt a bit wrong to be living in that little pocket of wealth when other places were struggling so hard. But I think that I realised that if I could just let myself go a bit it could be a very comfortable place to live and, above all, a very charmed existence for our daughter. Because when you have a child the world turns into the theme park of possible dangers. And Cambridge suddenly felt like a very reassuring place for her to be.

Eventually the sun went down and it got a bit chilly, so we all divvied up into the boats again and headed back. I had decided that I really liked Mags and I had decided I would make her my friend, so I made sure I was in the same boat heading back.

I asked her if she had a boyfriend, and because she looked embarrassed and said no, I thought for a minute that I'd made a boo-boo, so I asked her if she had a girlfriend. She laughed so much she made the boat rock. She then said something that has stuck with me the whole time I've known her. She said, "I'm not very good at relationship stuff." It seemed a strange remark to me, because I had never considered relationship stuff as a thing you could be good at or bad at. Up until then I thought it was just something that happened to you. But when I asked her about it, she was adamant that it was like a subject you might learn at college. There were many aspects to it, she explained. There was choosing the right person and wooing them correctly. There was the ability to resolve conflicts and choose gifts and remember important dates. "They should run courses on it," she said. "They really should, if only for people like me."

Over the years, I think we've both come to see that she was right. She always has chosen the wrong guys and when she *has* chosen someone nice it's always gone wrong, even when, like with gorgeous Ian, that wasn't her fault. But I feel sad for Mags. I feel a little guilty even, that she never had what we had. But more of that later. I'm tired now. I need to sleep.

• • •

On Sunday, Sean accepts an invitation to a pub lunch with Maggie and Dave.

Maggie pulls up outside his house just before twelve and hoots her horn.

174

"Hello!" she says, beaming from the side window of her little Fiat. "Jump in. You'll have to fight it out with Dave over who gets the back seat."

"Sean does," Dave says, leaning down over Mag's lap and waving up at Sean. "There's no way I'm getting in there."

"We can take my car, if you want," Sean offers hopefully. "It's parked down the end. You can take my space, Mags."

"Oh, stop being such a wimp," Maggie laughs. "It's only five minutes to Grantchester."

"Fifteen," Sean corrects. "But, whatever."

Dave stands to let Sean access the rear seat. "Sorry, dude," he says. "But my legs are even longer than yours are."

"You can swap on the way back, maybe?" Maggie offers, as Dave fastens his belt and then shifts his seat forwards providing Sean with an entire extra inch of leg room.

"It's fine," Sean says, twisting so that he's sitting sideways. "Go, Mags. Go!"

Though it's still early when they reach the Green Man, there is only a single free table left outside, so Dave and Sean leave Maggie to defend it while they head into the dark interior to order.

"Jesus," Dave says, when he sees the menu. "Thirteen quid for fish and chips?"

"It's a bit of a gastro pub," Sean says. "So, hopefully it's worth it."

"Damn," Dave jokes. "Mags didn't warn me. If I'd known I would have brought the Imodium."

Sean looks up from his own menu to find the owner leaning on the bar in front of them. "It stands for *gastronomic*," he says, drily.

Sean senses himself blush.

175

"That's what I was just saying," Dave quips. "Astronomic."

Sean clenches his teeth and beams a message of sympathy and apology to the owner. "Right," he says. "Well, I'll have the *celeriac, mushroom and chestnut pasty*, I think. That sounds great."

"Ooh," Dave says. "Fancy, fancy. Astronomical cod and chips for me, I think. Sorry, gastronomical, I mean. And the mackerel for the missus. She likes a bit of mackerel."

"Do you not want to show her the menu?" Sean asks. "I mean, that's what we said. That we'd take out a menu."

"Nah," Dave says. "The mackerel will be fine."

"There's a bit of a wait," the owner tells them. "We're a bit short staffed at the moment."

"That's fine," Sean says. "We're in no hurry, are we?"

"It depends," Dave says. "How long is 'a bit of a wait'?"

"Thirty, forty minutes max," the man says. "It's this Brexit business, I'm afraid. They all keep buggering off home."

When they get outside, Maggie smiles up at them. "Isn't it a lovely day?" she says.

"It is," Sean agrees, placing his pint on the table and climbing onto the built-in bench.

Dave hands Maggie her white wine spritzer. The bubbles glisten in the sunshine.

"Menu?" Maggie asks.

"I ordered you some mackerel," Dave says, handing her back her bank card. "That OK?"

"Um, yeah..." Maggie says, doubtfully, slipping the card into her purse and then sipping at her drink. "Yes, mackerel's fine," she says, with forced positivity. "What's it come with?"

"I forget," Dave says. "Anyway, I hope you're not hungry. Apparently all the staff have buggered off back to Romania."

176

"They were Italian, I think," Maggie says. "The last time I came here they were, anyway."

"A lot of people are leaving, apparently," Sean says. "I read about it in the Graun. The NHS is really struggling."

"They can *all* fuck off as far as I'm concerned," Dave says.

"Oh," Sean says quietly, almost imperceptibly wide-eyeing Maggie.

Maggie sighs and runs her tongue across her lips, visibly trying to decide whether to say something.

"So, Mags," Sean says, deciding to save her from the dilemma. "How do you feel about taking up rowing again?"

"Rowing?" Maggie says. "Gosh! Where did that come from?"

"Again?" Dave queries. "Why, *again*?"

"Oh, we used to row together years ago," Maggie explains. "Well, Sean did. I just dabbled, really. You did it for years, didn't you?"

Sean nods. "Five or six years, yes."

"Whereas I only went a dozen or so times, I think."

Sean laughs. "At a push."

"Yes," Maggie says. "Yes, you're probably right. Half a dozen, then."

"I don't think rowing's my kind of sport," Dave says. "More of a rugby man, me."

"Right," Sean says. "So, what do you think, Mags?"

Maggie smiles and wobbles her head from side to side. "Sure," she says, finally. "Why not? It would do me good."

Dave frowns deeply at this and sips his pint, then clambers back out of the bench seat. "I'm gonna get some crisps," he says. "I'm starving. Anyone else?"

Sean and Maggie shake their heads.

Once Dave has gone, Maggie leans in, grasps Sean's wrist and asks, gently, "So, are you all right, pumpkin?"

Sean nods vaguely.

"Have there been any more pseudo-revelations? In your tapes, I mean?"

Sean shakes his head. "No, but why the *pseudo*?" he asks.

"Oh, sorry. I didn't mean to be... It's like I said, the more I think about it, the more obvious it seems to me that the whole business, you know... about April... well, that's rubbish, isn't it? We've got a photo of you three at home and I looked at it when I got back. And no one could *ever* doubt that you're April's dad. I mean, things like that... You just have to think of Harry and William to know what I mean. One of them looks like his dad and the other one, well, he's gorgeous, isn't he?" She pulls a face.

"Yes, I see what you mean," Sean says.

"It's like I said before. It's all those drugs she was on, sweetie. That's all it is."

Almost as soon as Dave returns with his packets of crisps, the food arrives. "Fastest bloody forty minutes I've ever seen," he says, glancing at the screen of his massive Samsung telephone which he has placed in full view on the table before him.

"Don't complain about the food being too *early*..." Maggie berates him, glancing apologetically at the waitress.

"I just wanted to eat my crisps," Dave says. "Still. Never mind. Let's see what fifteen quid fish and chips tastes like."

"Thirteen," Sean corrects him. Dave is starting to get on his nerves. "Actually, it's not even thirteen. They were twelve-fifty."

"*Seven*-fifty down from ours," Dave says, cutting into his cod.

178

"Just..." Maggie says, closing her eyes for a little too long. "Just try to enjoy it, hum? You're not paying for it anyway, so just... Can you do that for me?"

Dave shoots her a glare and then raises a chunk of cod to his lips. "It's nice," he says, through a full mouth. "It's tasty."

After lunch, they walk down to the river where they watch a group of youngsters struggling to control the direction of their punt.

"Do you remember the picnics we used to have?" Sean asks.

"You two?" Dave asks. "Rowing and picnics together... Aye, aye."

"It was just a work thing," Maggie says. "Nothing to be jealous of. A whole bunch of us used to rent punts and come out here with our picnic."

"All the way from Cambridge? On a punt?"

Sean laughs and nods towards the river. "They're all from Cambridge," he says. "It's not as far as you think."

"How long did it used to take?" Maggie asks. "An hour? An hour and a half?"

"Something like that," Sean says. "We should do it again sometime."

"Ooh, yes," Maggie says. "That'd be a right laugh."

"You wouldn't get me on one of those," Dave says.

Maggie wrinkles her nose. "Dave can't swim," she explains in a confidential tone, reaching out to caress Dave's arm.

"Loads of people can't swim," Dave says. "There's not a lot of call for swimming when you grow up in deepest Derbyshire."

By the time they drop Sean off at the end of his road, he's feeling exhausted.

Being sociable, he thinks, as he walks along the road, is like a muscle – a muscle he has allowed to atrophy. And the sheer effort of making polite conversation for three hours with Dave and Maggie has completely worn him out.

Still, the good side of that, he realises as he closes the front door, is that he's glad for once to find himself alone in the house. He hurls himself onto the settee and lets out a long deep "Ahhh" of satisfaction.

And then he remembers it's Sunday. Maggie's description – her *pseudo revelations* – is still ringing in his ears. She'd annoyed him by saying that. He pulls a face. He should, perhaps, have said something.

He levers himself from the sofa and heads through to the kitchen where he switches on the kettle and pulls the box from the kitchen cabinet.

Snapshot #16

35mm format, colour. A man looks out through lace curtains at the street beyond. The light from outside is cold and harsh, making the man's features look sharp and angular. He looks pensive, or perhaps sad.

Sean studies the photo and remembers instantly what had been wrong. He had made a terrible, terrible mistake at work. He had chosen to clad a small office block on the Cambridge Science Park with marble. But even before all of the marble had been clipped onto the walls, it had started cracking and falling away. One lump had punched a hole right through the roof of a contractor's car. Had he been in the car, he might have died. Estimates to remove the marble, change the clips and replace it all with granite (which unlike marble would not crack and shatter in the summer heat) had been estimated at almost two-hundred thousand pounds. So he had been going to work each morning wondering if today was the day he'd be sacked. Or even worse, sued. He hadn't been sleeping at night either, and on multiple occasions, Catherine had come downstairs at three a.m. to find him staring into the middle distance.

He had told her what was wrong but, as often where his job was concerned, she had failed to grasp the seriousness of the situation. She had said, "Oh, you're only human. Everyone makes mistakes." It had been as if she didn't really believe that anyone could get that upset about work.

So, yes, he remembers this photo being taken. He had been jerked out of his worried daze by the flash of the camera. "Don't look so sad, it may never happen," Catherine had said. But it already had happened. Sean just hadn't known what that meant for his career quite yet.

Eventually he had started rowing, and not only had the hard physical effort of it diminished his stress levels enormously, but it had given him the opportunity to socialise with one of the partners who was also a rower, and with him on-side, the situation had eased.

Eventually the client had accepted a new composite cladding for the building which cost less than a third of the original marble, and the supplier of the marble had agreed to take half of the financial hit. So the whole business had just melted away like an ice cube on a hot day, leaving Sean wondering why he had been so worried about it in the first place.

Cassette #16

Hi Sean.

I'll bet you don't remember this one. It's a pretty ordinary photo, after all. I only took it, I think, because I had a new compact camera and I wanted to finish the film off. But it is, as it turns out, very evocative of a certain time and specifically of another thing we never spoke about: your affair.

Just so you know this from the outset, I never knew for sure who it was with; in fact I'll go as far as admitting that I was never one hundred percent sure there *was* someone else. But back around the time this photo was taken I thought I was pretty sure, at any rate.

It was partly my fault, I suppose. I hadn't been "putting out" since April was born. Oh, we'd done it once or twice, but it had become rarer and rarer for the simple reason that I no longer enjoyed it. As I was never very good at faking these things, you had slowly stopped trying.

Some nights I'd wake up and realise that you were doing it on your own at the far side of the bed, and I'd feel horribly guilty. But even then it was somehow beyond me to roll towards you and join in. And then after a while, once I'd realised (or convinced myself) that you were having an affair, I had a whole new reason not to join in – seething resentment.

The thought crept up on me, really, without me even noticing it. To start with, you were distant, distracted. And then you seemed sad whenever you were at home. It was like you always wanted to be somewhere else. That was the impression I had.

And then one day, I woke up and realised that I knew. It was as if I had realised in my sleep.

I did all the usual cliché things. I went through your pockets; I checked your wallet for receipts while you were in the shower. But there was nothing I could point to and say, "What the hell is this?". So I watched and waited and got angrier and angrier.

I got scared too. I became terrified that you were going to leave us. I used to cry about it some days while you were at work. I used to imagine myself turning up at Mum's with April and having to explain that, like all of Mum's own relationships, it was over – that, like mother, like daughter, I had failed. I used to try to picture the type of woman you were seeing and I'd always imagine some clever, young, vivacious, rich degree student and then feel overwhelmed by the knowledge that there were hundreds, thousands even, of women in Cambridge for whom I'd be no competition at all.

Things changed a bit when you started rowing, at first once a week, and then twice, and then three times. You suddenly seemed happy again. Sometimes you seemed almost unreasonably happy. Ecstatic, I suppose, is the word.

I decided, God knows why, that you'd replaced your extra-marital adventure with sport. I convinced myself that you were coming back to us. But then I became doubtful again and wondered if you were really rowing at all.

One particular morning it all got the better of me, so I waited for you to leave and then bundled April into the pushchair and almost jogged with her down to the river.

You were there, in a racing eight, looking red cheeked and sweaty, whizzing down the river at quite a shocking speed. So I felt reassured, for a while.

I discovered, too, that it did me good to get out of the house first thing. So the race down to the river and back became a regular morning adventure for April and me. Sometimes we would see you and sometimes we wouldn't. Amazingly, you never noticed us. I suppose you were too busy being shouted at by that horrible woman cox with the megaphone. April only ever once mentioned seeing you rowing and, surprisingly, you didn't seem to think anything of it, so I got away with it.

But then, one morning, all my certainties fell to pieces again. Because I saw Maggie was rowing too. You both looked ecstatic, and again it felt like a realisation of something that I had always known.

I sat a way back from the boathouse and I watched until you got back, and then I watched until you left.

Maggie was running her fingers through her hair, still damp from the showers, and you were laughing at something she had said. And then you put your arm around her shoulders and squeezed her.

I cried when I got home and then I sat and tried to reason with myself all afternoon.

When you got home that night, I suggested we have Maggie and Drunken Duncan, her boyfriend of the moment, round for dinner. I just wanted to see how you'd react.

"Oh, she's split up with Duncan," you told me nonchalantly. "Didn't I tell you that?"

"No," I said. "You didn't."

"Well she has," you said. "But we can still invite Mags around if you want."

I was left wondering how I'd get out of that one.

. . .

Sean pushes the dictaphone to the far side of the table and covers his eyes with his cupped hands. He feels like he wants to weep, but realises, after a moment, that the tears are not going to come.

He feels angry, too. For how could Catherine possibly have convinced herself he was having an affair with Maggie?

OK, perhaps he can see how that could have happened. They had been close over the years. Perhaps, at times, too close.

But why on earth hadn't she simply asked him? He could have put her mind at rest. He could have saved her months of anguish – years, perhaps. Now he does know, it's too late to tell her the truth. And that feels devastating.

●●●

On Thursday evening, Sean is invited to join a group of friends for a pub quiz at The Brook.

Quiz night had once been a fairly regular occurrence and Sean can't quite work out when that ceased to be the case, nor why. Certainly, he hasn't seen any of the gang since Catherine died, but now that he thinks about it he can't remember having been out with them for a while *before* she died either, so perhaps the two are unrelated.

Whatever the reason, he accepts the invitation. He's grateful for any kind of distraction at the moment and is looking forward to seeing his old friends again.

When he gets to the pub, five familiar faces are already lined up along a bench seat, drinking.

Sean buys a round of drinks for those whose glasses are nearly empty and then sits down on the other side of the table, feeling, for some reason, as if he's being interviewed.

"So!" he says, scanning the smiling faces. "It's been ages. I was trying to work out how long it's been and why we never do this anymore."

Jim, the youngest of the group, glances along the row and then shrugs and says, "We've all been too busy, I guess. You know what it's like, what with work and the kids and everything else."

"Sure," Sean says.

"How have you been?" Pete asks.

"OK," Sean replies. "You know."

A silence falls over the group. Everyone sips their drinks.

"The missus saw you out in Grantchester," Pete says.

"Sylvia?" Sean says. "She should have said hello."

"You were with someone," Pete says, coyly. "I don't think she wanted to interrupt anything."

Sean frowns. "I was with Maggie," he says.

"Maggie, was it? Fair enough," Pete says.

"And her partner," Sean adds, furrowing his brow and smiling in amusement. "Dave, his name is."

"Ah," Pete says, sounding disappointed. "Oh well."

After another awkward silence the talk turns to Jim's wife who is pregnant again, and then to Pete's upcoming retirement party, and then finally to their standard staple: football. And it's a relief for Sean to have an hour of mundane, everyday conversation.

It's strangely calming to discuss things which really don't matter, he realises, but it also occupies his mind so that it doesn't go hunting under rocks. Because Sean's pretty sure there's something lurking in the shadows here that he doesn't want to see.

By ten-thirty, when the quiz ends, they're all pleasantly drunk. But despite their alcohol intake they have done well, in no small part due to Sean's grasp of eighties pop music. When the results are tallied up, it is their group that has won. First prize. An eighty pound bar tab for future use.

"Yay!" Pete says, raising one hand in a victory gesture and almost knocking over his pint in the process. "Result! Third time in a row! We rule!"

Despite his attempts at not thinking about it, the truth that has been tugging at Sean's sleeve, trying to get his attention, finally takes centre stage. Because evidently, the group never stopped coming to quiz night. They simply stopped inviting Sean.

Sean makes his excuses and leaves the table, but a shadow must have crossed his features because when he stands and heads for the bathroom, Jim, who has always been one of the more sensitive souls in the group, follows him.

Side by side in the urinals, Jim says, "I'm glad you're back, mate. We missed you."

"I never went away, though, did I?" Sean says. The alcohol has loosened his tongue.

Jim clears his throat. "No," he says. "Sorry about that. It's just, you know..."

"No," Sean says, buttoning his jeans. "I'm not sure I do."

"It's just, you know, when Cathy got ill," Jim says awkwardly. "It was a real downer and no one knew what to say, really."

"Right," Sean says.

"And then Pete's missus went and got cured and everything. And she started coming out with us, for a while. And it seemed... I dunno. It just seemed a bit awkward, really. To be rubbing her good health in your face, like."

"Right," Sean says.

"It was nothing personal," Jim says. "It was nothing against you. It was just, we... I dunno really."

Sean washes his hands and dries them on the roller towel.

"Still, you're back, now," Jim says, slapping him on the shoulder.

"Yeah," Sean says, sounding unconvinced. "Yeah, I'm back now."

Snapshot #17

35mm format, colour. On a pub lawn, two women in summer dresses lie either side of a handsome man with slicked back hair. He's wearing a waistcoat and rolled up shirt sleeves. A small girl stands behind them holding a glass of orange juice. Of the four people in the photo, only the man is smiling.

Ouch, Sean thinks, the second he sees the photo. Because something had gone wrong that day between Catherine and Maggie. Despite the summer sun and the alcohol, the ambiance had been bitchy and glacial, so difficult, in fact, that Sean had been forced to abandon the whole mission and drag Catherine and April away.

It was a shame because Sean, for his part, had been feeling on top of the world. The *Marble Drama,* as it had come to be known, was over, and he was working on a new sheltered housing project out in Chesterton. The building did *not* require cladding.

Maggie had met Stephane, the man in the photo, and was as happy as he had ever seen her. Actually, thinking back on it, now, Maggie had been unreasonably, hysterically, irritatingly happy, and he had thought that it was this that had put Catherine's back up that day. Of course, knowing what he knows now, she must still have been fuming, quite simply, over their supposed affair.

But Catherine should really have felt reassured. Because Maggie could only talk about one thing. Stephane. Bloody Stephane. She had talked about him for weeks at work and she had talked about him that day, as well. Stephane who had a gym in his London flat; Stephane who knew *all* the best restaurants. "And guess who bought me these gorgeously tasteful earrings? Why, Stephane, of course!"

If the truth be told, even though he hadn't even *considered* having an affair with Maggie, he had, once Stephane came along, felt vaguely jilted. There was something about the guy that just really annoyed him.

Cassette #17

Hello, honey.

So here's a photo of Maggie and me with Stephane keeping us from each other's throats by lying in the middle. He actually seemed to think that all the bitching that was going on was funny. Perhaps he thought we were fighting over him. He had that kind of outlook on the world. And look at little April there scowling at the back. She looks like she's about to glass him with her orange juice. God though... I had forgotten how good looking he was.

I had worried about you and Maggie for most of the summer. Your moods seemed to be all over the place and I was constantly trying to decode if you were still having a dalliance behind my back or not.

Once I knew that Maggie had split up with Duncan, I avoided her like the plague. It was bad enough that you worked together and rowed together. I was damned if I was going to be the one to organise little get togethers for you both at the weekends.

But it was a difficult time, that's for sure. I suspected you of being unfaithful during every instant that you were out of my sight, but whenever you were late and I invented an excuse to phone you, you were always there, perfectly reachable at your workstation, and unless you and Maggie were doing it there in the middle of the open-plan office (which I did manage to visualise, by the way), I couldn't work out where or when you might be doing it.

By September, when this photo was taken, everything except my own lingering paranoia was back to normal. You seemed calm and interested in home life. It was as if nothing had ever happened. I suspected you were very good at pretending that nothing *had* ever happened. And when I went down to the river and saw that Maggie was no longer rowing, I was able to convince even myself that it was over.

And then we met them, that sunny September day on the green outside The Fort. Maggie was with Stephane, her French banker, or trader, or whatever they call them, that we had all heard so much about. He was beautiful and smooth and stunningly well dressed, if perhaps a little oily in that way that Latins sometimes can be. Does that sound racist? I don't mean it to. I'm sure you know what I mean. Anyway, Maggie was clearly in love with him and frankly I could understand why.

You behaved most strangely around him. It was as if his very presence upset you, and I deduced that you were jealous. Maggie had dumped you for shiny, wealthy, bilingual Stephane, and I felt angry on your behalf while being still angry on my own account, mixed with a dose of what I suppose one can only call jealousy.

He only ever wore those expensive double-cuffed shirts, and braces, and waistcoats, and stunningly sheer suits. I've always had a bit of a secret thing for a man in a suit, but more of that another day. He was whizzing Maggie up and down the country on mini-breaks in that open top BMW of his, and neither of them were tied to home by a petulant daughter. April, you will remember, was at her absolute worst back then so I was feeling jealous of pretty much anyone who didn't have kids. But Stephane, well, he pressed just about every jealousy button that I had.

The feeling soon wore off, because as we all know, Stephane turned out to be a bombastic, arrogant nob.

Do you remember the champagne incident? It just came back to me.

We met up in a pub somewhere, it was around Christmas, I think. And you ordered a beer only to find that Stephane, who was at the bar, had cancelled it for you. He had ordered a magnum of some ridiculously expensive champagne for us all and couldn't even imagine that anyone would rather have beer.

You were quite assertive and explained, very calmly, that you didn't like champagne but that you did, very much, like Harvey's IPA.

And Stephane just laughed. He made this shooing gesture with his long manicured fingers, and said, in that smooth French accent of his, "Nonsense. You will like *this* Champagne. Believe me!" We all looked at each other and no one said a word, and then, while he was pouring the Champagne, Maggie mouthed, "Sorry". Or perhaps, looking back, she mouthed, "Help!"

It's a horrible thing to admit, but I was glad he had turned out to be such an arsehole. I was still angry with Maggie, but not, surprisingly, as angry as I should have been. Perhaps I was already starting to doubt myself.

. . .

The tapes trouble Sean all week. Looking back on his relationship, so many things, so many of Catherine's seemingly inexplicable mood changes, suddenly make sense. Stupidly and, he now realises, in a rather macho way, he had assumed that his wife's ups and downs were simply part and parcel of living with someone. All men know that women are mysteries, don't they? Everyone knows that women are from Pluto and men are from Mars or whatever it is.

But perhaps he should have tried harder to understand. Perhaps he should have forced her to open up and tell him what was wrong. Perhaps he should have sat her down and refused to budge until everything was out in the open.

Then again, there were plenty of times when he had tried. Catherine had been perfectly happy for him to assume that her moodiness was normal even as she berated him for being a macho man when he did. Lord, if he had been told one small truth for every time Catherine said, "Oh, don't mind me, I'm all over the place at the moment," then there would have been no secrets at all. So it's a shame. They wasted precious time tip-toeing around each other when clearly all that was required was a good heart to heart. And now it's all over. There is no more time.

On Friday morning, as Sean pulls up his chinos, his iPhone makes a spectacular leap for freedom from his trouser pocket and lands in the flushing rapids of the toilet bowl. Sean looks on the Internet for tips and doubtfully leaves the device in a sealed packet of rice for the weekend, but when, by Sunday afternoon, it's still refusing to resuscitate, he walks into town to drop it at the Apple store. *It'll be "sorted"*, the genius tells him, *by Tuesday.*

As he steps out into Corn Exchange Street, he almost bumps into Maggie, who is hurrying past.

"Hello stranger!" she exclaims. "What brings you to civilisation?"

Sean kisses her on both cheeks. "I went and dropped my phone down the loo," he explains. "I've just left it with an Apple 'genius'." He raises two fingers to indicate the quotes around the word "genius".

"How did you manage *that*?" Maggie asks.

Sean grimaces. "You know, I really have no idea. It pretty much jumped out of my pocket, if you can believe that."

"I thought they were waterproof or something, aren't they?"

"Not mine," Sean says. "Too old."

"But they can fix it, can they?"

"The guy was too busy being cool to give me any actual information. But by Tuesday I'll have it back, theoretically. Or one like it."

"Oh well," Maggie says. "That's still pretty good service, I suppose."

"For three hundred pounds..."

"Ah..." Maggie says. "Quite expensive good service, then."

"And you? What are you doing here in consumerville?"

Maggie waves her shopping bag at him. "New swimsuit," she says. "I don't think I can get into the old one anymore. Though I didn't even try, to be honest. Too depressing."

"You're still thin," Sean says, eyeing Maggie's figure in mock appraisal. "You're looking good."
194

"For my age," Maggie says, completing Sean's phrase. "I know."

"No, you're looking good, full stop, Mags."

Maggie blushes. "Well, thanks Mister Patrick. Hey, you don't fancy a coffee in Clowns do you? It's not every day I get a compliment. I want to make the most of it."

Sean nods and smiles. "Sure," he says. "I haven't been there for years. Plus it's on the way."

Maggie takes his arm and starts to walk. "Just don't let me eat cake," she says, confidentially. "No matter how much I fight for it, just say no."

"All right," Sean says. "I'll keep you away from the cake."

"Huh!" Maggie laughs. "I'd like to see you try. Have you *tasted* their chocolate cake?"

"So talking of being fit and slim and everything..." Sean says.

Maggie releases his arm. "God, you're going to ask me about rowing, aren't you?"

"You've changed your mind then? That's OK."

"I haven't really. Well, I have, I suppose. It's just Dave. The idea of me and you doing it together, rowing, that is, well, it seemed to get his back up. So it's probably safer if I don't."

Sean frowns as he guides Maggie across St Andrew's Street. "No one's stopping Dave joining us."

"Oh, I know. But he can't swim, can he? The poor love."

"Hum," Sean says, pointedly.

"Hum?"

"I just think it's a bit weird stopping you doing something because he can't join in. It sounds a bit controlling, that's all."

Maggie sighs deeply. "Look, I know you don't like him much. But he's not stopping me. Not as such. And I know he doesn–"

Sean raises his hands to interrupt her. "Hey," he says. "I really do not have an opinion on the guy. Other than to say that I think you deserve someone who's nice to you."

"He is nice to me."

"Then good. That's all fine, then."

"You're talking about the pub, right? When he chose for me? And paid with my card? But it was fine. It's just that he knows my tastes so well."

Sean laughs. "*I* didn't mention that, Mags. You just did. But seriously, I didn't mean anything."

"And as for the rowing," Maggie continues. "I mean, of course, the *ideal* is to have a wonderful partner who caters to your every need and supports you to do whatever you want to do. To be with someone who says, *enjoy rowing with your best friend, darling. I'll have dinner ready when you get home.* But life's not like that, is it? You don't... Well, *I* don't get to choose between some perfect partner or Dave, do I? I get to choose between Dave or being on my tod."

Sean glances at a shop window and pulls a face. Maggie is sounding distinctly edgy today. Fearing that she may have seen his expression reflected in the shopfront he turns back to check on her, but all is well.

"That sounded terrible, didn't it?" she's saying. "Am I sounding mad today? I am, aren't I? Shut up, Maggie! It's just that I get a bit defensive. I mean, I know he's not an easy person to like. But his heart's in the right place, honest it is."

Sean reaches out and gives Maggie's shoulders a quick squeeze. "Of course his heart's in the right place," he says. "And that's fine. And no, you don't sound mad at all. You sound a bit... stressed, maybe. But not mad, per se."

"Do you hate him? Dave, I mean?"

Sean laughs. "You're not listening, Mags. I *really* don't have an opinion of the guy. I just want to make sure you're happy."

"Well, I am. And I'll be even happier once we get to Siena tomorrow."

"Tomorrow? And Siena is it now? I thought it was Portugal. Or Bali."

"Nah, we couldn't agree on those. But Tuscany is going to be gorgeous. Especially if it's like this." Maggie looks up at the blue sky.

"And there was me thinking the cossie was for Jesus Green Pool."

"God, Jesus Pool!" Maggie says, fondly. "I'd forgotten it even existed. We used to go there all the time, didn't we? What happened, eh? What happened to our youth?"

As they have reached the entrance to Clowns, Sean gestures for Maggie to enter first.

"It looks busy," she says, pushing at the door. "But let's try, anyway."

Once they have ordered their coffees (and, for Maggie, cake), they take the only free table, crammed in the corner, and sit.

"You were so lucky, you know, to meet each other," Maggie says, as if this is somehow the continuation of a conversation they've been having.

"Me and Cathy?" Sean asks, then, "I suppose so. Though it doesn't feel that lucky right now."

Maggie rolls her eyes. "What is *wrong* with me, today? God, I'm such an idiot sometimes. I'm so sorry, Sean."

"It's OK," Sean says, flatly. "I know what you mean. And we *were* lucky, I suppose."

"It's just the way you got on," Maggie says. "About everything, really. Whereas for most of us, well, this is about as good as it gets." She sips at her cappuccino. "God, this is good coffee," she says, wiping the froth from her lips. "I wonder if it will be as good in Italy?"

"I'd think so," Sean says, then seriously, "So, Mags. *Are* you happy? I mean, you say you are. But *as good as it gets* doesn't sound that satisfactory."

"I'm OK," Maggie says, forking a lump of cake and pointing it at Sean, then eating it herself when he shakes his head. "Like I said, I've got someone to go on holiday with this year," she says, speaking through crumbs. "And maybe that really is as good as it gets."

"You could have the pick of the pack if you just believed in yourself a bit more," Sean tells her. "You're funny, clever, good looking..."

"Well, thank you for your vote of confidence," Maggie says. "Now I remember why I like you so much. *And* Clowns! God, this cake!" She pulls a face expressing ecstasy. "You really don't know what you're missing."

"I just ate late, that's all," Sean says.

"I was never very good at relationships," Maggie says, sucking her teeth. "That's the thing. Or choosing men. I never have been. It's like a skill set that I just don't have."

"I remember you telling Catherine that, years ago."

"Really?" Maggie asks. She looks puzzled. "Well, it's true anyway."

"I'm not so sure it is."

"Oh, it is! Trust me."

"Maybe. I guess, I mean that, well, you believe in it. So it's true."

"Like a self-fulfilling prophesy, you mean?"

198

"That's exactly what I mean."

Maggie pulls a face. "Well, I've certainly spent most of my life self-fulfilling. When I wasn't busy being in some rubbish relationship, that is."

"Now, come on. Even you have to admit that they weren't *all* rubbish," Sean says.

"Really? Which ones weren't?"

Sean shrugs. "Ian was pretty lovely. We were *all* in love with Ian."

Maggie laughs genuinely. "Yes, and look what happened there!"

"Yes. I suppose."

"Look, I don't know," Maggie says, another chunk of cake hovering in front of her mouth. "But it's always felt a bit like destiny to me."

"Destiny?"

"You don't believe in destiny, I take it?"

Sean shakes his head.

"You don't think it was your personal destiny to meet Catherine in Dreamworld that day, all those years ago?"

"In Dreamland? I don't know," Sean says. "Perhaps if it hadn't been Catherine, it would have just been someone else."

"Sorry, but I can't even imagine that."

"No. Nor can I, to tell the truth," Sean admits.

"I often think that there's just one person on the whole planet for you," Maggie says. "But sometimes your paths never cross. Or they cross and you're busy looking the wrong way or at your phone, or whatever. Or they cross at the wrong time in your lives when one of you isn't ready."

"Again, I don't believe that," Sean says. "It's just not... I don't know. It's not scientific, I suppose."

"Maybe not," Maggie says. "But I'll tell you this much. Dating in your fifties feels like licking out someone else's dog bowl. It feels like all of the decent food has been eaten and you're left with all the mangled leftovers that no one wanted, the bits that even the dog couldn't digest."

Sean's brow furrows. Maggie *is*, he decides, sounding a little fragile today if not quite mad. And the tone of the conversation is definitely darkening. In an attempt at changing direction he says, "Anyway, here's a shocker for you. Here's a little snippet from my *perfect* relationship with Catherine. She thought we had an affair."

Maggie frowns at Sean uncomprehendingly. "What? Who did? Who had an affair?"

Sean gestures at the space between them. "You and me, apparently."

Maggie's mouth drops. "What?" she says.

Sean nods. "It was on the tapes. She thought we had a thing together. And she thought it all ended when you met that French bloke."

"Really? But why? I mean, that's madness. Based on what?"

"The fact that we were... *are*, close I suppose. The fact that I was stressed and distant, which was actually a work thing, as it happens, but Cathy didn't know that."

"The Marble Drama?"

"Ha! You remember. Yes, that's the one. And to explain it all, to explain the fact that I was being weird and distant and stuff, she invented an affair. Plus we were rowing together at the time, of course."

"You see... *rowing*..." Maggie says, with meaning. "It makes people *very* suspicious! But that's really... I don't know..." She stares into the middle distance for a while then adds, "It's a bit icky, really. It's tawdry."

"Yes," Sean says. "It's not very nice, is it?"

"She was a bit sulky for a while," Maggie says, evidently trawling back through her memories. "But never a clue that she thought anything like *that*. She never said a word."

"No."

"How long?"

"How long did she think we were together?" Sean asks. "A couple of months, I think."

"Ooh," Maggie says, looking worried. "But, no... I meant, how long did she believe this? Not until... not the whole time, surely?"

"I don't know. I don't think so. I think she believed it for a while. And then when Stephane came along she started to doubt herself."

Maggie rubs her brow for a moment, then blows through pursed lips. "I'm not sure I know what to do with that information," she says.

"No," Sean agrees. "Me neither. I'm sorry. Maybe I shouldn't have told you."

"Oh, it's not that. No, it's better out in the open. Everything always is, really. And I can see *why* she could have thought that, I suppose."

"You can?"

Maggie shrugs. "We were always close. Stephane was jealous of you, actually. So is Dave, hence the rowing troubles." Maggie pulls a face like she has toothache.

"What?"

"Oh, sorry. I was just thinking about Stephane, actually. What an error of judgement *that* one was."

Sean smiles at Maggie whimsically. "You enjoyed it at the time, as far as I recall. You wouldn't shut up about him."

"Well, yes," Maggie says. "Yes, I always enjoy it *at the time*."

Sean winks at her. "Yes, you do," he says.

"But anyway, I still don't think that's right," Maggie says.

"You don't think what's right?"

"Well, it's like the April thing, isn't it?" she says, fiddling with one earring. "Catherine and I were best friends, really, weren't we? She can't *really* have thought that, or I would have known. I would have picked up on it, surely?"

"Maybe," Sean says. "At any rate, the tapes certainly aren't proving to be boring."

"No," Maggie says. "No, I can see that. But I still think you shouldn't take them to heart. I still think we're basically talking about morphine, here."

Sean nods thoughtfully. It crosses his mind that for many of these recordings, particularly the early ones, Catherine was hardly taking any drugs at all. She certainly wasn't on morphine until the end. But then he decides to leave Maggie with the option to believe what she wants to believe. "Maybe," he says. "Maybe you're right."

When Sean gets home that evening, he re-listens to all of Catherine's tapes, just to be sure. But the sad truth is that, no, she doesn't sound out of her mind. In fact, with the exception of the first tape, which was recorded last of all, she sounds perfectly compos mentis. Which would seem to imply that she really did spend much of their married life believing he had cheated on her. "What a shame she never asked," he murmurs sadly as he reaches for the next envelope in the series.

Snapshot #18

35mm format, colour. A small girl stands at the school gates, holding her mother's hand. She is sucking her thumb and her cheeks are wet with tears.

They had argued, Sean remembers. They had argued at the school gates because Sean had felt that Catherine was doing just about everything that she shouldn't be doing.

He had spent the preceding days attempting to reassure April. He had told her what fun school would be, how exciting learning things was. He had said that there would be toys and climbing frames and new friends to play with.

Catherine, for her part, had been all over the shop. And her unpredictability had peaked at the school gates when she had burst into tears and hugged April as if she was never going to see her again.

An onlooker might have thought she was putting the poor girl on a train for a concentration camp rather than dropping her at school for the day, such was her desperation. And April had picked up on all of it. She'd been terrified, a terror that she associated with school long after Catherine, herself, had got over it.

And so, just to make everything even worse, they had argued. Watched by other nervous parents and poor, tearful April, they'd had one of their rare all-out shouting matches.

Sean frowns as he tries to work out whether the dates match up with his hypothetical fling with Maggie. Because that would certainly explain a lot.

Had Catherine's tears that day – indeed had the argument itself – been about Maggie, and not about April at all?

Cassette #18

Hello, darling.

I'm feeling quite well this morning. In fact, I'd go as far as to say that I'm feeling positively chipper. But don't ask me why. I don't know. Perhaps it's just that after a week of rain, the sun has come out.

I wish this communication was a two-way thing. I wish I could ask you how *you're* doing, too. According to my calculations, it must be summer by now. God, I'll miss not being able to walk along the Cam with you. Well, I *would* miss it, if I wasn't dead.

So, April's first day at school.

I know you've had to wait too long for this, but here goes: I was wrong.

I fell apart at the seams that day. And yes, I was a terrible mother, a wicked mother who completely forgot about her daughter's needs. And yes, you were totally right to point that out.

I got lost in myself, that's the thing.

As a mother, you spend all of your time trying to make everything right for everyone else. But that day, I got lost in me.

Everything welled up: how inferior I felt, to you, to your family, to the people we knew in Cambridge, to the pretty students wafting around in summer dresses showing off their slim, child-free figures and their smooth brown legs. And yes, inferior to Maggie, too.

Up until that day I at least had April. Until that moment at the school gates, my existence had been justified. I had a baby. She needed me. She needed me twenty four hours a day. Only suddenly she was off out into the world on her own.

I felt so lost, Sean. Once she started school it felt like the only thing tethering me to planet Earth had been cut free. I was terrified I'd just float away.

You never knew it, but I used to spend the entire day in bed and then get up in time to meet her from school. You were working pretty late back then, so I usually had time to cook and clean and shop before you got home. I tried to keep everything looking normal.

I suppose, looking back on it all, I was depressed. Then again, perhaps that's just a label people use too much. Half the time, when people tell me they're depressed these days, I think, *No, you're not, you're sad!* Or confused. Or lonely. Actually, I think I must have been all of those.

Whatever it was, I wasn't right in the head, and I'm sure you must have noticed how nutty I went for a while.

It didn't last too long, thank God, because Maggie found me that job at the RSPCA shop in October. She had been laid off from Nicholson-Wallace (which, I hate to admit, I was glad about. I got to stop worrying about you and Mags on that open-plan carpet). She had split up with Stephane, too, so I

205

was extra glad you'd no longer be working together. It turned out that Stephane had a wife hidden away in Paris. How French of him!

Anyway, Maggie suddenly had loads of free time to interfere in everyone else's lives and because my own was so empty and perhaps because I wanted to keep an eye on her, I accepted her interference.

At first, I thought this was her way of making up for the fling you two had had, and if I'm honest, I got a certain amount of pleasure from watching her grovel.

I eventually managed a rather special kind of mental gymnastic whereby I managed to forgive you both, superficially, at least, for the simple reason that you'd come back to me. I felt, somehow, that I had won that particular round and that Maggie had lost it. And I even, in my finer moments, managed to feel sorry for her loss.

But I did my best never to leave you two alone together again. Because from that point on, she always seemed a little dangerous to me.

She was so present, though, and so seemingly natural towards me and April, and even towards you, that I think I must have begun to doubt myself. I think I started to wonder, first if it was really Maggie you'd had a fling with, and, later, if you'd actually had a fling at all.

I struggled, the more I thought about it, to imagine her able to be that bare-faced about it all. But who knows? Women can be surprising.

* * *

Sean takes the following Friday off work in order to help his daughter move house.

He offers to drive down, but April insists they don't need an extra car. Ronan, she tells him, has booked a van.

He leaves the house just after seven and, sandwiched between commuters in suits, manages to snooze on the train. He makes it to Hyde Park Gardens before nine and is surprised to find that April's move is almost completed. As the previous flat had been rented furnished she only has her personal effects to move. With all of her housemates present, they have made light work of the task. Sean finally gets to meet Matt, as well. He almost thanks him for the use of his room, but then wonders if April even told him. Sean can understand April's attraction to him, though. He seemingly buzzes with energy and looks like a young, prettier version of Pete Doherty.

"Don't worry," April says, pushing a wisp of hair up behind one ear. "There's still Ronan's place to do, and he's got loads of stuff and only one friend. So you're still needed, Dad."

"I don't only have *one friend! My* friends will all be at work by the time we get there," Ronan explains. "Otherwise that sounds a bit sad. Jesus! Only one friend, indeed."

Ronan drives the van to his current place, which turns out to be at the top of Finchley Road. April and Sean follow on in April's Mini. "We can talk that way," she insists.

And talk is exactly what April does. She tells Sean about the "goodbye" party they had the previous weekend and how drunk everyone got, and how bored she was because she *couldn't* drink. She tells Sean, with apparent pride, that Matt seemed a bit tearful as they were loading up the van. "But then again, he might just have a cold," she admits.

"You sound quite happy about that," Sean teases. "You're not still carrying a torch for him, are you?"

April giggles. "Oh, don't get me wrong," she says, indicating to overtake a bus. "I wouldn't touch him with a bargepole now I know him. And Ronan's worth three Matts. At least. But, well, it's nice to imagine that he's regretting missing his chance, if you know what I mean."

She tells Sean about her work life and about Ronan's job as well. She recounts an article she read in *The Guardian* and going bed-shopping with her friend Lisa and being mistaken for a couple of lesbians and how Lisa's gone vegan, which has always struck her as a bit of a lesbian thing, so, perhaps, she's going to go lesbian as well.

Eventually, Sean interrupts her flow of almost random words to ask, "April, honey. Are you feeling OK?"

"Me?" April asks, turning to look at Sean just long enough for him to worry about the traffic. "Of course I'm OK. Why? Don't I *seem* OK?"

"You just..." Sean shrugs. "You're reminding me of Maggie, that's all. She gets a bit manic sometimes. Generally when she's worried about something. So I'm just checking."

"Oh," April says. "That. It's just that I had a coffee because of the early start. I stopped when I got pregnant, because you're not supposed to, really. But I thought today I needed a little boost. So I let myself have just one. And I think it's sent me over the edge a bit. Sorry. Am I blathering?"

Sean laughs. "There's no need to apologise."

"Plus I'm excited!" April says. "I'm moving in with my boyfriend. I feel all grown up, Dad."

"You *are* all grown up."

"I know!" April says. "When did that happen?"

At Ronan's, his friend Toby is waiting, sitting on a wall in the sunshine ready to help and, apparently unexpectedly, two flatmates have stayed home to give a hand as well. Which is just as well, because the flat is on the third floor and, despite having been rented furnished, contains a not inconsiderable amount of Ronan's furniture. "Car boot stuff, mainly," Ronan explains. "Still, at least we have a couple of bits for the new place."

Once the van is loaded, they drive back down Finchley Road to the new place which is just off Primrose Hill.

"My knowledge of London's not great," Sean says, sounding puzzled. "But isn't this right next door to your old place?"

"Yeah, it's not far," April says.

"So, why didn't you do Ronan's place first?"

"Oh," April says. "That's what I said. But the van has to go back to South London. Ronan worked out the optimal route on Google or something. You'll have to talk to him about it. It's boy logic."

Eton Avenue, where the new flat is situated, is a pretty, tree-lined street of imposing red brick houses. April and Ronan's place is set in the basement and when he steps inside Sean inevitably thinks of Mitcham's Corner.

"Huh!" he says, once April has let him in.

"I know it needs a lick of paint and everything, but..."

"It'll be nice," Sean tells her. "Really."

"D'you think so?" she asks, sounding doubtful. "And through here is Ronan's office-cum-nursery."

"An office-cum-nursery?" Sean says, doubtfully. "That's an interesting combination."

"Yes," April says, running her fingers across a dusty mantelpiece. "Can't use the fireplaces, unfortunately. Never mind. I still think they look pretty." She wipes her fingertips on her dungarees.

Ronan appears in the doorway. "I'm sure you're having a lovely chat and everything," he says, "but the van's rented by the hour. So if you *could* see your way clear..."

"OK, OK," April says, pretending to be offended. "God, I didn't even know you'd managed to park."

As they carry the first boxes in from the van, Sean asks April if she remembers the flat on Mitcham's Corner before answering the question himself. "Of course you don't," he says. "You were three or four when we moved out. But it was a basement flat, like this. Smaller, but it had a similar feel about it."

April shakes her head. "I don't. But maybe that's why this place felt so familiar," she says. "It was like it was talking to me, beckoning me in. And it's called *lower ground floor* if you don't mind, Dad. No one says *basement* anymore. It probably sounds a bit too gimpy."

"Gimpy?"

"Did you not see *Pulp Fiction*?" April asks. "Bring out the gimp and all that?"

Sean shakes his head. "Not that I recall."

"Oh, never mind. It doesn't matter," she says. "Put that one in the kitchen, can you?" she adds, nodding at the box he's carrying.

As they head back outside, Sean says, "I can understand your excitement, though. I remember how it feels to have your own place. I felt dead proud, really. I feel pretty proud of you today, for what it's worth."

"Aw, thanks," April says cutely. "Was it nice? The place on Mitcham's Corner?"

"It was OK," Sean says. "Actually, it was mouldy, to be honest. And the lack of light drove your mother a bit crazy."

They head back outside and find Ronan and Toby wrestling the small, wooden-armed sofa from the van. "Can you two manage the armchair?" Ronan asks. "It's pretty light."

"Of course," Sean says, then, "And you be careful, April. Don't take any risks."

April climbs into the van and lifts one side of the armchair, then laughs. "It weighs about the same as a packet of crisps," she says.

"Yeah," Ronan shouts back. "It's just bulky. But do it together and you'll be fine."

"So the lack of light is going to drive me insane, basically," April says, once they're on the move with the chair. "That's always good to know. Did I have my own room in Mitcham's Corner?"

Sean smiles. "No. We used to put you in the bedroom and then move you to the lounge when we went to bed. Nothing ever woke you up."

"Still doesn't," April says. "I could be abducted by aliens while the house burns down and I'd still carry on snoring."

"Well, now you know why," Sean says. "But do get yourself some good, strong lightbulbs," he adds, returning to her previous comment. "And maybe one of those SAD lamps before winter strikes. Because the light thing, that's real. Believe me."

"That'll be Ronan's problem, not mine," April says. "And he doesn't care about sunlight. He could live in a cave, that boy. He even likes it when it rains. The freak."

"I'm Irish," Ronan says, as he walks past. "Of course I like rain."

"But when the baby's born," Sean says, once they have squeezed the armchair through the front door. "Then you'll be at home all day, won't you?"

"Actually, no, I probably won't," April replies. "Ronan says he wants to try baby rearing. He's home all day anyway, so he reckons he can combine working from home with looking after the baby."

"So Ronan's going to work *and* look after a newborn baby?" Sean asks, once they have placed the armchair next to the sofa.

"I know. Don't you think we're terribly modern?"

Sean laughs. "Modern wasn't the word that came to mind," he says. "I was thinking more along the lines of *optimistic.*"

Snapshot #19

35mm format, colour. A scabby, semi-furless black and white cat is sleeping on top of a pile of clothes in a laundry basket. The laundry basket is perched on top of an old front-loading washing machine.

Sean reaches behind himself and winces as he rubs the base of his back. His spine is still sore from all the box carrying.

He looks down at the photo of the cat and thinks, *Solo! I might have guessed that you'd be in there somewhere.*

Sometimes Sean had worried that Catherine loved Solo more than she loved him.

He wonders if there *were* to be an afterlife, whether cats and humans might end up in the same place. A space filled with floating, angelic cats would certainly fit Catherine's idea of heaven.

To begin with, they had argued about the cat. Sean hadn't wanted a cat, that was the thing. He didn't much like them. He thought cats were selfish and aloof. Plus, since he had been promoted, their finances had been improving to the point where they were beginning to envisage the possibility of foreign holidays. He didn't want the presence of a cat throwing a spanner in the works.

But April's friend Sophie had a cat and so, of course, April wanted one too.

Their new little house in Thoday Street had a long straggly strip of a garden and the back door even had a cat flap, left by the previous owners.

Once Catherine had joined the battle, reminding him constantly that their daughter was an only child and explaining all the different ways a cat would be good for her, he had known it was only a matter of time.

Cassette #19

Hello Sweetie.

I bet you weren't expecting this one. A photo of old Solo looking his worst. That must have been just a couple of days after I brought him home.

April wanted a cat so badly – do you remember when she tried to smuggle Sophie's cat home in her backpack? And you really *didn't* want one. But I knew I'd wear you down in the end.

I pretended to be some kind of impartial judge, pondering the *fors* and *againsts* of your cat dispute and deliberating my decision. But the truth was that I wanted a cat too, probably even more than April did.

It was either that or another baby, but the only time I ever hinted at the idea you looked at me with an expression of such utter incomprehension that I knew it was a no-go. So a cat it had to be.

I was working three mornings a week in the RSPCA shop by then, but I was still, if the truth be told, bored and not a little lonely.

I was no longer spending my days moping in bed – there was so much decorating to do in Thoday Street – but I felt a cat would provide a presence in the house. It would mean that the place wouldn't be entirely empty when I got home from the school gates. I've never liked that feeling of closing the front door behind you and listening to the creaking of an empty house. It has always put the willies up me, I really don't know why.

And so, eventually, after what seemed a reasonable period of listening to April's whinging (which I encouraged, by the way – she would often forget all about the cat and have to be reminded) I declared that my period of deliberation was over, that I'd judged in April's favour and got Iris from the shop to drive April and me out to the shelter after school.

Do you remember how excited I was about the job offer I saw while I was there? I was more excited about that job than I was about bringing poor Solo home.

I know you always thought that I should aim higher. You were always pushing me to do A levels so that I could do an OU degree, or go to evening classes and learn to paint, or even just learn to drive. But it was never what I wanted.

All I ever wanted was to carry on being happy, and just as I knew I wanted you the second I met you, I knew I wanted that job the second I saw the card on their noticeboard. It was a perfect fit that would contribute to the family budget, leave me time to spend with April and make me as happy as any job could. And I was right. I never once regretted it.

Oh, there were frosty, foggy winter mornings when I had to clean up cat-vom or cat-shit, or sometimes both, when I'd whinge and moan about my lot. But I never once struggled to go to work of a morning. And I never once, in twenty years, took a day off sick.

As for Solo, well, that was a bit like the job, really. You thought that I should have aimed higher and come home with something that looked like a Bengal Tiger.

Instead, Solo had some skin complaint, a sort of cat eczema that they suspected was probably nervous in origin. He'd been beaten and kept in a cellar before he came to the shelter, so he had reason, it seemed, to be nervous. The poor cat had hardly any fur and more scabs than the Orgreave picket line. He had been living in a concrete-floored cage, albeit with a basket, out there at the shelter for years.

But he loved April instantly. I know you never really believed this story, but it's true: he kept standing on her feet, which was quite a challenge back then as they were only tiny.

He'd been with the shelter so long that they used to leave the door to his cage open and he quite literally followed us around perching with his four paws on April's school shoes whenever we stopped to pet or even look at another cat.

As we walked around, the woman at the shelter – it was Sally, in fact – explained how the shelter worked and how the unadoptables like Solo usually had to be put down, but how everyone loved him so much that they simply hadn't been able to bring themselves to do it.

I have to admit that it crossed my mind that being that person, being the kind hearted soul who adopted un-adoptable Solo would be a sure-fire way to jump to the top of Sally's pile of potential CVs for the job, but that wasn't all it was. There was something lovely about him that I could sense despite the scabs.

Solo's fur grew back almost immediately; it was true, in the end, that all he needed was a little love. And he gave that love back to us by the bucketload.

He knew that we'd saved him and he knew what we'd saved him *from*, and he loved us for it, I'm convinced of it. Oh, I can hear you sighing at your soppy wife, but just listen to me and try to believe for once.

He followed April around the house like a dog, you'll remember. He used to sit on the table and watch her do her homework. And during the days when I was home the place was no longer empty. When I was out at work at the shelter, he would sleep, I think, non-stop. He was always in the same spot when I got home as he had been when I left. And he'd always have a sniff at my shoes as if to remind himself of the unpleasant past he'd escaped thanks to us.

When I was off and at weekends, he was never far away. Whatever I was doing, whether it was cooking or decorating, or mending, I'd look up and always find him there keeping an eye on me and purring. Did you ever hear another cat purr as much as Solo did? I'll answer that for you: no you didn't.

It took a while for him to worm his way into your affections, but about six months after we got him and about three after his fur had grown back, I came home to find you asleep on the sofa. April was snoozing between your legs and Solo was asleep with his head on your shoulder like a baby, and you were smiling in your sleep. Solo looked up at me and I swear that he winked, and I knew then that he'd won you over. I actually got a bit choked up about it, seeing the three people, or the three beings, I suppose, that I loved most in the world, all sleeping together like that. I'm actually getting a bit misty-eyed right now, just telling the story. Isn't that funny?

You'll perhaps think it strange that I've included a photo of the cat as one of my precious photos, but I loved that cat. And that's not a euphemism either. I loved him.

He was with us for just over ten years, that's almost twenty percent of my life and over fifty percent of his. He really was one of the family.

And I know that everyone says this about their cats, but he was the loveliest, cleverest, purriest, most empathetic cat that ever existed.

Do you remember how he used to like sleeping in the laundry basket on top of that awful, shuddering washing machine we used to have?

When they invented those Power Plate things that people like to wobble on in order to lose weight, I remember thinking that fatty Solo had invented it first. And had proven, over many, many years of self-inflicted clinical trials, that it didn't work at all.

• • •

The following Friday, on arriving home from work, Sean notices he has voicemail on his phone. Which is strange, because it's been in his pocket all day, and he could swear that it hasn't buzzed once.

"Back already?" Sean asks, as soon as Maggie answers.

"Hello!" Maggie says, then, "Yes! Got back yesterday."

"That was quick, wasn't it?"

"Ten days. Nine nights. Lovely, though. Sunshine every day."

"Lucky you," Sean says, wedging the phone between his shoulder and his ear so that he can hunt for a snack to eat. "The weather's been rubbish here."

"Look, I can't talk for long," Maggie says, "but did you do anything about the rowing business, yet?"

"No. I was busy helping April move last weekend. But I've promised myself I'll phone around tomorrow and see what's what. Why, have you changed your mind?"

"Perhaps," Maggie says. "There's a learning to row thing at Cantabrigian on Saturday mornings."

Sean has found a previously opened packet of crisps, but when he pops one into his mouth, he realises that they are stale and has to spit it out into the bin.

"You OK?" Maggie asks.

"Sorry, stale crisps. They make me gag. I don't know why. Anyway, I *know* how to row, Mags."

"I know *you* do. But I only went about six times and *that* was twenty-odd years ago. Maybe *I* should do the learning one and you–"

"So you *have* changed your mind?" Sean asks, interrupting her. "I thought Dave had vetoed rowing."

"Let's just say I convinced him," Maggie says. "But seriously, if you want to do a different one then go ahead. I think I'll head down there and try this newbie thing tomorrow morning, myself. Strike while the iron's hot."

"No, that's fine," Sean says. "Let's *both* pretend to be newbies. We just head down there, do we? No need to book or anything?"

"Apparently not. But it's at eight, I'm afraid."

"Par for the course," Sean says. "Let's do it."

On Saturday morning, Sean peers doubtfully through the bedroom curtains. He's comfortable in bed and is having second thoughts. But as it looks like the beginnings of a beautiful day, he steels himself and heads downstairs.

He walks, with pleasure, through the early morning streets, past not-yet-open shops and pub staff unloading delivery vans.

He crosses the green to the Cam and then walks to Riverside and then over a bridge towards their meeting place. In the quiet of the morning, with the sunlight dappling the river, he feels like he's in some foreign country, perhaps Italy, or Spain.

When he reaches the association boathouse he finds Maggie sitting on a wall looking glum. "Oh, hello," she says. "Did you not get my message? I thought you might not have, which is why I hung around."

"I left it at home," Sean says, patting his pocket. "I'm trying to keep it away from large bodies of water these days."

"I fucked up, I'm afraid," Maggie says. "I must have misread the website or something. I thought we could just bowl up but he says we have to book in advance online and then wait to be invited or something."

"Oh," Sean says.

"He was pleasant about it. But, let's say, *unyielding*."

Sean snorts. He can imagine Maggie trying to persuade the guy and is surprised, knowing her, that she gave in while he was still being polite. "Coffee?" he says, tilting his head townwards.

"Sure," Maggie says, jumping up and grabbing the bars of her pushbike.

As they cross back over Riverside Bridge, Sean points at the building site where foundations are now being laid. "That's one of ours," he says.

"Flats?" Maggie asks.

"Yeah. Small. *Very* bijou. But nice."

"I should hope so," Maggie says. "That's prime real estate."

"It's a shame about the rowing. I was feeling quite in need of some exercise." Sean pats his stomach. "All those ready meals are starting to take their toll."

"Tell me about it," Maggie says. "I thought the Italians were supposed to be the voluptuous ones, but I felt like a beached whale around that pool."

"Was it good though? D'you have a nice time?"

"Yes, it was OK," Maggie says, sounding determined to see the upside. "The weather was heavenly and Siena was beautiful. I hated Florence. We both hated Florence."

"Really?"

"Oh, I know it's pretty and cultural and everything. But we got ripped off everywhere we turned. We ate horrible overpriced food, got woken up at eight by a building site and managed to queue for a whole morning to get into a museum where we couldn't even see the wall for Chinese tourists."

"The Uffizi?"

"That's the one. I'm sure we were just unlucky. But... Anyway, Siena, as I say, was gorgeous."

Sean glances regretfully at a double scull whizzing along the river. "We could rent a rowing boat or a punt, I suppose," he says. "If they're open. What time do you have to be back?"

Maggie shrugs. "We *could*," she says. "I haven't been on a punt for years."

They continue towards the town centre, past Midsummer Common, then diagonally across Jesus Green and by the time they get to Scudamore's, the employee is just opening up shop.

"You first," Maggie says, clambering on board once the formalities have been done. "I need to get my sea legs first." And so, bare footed, trouser-legs rolled, Sean pushes off.

His ankles go into a kind of spasm making the boat shudder from side to side and inducing a fit of giggles on Maggie's part.

"I think it's always like this to start with," he says, frowning with concentration. "It'll get better. You'll see."

"Hey," Maggie says, "If you're still dry, you're doing OK in my book."

Soon enough, Sean has settled into the rhythm of it and the punt is gliding upriver. "See, I knew I'd remember," he says.

"God, this is the life," Maggie says, as the same boat they saw before whizzes past in the other direction. "Much better than being slave-driven in a rowing boat. This is *exactly* my kind of exercise."

"Don't get too smug," Sean tells her. "You're punting back."

He pauses to remove his jacket which he throws to Maggie who puts it over her shoulders. "... a bit chilly," she says. "But then it's only just past nine."

"Toasty warm up this end," Sean comments, wiping sweat from his brow with his shirtsleeve.

"Such a winger," Maggie jokes. She points towards a block of staggered apartments on the river bank ahead and says, "That's one of yours, isn't it?"

Sean follows her gaze and nods. "Probably the nicest thing I ever designed," he says. "Do you remember the sliding out kitchen business?"

"I can't say I do," Maggie admits. "Was it good?"

"About the only time anyone's ever let me do any interior design," Sean says. "It was brilliant. We should have patented it."

"You should think yourself lucky," Maggie says. "I do miss the old days at Nicholson-Wallace, you know. At Wainbridge's we never seem to do anything more exciting than bloody verandas these days."

"Yeah, I noticed that. They're not exactly picky, are they?"

"No," Maggie says. "Not picky at all. Still, a job's a job, eh?" She raises her hand and points. "That one's got a *For Sale* sign

– look! You should buy it and cook curries in your patented kitchen."

Sean laughs.

"Why are you laughing? I'm serious."

"Well, I've designed at least thirty buildings like that, but I still couldn't afford a one bed flat in there."

"I'll bet you could," Maggie says. "Your place must be worth a bomb by now. Those town centre places have rocketed."

"I'll bet you I couldn't. You're talking at least half a million for one of those." Sean stops punting and bends over, visibly out of breath. "Not as fit as I was," he says. "D'you want a go?"

"I thought I was doing the easy bit on the way home," Maggie says. "It's a boy's job punting up-river. You know it is."

"Oh, come on, Mags. I'm knackered."

"Oh, fair enough," Maggie says. "God, chivalry. It ain't what it used to be."

Snapshot #20

35 mm format, colour. A man, woman and child are posing for a photo. Behind them the glass pyramid of the Louvre Museum is lit up against the night sky.

Paris! Their first ever trip abroad as a family. It had been the first time Sean had ever thought about parallel lives, about the fact that there were a million other lives they could live if they just chose to.

He had loved Paris. He had loved the food and the architecture – he had even managed to love the snooty waiters they seemed to encounter everywhere.

Catherine had been in a state of constant ecstasy over every single thing, whether it was the Louvre itself, a funky chair in a bistro, the tiny tubes of toothpaste provided by the hotel, or the fact that the waiters still wore white shirts and waistcoats. She had spent the entire three days raving about everything she saw.

Even April, who Sean had been worried about taking along, had been on her absolute best behaviour. She had even learnt some French words, and had said "Bonjour" to almost every person whose path they had crossed. And in central Paris that was a lot of people.

The thought had come to him, he remembers, when they were sitting in the sunshine opposite the Fontaine des Innocents waiting for their very expensive, very tiny coffees to be delivered.

A man who looked a bit like Sean had stridden purposefully past. He had been smoking and left a blue trail of Gauloises smoke behind him. He had been carrying a baguette, the top of which he had snapped off and popped into his mouth as he walked past them with visible pleasure. And Sean had thought, *Why don't we live here? Why do we live in England? What's stopping us learning French and moving to Paris?* With Britain being in the EU it was easy to move just about anywhere, wasn't it? That, after all, was the whole point.

It was all just daydreaming, of course. It was a life change that was so complex that Sean couldn't even envisage how he might put it into practice. Especially with a wife and daughter to worry about. But that feeling, his Paris-envy, as he nicknamed it in his own head, had stayed with him for many months after they got home to their "pleasant little lives in Cambridge", as he suddenly had come to see them.

Cassette #20

Hello Sean.

Today, as you can see, we're in Paris. I think it's '90 but it might be '91. For once, I failed to be my usual organised self, so there's no clue pencilled on the back.

Anyway, it was one of the absolute high points for me. It's such a cliché to say that Paris is romantic, but boy is it ever. Neither of us was having affairs and neither of us was unhappy at work, and April became, for three days only, this perfectly behaved little child. On top of all that, we got sunshine, too!

We walked along a canal somewhere at some point and I remember I looked across at you and my heart fluttered and I thought *Oh good, it's still there.* I had doubted, for a moment. Forgive me.

I don't remember that many specifics of the weekend except that the whole place seemed to glow in the April sunshine and everything seemed beautiful and chic and delicious.

You started smoking again briefly (you had stopped for some time) but the smell of Gauloises was everywhere and you just couldn't help yourself, or so you said. I think you thought it would make you into a Parisian or something. April kept asking what Daddy was doing, and I kept saying "a bad thing". But she liked it. "It looks pretty," she said, "like Thomas the Tank Engine."

We had a gorgeous meal with a horrible waiter. I remember that. And I bet you do too.

You made the *unforgivable* mistake of pouring wine into your water glass and he came bustling out of the back to tell you off. "You ruin it!" he kept saying. "You English! You know nothing!" So of course we both cracked up laughing which made things even worse. But it's one of the fondest memories I have of the trip. Isn't that peculiar?

He was lovely to April, though. I remember that because it seemed like the exact opposite of home. Here in England, there's nothing more likely to get a waiter's back up than taking your seven-year-old to a posh restaurant. But Monsieur *Wrong Glass*, as we used to call him, brought her a booster seat and special kiddy sized portions and then a handful of complimentary chocolates at the end. I think he felt sorry for poor April being brought up by such terrible heathens that we didn't even know our water glasses from our wine glasses. All that fuss! It was the cheapest wine on the menu, too!

. . .

Sean plays the tape over and over and over again, but all he can hear is that one phrase: *Neither of us was having affairs.*

Does that mean what he thinks it means, or could it just have been a slip of the tongue? Is it even possible to wait until next Sunday to find out? Does he want to carry on listening at all, anymore?

Once he has convinced himself that there are no further clues, not in Catherine's tone of voice, nor in her choice of words, he pushes the dictaphone to one side and stares at the photo.

He looks at little April in her blue plastic mac. (The red one which April wanted had reminded Catherine too much of *Don't Look Now.*) She's smiling and waving in the photo. They all are.

He tries to remember who took the photo. A random passer-by, presumably.

And then eventually, without any conscious decision having been taken, he slides his phone across the tabletop and calls Maggie.

It's Dave who answers. He tells Sean that Maggie is occupied for a few minutes, which Sean takes to mean that she's on the loo.

He's just reaching for the dictaphone again when his phone starts to vibrate.

"Mags?"

"Yes. Sorry about that. What's up?" she asks, sounding flustered.

"Sorry..." Sean says, "but..."

"Yes?"

"Mags, do you think Catherine had an affair?"

"What?"

"Do you think–"

"Sorry, I did hear you. It's just... Why are we asking this?"

"I don't know. I..."

"Did she say she did? Is this another one of her tape revelations?"

Sean frowns at his phone. Maggie is sounding brusque and unsympathetic, which is not like her at all. "Not really," he says, starting to wish already that he hadn't phoned. "But she said that at one point, in Paris, *neither of us was having affairs.*"

"Oh," Maggie says. "She says she *wasn't* having one, then? And her saying that makes you think she *was* having one for some reason? Have I got that right?"

"She said she wasn't having one, *then,*" Sean says, pedantically. "Which surely implies that at another point she was, doesn't it?"

Maggie sighs deeply. "I don't see how that implies anything, Sean," she says.

Sean shakes his head in frustration. He realises that without the context, without Maggie actually listening to the tape, he's not making any sense. "You know what? Forget it," he tells her. "I'm sorry. I'm being daft. Have a good Sunday." And then he ends the call.

Maggie phones him back immediately but he doesn't answer and she doesn't leave a message.

He puts the recorder back in the box and puts the box back in the kitchen cabinet where he hopes he'll be able to forget about it, even as he knows, with certainty, that he won't.

A text message appears on the screen of his phone with a ping.

"She didn't have an affair, Sean," it reads. "I'm certain of it. And if she says or implies that she did, it'll be like the rest. Another morphine induced anomaly. Relax. And give yourself a break from those damned tapes. As I keep saying, it's really not healthy."

● ● ●

Sean sleeps badly for three nights in a row.

Twice, in the wee small hours of the morning, he gets up, descends to the ground floor, and removes the tape recorder from the box. One time, at three a.m. on Wednesday, he goes as far as inserting the next tape and pressing play. But Catherine's voice gets no further than explaining that it's likely to be a shorter message than usual because she isn't feeling well before Sean, overcome by guilt, hits the stop button.

On Thursday, at work, Jenny asks him if he's feeling OK. "You're looking a bit peaky," she says.

When Sean tells her that he's not been sleeping well, she suggests exercise. "It always fixes it for me," she explains. "Go for a really long walk after dinner. You'll see." And as it's a beautiful evening, that's exactly what Sean does.

He heads, quite automatically, down to the river, where he hesitates momentarily about which way to walk. Right will take him to Riverside, which feels a bit too much like work. Left will take him towards The Backs, and then on towards Grantchester. He thinks of "his building" and decides, for want of a better destination, to make his way there. It should be lovely in the evening light.

By the time he has zigzagged back and forth to the river bank (there is no continuous footpath along the Cam) it takes him almost an hour of quite sporty walking, to reach the building.

He scrambles though the scrubby undergrowth beyond the furthest side wall, then down the bank to the river's edge from where he can look proudly back up at the building he created. The evening sun is low in the sky and illuminates all sixteen windows quite magnificently. For once, the reality looks better than the artist's impression he once drew.

Sean remembers quite clearly the late nights he put in designing windows that would fold back entirely, effectively transforming the lounges into balconies. He studies and congratulates himself upon the perfect way the building is staggered to make the most of the evening light. He remembers, again, the funky kitchen units he designed, complete with integrated, rotating, vanishing dinner tables. He wishes he could step inside and sense the smooth sliding movement once again. They had been so beautifully crafted by a local carpenter. He wonders how well they have aged.

A man, fifties, shirtsleeves, appears at one of the third floor windows. He pulls the handle of the vast sliding window, effectively sealing the interior against the cooling night air, and Sean remembers thinking, when he designed the building, that one day he would live there, that one day he would be that guy. He remembers, too, how on seeing the prices, he had understood that he would never be able to afford it.

The man returns to the window with a tumbler of golden liquid in his hand, perhaps whisky, perhaps just apple juice. He stares down at Sean suspiciously and then turns and says something to someone behind him. A woman, young, pretty, well dressed, comes into view. She follows the man's gaze and takes in Sean's presence before simply shrugging and vanishing again.

Sean turns his back to the building and takes in the splendid view one last time. The sun is just starting to dip behind the trees on the opposite bank and a couple are cycling along the footpath, their young daughter strapped into a child seat on the back. She looks like April.

He clambers back up to the road where he takes a photo of the *For Sale* sign before turning and heading for home.

Snapshot #21

35mm format, colour. A cluster of white buildings with curved roofs clings to a barren, rocky outcrop, rising from a ripple-free sea of blue. Tourists are massed in the narrow streets and many are holding cameras. A blue and white Greek flag flutters in the breeze and the entire scene is bathed in orangey evening light.

Sean smiles at the photo. He remembers the iodine odour of the salty evening air. *Could Catherine have had an affair in Greece?* he wonders. No, of course not. They had been together twenty-four hours a day. And they had been happy, too, hadn't they?

It had been their second holiday in two years, with Maggie and Ian this time, and they had felt sun-soaked and relaxed, and blessed.

April had been dropped off in Margate with Catherine's mother. Catherine had been terrified that two weeks in Margate would turn her into a hooligan but the only noticeable change on her return had been a sudden, determined predilection for oven chips and Coke. Some things, it seemed, never changed.

Santorini had been amazing, though. The light of the place, that was the thing. The light and the stunning blue of the sea and the sky everywhere you looked. The beauty of the island had literally taken Sean's breath away on a number of occasions.

After Santorini they had gone on to Mykonos, and that had been a mistake. For whereas Santorini, in the early nineties, still felt uniquely Greek, even Middle Eastern and undeveloped in places (donkeys were still considered a means of transport back then), Mykonos had felt more like Cannes. The streets had been lined with luxury shops selling ridiculous fashions from Jean-Paul Gaultier or Dolce and Gabbana and the bars had been serving not Retsina to traditional bouzouki music, but expensive cocktails to a background of techno. And then Maggie and Ian had unexpectedly split up, and the whole thing had gone tits up.

Still, the sex had been good. That's one thing Sean will never forget. For once Maggie and Ian had gone their tearful separate ways and Sean and Catherine had the whole place to themselves, Catherine had become quite rampant. Sean had never known anything like it. Perhaps Catherine, too, had been worried that Sean would run off with someone else?

Cassette #21

Hello Darling.

I'm not sure how well I'm going to manage this, today. I've been throwing up all morning, and even though they've now given me an antiemetic, I still feel pretty dodgy. We'll see.

Today, we're off to the Greek islands.

It had been your idea to go, and I'll admit it, I wasn't keen. I don't know why that's the case, really, except to say that I had always thought that Greece was a bit third-worldy and, though in ways it was – do you remember all those poor donkeys there were everywhere? – I loved it. It blew my mind, really.

Paris had been amazing and I believed that it would be a tough act to follow. In fact, I even campaigned for a return trip to Paris instead of Greece. But Maggie wanted to go somewhere hot and Ian wanted to practise his Greek and you wanted to swim, so I caved in.

Where Paris was like a prettier, chic-er version of London, stunning but somehow familiar, Santorini was a completely different experience, a sharp, gorgeous shock to the senses, like landing on a different planet, really.

It smelt different – that was the first thing I noticed when we stepped off the ferry. It smelt hot and dusty like one imagines the desert might smell. And the sea, just everywhere, that blue... God, I fell in love instantly.

On the third day you rented a moped so that we could explore, and we whizzed off around the island. There was hardly any traffic back then, just other tourists on mopeds and the occasional truck or donkey. A girl from work went there a couple of summers ago and what she described sounds very different. It sounds like it's become like Mykonos, really, so God only knows what Mykonos is like these days.

Anyway, the moped thing was amazing, definitely the best bit. I felt so carefree and young bombing around those dusty roads with my arms around your waist. I'm pretty sure we wore shorts, didn't we? How irresponsible were we?

Maggie and Ian stayed behind because Ian insisted that mopeds were too dangerous. I thought, at the time, that they'd stayed behind in order to have the place to themselves, that they wanted to have their holiday fun-time, but knowing what we know now, I suppose that's unlikely.

At lunchtime we followed a sign that said "restaurant", and rode miles and miles down this terrifying gravelly track that I thought we'd never get back up again, and came, in the end, to a tiny restaurant on a deserted, scrappy beach. We were the only people there.

An old woman dressed in black – they were all dressed in black – came out to serve us. She had fish or feta, she said. That was it. So we ordered feta for our starter and fish for our main course, and I can still remember the exact taste of that feta. It was rich and creamy and tangy and it came drenched in olive oil from the woman's own olive trees, and with bread that she had baked herself.

And then, just as we were finishing our feta first course, a little fishing boat came buzzing up to the beach. It was her husband with the day's catch: the fish for our main course. It was the scariest, ugliest looking fish I had ever seen, but she drowned it in more olive oil and threw it on the barbecue, and it was the best fish either of us had ever tasted.

After that, we got the Flying Dolphin to Mykonos, and everything went pear shaped. If we had gone there first, I think we would have thought that it was lovely but after Santorini it felt like civilisation – it felt like the holiday was over.

Ian started vanishing almost immediately, and I kept on and on asking Maggie if they had fallen out, and she kept on and on insisting that, no, everything was fine, and Ian was just practising his Greek on the locals. Which, in a way, he was.

But even before the big secret was revealed, it put a bit of a downer on the holiday, because we all loved pretty, clever, Greek-speaking Ian and we all thought that he was finally "the one" for Mags. Mags even mentioned marriage one night in Santorini when we were all alone and drunk.

Poor Mags. She fell to her knees when he told her what was going on. We'd gone out to eat, I think, so neither of us was there to witness any of it. She told me afterwards, when we got back; which is strange, because it's as if I have the image of it in my mind's eye. It's as if I was there. It must just be because I've imagined the scene a hundred times: Ian telling her that he needed to explain something. And then telling her that he had met someone. And finally that this person he had met was called Dimitri.

"I should have known," I remember Mags saying. "The sex was awful. Everything else was wonderful, but the sex was bloody awful."

We let her stay in bed the next day and then the day after that we rented a car and dragged her across the island with us to some beautiful beach you'd read about in the *Rough Guide*.

They had sun loungers and big suspended parasols which looked like ship's sails, fluttering in the breeze. The waiters all wore matching white pareos.

Poor Mags, she walked off to the far side of the beach and sat on a rock staring out to sea all day, while you and I studied all the gay couples around us, scared and a little intrigued by the idea that we might spot Ian and Dimitri together.

Mid afternoon, Mags came back – she was burnt to a crisp – and said that she wanted to go home, which we both took to mean that she wanted to return to the holiday apartment. But no, she really meant *home*.

Ian stayed on, though not, of course, in the flat that we'd rented. We bumped into him coming out of a bar one evening. He was with a Greek guy who was even more beautiful than Ian was. He turned out, of course, to be the famous Dimitri. It's a funny thing to say, but in that moment, Ian made sense to me in a way he never really had before. I had that sort of *of course* feeling you sometimes get when Barry Manilow finally admits that he's gay, or someone tells you that Michael Jackson has died. Of course, he is. Of course he has.

You couldn't fault Ian's taste, though. Dimitri was incredibly good looking. He had olive skin and jet black hair and blue eyes that perfectly matched his open-necked denim shirt. I think he could have turned a few men's heads even if they hadn't been gay, to be honest. And he smelt incredible, a mixture of aftershave – something subtle – and a sort of salty, spicy Mediterranean animal smell. He smelt a bit like barbecue smoke and sea and sex, if that makes any sense.

Ian asked us if Mags was OK, and I had to be the one to tell him that she'd gone home.

"If hell exists, I'll go to hell for what I've done to her," he said, looking like he was about to cry.

And you replied, "Luckily for you, it doesn't, then."

I loved you for saying that, because it summed up the whole thing for me. It somehow nailed it shut.

We were there three more nights, I think, but I don't remember any of it really. The whole thing seemed spoilt by the fact that we knew Mags was back in Cambridge crying her poor eyes out. I still wonder if we shouldn't have changed our own flights and travelled back with her. I almost suggested it – in fact was about to suggest it, even – when Mags said something which upset me, causing me to keep schtum.

She told me that she had only ever been in love with Ian and, because I wanted her to realise that she'd been in love on more than one occasion and by consequence would be again, I challenged her on this until finally she admitted that it was true.

"You're right," she said. "I *was* in love one other time. But he was married, so that doesn't count."

Well, it seemed obvious to me that she was talking about you. In fact, I was terrified that she was about to admit to the whole affair thing bang in the middle of my summer holiday. It crossed my mind that she might have a vindictive streak – that she might think she'd feel better if she torpedoed our holiday by chucking everything out there in the open, so that we could all be miserable together. I thought, too, about the fact that she was now single again and, as such, was now dangerous again, as well.

So I selfishly decided to keep you safe from her for a couple more days while I did my best to prove to you how much better you were off with me. Plus, to be totally honest, which is supposed to be the whole point here, thinking about Ian and Dimitri together had made me feel strangely horny. They were both so very, very pretty...

When we got back, I went down on the train to pick up April from Mum's.

She was so happy there, Sean – it was as much as I could do to drag her home. It had been a hot fortnight and Mum said that they, too, had spent every day on the beach. When I asked April what she'd been eating, she said, "Chips and Coke and chocolate ice cream," which I knew, instantly, was the entire truth.

When I got back to Cambridge, I found you and Mags together, staring at the TV screen. Something strange was going on and you both looked concerned, and I worried, for a moment, that you were going to make some devastating announcement to me.

When I looked at the TV screen, it was covered with red percentage numbers that I didn't understand. "We've crashed out of the ERM," you said. I had no idea what that meant but you looked pretty worried. It was the day after Black Wednesday.

• • •

Sean rolls onto his side and sunlight warms his face. He writhes and stretches and luxuriates in the sensation of the crisp, white sheets against his skin. The odour of fresh coffee reaches his nostrils, mixed with something different, something spicy and tangy.

He rolls onto his back, stretches again, his arms above his head, and then opens his eyes. The sunlight flickers and strobes as the leaves of the tree outside bristle in the breeze.

He throws back the covers, and stands. He yawns and then begins to walk towards the lounge, conscious as he leaves the bedroom of his nakedness yet aware by the time he reaches the lounge of the soft plush dressing-gown he's wearing.

A woman is in the kitchen area, a woman he loves. She's in the process of squeezing oranges, and this, he realises, is the origin of the second, tangy odour he detected from the bedroom. The woman is wearing one of his white work shirts and the sunlight is revealing the shadow of her enveloped body through the material.

"Coffee and juice?" she asks, and as she turns to face him, he realises that this is not Catherine. She is somehow of the same essence as Catherine, but she is not Catherine.

He turns to look at the picture window at the far end of the room and sees that the woman is now seated outside, waiting for him, so he crosses the room and pushes at the window which glides effortlessly before vanishing into the wall. He steps onto the balcony and then grips the cold railings and looks down at the scene below.

Beneath him is the Cam, complete with rowers and punts and wind-surfers, and beyond that, a daffodil spotted river bank, and beyond that, a vast sea of blue, dotted with tiny islands in a pink sunrise.

"The sea!" Sean gasps.

"Yes, they moved it," the woman replies. "Isn't that the funniest thing ever?"

"They moved it," Sean repeats, and he begins to laugh, and once he has started, he can't stop. He laughs and laughs and laughs. And when he opens his eyes to find himself in his usual, darkened bedroom, he realises that he is *still* laughing. He wipes the tears from his eyes and glances over at the alarm clock. It's six-forty-eight.

It is now ten o'clock on Saturday morning and Sean is out of bed, out of coffee and out of orange juice. So he makes Marmite on toast and a mug of tea instead and looks out at the rain-soaked garden and thinks about the dream.

It's the first happy, sexy dream he has had since Catherine fell ill, two years ago, and he wishes, in a way, that he could close his eyes and go back to that sunny apartment.

He tries to remember the woman's face, but it's a blur, like one of those frosted-window faces you see in crime documentaries.

But the flat, he remembers and recognises. It was one of the Cantabrigian Rise units, albeit stretched to dream proportions and re-situated on the Aegean. That sensation, of simply being happy, remains so sharp, so well remembered, and so lost to him now he's awake, that it makes him want to cry. He reaches for his phone and flicks through the recent photo list until he comes to the picture of the *For Sale* sign. And then he fetches the landline handset and dials the number.

By the time he hangs up, he knows the price of the apartment. Six hundred and thirty thousand for a one bedroom flat! And by the time he folds his laptop away and heads to the bathroom for his shower, he knows the estimated price of three bedroom houses in his street: Five hundred and fifty thousand. Which leaves a gap of eighty, at least.

Snapshot #22

120 format, colour. A teenage girl poses reluctantly for a school photo against a painted backdrop depicting clouds. She is rolling her eyes and wearing school uniform. Her school tie is knotted in such a way that it hangs halfway down her chest and has a total length of about three inches.

April's moods had come and gone. For certain periods, sometimes for an entire year or so, she would become angelic. And then something inexplicable would change somewhere in the cosmos and she could shift from angel to devil in about half an hour, a state which, once again, could last for an hour or a year.

As a general rule, both Sean and Catherine shared the brunt of whatever was going on in April's psyche, but sometimes one parent would be favoured, while the other was detested; you could never really tell which way the lines would fall, nor why. One such period had begun on April's twelfth birthday, and had lasted, almost precisely, until her thirteenth. For one year, exact to the day, April had become so utterly refractory to anything that Sean might suggest, or think, or do, that he had truly struggled to like his own daughter. It had been a learning experience for him, though, because he had discovered that loving and liking were very different things. For yes, it was entirely possible to continue to *love* his daughter even as he actively disliked everything about their relationship.

Catherine, Sean deduced, had attributed at least part of the blame for this breakdown to him, which he had thought, and still thinks, was unfair.

Catherine, he knew, believed that he had been thrown into a crisis about April's lineage by a throwaway comment from a work colleague they had bumped into in the street. His wife believed that he was troubled that April might not be his when, in fact, the problem had been far more complex and, in a way, quite the opposite.

For that one, fractious year, it seemed as if April had distilled every single thing that Sean disliked about himself, every single character trait he had worked so hard to suppress: his sarcasm, his cynicism, his intolerance for stupidity... Yes, it seemed for a while as if his eye-rolling, huffing, puffing daughter had become some kind of dark mirror. "You can pretend all you like, Dad," she seemed to be saying, "but I can see exactly who you are, because that's exactly who I am."

It was at this time that Sean had finally allowed Catherine's doubts about his paternity to surface into consciousness. Her constant comments as to all the ways that he and April were similar had made such doubts impossible to ignore. But her comments had only made the situation worse, really, because Sean hadn't wanted, right then, to accept the fact that April's cynical sneering came from *his* DNA, any more than he wanted to be constantly reminded that they might not be anything to do with him at all. The whole subject was something of a lose-lose situation no matter how he tried to look at it.

Cassette #22

Hello beautiful.

It's Saturday morning, and you and April have just left. You were both so beautiful today, and I tried to tell you that, but you both just rolled your eyes and looked embarrassed. Neither of you ever could take a compliment. But you were sitting holding my hand and at one point the sun came out and it looked as if you had a halo. So, know that I wasn't joking. You both really *did* look quite stunning.

It hardly seems fair on a day when I love you so much to drag you back to 1995, your horrible year with April, but I'm afraid that's the next photo I picked out and if I don't do them in order I'm worried I'll end up in a right old mess.

So here goes: things got so bad between you two that I used to daydream that I'd have to leave you, just to keep you and April from each other's throats. Sometimes I used to come home and worry that one of you might have stabbed the other.

It didn't last, thank God, and by the time she hit thirteen you'd both got over yourselves (and each other) and everything was peaceful and lovely again. But for a while, back then, it felt a bit like a war zone. It really did.

I knew what it was about, of course. It was all to do with you worrying about who April's father was, and that all started because that stupid secretary from your workplace bumped into us and commented that April didn't look anything like you. It was just a couple of days before her 12th birthday and,

245

from that point on, you just never stopped sniping at each other.

I did my best to placate everyone, but I don't think I was very good at playing go-between. Because, while I could understand April behaving like a twelve-year-old schoolgirl, I really did think that you should know better and I really did just want to shout at you to grow up.

I tried to talk to you about it all – I must have asked you what was wrong a hundred times. I wanted you to name it, you see, so that we could get it out in the open, so that we could finally discuss the whole thing. But until you did, I dared not mention it myself, because I was never quite one hundred percent sure that you knew. And as far as bringing things out into the open was concerned, you were never any help at all. All you ever did was insist that nothing was wrong, that everything was fine. You always reverted to being such a blokey bloke whenever the subject was our daughter.

About four years ago, a woman at work mentioned a friend of hers who'd had a paternity test done, and I realised that putting the whole subject to bed had become not only possible, but relatively inexpensive. So I paid a few hundred pounds and got one done. You may remember being quite surprised when I suddenly attacked your feet with the toenail clippers one morning...

I cried when the results came back. Because April is yours, after all. And as soon as I saw those results, I knew that it had been obvious all along, even though I had wasted years and years worrying about it.

Had it not been the case, had Phil been the father, I'm pretty sure I would have never mentioned the subject again. But it's done, honey, and it's all OK. Nature or nurture, everything that April ever becomes is directly down to us! In fact, if you ever find that second box of photos, you'll probably find the test results stuffed down the bottom.

Now, I know that you've probably thought about it a thousand times and I know that you've decided, or convinced yourself, that it doesn't matter one way or the other. You love each other so much, why should it matter, right?

But I want to thank you from the bottom of my heart, all the same, for being so God-damned classy about the whole thing, for never mentioning it once. For there were plenty of times when I was being unreasonable and when you needed ammunition to get your own back; there were lots of times when you could so easily have thrown that back in my face. So thank you, honey, for *not* doing that.

God! I just realised that with you listening to these over such a long period, you'll have to worry about this whole DNA thing for weeks on end. So, now I'm going to have to go back through the tapes and find the "Phil" one and erase it or record an addendum or something. Note to self: do not forget!

• • •

Emily, the estate agent – young, professional, pretty, albeit with somewhat severe features – talks constantly as they make their way from the car park to the third floor.

She tells Sean random facts about Cantabrigian Rise, most of which he knows already and some of which he knows to be patently untrue.

He had fully intended to come clean about his relationship to the building, but quickly realises that it's much more fun to say nothing, effectively giving her enough rope to hang herself.

"The roof is completely covered in photovoltaic panels," she is saying as they reach the top floor, "which means that the electricity bills are almost zero for these units."

"Photovoltaic, huh?" Sean says, doing his best to suppress a wry smile. "Not just a solar hot water system then?"

He sees Emily's confidence splutter momentarily; he sees the shadow sweep across her features. "Um?" she says, then, "No, no, the proper, um, photovoltaic ones. Which heat the water too, so that's one less thing to worry about, obviously."

"Obviously," Sean repeats.

They have reached the bright orange door of unit 3F. "Here we are," she says, sliding the key in the lock and pushing the door open.

Sean starts to frown even as he steps over the doormat. Because the floor-plan, he can see, has been modified. The apartment-width wall which originally divided the living space into living room at the front and bedrooms at the back has been removed and replaced by a long wall running from the front window to the rear wall.

"Now, this unit is quite unique, as it happens," Emily continues, "because the rooms run front to back so that they get both morning and evening light."

"At the cost of making them very long and thin and removing the utility of the retracting front picture window," Sean points out, savagely.

"Yes, well, you can still open the one on the lounge side," Emily explains.

"Well, thank God for that," Sean comments, extrapolating, as he penetrates further into the apartment, that the original kitchen must also have been removed. He wonders, briefly, if his heart is strong enough to acknowledge such destruction, then braces himself and steps through the dividing wall. He

248

breathes in sharply as he takes in the utterly standard oak-fronted kitchen units in the narrow galley-kitchen they have created on the other side.

"These are all brand new," Emily says, running her finger across the worktop, "so that's lovely for you."

"Yes," Sean says, flatly. "Lovely." He's already attempting to tot up in his mind how much it would cost to put the walls back where they belong and restore the original kitchen units. He's not sure the workshop, out in Fen Ditton, even exists anymore. "So, on price," he says, "how much room for manoeuvre is there?"

Emily looks at, or more specifically, pretends to look at, a sheet of paper in her ring binder. "I'm afraid the answer to that one is *none at all*," she replies. "It's only been listed for three weeks and we've already had more than ten offers, all of which have been refused. It's a seller's market, I'm afraid. People sometimes offer *more* than the asking price to secure unique properties such as this one. I'm not sure how well you know Cambridge, but these river front properties are few and far between."

"Right," Sean says, "then I'm sorry to have wasted your time." It has suddenly become urgent for him to leave this building. Because more and more modifications that have been done are popping into his consciousness the more time he spends here, and not one of them is, to his eyes, an improvement. "My budget is more in the five-fifty bracket," he adds, starting to move towards the front door.

"Ah," Emily says. "Then unless one of the one bed units comes onto the market – which is frankly a once a decade kind of event..."

"There are two bedrooms here?" Sean asks, just for fun.

"Oh, no... No, they've been knocked into one. As you can see. But this *was* a two bedroom, originally. Which it's why it's ninety square meters. The one bed units are nearly all seventy square meters."

"Sixty six," Sean says.

Emily glances at him and half frowns, half smiles as she says, "Yes. That's right. Sixty-six."

When Sean gets home, he makes a mug of coffee before heading out to the back garden. He sits in the tatty old deck chair and looks back at the house.

It's probably for the best, he thinks with a sigh. He's not, if he's being honest with himself, ready to move at all. It would feel like a kind of infidelity towards Catherine, a sort of treason towards April who still, after all, has her bedroom upstairs.

Pages, the universe seems to be whispering, cannot be turned this quickly. If only they could.

He glances up at the top rear window and pictures little April peering out. A memory surfaces of one sultry summer afternoon when he had fallen asleep on a sun-lounger only to be woken by the unexpected sensation of raindrops. April and Catherine, hysterical with laughter, had been squirting a water pistol at him from April's upstairs bedroom.

Now April is going to be a mother in her own right and Catherine has ceased, quite simply, to exist. And yet this still does not feel like a collection of bricks and mortar to be quoted and traded. It still feels like home. And not just his home. *Their* home.

Sean covers his mouth with one hand and exhales sharply. He has a lump in his throat and his vision is blurring. "God, this is hard," he mutters, as an unexpected convulsion of grief rises from deep within his chest and sweeps, like a wave, through his body. He swipes at the corners of his eyes. "Jesus," he says.

Cantabrigian Rise continues to play upon his mind and he finds himself sketching the modified floor plan and the original. He finds himself mentally listing costs and delays and the names of potential contractors who might owe him a favour. He dreams of restoring 3F to its former glory. But he knows that it's nothing more than a daydream. The place is too expensive even before factoring in all of the renovations.

Yet, despite all of his rationalisations, the idea is still floating around on Sunday afternoon as he pulls the shoe box from the kitchen cabinet.

"What do you think?" he asks the box, as if it might somehow reply. He lifts the lid. He waits. He listens. The air inside imparts no wisdom.

But then, just as he reaches for the next envelope, he thinks, *"Wait. When the time is right, you'll know it. When the time is right you won't have to force anything. So wait."*

It's something Catherine could have said. In fact these are the exact words that Catherine would have said. And in some strange way, it suddenly doesn't seem to matter whether Catherine still exists, in heaven, or in the ether, or merely as a well known, much loved construct inside Sean's own mind.

It's not something that he could easily explain, more of a feeling, really, but in that instant, they amount to the same thing. In that instant whether Catherine exists or doesn't exist outside of Sean is immaterial, because it seems to him that all we ever see of each other is the representation we hold inside our own minds. And Catherine *does* still exist inside Sean's mind. He still knows her favourite flavour of ice cream and he

251

still knows that she doesn't like his carrot soup, and he can still hear her saying, as if she was here beside him looking at the box, thinking about his dilemma, *"Wait. When the time is right, you'll know it, Sean. So wait."*

Snapshot #23

35mm format, colour. Two women of different generations and a child are standing at the end of a jetty. Behind them, the sky is wispy blue, but their wild hair conveys the fact that a savage wind had been blowing that day.

Sean swallows hard. Because only now that he is looking at this photo does he realise that he has been dreading it.

He raises it close to his eyes and studies Catherine's face, and wonders if he imagined it, if time has, perhaps, played tricks on his mind. But no, there it is, that vacant expression, that tongue just visible in the corner of the mouth, that pale transparency, an impression that she was there and yet not there, like a hologram, perhaps.

They had gone down to Margate to visit Catherine's mother who had recently become single again. But Catherine had been absent, distracted and generally peculiar all weekend, like a bad, amnesic actor unconvincingly playing the role of wife, mother and daughter. Even Wendy had spotted that something was wrong with her. "What's wrong with that one?" she had asked Sean, nodding towards the lounge.

"Nothing," Sean had said. "Nothing at all."

But even as he pretended to Wendy, as he pretended to himself, he had known that something was wrong and that it was no little, insignificant thing, either.

He had avoided any kind of reflection on the subject for the entire weekend; he had resolved to simply hold the question until his wife returned to him long enough to answer it. But when they'd got the photos back a few weeks later, he had bravely asked the question. "What were you thinking about when I took that photo?"

"Um?" Catherine had said.

"What were you thinking about all weekend in Margate? For that matter, what are you thinking about now? Because whatever you are thinking about it's not *here* and it's not *now*, is it?"

"I don't know what you mean," Catherine had replied. "Everything's absolutely fine." And because "absolutely fine" had never once before figured in Catherine's vocabulary, he had known, definitively, that she was lying.

He had pretended to believe her, though – not for any altruistic reason, but because it had been easier for him.

He had just been made a partner at Nicholson-Wallace and was having to work all hours. He didn't have, he feared, the time nor the energy to deal with whatever was going on in Catherine's head, so he chose, selfishly, to leave it be.

He had surprised himself by his ability to pretend. There had been a feeling, deep inside, like a stitch when you run, like a sorrow, like a shadow, like a loss. Of course there had been. But he had managed, by concentrating on the demands of work, to keep it for the most part out of consciousness.

Cassette #23

Hello Sean.

I've really not been looking forward to this, but in the interests of full disclosure, here goes. I'm so sorry, baby.

I'm not sure if I've mentioned this before and I'm not sure if you'll remember it now, for it was such a long time ago. But you once said, "One day, we'll be dead, and we still won't have known each other. Not properly. Because no one ever does."

What followed was this long and complicated discussion about how well it was truly possible to know another person. We all had, you said, secret gardens, sexual fantasies and shameful things we have said and done, things we would never admit to another living soul.

I deftly turned the conversation to you by pretending to be shocked and asking you what *your* secret fantasies were. Which put an instant end to that conversation. You didn't, evidently, have any. But the reason you'd asked me that question was that weekend in Margate, when you'd accused me of being distant, and had quite rightly sensed that something was wrong. You were totally right, actually. I was there with you in body, but my mind was somewhere else entirely.

Everything had been great between us, so don't ever think that what happened reflects on you in any way. Everything was hunky-dory: you'd been promoted, April was being lovely, Solo's fur had grown back and our home was a happy home. I wasn't looking for anything at all; in fact, had you asked me, I would have said that I didn't even have room in my life for anything else. But then I met someone. I met Jake and for a while he knocked me off my feet.

He came into the shelter one day to get a kitten for his daughter. He was divorced but his daughter came for weekends and school holidays, he explained, and he wanted a cat so that she'd feel like his place was still home. It was early June and we were overrun with abandoned kittens but, though there were plenty to choose from, most were still too young and were waiting to be weaned or waiting for their shots, or to be sterilised, before we'd let them go.

Anyway, Jake walked through the door one evening, just as I was about to close up, and I thought, simply, *wow!*

Now this is where the whole thing is going to get tooth-numbingly embarrassing and where it's probably all going to sound horrifically shallow, too. But this is all supposed to be about honesty, and part of that honesty is for me, as well. It's about admitting to myself that we humans are still animals at heart, no matter how much we try to pretend otherwise, no matter how sophisticated we'd like to think we are.

So here it is: the first thing that struck me about Jake was his clothes. I've always had a *thing* for guys in suits, and I know that you know that and I know that you've always done your best to ignore the fact for the simple reason that you pretend to hate wearing one. You and I both know that the truth is that for some inexplicable reason, dressing up in anything out of the ordinary embarrasses you. But that's been a shame, really, because my so called *thing* for men in suits is actually quite a powerful thing. You see? I told you that this would make your teeth hurt. It's certainly making mine hurt to say these things we never say.

Jake was a lawyer. In fact he almost certainly still is. And not a humdrum lawyer either, but a fairly high-flying, corporate lawyer. So he walked into our lowly, shabby cat shelter wearing a sheer, perfectly tailored, five-hundred pound suit and a silky, perfectly knotted polka dot tie, and a crisp white shirt with cufflinks and braces. And it's entirely silly, but it all made me go a bit weak at the knees.

He had electric blue eyes and what people like to call a strong chin and good skin and a nice arse and big smooth hands coming out of those thick white cuffs and when he smiled, which was often, he revealed a set of nice white teeth.

He smiled and reached out to shake my hand and said, "*Hello.*"

When I tried to reply, I just croaked. It took me three attempts before I could even speak.

I hope you don't think that I'm trying to rub your nose in all of this, because that really isn't my intention. I'm just trying to explain what happened in a way that, perhaps with time, you'll be able to understand. It wasn't a choice, you see. At any rate, it never felt like a choice. It felt like ... I don't know. A compulsion, maybe?

Anyway, Jake strode in, shook my hand, smiled and said, "Hello." He touched his tie in a sort of straightening gesture, which somehow made him look nervous to please, which was cute. And something strange happened to me. I felt drawn to him. I felt hot and a bit faint and my throat constricted.

He came back three times before he made his final choice, always after work and always in his work clothes. He was always very nice and always hung around a little longer than required asking questions about the shelter, and every time he left I spent half an hour thinking about him and then another hour convincing myself that I was being stupid, foolish;

257

reminding myself that I was married, and happily married at that.

The third time he came, he touched my arm very gently and asked if he could buy me a drink. And it took truly every bit of energy and determination I could muster to say, "No."

But I kept bumping into him, that was the thing. I bumped into him in Sainsbury's and I bumped into him at the petrol station. I bumped into him walking back from school, and I came upon him when I was walking across Midsummer Common one morning. That was the first time I had ever seen him dressed casually, in a polo shirt and chinos. And I realised that the reason his suit hung so well was because he was incredibly fit beneath it. He later told me that he had been a competition swimmer in his youth and the least that I can say is that it still showed. Anyway, we were both heading the same way – towards the town centre – so we had to walk side by side for a bit, which felt awkward.

We made polite chit-chat. I asked him how the kitten was doing; he asked after Miaow, the kitten's mother and I told him the truth, that the mothers were often un-adoptable and that many of them spent the rest of their days in the shelter.

Jake was shocked about that and he asked me whether she would still get on with her kitten if he adopted her as well, to which I replied that, yes, she almost certainly would. And he said he couldn't bear the idea of Miaow spending her life kitten-less at the shelter. That glimpse of kindness softened the heart I'd been trying so hard to harden. It provided Jake with an opening; it gave him a way in, if you see what I mean.

It also meant, of course, that he had to come back to the shelter again and that I *knew* he was coming back in advance. And though I promise you I tried incredibly hard not to do so, I started to fantasise about him. I used to try to balance these

258

fantasies out by overwriting them with another one about you, but the new is always so much brighter than the familiar... It never worked that well.

I was scared, in advance, about what I might do, and a couple of times it was on the tip of my tongue to tell you about him. I thought that perhaps the shame might cool things down; I thought your anger might save me. But I never did manage to tell you because I could never quite put the words together to express something so complex and sordid and exciting and stupid. I still wonder how that conversation might have gone.

He turned up the following Thursday night just as I was locking up. He had come straight from work, but his train had been late, so by the time he had driven from the station it was almost seven. He was wearing a silky, sharkskin three piece suit. He looked stunning.

I gave him some tips about reintroducing the two cats and then – and I'm sure you've seen this coming, because I had, too – he said that it all sounded terribly complicated and asked me if I had time to come back with him.

And I heard my mouth say, "Sure. Why not?"

That will sound like me shirking my responsibility for the whole thing, and perhaps that's what it is. But I really *was* thinking, *No, no, no!* even as I heard my mouth say, "Sure, why not?"

We filled out the paperwork for Miaow and he paid the fee and added on a generous donation, and all the time I was thinking, *You have to say, 'no.' You have to remind him you're married and say 'no'. It's that easy.* But I didn't seem to be able to speak.

He asked me which was my car, and I explained that I took the bus on Thursdays. He offered to drive me home afterwards, and I remember thinking, *After what?*

We caged up the cat and went outside to the car park.

He took his jacket off and threw it on the back seat – he had this lovely old racing green MG – and as he drove I kept glancing across at his white shirt and his waistcoat and his tie which jutted out from his collar, and it was as if my mind had split in two. One half was saying, *What are you doing, girl? Stop!* And the other half was lost in the fantasy of kissing him, thinking about what it would feel like to put my arms around his stiff, starched collar. And I thought that one day, I'd be dead, and it would be a shame to miss the opportunity, because, somehow, surely everyone deserved the chance, once in their lives, to live out their fantasies. I told myself that we'd married so young and that if we'd met later on then perhaps I would have got the pretty, arrogant Jakes of this world out of my system. I told myself that you'd had your fling with Maggie, so it was my turn now. I told myself so many things in an attempt to make it all OK, Sean, but the sad truth is that his aura, his confidence – the confidence that meant he at least *wasn't* embarrassed to dress like that – these things were like a magnet to me, and I didn't seem to have the power to resist. Sitting beside him, my heart was racing and every part of my body seemed to be waiting for his touch. But even then, I was promising myself that nothing was going to happen. I don't know who I thought I was kidding.

When we got to his flat it was a huge, modern place out in Trumpington and I wondered if you'd perhaps helped to design it. We put Miaow in one room and Mitsi (his daughter had named the kitten Mitsi) in another, and fixed the door so that there was an inch through which they could peep at each other. But Mitsi went crazy, in a good way. She hadn't forgotten who her mother was yet and so, within a minute, we opened the door and they were all over each other in a big love-in. It was so cute watching their reunion, it made me well up.

Jake offered me a drink, and I said, "No," and then changed my mind and said, "Yes," so he mixed me a gin and tonic.

"There's something I've been meaning to ask you," he said, gently stroking his chin. "And I'd never forgive myself if I didn't."

I asked him what that was.

"I've been meaning to ask you if you'd mind terribly if I kissed you," he said.

"Best not," I croaked. "You know... married and all that."

"Oh, of course," Jake said. He seemed quite cool about it.

I stayed and sipped at my drink, and all the while I was imagining my body pressed against the formal crispness of his clothes, imagining the feel of them against me, imagining how it would feel to kiss his lips. And it was as much as I could do to stop myself launching myself at him right there, right then. Does that make any sense to you? I bet it does. I bet you've felt that too, at least once in your life.

But it was all getting to be too much for me. I put my gin and tonic down, stood and walked to the door. "I'd like you to take me home, please," I said. And Jake, bless him, did exactly that.

The weekend after that, I tried to get *you* to buy a suit. Do you remember? We were in the town centre and I attempted to drag you into Moss Bros.

I was thinking, praying, that perhaps, just perhaps, dressing *you* like Jake could save me from this madness, because even as it was happening, I knew it *was* a kind of insanity. But you just

261

laughed at me and said something like, "What the fuck would I do with a suit? When would I even wear it?"

And because you're right, because there are always things that we never can say to our partners, I did not reply, "Well, you could wear it in the bedroom, for starters," and I didn't say, either, "Because otherwise, I'm going to have an affair with a stunningly well dressed lawyer called Jake."

The following Thursday when I got out of work, Jake was there again, waiting in his MG in the car park. "I wondered if I could drive you home," he said. "You said you take the bus on Thursdays, so I just thought…"

I agreed. We needed, I had decided, to talk. I needed to tell him that there was no hope for us, once and for all.

He drove to that big roundabout at the end of the road, then said, "Do you have to be back quickly?"

I told him that I didn't, and it was true. April was staying at Stacy's and you'd texted to say you were working till at least ten.

"Perhaps we could go for a walk out in Brampton Wood?" he said. "It's a lovely evening."

And because I had decided to tell him that nothing between us was ever going to happen, and because I was going to tell him to stop stalking me, and because I was in no real hurry to do either of those things, I said, "Yes."

When we got to Brampton Wood, he pulled on the handbrake and then gently touched my knee. I didn't move. I bit my lip. I stared straight ahead.

"Please," Jake said. "Just a kiss."

And I caved in. I know, I know, I should have been stronger. But I wasn't, and I lost track of myself. I launched myself at him. I ran my fingers over the cotton of his collar, over his silky tie, and then I wrapped my arms around his neck and kissed him. And just for a moment, I wasn't myself. For one fantasy instant I was a completely different person, a woman in a film, perhaps, kissing a very elegant, confident man on the leather seats of his perfectly restored MG. I'm pretty sure a shrink would say that it all came back to my lack of self-confidence. The bit of rough from Margate was still haunting me, I think.

We kissed for a bit and then I pulled away. I said something like, "I thought you wanted to *walk* in the woods, not frolic in them."

Jake laughed and said, "All right then." He was always the gentleman. He was never pushy. It was always as much my fault as it ever was his.

He pulled on his jacket and we walked into the woods together. The bluebells were in flower and it was like a sea of blue and I wished I'd had my camera with me. But then I realised I'd never be able to convincingly explain why I was out in Brampton Wood in the first place.

As both of our "real" lives were off-limits, for obvious reasons, it seemed hard to find things to talk about. Jake spoke about the cats, I seem to remember, and I eventually mentioned what a snappy dresser he was. He told me that one of the partners in the law firm had walked him to his tailor on the day he had started twenty years ago and he had never changed tailors since. "It's just a uniform, really," he said. "As a lawyer, you can't even vary it very much. I allow myself some quirky cufflinks and a flashy tie or two, but there's not much else you can do, really. It's a bit boring, if you ask me."

I told him that I didn't find it boring at all. I said that jeans and t-shirts were boring.

"Yes," he said. "Yes, I've heard that before. Women do seem to like a man in a suit. Considering how much effort guys seem to put into attracting the fairer sex, it's a wonder more of them don't wear them."

When we got back to the car, we sat, side by side, in silence.

"We need to stop this," I said, eventually. "I'm married."

"I know," he said sadly. "I'm sorry. I'll stop if you want me to."

"I think that would be best," I said, "for everyone concerned."

He nodded, stroked my fingers briefly with his big smooth hand – the contact felt electric – and then started the engine.

We drove in silence all the way back until we reached the first roundabout on the ring road, when he said, sounding miserable, "So, left, or right?"

"Oh," I said.

"Right," Jake said. "Please say, *right*. Just for five minutes?"

I nodded silently. I don't know why I did that. I really don't. I seemed to be on some kind of autopilot.

When we got to his place, he closed the front door and we kissed against it, and there really was something powerful and animalistic, something fetishistic, almost certainly, about being forcefully kissed by him dressed like that. Between the smooth wool of his suit, the satin back of the waistcoat and the crisp white collar, between the softness of his skin and the stubble of his five o'clock shadow, there seemed to be so many textures to run my fingers over. I've always had a thing for textures, and I couldn't get enough of the feel of him. I couldn't, somehow, get close enough to him.

We kissed frantically for a few moments and then I let Jake pull my top over my head and lead me by the hand into the lounge.

A big candle was burning in a glass lantern and there was a bottle of champagne sitting in an ice bucket. The ice had almost melted.

It had all been planned from the start, I realised, and I suddenly had second thoughts. I suddenly wanted to stop the whole thing and run away. But Jake was pouring champagne and walking towards me and I felt bad for him and bad for you, and confused and guilty. It seemed like an insolvable riddle.

He kissed me and pulled me towards him, and it felt heavenly again, and the sensible, doubtful, faithful parts of me were all momentarily drowned out by a rush of hormones or endorphins or something.

We did the wicked deed just once, there on the couch, and the truth is that even as it was happening, I had already changed my mind. But I liked Jake. He really was a very likeable guy, and I suppose I didn't want to hurt his feelings either. And there was something about his willpower to move forward that overwhelmed my own desire to stop. When he pulled a condom as if from nowhere, I realised again what I already knew, that this had all been planned and that Jake was way too cocky – way too sure of himself. What had attracted me to him was already pushing me away.

Nothing about it was violent or unpleasant, Jake was nothing but respectful and, though I thought about it a hundred times, I didn't say, "No," and I didn't say, "Stop." And yet, by the time it was over, everything felt wrong. It was as if I had come back to myself, as if I had woken up and couldn't work out, suddenly, what I was even doing there. I had broken out in a cold sweat.

Jake was looking smitten. He re-zipped himself up (sensitive to my fantasies, he had remained fully clothed, throughout) and refilled his glass with champagne and said, "Sorry, I'm not usually that quick. It's just that I've been thinking about you for–"

"*Don't,*" I interrupted.

"I'm sorry?"

"Just don't," I said. "I can't do this."

Jake put his glass back down. "What's wrong, darling?" he asked.

"I can't do this, that's all. That was a mistake. And don't call me darling."

I was already pulling on my top. "I'm sorry, but I need to go, now."

"Don't be silly," Jake said. He crossed the room, and tried to grab my arm, but I pushed him away.

"I'm married, Jake," I said. "You're very lovely and you're incredibly good looking. You're like this perfect photo-fit fantasy man. You really are. But I can't do this. I'm sorry." And then I grabbed my own jacket and walked out the front door. I was shaking so much I could barely walk.

Jake came running after me eventually. He caught up with me in the street. "Catherine!" he said. "For fuck's sake, at least let me drive you home!"

I just waved over my shoulder and continued to walk and, after a while, I flagged down a taxi.

If I'm being completely honest, I'd have to admit that I continued to fantasise about Jake for a while, but thinking about him always made me feel sick, too. It was a very complicated set of feelings. I sometimes thought about getting a taxi over there again. I once looked up his phone number on the computer at work, but I never used it.

When Mum died, the shock killed off, for a while, any remaining desire I had for anyone at all. And it threw you and me back together, too.

But I'm too tired to go into all that today, sweetheart, so that'll have to wait until next time. I am sorry, though, that I broke my marriage vows. I love you so much. It lasted less than ten minutes out of thirty years of marriage, but I broke them all the same. It was short and stupid, and by the time it was happening I understood that I didn't want it anymore, but I know that won't help. But what can I say? Humans are human, desire is desire, and life's life, isn't it. And you know what? Now I know that I was right, now that I know that I really *was* going to die one day, and sooner than I thought, I don't regret the Jake thing at all. It just feels like something I needed to experience, and I'm glad that I gave myself that leeway. Because, for a while, it was fun. Actually, it was more than fun. It was a passion that came and made me realise that I was alive again, before vanishing, just like that.

I bumped into Jake only once after that. I was in the Grafton Centre, and he asked me to have a coffee with him. I felt I owed him that, at least.

I didn't feel any danger in doing so because whatever had drawn me to him – the beginnings of love, or just empty lust, perhaps – was gone. I explained, over coffee, that I was sorry but I was married and I loved my husband and I loved my daughter, and that was all there was to it. I said that what had happened had been a terrible, terrible mistake. I told him lots of wonderful things about you for some reason. I think I was brandishing you like a crucifix to keep the vampires away. I told him that some other woman would be very, very lucky to snag him, but that woman wasn't me. I thought, too late, of

Mags. It seemed such a waste that I had used Jake for myself rather than introducing him to Mags.

Poor Jake. He was so sure of his irresistibility that when I told him it was over, it was as if he couldn't even understand the words I was saying: he made me repeat it three times. And then he straightened his tie, buttoned his jacket, did that Prince Charles thing with his cuffs, pecked me on the cheek and stood and walked away.

• • •

Sean is angry. Sean is so angry that he can't think, he can't eat, and he isn't sleeping properly, either. His mind obsesses about Catherine, about Jake; it creates visions of their entwined bodies that are so real and so painful, that he finds himself wincing.

When he opens the laptop of a morning, the previous evening's Google search is there, full screen, waiting for him. "My dead wife cheated on me: About 3,230,000 results."

He moves the pointer so that it hovers over the little cross that will close that window, but then he clicks on one of the links instead. He has found an entire forum of people who discovered that their partners cheated on them, but the fact that out there, in the myriad randomness of humanity, someone, somewhere is feeling the same as he feels, doesn't seem to help either. It doesn't seem to help at all.

He asks himself who he hates the most – smug, suited Jake, who shagged his wife, knowing that she was married, or Catherine herself, for cheating on him, for breaking her marriage vows, or perhaps, above all, for having waited until now to tell him, for waiting until she was no longer present to bear the weight of his anger.

His memory of her is sullied – that's the thing – and he can't see how that can ever be undone. He hates her. And the reason he hates her the most is because he had been happy to have spent his life loving her. Even if it was over, at least his life had been built upon that rock of certainty. And now she's taken even that away from him; she has retrospectively made their years together seem false and stupid and cheap.

His anger comes and goes like ripples of red-hot energy from an unpredictable nuclear reaction and, because he can't think what to do with all that heat, he punches a wall and hurts his knuckles; he throws a chair, albeit feebly, across the room. And then finally, on Wednesday evening, after pacing around the suddenly hated house for an hour, he pulls on shorts and trainers and goes running.

It's drizzling outside, but he doesn't care. He imagines the rain sizzling against his angry skin as he runs and runs, driven by the spiritual pain borne of this anger that's too big to even be thought about. Eventually, after almost an hour, he finds that he has been lost to himself for the last mile or so, and when he takes stock of the sensations within his body he finds that the fizzling molten heart of the pain has gone, that the fire has died. He discovers that his anger has been consumed and transformed into a different physical pain in his legs, in his chest, in his lungs. And where the anger sat, only emptiness remains. He turns and starts to walk homeward.

By the following weekend, Sean's feelings towards the house have morphed so radically that his thoughts from the previous weekend – that the house was a shrine to Catherine, to their daughter, to their life together – seem little more than sour, slightly embarrassing memories. The house, now, feels like salt to a wound, so much so that he can hardly bear to step through the front door of an evening. But autumn is closing in fast, the evenings are cooling, the Cam is punt-less and the drizzle almost constant, so he finds himself forced indoors, angry and resentful as he looks around, scowling, at the many reminders of Catherine's long shadow.

On Saturday morning, a young, smooth, estate agent named Irvine arrives, as requested. He has a Scottish accent and is wearing a tonic grey suit and a hugely knotted tie. Sean wonders if this is what Jake looked like and has to fight his desire to slam the door in the poor guy's face.

Irvine wanders around opening cupboards and taking measurements with his laser device, before sitting at the kitchen table and, after tapping away at his smartphone screen, announcing a price bracket. The house is worth a little more than Sean had thought, but still not enough to buy and renovate the apartment in Cantabrigian Rise.

"You're thinking of selling up soon?" Irvine asks.

Sean sighs. "My wife died," he says, and he hears that he has said this without sadness, without kindness, and feels suddenly scared of himself, feels unexpectedly frightened by the power of his own anger. "And my daughter's moved out, too. So yes, I'm toying with the idea of a riverfront bachelor pad, actually."

"I'm so sorry for your loss," Irvine says unconvincingly. "Do you have a property in mind?"

Sean shakes his head. "I'm really just at the start of the whole process," he says, scratching his ear.

Irvine nods thoughtfully.

"I looked at a place out at Cantabrigian Rise," Sean explains, "but it was too expensive and needed too much work, so…"

Irvine laughs. "That's funny," he says. "I valued that place yesterday. 4A, was it?"

Sean frowns. "No, actually. 3F."

"Ah," Irvine says. "They're two-beds on the third floor, are they not?"

"That's right," Sean says, suddenly intrigued. "So how much is 4A going for?"

Irvine laughs again and fiddles with his tie which provokes, in Sean, an unexpected shudder of disgust. "Aye," he says, "that would be telling. It's not even been listed, I don't think." He pulls a business card from his pocket and writes *Bonnie Fleetwood* on the back. "I just do the valuations, but you should give Bonnie, here, a call. It should be in your price range. Well, if they listen to me it should be, at any rate. Anyway, I'd better be off. I'll get this typed up and posted to you by Wednesday, OK?"

Despite his aching legs, Sean goes jogging again on Saturday evening, and it seems to do him good because on Sunday morning he wakes up feeling calmer. It's as if he has managed to place Catherine, Jake and even this damned house in a box labelled *The Past*. It's probably only temporary respite, but that is at least something.

He makes a pot of coffee and opens *The Guardian* website on his laptop. "Let's have a *calm* day today, shall we?" he mumbles as he opens the kitchen cabinet and pulls out the box of muesli. He has exhausted himself with his own anger, he realises. But then his eyes stray to the shoebox, there, on the top shelf. And it's Sunday, of course, isn't it. Is he going to listen to another tape? Does he have any spare capacity for further sordid revelations? He hears Maggie's voice, saying, "They're not doing you any good, you know."

"No, Mags, they're not," he mumbles, answering her out loud as he stares at the box. "You're right. They're not doing me any good at all."

He reaches for the box. He looks down at it in his hands. He traces the curve of Catherine's handwriting with his eyes, and his lip curls. And then after less than a second's hesitation, he exhales deeply and strides to the back door.

Outside, in the wet, cold garden, he lifts the lid on the wheelie bin. He holds the box over the opening and hesitates anew. "Freedom," he says, forcefully, as if trying to convince himself. And then he drops the box into the void.

He swallows with difficulty, then peers down into the darkness and sees that the box has landed straight, has fallen intact. The envelopes and tapes and photos of his life with Catherine have remained inside. He thinks of the photos, photos that feature not only Catherine's life, but his and his daughter's, too. "Fuck, fuck, fuck!" he mutters, as he reaches down to retrieve it.

He shakes his head and places it on top of the bin. "Take your time," he tells himself. "You'll know when you're ready." And then he picks it up and walks back indoors.

• • •

Despite everything, the fact of not listening to this week's tape leaves a gap in Sean's life that he struggles to fill. The box of envelopes plays constantly on his mind, but he remains steadfast. He's unsure, for the moment, if he'll ever be able to listen to the remaining tapes, but for now, at least, it's an impossibility.

Finding nothing of interest on the television that evening, he phones April for a chat instead. "Time to concentrate on the living," he murmurs, as he dials her number.

April is in fine form. She tells Sean that her morning sickness, which she has never even mentioned before, is now over. She tells him excitedly that she is only going to work for another six weeks before going on maternity leave. They have painted the lounge and she's going to do the bedroom once she's off, she says. She refuses Sean's offers of help, reminding him that Ronan is at home all day working if she does need another pair of hands. "But you can buy us a crib once the monster arrives," she tells Sean. "How does that sound?"

"That sounds lovely," Sean says. "I'd be proud to."

April is just about to wind up the conversation when Sean says, "Can I ask you a serious question, Little Daughter?"

"Sure, Big Daddy. Fire away."

"How do you feel about your room here?" Sean asks tentatively.

"My room?"

"Yes."

"How do I *feel* about it?"

"Yes. How attached to it are you, I suppose? To still having your own room here, I mean. Be honest."

"Oh, I don't know," April says. "A bit. Not much, I guess. But a bit. Why, are you thinking of getting a lodger to keep you company?"

Sean laughs drily. "No, no, nothing like that. I just... I mean... Look, it's early days, OK? Very, very early days. And I'm really only just *beginning* to think—"

"Oh, God," April interrupts. "You're moving house, aren't you?"

"No... Look... Yes... I might be, *perhaps*. But only if you're OK about it. And as I say, I'm really not even at the beginning of anything yet." Sean hears her sigh deeply, causing him to prompt, "April?"

"Oh... I knew this was coming," she says. "Of course I did. I even discussed it with Ronan a few weeks ago."

"You did?"

"Yeah. And we both agreed that it makes sense, that it would be good for you, that it would be healthy, I mean. We both see that you need to move on with your life at some point. And part of that is... part of that *has to be* moving out of that house. There must be so many memories tied to the place, Dad. I don't know how you stand it."

"So you *don't* mind?"

April exhales deeply again. "Look, I'm going to be honest, Dad, if that's OK? I didn't *think* I would mind. But now it's happened..." She pauses for a moment, then continues, in a far more up-tempo voice, "You know what, Dad? Don't listen to me. I'm talking bollocks, here. Absolute bollocks. Of *course* you should move. If you want to move, you absolutely should. The house will still be there. I can go and stand and look at it any time I want to. But ultimately, it's just a house, isn't it?"

"Hum, you don't sound very convincing. Or convinced."

"No, really. I'm certain. You won't be leaving Cambridge, though, will you? You're not going to move to London and live in a squat and be a DJ or anything scary like that?"

"Well, maybe," Sean jokes. "I was thinking about a sect, actually. Scientology seems quite groovy."

"That's a fabulous idea," April says. "You can introduce me to Tom Cruise."

"But, no. Just a flat, I thought. Something on the riverfront, maybe. One of the places in a building I designed is up for sale, so I may go and look at that for starters."

"Cantabrigian Heights or whatever?" April says.

"Rise," Sean says. "Cantabrigian *Rise*. Yes, that's the one."

"Gosh, I remember you taking me to the building site when I was little. You've always had a thing for that place."

"I know. I still think it's one of the nicest things I've ever done. That's all it is, really."

"You should go for it, Dad," April says. "Really. Mum would totally approve, too. She once said it was a shame you didn't have the wherewithal to live in your own buildings. Maybe I'll come down and we can go to see it together?"

"That'd be nice. But anyway, if you're sure you're OK about it?"

"I really am."

"Then I'll let you get back to whatever it is you pregnant lassies do on Sunday nights."

"We're just binge-watching something on Netflix. The Bridge. It's Swedish. Or Danish. A bit of both, actually. Have you seen it?"

"No."

"It's brilliant. We're both addicted. Go watch it now. Oh, before you go, Dad?"

"Yes?"

"Have you heard anything from Auntie Maggie?"

"Mags?" Sean says. "No, I can't say that I have. Why d'you ask?"

"She's gone quiet, that's all. On Facebook. I mean, she never posts much, but she still *likes* stuff, especially baby stuff. And anything with animals. But for the past month or so there's been no reaction to anything. Zilch. Nada."

"You could phone her, maybe?" Sean offers.

"Yeah," April says doubtfully. "Yeah, I suppose I *could*. It's just we don't tend to do that these days. It's not, like, our usual mode of communication. But you're right. I'll give her a ring."

The call ended, Sean struggles to remember his last interaction with Maggie. It's as if his internal filing system has been shaken up by the trauma of Catherine's revelations. But eventually it comes back to him: his call asking Maggie if Catherine might have had an affair and Maggie's text informing him that such a thing was an impossibility. If only she knew the truth.

Wondering if he might have upset her by not answering her call, by not replying to her text either, he reaches for the phone. Maggie answers immediately.

"Hello Mags!" Sean says, trying to sound chipper and, he suspects, probably overdoing it a little.

"Hi Sean," Maggie replies without enthusiasm. After a pause, during which Sean waits for her to become her usual voluble self, she adds, "Yes?"

"I just... I was wondering how you are, really," Sean says.

"Oh, that's nice," Maggie says. "I'm OK, really. Considering."

"Considering what?"

"Oh, nothing much," she says, sounding falsely disinterested. "I split up with Dave, that's all."

"Oh, no!" Sean says. "I had no idea, Mags."

"It's no big deal; really it isn't. I'm getting quite good at it these days. Hardly makes a ripple, really."

"I doubt that's true," Sean says.

"No, no I suppose not."

"What happened, Mags? I mean, if you want to talk about it... Perhaps you'd rather not talk about it."

"Girls always want to talk about it, Sean," Maggie says, flatly. "Do you not know that yet?"

"Apparently not."

"Not wanting to talk about things is a boy thing."

"*OK,*" Sean says, sounding dubious. "So, what happened?"

"He wasn't very nice in the end. Like you said. You spotted that before I did. We were having a row the last time you called, actually."

"Oh, I'm sorry, Mags. And that call... it was... I know I was strange. I was just having a bad day."

"I don't even remember what it was about, to be honest. What *was* it about?"

"Nothing," Sean says. "Nothing that matters."

"No? Anyway, we were in the middle of a shouting match. So if *I* was a bit weird, I apologise too."

"What about? The barney, I mean. That is, if you're sure you want to go–"

"Money," Maggie interrupts. "It was about money, mainly."

"Money?"

"Yes. I was paying for pretty much everything. Which I honestly didn't mind. Dave's not, as I'm sure you spotted, very wealthy."

"Neither are you, are you?"

"No. Well, *quite.* But we went to the pub and I paid for the food and drinks, as usual. And then I went home – I had an early start the next day, you see. Only after I'd gone, Dave bought *everyone* drinks."

"But he didn't buy *you* a drink?"

"No, but that's not it. That wouldn't have bothered me. No, the thing was that he bought everyone drinks and then told the barman to put them on a tab in *my* name. He said that I'd pay it the next time I was in."

"*What?*"

"I know! Because I'd gone and he couldn't use my card, he told them to keep a tab. So the next time I went in there to meet him, there was a bar tab waiting for me. It was thirty-six pounds eighty."

"Jesus, Mags. What a weird thing to do."

"I refused to pay it, of course. Which became this big row with the barman who said he was just doing his job and what-have-you. And so I walked out and went home."

"Wow, I can't think what to say to that."

"Dave arrived about an hour later. He'd gone to the pub to meet me, but hadn't had his card with him, so he claimed. And the barman had told him that if he couldn't pay, he was barred. Actually, we both were. It's the first time I've ever been barred from a pub. So Dave went all shouty on me about how he'd been barred because of me, and how embarrassing that was – that's when you phoned, bang in the middle of that – and then I told him to get out. So that was the end of that, really."

"That's awful, Maggie. I'm really sorry. Is it all definitely..."

"I went back to the pub to pay the tab afterwards," Maggie continues, "because... well, because I'm a sop, I suppose. But I felt bad about it, really. Because it wasn't the poor barman's fault, either, was it? He's ever so cute. And I was worried they'd take it out of his earnings or something, you know, like they do in banks? But I told them not to let Dave know it had been paid and that they should get him to pay it again if he wanted to be un-barred or whatever it's called."

"Mags..."

"Anyway, I'm out of it all. Which is probably a good thing, even if it doesn't feel that way yet."

"I'm *really* sorry. You should have phoned me."

"Don't be. It's all thanks to you, in a way."

"Thanks to *me*?" Sean pulls a face at his phone. He's not entirely comfortable with being responsible for Maggie's breakup.

"Yes, you said I deserved someone who was nice to me, and that kept going around my head whenever I was with Dave. Like a sort of mantra, really. And he wasn't, that's the thing. He wasn't very nice to me at all."

"Gosh, I hope it's not *my* fault," Sean says. "I really wouldn't want to think–"

"Stop, Sean. Dave's a loser. It just took your friendly nudge for me to see that. So, if anything, I'm grateful. Really. If it's anyone's fault, it's mine. I bring these things on myself, you know?"

"Not really. No. I'd be tempted to say that if it's anyone's fault, it's *Dave's*."

"Yeah. But *I* chose him, didn't I? I think I do it subconsciously or something. I've been thinking about going to see someone, a shrink maybe."

"If you think that might help," Sean says, "then you should do it."

"Because ever since... well... ever since Ian, really, I've believed, I think, that nothing can ever work out. I think that's why I go for these hopeless types. To sort of *prove* myself right. Does that make any sense?"

"Sort of. Yes, I think so."

"I wonder what he's doing now? It's such a shame we never kept in touch."

"Dave?"

"No, Ian, silly. He was so lovely."

"I thought you hated Ian more than anyone else on the planet."

Maggie sighs loudly. "Oh, you can't hate people forever, can you? Sooner or later it always becomes clear that however awful they were to you, they were still trying to do their best. Nobody sets out to be awful, do they? But we're all this collection of traumas and hurts and dysfunctional mumbo-jumbo trying to be functional and logical and wise. And Ian, well, he never set out to hurt anyone, did he? His true nature just sort of caught up with him, I think. He seemed as shocked as everyone else about it, the poor boy."

"Well, that's a generous way of looking at things," Sean says. It crosses his mind that this conversation has relevance for his own life right now, but he can sense, even before he starts to think about it, that it's a subject which requires time and calm and space, so he mentally files it away for later when he's alone.

"Generous?" Maggie says. "Maybe. Or maybe it's just called survival." She thinks about this for a few seconds before adding, "But no. It wasn't Ian's fault. It was just bad luck on my part that I met him when I did. He's still the best husband I never had."

• • •

Sean spends the week feeling strange, confused – more blank, really, than disappointed.

When he tries not to think about Catherine's affair, he's aware that it's there, just out of view, waiting for him. But when he tries *to* think about it, the overriding emotion is no longer anger, or pain, but emptiness.

It is as if his memory of his wife, once so solid, so certain, so integral to his own being that it was impossible to believe
280

that she was no longer here, has become blurred and confused by her horrific revelations.

She has become, in the space of a ten minute cassette recording, a different person from the one Sean thought he knew. And in becoming that different person, he has lost his claim to her and, perhaps, even his capacity to be surprised, shocked, or even angry. For once you accept that you *don't* know someone, how can anything they do surprise you?

There is also, Sean realises, a part of him that wants to understand her. And the key to understanding lies within him. For did he not, once upon a time, meet a Swedish girl at a party? Did he not, himself, acknowledge that sexual attraction could be so powerful as to be quite literally irresistible? But he *hadn't* slept with her, had he? Sure, he hadn't had the opportunity, but he still *hadn't* slept with her.

The weather remains cold and damp, but Sean continues going jogging every evening for the simple reason that it makes him feel less mad. It makes him feel calm and sated, almost as if he has popped a Valium or smoked a joint, and so he runs until he can run no more before showering and zoning out in front of the television.

When, on Sunday, the bad weather makes running an impossibility, Sean realises that the running thing has become more than a habit, that it really is like a drug. He paces the empty house, peering out at the torrential rain like a frustrated, caged animal, unable to even imagine how to get through the evening without his fix. He repeatedly pulls his running gear on, and once even makes it to the end of the street. But the temperature is hovering just above zero and the rain is icy cold and biblical in its intensity. So he turns and runs straight back home.

Without his drug, frustration, boredom and resurfacing anger drive him back inexorably towards the tapes. *Perhaps I should just get them over with,* he thinks. *Then I really can bin them. Then I'll never have to think about them again.*

But still he hesitates until the grey, depressing daylight fades to utter darkness.

Only then, realising that he's behind, that he can listen to *two* tapes, realising that, *hell, he can listen to all of the damned tapes if he wants to,* does he stride to the kitchen to retrieve the box.

Snapshot #24

120 format, black and white. Two children are playing in a sandpit with buckets and spades. The little boy, in a woolly jumper and jeans, is staring at the camera and smiling broadly. The little girl, wearing dungarees and a sweatshirt, has her face obscured by a mop of unruly hair which has fallen forwards as she plays.

Sean covers his mouth with his left hand as he studies the photo held by the trembling right.

He knew that this photo would be here – of course he knew. He should have been ready. But he hadn't expected it here, not in the middle. At the beginning, perhaps. Or at the very end. But not here. Why here? Could this no-longer understood woman called Catherine have chosen it this way? Had she wanted to twist the knife?

It's a shock; it's such a shock that it feels like being stabbed in the heart. Because this image reminds him just how deep and important this thing between them was, this thing that Catherine threw so lightly away, and for what? For a fling with an idiot in a suit?

For their story had not been mere chance, mere science, as Sean has always liked to think. He's not comfortable with the metaphysical, never has been. But here, in the privacy of his own mind, he admits it, now. Their relationship had also been built, as Maggie would say, on destiny. And that destiny had revolved, repeatedly, around the tatty, out of focus, utterly magical photo that Sean is holding in his hand – a photo so profoundly symbolic of their life together, that he can barely see it for tears.

Cassette #24

Hello Sean.

You're still listening, then? I'm so glad about that. Because I've still so much I want to tell you. And don't worry. There are no more lovers in the pipeline. What happened with Jake is awful and terrible and unforgivable, I know. But it was truly a one-off, for whatever that's worth.

So, the third of April, 1996. Do you know, I can hardly remember any of it?

Oh, I remember bits and bobs. I remember opening the door to the policeman. I thought something had happened to April at first. I was relieved, even, when he said that April was fine.

I remember random words from that conversation, too. "In the supermarket" for instance, and "heart attack" of course. Then everything jumps to Margate General, to that cold green room. I have no memory, for instance, of how we got from one place to another. You must have driven me, I suppose.

After that, there's another blank space and then the funeral. April cried and cried and cried until I wanted to shake her. I had no room for her grief. I didn't even have room for my own.

It had been so unexpected, that was the thing. She was only fifty-one. Which is what trying to live on oven chips, Stella Artois and Silk Cut will do for you, I suppose.

As to how it was all organised, how all the little things one has to arrange came to pass, I really don't have the foggiest. I can only assume that you did all of it.

I remember you as this great presence, this warm, benevolent mass beside me. You were there when the doorbell rang and you were there when the coffin sank into the floor. And you organised it all, you paid for it all. You must have. And you held us all together. I don't think I ever even thanked you.

The grief lasted for months. There were different phases and different intensities. There were different styles of grief, from the wailing screaming of that first day through the weak-kneed collapse at the morgue and finally those hopeless, seemingly endless weeks of grinding, grey misery.

Eventually, though I never thought it would happen, the fog started to lift. And as I came out of my grief for Mum, I fell headlong into my love for you. It was as if I had such intensity of feeling back then that I needed somewhere new to put it. And what better place than in you?

I became able to see you for who you were again, and it was like a revelation. You were suddenly this brand new shiny thing in my life all over again.

As my needing you faded, my love for you returned and I became aware, very gradually, that you were on your way out. You were heading for the door. That came as a terrible, terrifying shock to me.

Between Jake and Mum, I'd been gone too long. I had left you on your own and I hadn't even been aware of the fact. The more I analysed it, the more convinced I became that you had worked out about Jake, you had seen just how selfish I was, and you were just waiting for the right time to leave me. You had been, I decided, on the verge of leaving when Mum died.

This selflessness was, I came to understand, your final act of kindness before you walked out the door.

For months, every time you sat down to say something to me, my heart leapt into my mouth. Because every single time, I thought you were about to announce our end-date.

I was, by then, as in love with you as I had ever been. It's amazing how imminent loss concentrates the senses. And you'd been so incredible about Mum's death, so... *empathetic*, I suppose, is the word.

Other people expressed sympathy, they said, "Oh, I'm so sorry. But at least you loved her, right?" Or they said, "I'm so sorry, but it will get better, even if it doesn't feel like that right now." Or, "At least you have Sean and April." None of that was of any use to me.

You were different, though. You had this ability to join me in the darkness. You would press your forehead to mine and cry with me. You would pull April to your chest and cry with her. And that readiness to go there, to *feel* the pain, even when it wasn't your pain, was magnificent. And unique. And, to me, infinitely loveable.

I couldn't stand the idea of you leaving, I really couldn't. I used to imagine committing suicide if it came to pass because a world without you and a world without Mum – a world without *either* of you – felt like trying to survive on Mars. I imagined it would be like trying to breathe on a planet with no oxygen. Something like that, anyway.

I wanted to get back to you, but there were still walls between us, walls I couldn't even seem to name – a barrier I had built because of Jake, perhaps, and a wall of grief from losing Mum. And I couldn't work out how to break through them.

The letter came from the council in June – recorded delivery. By the time we got around to picking the letter up from the Post Office, Mum's house had to be vacated within ten days.

Selfless as ever, you took a week off work and we rented a van and left April with Mags, and drove down to Margate. You tried singing that awful Chas and Dave song to cheer me up. It didn't work.

I was useless all over again. I don't think I did anything much except stare at objects and burst into tears. And again, you did it all, filling the boxes and stuffing the bags and driving all Mum's rubbish to the tip. You cooked her remaining oven chips, which we ate as if it was a memorial service – I remember that. After I'd eaten the last one, you held me and I wept for the umpteenth time that day.

And then, while clearing out the bookshelf, you found the photo.

I was sitting in the garden having a "moment" by smoking one of Mum's cigarettes when you came rushing out waving it at me. You were so excited. You looked about the same age as you are in the photo.

"This photo!" you said. "Look what I've found! This photo. I have the same photo at home. Look!"

You sat down next to me on that damp, mouldy sofa and put your arm around me. "Look!" you said again. "Your mum's got the same photo I've got at home."

You were back. For the first time in months, you were back, but I didn't understand yet what was happening because I was only just realising that you had been gone. Yes, you'd been there to love and cherish and support me. But that magical thing of being *in love* was a distant memory for both of us. It was only then that I understood that perhaps this was what I had been looking for from Jake. So I must have just frowned at you, I think. I frowned at you and looked at the photo, and looked at your face. I noticed how happy you were. I looked at how beautiful you were. There was love in your eyes, deep, painful, bewildered love – like back at the beginning. For the first time in years.

"It's you, isn't it?" you said, pointing at the little girl hiding behind her hair. "Look, it's you and me. Christ, I've known you since I was *seven*. My Mum told me about it, too, but it was you! On holiday. In Cornwall. The inseparables. It was you! Was it? Was it you? Look, your mum's got the same bloody photo. Say something!"

And then you squeezed me excitedly and snatched the cigarette from my fingers and took a drag. "That's just... wow," you said. "Do you understand what I'm saying? Do you understand how mind-blowing this is?"

At that moment there was nothing in the world that I wanted more than to reconnect with you and I could see that there was nothing in the world that you wanted more, either. I nodded and smiled. And when you tried to get me to speak again, I kissed you.

Snapshot #25

35mm format, colour. Two women and a tall, skinny man look up at the photographer. They are lying on yellow sunbeds next to a turquoise swimming pool in which a young girl is floating on an orange airbed. All three adults are raising one hand to shield their eyes from the sun, and all are smiling.

The second Sean flips the photo over, his eyes mist with tears of confusion. Because, of course, their relationship had continued after Wendy's death. Things hadn't just ended after Catherine's secretive fling. And at the moment Sean had found that photo, at the moment he had discovered that there was a *reason* he had fallen in love with Catherine at first sight – namely, that it wasn't first sight at all – they still had eleven more years ahead of them.

Though Sean had never quite understood just how far away Catherine had drifted from him, he had understood, that summer, in Valencia, that she was back. And he had thanked the Gods for that.

Cassette #25

Hello Sean.

How heavenly was Valencia? I found a whole package of Spanish photos, but I thought this one summed it up the best: the long sweltering days lying around the pool, the endless gin and tonics, the fresh fish on the barbecue... But best of all were those long, sultry siestas we all used to have, the scorching Leveche breeze blowing those long white curtains in and out as if a giant was breathing outside the window. I used to wake up feeling as if I had been drugged.

The whole thing had been Craig's idea. He was a wine taster or wholesaler or negotiator. Whatever it was, he put half the cost of the villa and most of the meals we had in restaurants down on expenses.

Do you remember the way they used to wake us up at nights, the way their bed head used to bash against the wall and that little wobbling tremolo that Maggie used to make as they reached the end? The first time it happened, you nudged me in the ribs and whispered, "At least this one isn't gay, huh?" And we both fell about laughing.

There was something inherently sexy about the Valencian sun though, wasn't there? Because Maggie and Craig weren't the only two people burning midnight calories... We were so in love on that holiday. I felt like I was twenty all over again. I felt amazing.

April made friends with the gardener guy's daughter, Marina or Marisa or something like that. They hung out together for the full two weeks without ever, I don't think, exchanging a single word of conversation. Actually, they conversed plenty, they conversed constantly. It's just that April was doing it in English and Marisa was doing it in Spanish. But somehow they got along fine.

Anyway, everyone was happy and relaxed and sunburnt. Craig, whom we hadn't really known that well, turned out to be generous and easy-going and funny. And Maggie was so utterly, utterly relaxed that I finally convinced myself that I had made your whole affair thing up in my own head. And so I felt even more guilty about my own.

That said, I was never that comfortable about leaving you two alone together. It's funny how our brains can hold multiple truths, isn't it? Because, I mean, I really *did* believe both that you two *had* had a fling together and that you *hadn't.*

I read a thing about Schrödinger's cat the other day. According to our cleverest scientists, this theoretical cat is neither dead nor alive until someone opens the box to check. It's in a sort of suspended halfway state for some reason that I didn't quite grasp. But I think your affair is a bit like Schrödinger's cat in that it neither existed nor didn't exist, essentially because I decided to never look inside that box. That makes me, I suspect, something of a coward.

I actually intended to open the box while we were in Valencia – I fully intended to have a showdown with Maggie and find out once and for all. But we were having so much fun together that the moment never seemed right. And by the end of it, as I say, I'd pretty much convinced myself that it had never happened and that I would come over as an idiot if I asked her.

Do you remember that winery that Craig took us to on the final weekend? They had all of these bottles of fifty-euro Valencian wine lined up for us to try and Craig tried to tell us that we were meant to taste it and then spit it back out. We didn't believe him at first – he was always joking about one thing or another, after all – but then they brought us a bowl to spit in and these little white towels to dab our lips on, and we realised that it was true.

"This is the best wine I've ever had," you said. "I'm not spitting the bloody stuff out!"

Oh, we got so drunk, Sean, it was shameful. We even had to leave the hire car there and get a taxi back to the villa. You fell out of the taxi when we got home, too, and then I tripped over your legs and we ended up uncontrollably laughing in this writhing mass in the car park. That continued until Maggie arrived and yanked us upright and reminded us that we had a daughter to pick up from the gardener's cottage down the way.

I felt so ill the next day. That journey to the airport was one of the worst experiences of my entire life.

The next morning, I woke up to drizzle in Cambridge and felt as miserable as I ever have. My chest and jaw seemed to hurt, too, and it wasn't until you got home and said that you had the same symptoms that we worked out that it was from all that laughing. I don't think I had ever ached from laughter before, nor have since.

Getting home was even worse for Maggie because her American went back to Los Angeles. I'm not sure if you ever knew this – she didn't seem keen on anyone else knowing – but he asked her to go back with him, to live in America. He tried for ages to convince her – the phone calls went on for months. And I tried my best to convince her too, for both selfless and selfish reasons. But she just kept saying, "What the hell would I do in Los Angeles?" To which there was no simple answer other than, "Let yourself be happy, perhaps?"

But happiness, as they say, is an option. And I just don't think Maggie was ever very good at choosing it.

• • •

When April arrives on Saturday morning, Sean is busy vacuuming the sofa. He jumps visibly when April, behind him, coughs loudly.

"Jesus!" he exhales, stomping on the power switch of the cleaner which whines slowly to a halt. "Are you trying to kill me? Do you want your inheritance right now or something?"

April pulls a cute face and shrugs. "I rang. I knocked... I don't know what else I'm supposed to do. Send a telegram, maybe?"

Sean's regard drops to April's belly. "Oh, look!" he says. "You have a baby bump."

"I know," April says. "He's huge, huh?"

"He is!" Sean agrees. "And you're only..." Sean frowns, then adds, "*He?*"

April nods. "Twenty weeks. He's big for his age. He's going to be an American basketball player, I think."

"You mean he's going to be black?" Sean asks facetiously.

April nods with mock seriousness. "Of course. Ronan's going to be thrilled."

"Anyway, come in, come in!" Sean says, stomping repeatedly on another button until the cable starts to snake inside the cleaner. "I'll put the kettle on. Um, sit down."

April watches bemusedly as he puts the cleaner away in the cupboard under the stairs and then starts to fill the kettle. "I

293

don't think I've ever seen you with the Hoover before. I'm surprised you know how it works."

"Cheeky!" Sean says, glancing up at her. "You've seen me do the hoovering a thousand times more often than you ever saw your mother do it. And don't even get me started on how many times *you* did it. I can count those on two fingers." He joins finger and thumb to form a zero.

April frowns thoughtfully before saying, "Actually, that's true. I don't know why I even said that."

"Sexism," Sean says. "Just sexism. The river of sexism flows both ways Little Daughter. Actually, I'm going to have to stop calling you that, aren't I?"

"I think so," April says. "Try lardy daughter. Or roly-poly daughter."

"So, how have you been? How are you feeling?"

"Fine really. Full of beans. All the tests and everything are good. I'm not sleeping too well. I can't seem to sleep on my front anymore. But on my back, I snore. And then I wake myself up. So, that's a bit of a pain."

"And Ronan, you're waking him up too, presumably?"

"Nah. Nothing wakes Ronan up."

"And it's a boy, then?"

"Yes. We're thinking Jack or Jake or... *What*?"

Sean who is grimacing does his best to relax his facial muscles. "Just... not Jake. Preferably."

"Why not?"

"Jakes are always arseholes, that's all."

April's eyebrows twitch, and then she visibly decides not to pursue it. "OK, so, Jack, or Josh, or Jim."

"What's with all the Js, anyway?"

April shrugs. "I don't know. We both just like them. That's all."

294

"Fair enough. As long as it's not Jake."

"But they sound joyful, I think. Joyful Jim. Joyful Jake. I mean, Jack. Sorry. Anyway, enough of baby names. How are you, Dad?"

Sean pulls cups from the cupboard and drops tea bags into them. "I'm – oh, can you drink normal tea? You can, can't you?" April nods, so he continues, "I'm fine. Busy. But that's good."

"You know, you don't talk about it much anymore," April says. "The whole Mum thing, I mean."

"No?"

"No. And I've been struggling to know whether I should mention it or if I *shouldn't* mention it. I'm just, you know, putting it out there. So you can tell me. I hate worrying about stuff like that."

Sean nods as he pours the water into the cups. "I think I'm better *not* talking about it at the moment. If that's OK with you?"

He thinks he has managed to sound relaxed but that's perhaps not the case because April replies, "That's fine. But you sound angry. It's not with me, is it?"

"Angry?" Sean says with surprise.

"Yes. Angry."

"Oh..." Sean shrugs. "It's one of those phases, isn't it? Denial, numbness, whatever, and *anger*." He sighs. "I'm probably not doing them in the right order, though. I never was one for following instructions."

"OK," April says. "If that's all it is."

"But, really, I'm fine. And I'm better not talking about it right now. Really, I am. But I appreciate you asking."

"Good. Well, that's sorted, then."

A silence falls over them, a silence during which the only sound in the kitchen is the gentle throb of the refrigerator and the noise of the teaspoon against the side of the cup as Sean squashes the teabag with it.

"Right. When are we seeing this amazing flat of yours?" April eventually asks.

"Three o'clock," Sean replies, turning to look at his daughter and forcing a smile. "After I've bought you lunch down on the river."

• • •

"So this is 4A," Bonnie, the estate agent announces breathlessly. She is visibly overweight, yet has had to brave the staircase as the lift is in the process of being serviced.

"Oh, it's gorgeous!" April says, stepping inside. "There's so much light. And the sun's not even out."

Sean follows his daughter into the living area.

"Are those...? Those are the originals, aren't they?" April asks, pointing towards the kitchen units.

"They are. And look at this." Sean crosses to the worktop, fiddles with a catch and pulls out a long swivelling table. "Gosh, it's as-new," he says. "It looks like they never used it."

"Maybe no one told them it was there."

"Now, *I* didn't know that was there," Bonnie comments. "Have you been here before, then?"

"Not this unit," Sean says. "But they're all the same. At least they were, fifteen years ago."

"How nice," Bonnie says, as if she hasn't really been listening at all. "Now, it's only a one bedroom," she continues as she starts to waddle towards the rear of the unit, "but you could perhaps put a partition in here if you wanted to make a box room for baby."

296

Sean, who is suddenly feeling uncomfortable, opens his mouth to explain that April is his daughter and that she won't be living here.

But he is beaten to it by April, who says, "Baby? What baby's that then?"

Bonnie visibly pales. "Oh... I'm... Um..." She swallows. "I'm sorry... I just assumed."

April runs one hand over her bump and shakes her head. "Doughnuts," she says. "I can't get enough of them."

"Right," Bonnie says. "Well, I... I certainly couldn't fault you on that. Doughnuts are *famously* difficult to resist."

Sean catches his daughter's eye and has to bite his cheek to avoid laughing as April replies, "Yes. Well, too difficult for me, anyway."

Other than showing them around the apartment, Bonnie is unable to answer any of Sean's questions about the price, the availability, or who the seller might be. "I brought the wrong folder," she says, waving said folder at Sean. "And I've a memory like a sieve. I'm so sorry. I'm rubbish today – honestly I am."

Once they're safely in Sean's car with the doors firmly closed, he says, "Now, that was cruel. You completely threw poor Bonnie off her stride."

"Oh, don't be silly," April says. "It was just a bit of fun."

"It would have been. If she hadn't so clearly been a doughnut fan."

April sniggers and bites her lip. "Yeah. I didn't think about that until I'd said it. You know me. Shoot first. Think afterwards. But I don't think she thought I was getting at *her*, did she?"

"No," Sean admits. "No, I think she thought she'd found a partner in crime. Someone to eat doughnuts with. Which is why it was so cruel."

"Hey, I like doughnuts," April says. "Actually, I could kill a doughnut right now. Is there a cake shop anywhere?"

"We could go for coffee at Clowns," Sean offers. "But I don't think they do doughnuts."

"Ooh, Clowns," April says. "I wonder if they still do that carrot cake with all the–"

"They do," Sean interrupts, laughing. "It hasn't changed in twenty years. Can you drink coffee though?"

"I'll have decaf. Or tea. Or hot chocolate. I'll have anything as long as I can have cake."

As they are sitting down with their tray, Sean's phone rings. "It's Bonnie," he says, flashing the screen at April so that she can see. "She wants to join us for cake, I expect. Hello?" He spends a few minutes saying, "Yes," and, "No, I see," and, "Really?" before finally hanging up.

"More info?" April asks through a mouthful of cake.

"Lots," Sean says. "The sellers are German, apparently. And they're moving back to Frankfurt because of Brexit. His job's been moved there."

"There's a lot of that about," April says, looking concerned. "I think Britain's going to be like a big empty car park by the time they've finished with their Brexit bollocks."

"Anyway, that's good news for me, because Bonnie reckons they're desperate for a quick sale. She says I should make an offer."

"Gosh," April says. "So, what do you think?"

"What do *you* think?" Sean asks, sipping his coffee.

"Oh, how would I know? I have no idea how much places cost in..."

"No," Sean interrupts. "Do you think I should *move*? Do you *mind* me moving?"

April shakes her head, slowly but definitely. "No, I don't mind. And yes, you should definitely move."

"There's no spare bedroom," Sean reminds her.

"You'll have to buy a sofa bed, then. One of those good ones with a proper mattress and springs and everything."

Sean nods. "Plus, Bonnie was right. There really is room for a folding partition in the bedroom. So I could make a box room."

"For my doughnut?"

Sean laughs. "Yes, for your doughnut."

"So, you see," April says. "It's made for you. Hell, it's almost like it was *designed* for you, Dad."

"Hell," Sean says, with a smile, "It's almost like it was designed *by* me."

Snapshot #26

35mm format, colour. A group of adults, perhaps fifteen people, are frozen in motion by the flash of the camera. Their faces are animated and joyous. A young woman to the right, behind the sofa, is throwing streamers.

So are we really doing this? Sean wonders. *Am I really going to continue listening to these, one a week, as prescribed?*

He feels like a stooge; he feels as if he has been conned into something by Catherine against his will. He should be stronger, he thinks. He should just say "no" surely? But the truth of the matter is that he likes these tapes. He enjoys them. He needs them.

Even after the pain of discovering Catherine's infidelity, he needs them, perhaps even more than before. Because something has been broken, and who else has the power to fix it if it isn't Catherine?

Today's photo is of Sean's fiftieth birthday party.

He had wanted to invite a few friends to the local pub but Catherine had pretended to be ill.

"Please," she had said. "Can we do it in a week or so, once I've shaken this horrible flu thing?" Sean had acquiesced. He hadn't been feeling particularly enthusiastic about being fifty anyway.

But when he had returned home from work on the Friday night to a dark, apparently empty house, he had regretted the decision. Because nothing, it seemed, could be more depressing than *not* celebrating his fiftieth birthday at all.

When he had turned on the light, they had screamed. April had released party poppers which had thrown streamers into the air.

He studies the faces. They had all been there: Catherine (who had taken the photo) and April, Maggie, Steve and Cheryl, Jim and Pete... There's only one face in the image that he can't put a name to. A serious blonde woman, a German temp who had replaced their usual receptionist at Nicholson-Wallace. *Petra, perhaps?* Sean thinks.

There had been food and drink and Jim had brought a PA system and a pile of disco CDs. It had been a brilliant party, perhaps the best one ever.

The only negative, in fact, had been Maggie. For Maggie, still smarting no doubt from her separation from Craig, had bent his ear for almost an hour, beneath a streetlight, at the end of the road. She had been drunk and maudlin and uncharacteristically sombre about her future. "I'm going to get a cat," Sean remembers her telling him with drunken insistence. "I'm going to get ten cats. I'm going to become a cat lady." By the time she had finished, he had felt quite miserable.

Cassette #26

Hello Munchkin,

Here's another memory for you: September, 2013. Your fiftieth.

Maggie, who was single *and* out of work at the time, offered to do all of the organising. And because it was so much easier for her to do it than it was for me to sneak around behind your back, I gave in. She made quiches and sandwiches and nibbles on sticks. She drove out to some cheap booze place in Luton and came back with enough alcohol to open a nightclub.

April was upset because Ronan, who she had just met, couldn't make it, but she soon got over that when I gave her all the party poppers to pop. Even pushing thirty, she could never resist a party-popper. She actually let one off by accident just minutes before you arrived, and we had to scramble around to clean all the streamers up so that they wouldn't be a giveaway when you walked in.

Jim supplied the music, and it was wonderful to dance again. I hadn't really danced like that since Wolverhampton. In fact, even at college parties, I was always far too busy concentrating on looking cool to let myself go. But at that party, the music was brilliant and I was drunk and yet not a smidgen more drunk than required, and I danced, I think, from about eight until it ended.

April did a real John Travolta act, too, and I was glad about that. Because she'd been an amazing little dancer until she hit

303

twelve but then had stopped completely. It was good to see that, as so often, her confidence was returning with age.

Anyway, I danced with April and I danced with you and I danced with Pete. He was forever grabbing my hand and trying to get me to jive, which, as you know, I was never very good at. But it was great fun.

At one point I was doing a very silly rock-and-roll number with Pete and he spun me around and I somehow, through the blur, noticed that you were missing, so at the end of the song I broke away and set out to find you. But you weren't in the kitchen and you weren't in the bathroom, and you weren't upstairs having a lie down either.

As I came back downstairs, Jim asked me if I was looking for you. "He's out the front having a crafty cigarette," he told me. And so I opened the door and stepped outside.

It took me a few seconds to spot you. You were at the end of the street sitting on a wall smoking. And opposite you, talking seriously, was Maggie.

I watched you for a moment. I was trying to work out whether you were having another affair, or whether it had never ended, or whether you were thinking about having one, or perhaps angrily discussing the one that was over.

I started to walk towards you to have it all out. The drink had made me feel courageous and reckless. But as I passed beneath number twenty one, the top front window opened and a man's head stuck out. "Hey! I know it's a party and everything," he said reasonably, "and I know you don't do it often, but I'm up at six for work, so if you could at least keep the bloody front door closed then that would be great. I *like* the Bee Gees, don't get me wrong. But I can hear them up here with me earplugs in, darlin'."

I checked my watch – it was almost two in the morning – and then I apologised and returned to close the front door, which stupidly I had left open. By the time I got there, you and Mags were striding back to join me.

"Everything all right?" you asked. "That idiot giving you hassle?"

"No, he was nice," I said, glancing up in case the poor guy was still there listening. "And he's right. I suppose we should turn it down a bit. People have to work."

"All good things must come to an end," Maggie said, and I thought I detected an acerbic tone to the remark. I felt it was directed at you.

We went back inside and Mags went off to get the music turned down but I held you back in the hallway. "Has it?" I asked.

"Has what, what?" you said. You were quite drunk.

"*Has* it ended?"

"It certainly looks like it," you said sadly, and for a moment I thought that the phrase contained everything I needed to know. It said that, yes, you'd had an affair. And no, I hadn't been mad to imagine it. And yes, it was over. Your tone even expressed that you were sad about the fact. And momentarily I felt better about Jake. I felt justified. But then I realised that the music had stopped. I realised that you were talking not about Mags, but about the party.

"It doesn't matter, though," you continued, "because it's been brilliant. Best party ever." And then you leaned in to kiss me. You reeked of cigarettes and whisky. "And it doesn't matter," you added, "because I love ya. And what could be more important than that?"

Things went a bit strange, for a while, after that.

I suppose I must have been worrying about you and Maggie again, because I quite subtly pushed her away. We lost the habit of seeing her for a bit, which was a shame, really. As you seemed sadder than usual, I assumed that Maggie's absence was the reason and evidently that didn't help things either.

With hindsight, though, I'd say that something different was going on. I think that once you hit fifty, we started to become aware of our mortality. Up until that point we had pretty much carried on as if everything was going to continue forever.

Mum dying was the start of it all, I reckon. That threw the notion of random, unpredictable death into the mix. And then *your* Dad died, and then Iris at work, and then Pete's wife Sylvia got cancer. The prognosis for Sylvia's cancer was pretty bad at the time, but it looks like she's going to outlive me by a mile. I wonder if these things really do just come down to chance or if she somehow led a better life than I did and deserved a better outcome.

Anyway, death was in the air. I don't think either of us ever put any of this into words. It was just a thing that lurked in the ether around us, a feeling, a slowly dawning realisation, an awareness. But I know that you were feeling it too, because you came up with that harebrained scheme to move to New Zealand. We watched a couple on some terrible television programme who had done just that and you said you wanted to do one last amazing thing before we got too old for it. The subtext, I'm pretty sure, was *before we die.*

We never did move to New Zealand, did we baby? And though I'm sad that we never managed to have that adventure together, I'm also grateful that we stayed here in Cambridge. Because if we had moved, we would never have had all these people around us when we needed them. And we were going to need them sooner than we thought.

• • •

On Thursday evening, when Sean gets home from work, he finds Maggie sitting in her car outside with the windows open. She's reading something on her smartphone and only glances up when he leans in the window. "Oh, hello!" she says.

"Hi Mags," Sean says, bemusedly.

"Look, I'm not stalking you or anything. Please don't think I'm stalking you. I just thought I'd give it ten minutes before I gave up on you because I know you're always home about now."

Sean opens his palms towards the sky. "Well, here I am," he says.

Maggie closes the windows and then climbs out. She looks at Sean over the top of the Fiat. "So cold this evening!" she exclaims. "Is now a bad time?"

Sean shakes his head. "Now's fine, Mags. Come in. Have a cuppa."

Maggie follows him to the front door saying, "I know I should have phoned, only I was driving past and I wanted to congratulate you."

Sean stands aside and ushers Maggie through the front door. "Congratulate me?"

"On your move!"

"April," Sean says.

Maggie glances back at him and nods. "It's a good job she called me because otherwise I wouldn't even have known. You secretive devil."

"It's not definite yet," Sean says, hanging his jacket over the back of a chair. "I've just come from Barclays, actually."

"The bank? Oh, how exciting."

"No, it was pretty boring, actually."

"Oh? What did they say, then? Bad news?"

"No, they're agreed. In principle. For a bridging loan."

"Right," Maggie says, her brow furrowing. "A bridging loan. Is that when... Remind me, will you? I think I know, but remind me."

"They lend you money so you can buy a place and then sell yours afterwards."

"Right. Of course. I knew that."

"Tea?" Sean offers, gesturing vaguely at the kettle.

Maggie shakes her head.

"Coffee? Beer? Wine...?"

"Really," Maggie says. "Nothing. So is it all OK, the loan and everything? Have you made an offer?"

"Tomorrow," Sean says. "Once they confirm their agreement in principle. This was sort of in principle, *in principle*, today. He has to confirm it with his boss tomorrow morning."

"And it's one of the C.R. units, right?"

"Cantabrigian Rise? It is."

"The one with the *For Sale* sign we saw?"

"No, that was a two bedroom unit. I couldn't run to that one. No, this is another one. A one bedroom unit on the fourth floor."

"That's brilliant, Sean. I could hardly believe it when April told me. They're gorgeous. We were all so proud of those. And I always look at them when I go past."

"I know. Pricey, though."

"I'll bet."

"The one bed costs almost the same as this place."

"But it'll do you so much good to move."

"You approve, then?" Sean asks. He feels strangely as if, without Catherine to consult, his decisions are somehow illegitimate.

"Oh, how could I not?" Maggie says. "You don't want to be rattling around in this big place, do you?"

"No," Sean says, trying to stop his mind straying to the obvious loss which has caused this new status of *rattling around*. He opens the refrigerator and pulls out a bottle of beer. "Are you sure?" he asks.

Maggie rolls her eyes. "Oh, go on, then," she says. "Just one. Honestly, you're like a little devil on my shoulder."

Snapshot #27

Printed digital photo, colour. A man stands beside a shiny, racing green sports car. He is smiling but looking vaguely embarrassed at the same time.

Sean studies the printed page and remembers the day he swapped the Renault for the Mazda. He had taken the Mégane in for its yearly service and there, on the forecourt, freshly washed and polished, had been the little green sports car. It was priced at five thousand nine hundred pounds, which Sean knew was also just about the value of the Mégane (he had looked it up just a few weeks before).

He had handed in the keys at the service desk and then instead of jumping in a taxi back to work, as planned, had walked twice around the MX5 before trying the door and lowering himself into the driver's seat. He had caressed the steering wheel – it was made of polished mahogany. A salesman had quickly appeared and, less than an hour later, he had driven it off the forecourt, imagining how Catherine would laugh, her hair whipping in the wind, when he picked her up that evening. April was long gone from the family nest and it was just the two of them now, ready for a fresh round of adventures. The car seemed, to Sean, to be a symbol of that. Catherine would be thrilled, he thought.

But from the very beginning she had seemed to hold back her joy. It was as if the car was symbolic not of fighting against ageing, but perhaps of ageing itself. Whatever was going on in her head, even before her back pain made the whole thing impossible, there had been something reticent, something determinedly joyless about her reception of the car.

She had teased him about it endlessly, too, to the point where it started to annoy him. She had nicknamed the car his "Mid Life Crisis" and later refused to call it an MX5 at all, referring to it endlessly as the MLC instead. As in, "Can you meet me in town with the MLC so I can bring the shopping home?" or, "Do you want to go to April's on the train, or are we taking the MLC?"

It was undoubtedly true that the car *was* a symptom of Sean's midlife crisis. And the fact that a consequential chunk of that crisis was his desire to seduce his wife anew, to show her they weren't too old to have fun, to demonstrate that he could still surprise her, only seemed to make the bite of her mockery even harder to bear.

Cassette #27

Hi Sean.

I don't think I'm going to be able to talk for long today. I've just started another round of my trial chemo and it *definitely* isn't a placebo. This time around, it has knocked me for six, in fact, it has left me so utterly, utterly exhausted, that I barely managed to sit up and talk to you this afternoon. I'm so sorry.

The oncologist came around just after you left and said they were having a case meeting tomorrow to review my progress, and though I'm hoping, for your sake, that it will show it's working – I know that you're desperately clinging to that idea – I can't help but think what a relief it will be if they tell me that it isn't and that I can stop taking this poison, because poison, it is. From the second they hook me up to the IV I can feel it burning my veins. And the tiredness it induces is truly sapping my will to live. How ironic is that?

Anyway, it's time to get on with these tapes. I'm approaching the end of the photos I chose and though we're all still pretending that I'm going to live forever, it's probably just as well that these are nearly finished.

It's time to talk about that bloody car.

You came out to the shelter to pick me up one Thursday evening, and I couldn't believe my eyes.

The first thing I thought of was Jake's MG. It was even the same colour. So if my initial reaction was a bit off, that will be why. My back had been hurting all day, too, and the second thing I noticed was how difficult it was to clamber in and out of. That made me feel not younger, as intended, but older. And then you asked me, for some reason, if I wanted to drive out to Brampton Wood and I said "No," but couldn't explain why. You seemed put out by that and suggested dinner in Grantchester instead and I spent the whole drive out there wondering if you had somehow found out about what had happened with Jake; if this was all some elaborate scheme to take the Mickey, or to be more like him, or just, perhaps, to let me know that you knew.

So we didn't get off to the best start with the car, did we?

You were as excited as a three-year-old with a brand new tricycle, so I did my very best to be enthusiastic. I just don't think I was very convincing. I was too busy trying to decode the subtext; too busy fighting my own guilt, no doubt.

It was a cool, damp, September evening, but you insisted on having the top down and the music on – you were playing Van Morrison – and by the time we got to The Rupert Brooke my neck was so stiff that I could barely turn my head.

We went through a difficult patch after that, and it was largely to do with the car, though I'm sure, if we had seen a shrink, it would have turned out to be symbolic of something much bigger. You believed, I think, that I had invented my back pain as some kind of protest about the car, and to counter this I did my best to pretend that I loved the damned thing, even when I could barely lever myself out of it. We ended up acting out this dodgy drama of half-lies and unspoken truths, all revolving around the subject of my back and that stupid, stupid sports car.

The pinnacle of this idiocy was, of course, the trip to Edinburgh. Even the question, when you asked me, was a trick one.

"How do you fancy a romantic weekend in Edinburgh?" you asked. "Or will it be too hard on your back?"

There was no way I could say no to that, was there?

By the time we got there, I was virtually paralysed. I literally couldn't move for pain and you had to lever me from the passenger seat and almost carry me, whimpering, to the hotel room. The hotel organised for a doctor to visit and he prescribed some very strong painkillers which left me feeling woolly and stoned, but which still didn't completely dull the pain. And then on Sunday night, like a piece of clunky origami, you folded me back into the car, and drove me back home. I took a double (entirely prohibited) dose of painkillers for that, along with a double dose of Scotch at the hotel bar, and I'm happy to say that I don't remember a thing.

I was never quite sure whether you thought that I was actually lying about being in pain just to piss you off about the car, or if you thought that the pain was real, but psychosomatic. Either way, it amounted to pretty much the same thing. You were annoyed with me and, knowing that it was unreasonable, you did your best to hide it. And because you *knew* it was unreasonable, you lied and denied being angry the only time I ever tried to discuss it with you. Isn't that amazing, though? Isn't it incredible that as well as we knew each other after thirty-something years together, there were still things we simply couldn't discuss.

Your anger didn't fade, either, did it? As you ferried me back and forth to Addenbrooke's for X-rays and CAT-scans and God knows what else, none of which came up with anything, it was all just grist to the mill. It was all proof that, other than car-envy, there was nothing really wrong with me after all.

You know the way they say that dogs and cats can smell cancer on people? Well, I've often wondered whether we don't have the same gift. I've often wondered whether on some subconscious level you hadn't realised that I was dying – whether that wasn't the reason you felt so angry. And whether that wasn't the real reason you felt so desperate for us to go whizzing around in a sports car while we still could.

Eventually, about a year after you'd bought it, you gave in to the inevitable and swapped the MLC for something you were actually able to lift me in and out of, and around the same time, in desperation, I tried yoga with Maggie, which actually seemed to ease my pain, for a while.

I'm sure that even this coincidence you saw as some kind of victory lap on my behalf. My brief little pain-free celebration that I'd finally made you get rid of your beloved car.

So, secretly, you stayed resentful towards me, and I towards you for not believing me. And it wasn't until the real cause of the pain was found that the whole problem went away. Though I have to say that, in the end, I think I preferred it when we didn't know, even if that did mean we were angry with each other. Because even when we were angry I loved you. The loving never stopped.

• • •

Sean is eating a tuna sandwich in the landscaped gardens of Nicholson-Wallace. It's nearly the end of September, but it's a beautiful sunny day. An Indian Summer everyone keeps saying, and every time someone mentions it, Sean resolves to look it up and find out where the term comes from, before promptly forgetting all about it.

He's just picking up the second half of his sandwich when his phone, in his pocket, starts to vibrate.

"Hello Little Daughter," he says, on answering.

"I've told you to stop calling me that," April says. "I'm going by a new handle now. I'm calling myself *The Blob*. I'm on my break so I can't talk for long, but I was just wondering if there was any news on the flat front?"

Sean laughs. "You must have a sixth sense or something," he says. "I just upped my offer, like, a minute ago."

"They refused you then?"

"They did. But I did go in a bit low so I was kind of expecting it."

"And what about this time? If they refuse, are you going to carry on haggling or is that it?"

"I was just debating that," Sean says, watching a robin eyeing his crumbs from the far corner of the bench. "And I think I've decided to stop. To sort of leave it in the hands of the Gods. I *could* go higher, but things would start to get tight. And I'm a bit too old, I think, to start worrying about how to pay the electricity bill."

"Sounds fair," April says. "But I hope you get it."

"Do you really?"

"Yes. I think it would be great."

"Well, good. Let's cross everything. And how's the baby?"

"Oh, kicking like crazy. He's all elbows and knees at the moment. I think he's practising to be a gymnast."

"It was basketball last time."

"Maybe he'll do both," April says. "Simultaneously. Gym-ball or basket-nast or something. A whole new sport."

"I'd like to see that," Sean says distractedly. His phone has begun to vibrate again, so he pulls it away from his ear to check the screen. "Sorry, I've got another call. Hold on a second, will you?"

"Is it them? Is it the estate agent's?" April asks.

"Yes," Sean says. "Won't be long."

Two minutes later, when Sean attempts to recover the call, it's not April he finds on the end of the line but Maggie.

"How did that happen?" he says.

"I'm sorry?"

"I was talking to April. I didn't phone you."

"Ooh," Maggie says, with mock distaste. "Don't sound so *keen,* Sean. Just tell it like it is, won't you?"

Sean laughs. "It's not that I don't *love* talking to you Maggie. It's just I was on the phone to April. I put her on hold and suddenly I'm talking to you. I don't see how that happened."

"*I* phoned *you* Sean," Maggie says. "Do you want me to bugger off?"

"No, you're OK," Sean says, glaring briefly at the screen of the phone. The call with April seems to have been dropped. "Was it for something specific?"

"Not really. I just wanted to know what the news was. About the flat out at C.R."

"Did April call you?" Sean asks.

"No. Not at all. Why?"

"It's just... that's weird, that's all. You both calling me."

"Why, *is* there news?"

"I just found out. Literally ten seconds ago."

"You found out what?"

"They said yes. The sellers, that is. They just accepted my offer."

"Oh, gosh!" Maggie exclaims. "Gosh, that's brilliant news, Sean."

"Is it?"

"Yes. You're not having doubts, are you?"

"I'm not sure," Sean says. "I'm just a bit shocked, I suppose. Look... it's... lovely chatting, Mags, but would you mind terribly if I phoned you back this evening? I was on the line to April and I lost her. She'll be wondering what happened."

"Of course," Maggie says. "Kids come first. How about a pint somewhere? To celebrate? This evening?"

"Maybe at the weekend," Sean offers. "I need, I don't know, time to digest it all, I think."

When Sean tells her the news, April shrieks. "I'm so excited!" she says.

"Are you?"

"Yes! Of course. Aren't you?"

Sean swallows with difficulty. "I don't know," he says. "That's the truth. It suddenly feels very... I don't know... symbolic. Final. Do you know what I mean?"

318

"Sure..." April says, doubtfully. "Well, it isn't final though, is it? Not until you sign on the dotted line."

"No."

"When's that supposed to be happening, by the way?"

"Saturday morning. If I go through with it."

"Why the sudden doubts, Dad? Is it the hassle of moving? *We* could help with that. Or the money? Or is it ... it's not because of Mum, is it?"

"We lived there for nearly twenty years," Sean says. "We chose every bit of furniture together. Every roll of wallpaper. Your mother hung most of it."

"I know. But isn't that why?"

"Why what?"

"Well, why this is necessary."

"I thought so," Sean says. "But now that it's real, I'm not sure."

"Do you want me to come up, Dad? So we can talk it through? I could come this weekend – maybe even drag Ronan along. He's very sensible about things like this. Very logical. Very detached. That's helpful. Well, sometimes it is. Sometimes it's really bloody annoying."

"You don't want to be driving all the way to Cambridge," Sean says unconvincingly.

"Hum," April says. "OK. I'll see you Saturday morning, then."

"I'm *signing* Saturday morning," Sean reminds her. "Well, I'm supposed to be signing."

"OK. Then I'll see you Friday night."

• • •

Sean is just pulling three curries from the freezer when the doorbell rings.

He dumps them on the counter and walks to the front door. "Hello," he says as he opens it. "You're early."

"Hi Dad," April says. "I got off earlier than usual, so..."

"But mainly it's because she drives like a maniac," Ronan jibes.

"That's not very reassuring. Perhaps you should let Ronan drive?"

"Fast but careful," April tells Sean. "That's me. Whereas Ronan is slow and distracted. He's always looking at the clouds or the cows in the fields or something. Believe me, you *don't* want him doing the driving."

"I do tend to look around a bit," Ronan admits.

April follows Sean into the kitchen and Ronan dumps their bag at the base of the stairs before joining them.

"How do you feel about curry?" Sean asks.

"Ooh," April says. "*Your* curry?" As an aside to Ronan, she adds, "Dad's curries are the best."

"No, these are Sainsbury's, I'm afraid," Sean explains, moving to the counter and gesturing at the frosty packaging. "But they're all right. I've got Rogan Josh and..."

"Can we get pizza?" April asks. "Those aren't defrosted yet, are they?"

Ronan laughs heartily.

"Pizza?" Sean asks, then, "What's the joke, Ronan?"

"Oh, he's just taking the piss out of me because all I want to eat is pizza," April explains. "It's a kind of craving, I suppose."

"Kind of, you say? No, that's exactly what it is," Ronan says. "We've had to have pizza five times this week. And then she eats the remainders for breakfast and lunch."

"Four times," April says.

320

"Five. Saturday – in the restaurant – and then Sunday, Monday, Wednesday and again yesterday at home."

"Monday was leftovers," April says. "That doesn't count."

"It was pizza leftovers though, was it?" Ronan asks, grinning broadly. "Or was it not?"

"Oh, whatever," April says, batting away his words with the back of one hand. "Can we though, Dad? Have pizza?"

Sean laughs and shrugs. "Sure, whatever. Ronan you can still have curry if you want."

Ronan shakes his head. "Nah," he says. "Pizza'll be grand."

"Are you sure that's a balanced diet, though?" Sean asks, as he returns the packages to the freezer.

"Oh, don't you start," April says.

Ronan wide eyes Sean and nods exaggeratedly. "It's what I keep telling her," he says. "But Princess Pizza will not be told."

"Just stop, both of you," April says. "I can't stand it when you gang up on me. Plus I always get the one with all the veggies on it, so it's *fine*. It's what the baby wants. He's asking for it."

"He's Italian, not Irish, apparently," Ronan says.

April puts one hand on her hip and looks at Ronan with exaggerated disdain. "Well, maybe he *is*," she says. "Maybe I had a secret fling with the guy at Domino's."

Ronan pulls a face. "You remember what your man at Domino's looked like, do you?" he says. "Good luck to you there, girl."

Ronan returns to the car for two six-packs of beer he has in the boot.

"I'm not sure we need twelve bottles, do we?" Sean comments. "Especially with April not drinking."

"It's all part of Ronan's theory," April says.

"I call it the beer oracle," Ronan explains, removing the cap from a bottle and handing it to Sean. "If you can't make a major decision you just have to spend a night talking about it and getting blathered. By the morning, you'll know."

"Is that an Irish thing?" Sean asks.

"Nope. It's a Ronan thing," April says. "Be afraid. Be very afraid."

Ronan raises his bottle to tap it against Sean's. "Cheers," he says.

After much discussion about who does the best pizza, Sean gives in to his daughter's wishes and orders them from Pizza Express via Deliveroo.

They then move to the lounge and, while they wait, Ronan keeps them supplied with beers from the refrigerator. April, for her part, drinks the best part of a litre of apple juice.

They discuss April's job. She's in the process of handing over to a guy who will be replacing her during her maternity leave, but it's not, she says, going smoothly.

Sean asks her what the problem is and she laughs. "Basically, the problem is that he's an *idiot*."

"Then again," Ronan interjects, "she's always telling me that *I'm* an idiot, so..."

April pulls a face at her father. "He pretty often *is*," she says.

They discuss the baby for a while, with a repeat detour via the subject of April's pizza diet. "You've never had a craving," April says, "So you wouldn't understand."

"Did April's ma go through the whole pizza thing?" Ronan asks.

There follows a momentary pause; a stolen, awkward glance from April to her partner, and an involuntary wince, just visible around Ronan's eyes, before Sean says, "It's fine,

Ronan, really. And no, not really. She ate quite a few bacon sandwiches. So maybe that was her craving. Oh, and cheese. Lots of cheddar cheese."

April raises her palms to the ceiling. "Cheeeese," she says, exaggeratedly. "Cheese? Pizza? Any connection there? I rest my case."

"So, on names," Ronan says, clearly trying to change the subject. "April says you don't like 'Giles'. So we were thinking about—"

"Hang on," April interrupts. "*I'm* the one who doesn't like 'Giles'. It's a wanker, banker sort of name, that's all."

"Is it?" Ronan asks.

"It's quite posh," Sean comments. "But I quite like it actually. Giles. Yes, I had a friend at school called Giles. Giles Anderton. He *was* quite posh. But very nice."

"He's *not* being called *Giles*," April says, rolling her eyes. "No, we're almost settled on *Jack*, actually."

Sean purses his lips and nods thoughtfully. "Yes," he says. "Jack's a good name."

"It's nice, isn't it? Sort of unpretentious?"

"Jack Nicholson," Sean says. "Jack Dempsey. Jack the Ripper..."

"Ooh, they're all pretty butch, aren't they?" April says, doubtfully.

"Especially Jack the Ripper," Ronan says, laughing. "He was as butch as butch can be."

"Jack Twist," Sean offers.

"Who's Jack Twist?"

"He was one of the gay guys in whatsit Mountain, wasn't he? In Brokeback..."

"Ah, all right," April says. "Well, as long as my son has the possibility to explore his feminine side too, then that's OK."

"You boys sure found a way to explore your feminine sides up there on Brokeback Mountain," Ronan says, mockingly.

"And there's always Jack Kerouac," April offers, ignoring him.

"And Jack Dee."

"So, Jack Patrick?" Sean asks. "Or will it be Jack Connolly?"

"We haven't decided yet," April says. "It might end up being Connolly-Patrick. Or Patrick-Connolly. Would you mind?"

Sean shrugs. "Not at all," he says. "But no second name, then?"

"Oh, don't get us started on that," April says. "It's taken us a month to settle on bloody Jack."

Once the Deliveroo guy has been and gone, Ronan heads to the kitchen for more beer.

"I'm not sure I want another one," Sean says, when he returns.

"Just trust the process," Ronan instructs.

"The thing is, I think I've decided, really," Sean tells him. "So, I'm not sure I need to spend the weekend with a hangover after all."

"Hangover, shlangover," Ronan says, pushing the bottle forcefully into Sean's hand.

They eat in the lounge, the three pizza boxes open on the coffee table.

"Oh, God, I'd forgotten how good these are," April says, tipping back her head and lowering a slice of her Romana Padana into her mouth.

"So, you've decided, you say?" Ronan says. "That sounds positive."

"I think so," Sean replies, between mouthfuls. "Gosh, these *are* good, aren't they? Yes, I've tried to be logical about it all. I even wrote out a list of pros and cons."

"That's good. That's my kind of thinking," Ronan says.

"And?" April asks. She rubs her belly and adds, "Umm... See, happy baby! Baby like pizza. He says it's molto bene. What are your pros and cons, then, Dad?"

"Well, the apartment *is* perfect," Sean tells them.

"Right..."

"And I do have to move at some point. Because it's crazy staying in such a big house."

"That makes sense, too," Ronan says.

"And I hate gardening. That really *was* your mother's thing."

"Yes, I noticed that it wasn't looking its best," April says.

Sean takes a deep breath and then, speaking more rapidly than usual, says, "But I don't think I'm ready. That's the main thing I've realised."

April's mouth falls open. Realising it's full of pizza, she quickly hides behind her hand. "Oh!" she says, swallowing and then licking her teeth.

"I *might* be ready soon. Perhaps even in a few months. But I'm not quite ready now, I don't think."

"Not ready," Ronan repeats, sounding unconvinced.

"No. So that's where I'm at."

"But the place you've seen might be gone in a couple of months," Ronan points out, concernedly.

"That's true. It almost certainly *will* be gone. Especially at the price they're asking."

"So, what would it take for you to be ready?" Ronan asks.

Sean shrugs. "I don't know. Time, perhaps?"

"Don't push him, Ro," April says.

325

"I'm just saying that there might be a way for Sean to *feel* ready. If he wants to."

"I said don't push him, sweetie," April says. Then addressing Sean, she continues, "I think you should wait until you're good and ready, Dad. And I know that's what Mum would have said, too."

Ronan clears his throat. "Can I?" he asks.

"Can you what?" April asks, shortly.

"Can I say something without you biting my head off?"

"Of course you can, Ronan," Sean says. "Say anything you want."

April sighs. "Just don't try to–"

"No, let him speak," Sean insists. "It's fine."

Ronan puts his half-eaten slice of pizza down and presses his fingertips together. "So, at the risk of being called Mister Spock," he says.

"Mister Spock?"

"It's what I call him when he gets all logical on me," April explains.

"At the risk of being called Mister Spock," Ronan repeats, "I've never been much of a believer in being led by your mind."

"I'm sorry?" Sean says.

"It's *your* mind," Ronan says. "It's your organ, and waiting for it to be ready for something is a bit like waiting for your own hand to pass you a cup of tea instead of telling it to just do it." He reaches, theatrically, for his beer to demonstrate this. "Or a bottle of beer," he adds.

"I'm not sure I'm following you," Sean says.

April, who catches his regard, rolls her eyes again.

"If it makes sense for you to do it. Because, a) it's the perfect place for you – your words not mine, Sean – and b) you need to move, because this place is too big, and, c) it's at a good price, then *change* your mind. *Tell* it you're ready. Don't let some nebulous biochemical process in your head make the decision for you. Your brain is a tool. And you're the one in control, Sean. Or at least, you should be."

"Now, *that*, you see," April says through laughter, "is one hundred percent Ronan. I told you he'd be irritatingly logical. But in the end it comes down to what it always comes down to. Do you want to decide with your head or with your heart?"

Sean nods. "Yes," he says. "Yes, I suppose that is what it boils down to. My head says move, but my heart says I'm not ready."

Ronan laughs genuinely. "Your head or your heart?" he repeats.

April pulls a face. "Yes, Mister Spock. His head or his heart."

"Well, as far as I'm aware," Ronan says, swigging at his beer bottle and looking vaguely smug, "One of those two things is a biochemical computer, the most powerful computer on the bleeding planet and designed specifically for thinking. And the other one's a pump. So I know which one I'd favour for making decisions."

"A pump," Sean repeats, grinning and nodding. "That's good. I like it."

Sean sleeps badly that night. He dreams tortured dreams of heavy limbs which refuse to respond to his orders, arms that won't lift bottles of beer or cups of tea, legs that won't walk... He dreams of queues of people that never seem to advance and forms that for one reason or another cannot be filled. And because of all the beer, he has to get up four times to pee.

But when he wakes up in the morning light, the decision, despite his tiredness and despite the hangover, is clear. Perhaps Ronan's beer oracle works after all.

When he gets downstairs, April is already up, eating the remains of last night's pizza.

"Oh, hi, Dad," she says. "Ronan's gone out for a run. So, what are we up to today?"

Sean shrugs. "I don't know what you're up to," he says. "But I think I'm buying a flat."

Snapshot #28

Printed digital photo, colour. A man and a woman are sitting on an old grey sofa beneath a large, roofed porch. They are raising their glasses and smiling falsely. They are quite possibly mouthing the word, "Cheese."

It is Sunday evening and April and Ronan have just left.

Sean has placed the printed photo on the table and is caressing it gently with one fingertip as he struggles to remember.

His mind, though, isn't playing ball. It keeps drifting to other things, to yesterday's flat-purchase, or to April's coming baby, or to Ronan's cheeky Irish humour, or to Catherine's affair. Anything in fact except this photo.

He sits for almost half an hour trying to summon specific memories before he slips the cassette into the machine, but with the exception of a few facts, such as the town where they stayed – Fayence — and the fact that there had been a pool, it's all gone. The house had probably been lovely, he thinks. There had been noisy cicadas by day and even noisier frogs by night. And he remembers the sofa in the picture and the rainstorm. But that's it. It's not a lot from a ten-day holiday. But then, this was no ordinary ten-day holiday.

Cassette #28

Hello Sean.

It's been three weeks since the last tape – at *least* three weeks – and to be honest, I can't even remember what the last one was about. But I don't suppose it matters much. They're all just episodes, really.

These have not, as you know, been good weeks for me. The trial I was in has been interrupted because I'm not the only one, it seems, who can't take these doses of titty-bitty-marzipan, as we all call it around here.

That was my invention, by the way. Are you proud of me?

Anyway, three of the others in the trial have died already, so I suppose I'm lucky to still be here at all.

I've been in and out like a yo-yo these last few weeks, which is why I haven't been able to finish off my tapes.

You've been so sweet, Sean. So sweet and so brave.

We're all still pretending that I'm going to get through this; we're all saying that some miracle is going to happen. April, bless her, keeps bringing me printouts of the cancer curing properties of cannabis, and aspirin, and nettle tea, and God knows what else. And I keep promising to try them all when I get home.

I think April is the only person who really still believes that might happen. In fact, I chatted to the psychologist about her this morning. I wanted to know whether I should ram the whole thing down her throat, so to speak. I wanted to know if I should sit her down and chant, "I'm dying, April, I'm dying,

April; your mother is going to be dead soon." Perhaps if I said it over and over again she'd get it in the end. But the psychologist said that denial is sometimes a kind of protection thing. Like a circuit breaker or something. "She'll deal with it," he said, "when she's ready."

You're saying the same things as April, too. You're still talking about summer holidays and where we might go but I can see in your eyes that you don't believe it. But thank you, my darling, for pretending. It's so much more fun to look at those brochures of Lanzarote and imagine us all there. It's so much less depressing than sitting in silence waiting for me to pop my clogs and, believe me, that really is the way most of the visiting families behave around here.

So, back to today's photo, which is of our last *actual* holiday and, by the time you listen to this, our last *ever* holiday, I suppose. And God, what a waste of a great holiday that was.

I've been reading one of the self-help books from the hospital library; it's about dealing with one's own death, and there's this huge chunk about living in the moment. Because, like the Buddhists apparently say, there is no future and there is no past. They're both just things that happen in your mind. In reality, there is only ever the present moment. The problem, it seems, is that people with terminal diseases (*and* old people, apparently, facing old age and eventually their own deaths) lose their ability to live in the moment. They're so worried about the end of the journey that they fail to enjoy themselves getting there. Which is pretty understandable, but still a terrible waste. A waste that is perfectly illustrated by our time in the south of France.

Do you know, I hardly remember any of it? It's as if the whole thing happened behind a big, frosty window.

Because of my back pain, I had been going back and forth to the doctor, the clinic and Addenbrooke's Hospital, but still nothing had been found. (Though I do sometimes wonder if the doctors weren't looking through a frosty window, as well. They certainly didn't seem to be very good at spotting anything on those scans).

Anyway, the current theory we were working on was a slipped disc and it wasn't until my normal doctor sent me (finally) for blood tests, that anyone even began to suspect anything at all.

Because, ever since the car, my back pain had been, let's say, a difficult subject, I told you as little as possible about what was going on. You seemed to have exhausted whatever sympathy you had for my back and any mention of it, or doctors, or tests, seemed to be met with a blank expression, or occasionally even an eye-roll.

So I even used to hide the bus tickets so that you wouldn't know I'd been out there again. I felt, I suppose, embarrassed about it all.

The news came at the end of July. Because of something in the blood tests, too much Billy Rubin or something, they sent me for a fresh set of scans. I wasn't expecting anything much to show up – I'd pretty much given up hope by then – but when they phoned me up to ask me to come back in to discuss the results, it was unusual enough that I knew something was wrong.

By the time I got home from the meeting, I knew. Oh, I didn't know how advanced the whole thing was quite yet and we didn't know it had spread, either, but my back pain finally had a cause, and it wasn't a good one.

I didn't manage to tell you, though, did I? Even before I got home, you had sent me a text message saying something like, "Where are you? When are you home? I have a surprise for you!"

I was on the bus when I read it. "Oh boy, and do I have one for you," I thought, grimly.

You were all excited when I got in. You'd found, and booked, a villa in France, and you were on a website busily booking plane tickets and a hire car. Should I have told you there and then? I don't know. But I couldn't. It honestly felt as if the space for me to tell you at that moment simply wasn't there.

I thought we'd have to cancel. I thought the hospital dates would make the whole French escapade an impossibility. But when I phoned them up on the following Monday morning, the dates, miraculously, all fitted. I had a meeting booked with the anaesthetist two days before we were due to go away and the surgery two days after we got back.

Now, as you know, I have always been a sucker for a sign. And I took that as a sign. As big, pointy, unmissable sign. Is that silly of me? I expect you'll think so.

It's strange because even then, even before we really knew anything, the idea of one last holiday together was on my mind. So perhaps, deep down, that's why I kept it quiet. Perhaps, deep down, I knew.

Whatever the reason, I decided to say nothing. You knew something was wrong, of course, and you kept on asking me if everything was all right. You even thought I had the hump about going to France at one point.

There was only one moment when I nearly told you. We were in that pizzeria in that town on the hill – Mons, was it? Anyway, I almost told you there. The view was beautiful and the sky was so blue and I felt briefly happy and then overwhelmed with sadness – the way you can sometimes swing from one to the other – and it was on the tip of my tongue when that waiter tripped over with our wine. And again, I took it as a sign. I took his tipping wine over me as some kind of divine intervention.

I was weird for the whole ten days, I know that. And because I was weird, you, in turn, were worried. We didn't have much fun.

Everything about that trip, the flight, the drive, that gorgeous villa, the pool, the meals, even your presence, it was all wasted. And it was wasted because, as the book so clearly explains, I had lost my ability to live in the moment. Perhaps if I'd read the damned book beforehand it might have helped us have a better holiday.

On the last day there was that big summer storm.

It was very dramatic, with thunder and lightning, and rain like I'd never seen before. But it was warm, all the same – warm enough in the morning for us to still swim in the pool. I think that moment, swimming with you, with those cool hard drops whacking us on the shoulders, was the only moment in the entire ten days I was actually present. The rest of the time I was lost inside my head, lost in my fears for the future, I suppose.

The rain continued all day, and in the afternoon I put my jacket on and you that big blue jumper, and we sat on the tatty grey sofa they had on the porch and watched the raindrops hitting the surface of the pool. The outdoor sofa reminded me, bizarrely, of sitting in Mum's garden in Margate.

I'd pretty much avoided drink for the entire holiday for the simple reason that I was scared it would loosen my tongue. And that's the exact reason I let myself drink that afternoon. I had an operation booked in three days' time, after all. I *had* to tell you.

334

We drank the best part of two bottles of champagne between us and for a moment the alcohol enabled me to forget. It let me connect with you again and we snuggled together on the sofa and stared out at the crazy rain. You had two French cigarettes left, so we had one each and felt dizzy.

And then you said, as if from nowhere, "You know how we discussed moving to New Zealand?"

I started to tear-up immediately, because I knew instantly what was coming – I could sense it.

"Well, what about France?" you said. "What about somewhere like here? What if I took a year out or something? Maybe if we used our savings we could do it in a way that would allow us to..." Your voice, which had sounded manic, petered out halfway through. At first, you thought that I was laughing at you and you were hurt. "The idea's not *that* stupid, for Christ's sake," you said. But then you realised that my convulsions weren't laughter. You realised that I was sobbing.

You held me for a while, just like you did when Mum died. You pressed your forehead to mine and cried with me. You didn't even need to know what it was about to join with me in crying. You always had that amazing ability to empathise.

When I was all cried out, or at least I thought I was, you said, gravely, "It's that bad, huh?"

I nodded. I couldn't speak.

"Are you leaving me?" you asked, "Is that it?"

I exploded into fresh tears, because no thought could have been further from the truth. All I wanted, right then, was to stay with you forever.

Eventually, I managed to whisper the word, but you didn't hear me properly, or didn't want to believe that you'd heard me properly, so you made me repeat it, twice.

"Cancer," I said again. And then the third time it came out in a sort of annoyed shouty voice. *"Cancer!"*

We sat and stared at each other for a bit. It seems like it was ages, but that might be my mind playing tricks. And then your face crumpled again and you threw your arms around me and pulled me tight.

I felt so safe, wrapped in your arms. It's crazy, but momentarily, I felt happy – as happy as I have ever felt. I felt so cosy surrounded by you and that woolly jumper. It seemed impossible to me that I could feel that safe and yet still be in so much danger.

And as if you were reading my mind, you said, through tears, "We'll beat this. Whatever it is, we'll beat this together. You'll see. You can't... you know... You just can't. Not when I love you this much. I won't let you."

• • •

Sean does not listen to a tape the following weekend. He tells himself that it's because he's too busy; he tells himself that it's because he's too *tired*. And these things are true. He *is* tired. He *is* busy.

Between working and food-shopping and laundry, between repeated appointments at the bank and getting the flat tyre on the car fixed, and three separate surveyors' appointments at the house, Sean finds that for the first time in ages he is quite literally overbooked.

Even the weekend, generally so empty, turns out to be something of a rush. Sean has to visit his mother on Saturday lunchtime (Perry has had to rush off to Hong Kong for some reason) and Maggie phones repeatedly until Sean caves in and meets her for the promised celebration drink. But the real reason, he admits to himself, is that there's only one envelope left. And as much as Sean instructs his mind to make itself ready, he doesn't seem able to convince himself that he truly is.

He's scared of what Catherine will say to him in her final message, he realises. And he's afraid, above all, of reaching the end of this process – afraid of finding himself truly alone, once again. Because yes, for all the shocks and for all the misery, this has been a dialogue. Catherine has continued to make him happy and angry, and sad, almost as if she was still alive. And he has loved her and cried with her and, yes, raged against her, here in the confines of his own head. Of course he's scared of letting her go.

On Sunday evening – his usual listening slot – the fear reaches a crescendo, leaving him nervous and shaky and unable to settle, a state which only partly abates during his working week.

Amidst the sudden and surprising emptiness of the following weekend – the phone does not ring once, there are no visits – his fear of that final envelope becomes acute – a terror almost – and he finds himself unable to eat or sleep or even think about anything else.

By Sunday evening he's feeling trembly and shattered and, realising that he simply can't face another week of anticipation, he steels himself, downs a dram of whisky, and carries the box to the lounge. "Time to get this over with," he says, quietly. "Time to be brave."

He glances at the box and then looks nervously around the room, scanning for potential distractions before he starts.

Outside, beyond the window, a neighbour's child is learning to ride a bicycle with her father. He remembers trying to teach April – she had fallen off and scraped her knee and had cried for hours. She had finally managed it for the first time with Catherine while Sean had been out at work. He'd felt unreasonably jealous about that, he remembers.

He crosses the room and pulls the curtains closed. He doesn't want to see the little girl cycling past. He doesn't want any potential visitors peering in on him, either.

And then, finally, he returns to the sofa, lifts the lid and pulls the final envelope from the box.

He senses, immediately, that this one is different from the others, both heavier and more bulky.

He swallows with difficulty. His breath is laboured – it feels as if someone is sitting on his chest. He wonders briefly if he's having a heart attack. Wouldn't that be ironic? To die before he even reached the end of his late wife's messages? He rips open the flap. He tips the contents onto his lap.

A single photo, once again, but this time, not one, but two of the little cassettes. They are marked "A" and "B".

Snapshot #29

Polaroid, colour. A woman lies in a hospital bed. Sitting either side of her, their arms linked around her shoulders, are a man and a woman. The young woman is touching a necklace with her free hand, and a screwed up ball of discarded wrapping paper rests on the bed. All three people in the photo are smiling unconvincingly.

Tears well up in Sean's eyes the second they focus on the photo. For it's the last family snapshot ever taken.

It had been the Saturday before April's birthday and she had travelled up to Cambridge to collect her gift beforehand because, as she explained it, the following Friday, when her birthday actually fell, she'd be working. But they had all known the truth. They had all feared that the following Saturday might be too late. And tragically, they'd been right.

Though Catherine had picked out the necklace some months before, she had been so dosed up on morphine that day that she'd barely been present to hand it over.

Once April had left for London, her watery eyes belying her emotions, Sean had returned, for a while, to lie next to his sleeping wife. She had murmured something that sounded like "dream" a few times in her sleep. And Sean had prayed that she was having good dreams.

Cassette #29-A

Hello Sean.

I'm awake early this morning, and I'm just about with-it. I haven't had to hit the morphine much yet, and the pain, unusually, is bearable. That seems unfair, really. I'd so much rather have been awake like this when you and April were here yesterday – was it yesterday? Time stretches and shrinks these days, so it's hard to tell.

Still, my mind is clearer today so at least I can crack on with these damned tapes. I must say, I think I've had enough of them. I've had enough of it all.

I'm nearing the end, now. There are shadows closing in on me from the edges. I'll tell you about them maybe if I find the time and the energy, but both of those things are becoming precious and rare, so I'd better just get on with the things I need to say.

I've been dreaming about the day I met you, you know. I've been dreaming about Dreamland. Isn't that funny?

You know how people always say that your life flashes before your eyes? Well, perhaps that's what this is. Perhaps that's why I'm dreaming of the very beginning. Whatever the reason, it's a lovely dream.

In it, I'm there, sitting at my turnstile. I feel exactly as I felt, back then. Young and a bit horny, I suppose. And nervous, too. And insecure about... well, about everything, really. It's hell being young. We forget that as we get older, but the dream has reminded me just how scary everything seems when you're eighteen. The dream felt so real.

Anyway, I'm there in Dreamland, and I'm thinking about Phil and what a waste of space he is, and wondering if I should dump him, and I'm wondering if Mum has any food in the freezer other than chips, and I'm hoping that Stinky Dennis won't be there drinking beer in his underpants when I get home. My life feels small and dull and predictable. There doesn't seem to be much to look forward to, really. And then suddenly, there you are, walking past with your friends, that restrained smile on your lips, that glint in your eye.

Only because this is a dream, I can see things in the glint. In fact, I can see my whole life ahead of me reflected in your eyes. I can see our college years and April being born, and punting along the Cam. I can see our holiday in Greece and April's first day at school and almost losing you, and getting you back again. And I can see things that can't really be seen in real life, too. I can see your fears, and I can see the love, Sean. This won't make any sense to you, because it's all just a dream, of course. But I can see all the love that was in you, waiting for me. It has a pinkish sort of glow about it and it's soft and welcoming, like marshmallow. Perhaps I could see it that day. Perhaps that's how I knew.

It's been such a wonderful life, Sean. It's been so much better than I ever imagined things could be, especially for a girl like me.

This is the recording for my twenty-ninth photo, baby, and I think that it's enough. I need to do the initial one as a sort of covering letter – a covering tape, I suppose – to sort of... introduce the whole thing, but after that, I think I'm going to stop.

You know, I was twenty-nine weeks pregnant when we got married. Imagine that! Our beautiful baby daughter was a twenty-nine-week old prawn living in my tummy – actually a pretty huge prawn, by then – and it was enough time for us to know we wanted to spend our entire lives together, wasn't it? So twenty-nine weeks is enough. It's enough for a beginning and it's enough, I reckon, for an end.

I have one more thing to tell you. Actually, maybe I have *two* things to tell you, but I haven't decided about the second one yet. Maybe that's something I'll take with me to the grave.

The first and most important one is about love. It's such an amazing thing to go through life with someone who loves you, Sean. And if anyone knows that, it's me.

As I've been doing all these tapes, I've been thinking more and more – sometimes for days on end – about you and Maggie. I've been trying to decide once and for all whether you had an affair or not.

Some days I've convinced myself that you did. And not only has that made me feel a bit better about my own meandering off the straight and narrow, but I've found myself feeling glad for you. We all need a bit of fun in our lives, after all. We all need some excitement, some adrenalin. This idea that we should get everything we need from a single person seems a bit silly really, when it's put into perspective. And being in my situation really does put things into perspective.

On other days, like today, I'm pretty sure that you didn't. And on these days, I think that not only did nothing happen, but that you never even realised that she's in love with you. I actually think that you may even be a bit in love with Maggie, too, but I'm pretty certain you've never let yourself even think about that, either.

If I'm right – if I'm right today, that is, because I do keep changing my mind – and you do have a thing for each other only you've never spoken about it, then know that I'm not jealous, Sean. I'm really, really not.

Whether she slept with you or not, Maggie is an amazing person. Of course, she's an even better person if she managed to keep her knickers on for all these years, but even if she didn't, she's generous and funny and adventurous, and good-hearted. She really does have more qualities than just about anyone I know, and looking back on things, she's certainly been the best friend *I've* ever had. Well, apart from you, obviously.

So yes, I think that perhaps you two have always been secretly in love with each other. And I don't think that detracts from what we had in any way. We *can* love multiple people, and there's no shame in it either.

If it's true, then please don't waste it, Sean. That's the thing I've been wanting to say.

Nothing could make *me* happier than to know that you're happy with someone as good and as loving as Maggie. And nothing could make me happier than to know that Maggie, finally, got to date someone as wonderful as you. God knows, she's waited long enough, poor girl.

So that's it. I'm done here, my darling. I feel like I've lived my entire life twice. And that's enough for anyone.

Move on now, if you can. I've been fading for almost two years now, and by the time you listen to this, I'll have been gone for almost seven months more.

It's all coming to an end for me, Sean, and know that I've no regrets. It's been a wonderful life, baby. Thanks to you, it's been amazing.

But you still *have* time left on this planet, and that's precious and magical, and miraculous. So, don't waste it, eh? Move on with your life, whether it's alone, or with Maggie, or with someone else. Live every minute of it as if minutes were in limited supply. Because one day, like me, you'll find out that they really were.

If the "other side" does turn out to exist after all, then I'll be there when you arrive; I'll be there to meet you, I promise. And you'll be able to tell me what happened next. And you had better not say "nothing". Because if you've wasted it, I'll make your time in heaven, hell. And you can trust me on that. I just wish I could hang around to do it all with you.

Cassette #29-B

Hello there. Me *again*!

I've been um-ing and ah-ing about this one. I must have changed my mind twenty times about whether to include it or not. But as you know, I've never been very good at goodbyes. I've always had one final thing to say before I close the front door. And without this one, the truth, our truth, would never have been quite complete.

It's about that photo of "us" as kids. Picture number twenty-three or twenty-four, I think it is.

I have a horrible admission to make about that one, Sean.

That photo – the photo you found at Mum's after she died – well, it was *your* photo.

I'd found it in the boxes when we moved to Thoday Street and because Mum had told me about some kid I'd been in love with on holiday and because, like you, I wanted to believe that person was you, I'd taken the photo to show Mum. And I'd forgotten to bring it back.

When Mum died, you found it there – she hadn't tidied properly in years – and you assumed that she had the *same* photo. You were so bowled over by the whole thing that I didn't dare tell you the truth. We'd been through that difficult patch and I was desperately trying to find my way back to you. And the photo provided exactly the excuse we needed.

But the truth was that Mum was useless. I showed her your photo and asked if the girl in the picture was me, and she said that she doubted it. I'd never had dungarees, she said. I'd always been dressed in dresses. And that's true. I remember that. I was forever scraping my knees.

I really wanted to believe, so I begged her to look more closely, to study the surroundings, to look at the swings in the background or the toilet block on the right hand side. I asked her if she remembered that campsite, and she said that, no, she didn't think so. But she really couldn't remember. She didn't even know which boyfriend she'd been with at the time.

So, I'm sorry, again. I've always preferred to believe, like you, that it's possible. I've always chosen to think that maybe that *was* us in the photo, that perhaps we did meet when I was five, that we really might have been in love our whole lives, ever since that picture. But the odds, as Mum said, are against it. Still, eighteen onwards is still pretty good going, isn't it?

Oh, there's one more little story I want to tell you – yes, I know, I know, they keep on coming – but I've just thought of this one, and it seems a good way to end these tapes, if such a thing exists.

Do you remember when Mum died? Do you remember how, after the cremation, I went off for a walk around the graveyard and you found me in tears?

Well, I had come upon a handwritten gravestone – actually, it wasn't stone at all, it was made out of tin, roughly cut to the shape of a heart and painted with black enamel paint. On it, painted by hand, was a poem.

Now, I don't know if it's a well known poem or if it was written by the person who made the love heart, but I thought it was very touching, and I've never ever forgotten it.

It said: To lose someone you really love / is hard beyond belief / Your heart comes close to breaking point / and no one knows the grief / Many times I've thought of you / and many times I've cried / If my love could have saved you / you never would have died.

I wanted you to hear that little ditty, Sean, because it's exactly how I feel.

Just as I was reading the poem, a butterfly came and perched on the edge of the tin heart, and it made me think about the fact that everyone loves butterflies, but even they have to die.

If loving someone was reason enough to be able to stick around, then I'd still be there beside you. And if love was ever enough to save someone's life, then yours would have saved me, too. Because no one ever gave it more easily, or more generously, than you did.

I love you so much, Sean. I've been loved so much, Sean. But it's not enough to change destiny. And it's not enough to fight cancer. So goodbye, baby. And look after April for me. She takes up the half of my heart that isn't taken by you.

Epilogue

It is the fifth of January and Sean has been on holiday for three weeks. All that unused annual leave turned out to be useful in the end.

It's below zero degrees outside, but the snow, repeatedly forecast over the Christmas period, has never arrived. And that's just as well, really. With the exception of Christmas Day, which Sean spent with April in London, he's been doing his best to ignore the whole festive period. And by losing himself in his packing, he has pretty much succeeded.

But now, while cleaning out the loft, he has found that second box of photos, the one Catherine mentioned, and he can't decide whether to tape the lid down and simply move it, unopened, to the new flat, or whether to open it and investigate the contents.

He makes himself a mug of tea, and sips it while he decides. And then, thinking that it's likely to become an obsession if he doesn't look, he removes the lid and tips the contents onto the kitchen table.

The first thing he spots is a letter. It contains the typed results of the DNA test Catherine had mentioned having done. It proves, it says, his paternity of their daughter.

He gently folds this, caresses it and then puts it to one side. He starts to sift through the photos, and here is newborn April looking surprised, and then forward in time to Catherine in the pool in Valencia, and now fast forward again to April proudly leaning on the roof of her first car – a little green Vauxhall Corsa.

Amidst the loose photos is a much older, yellowed album containing photos of Catherine as a baby, then Catherine as a toddler, then Catherine at school.

Sean's eyes are misting now, so he puts these photos to one side. April, who is due to give birth any day, will love them, he thinks. He then re-stacks the remaining photos in the box and tapes down the lid.

Even though she never has anything much to say, Sean phones April regularly. "What have you been up to?" he asks every time.

"Sitting here feeling huge, mainly," she always replies. "I'm so over this whole being pregnant lark."

• • •

The weekend before the move, Sean drives down to Wiltshire to visit his mother.

She's on a new drug regimen but though Perry claims she has more good days than before, Sean has seen little proof of it so far.

When he arrives at The Cedars, she's sitting staring into the middle distance and working her mouth, as usual.

Sean kisses her on the cheek and hugs her frail, rigid body. He asks her if she knows who he is, and she says, shortly, "Of course I know who you are," but then fails to give any further information which might prove this to be so.

Sean sighs deeply and then moves a chair so that he can sit right beside her. "I brought some pictures to show you," he says, sliding a manila envelope from his bag. "I found them in the loft."

He starts with photos of his own childhood. Perry and himself in school uniform. A picture of his father fishing, a photo of the house they grew up in... It's finally a photo of Cynthia, looking youthful and pretty in an evening gown, which provokes the first reaction. She reaches out tremblingly as if to caress the fabric. "Such a pretty dress," she says.

Sean continues to go through the photos but Cynthia only seems interested in the ball gown, at least until he comes to a photo of himself, aged about five on his mother's knee. "He fell in the pond," Cynthia says, causing Sean to pause.

He looks up at her and smiles and says, "Who did? Who fell in the pond?"

"Um?" Cynthia says.

"Who fell in the pond?" Sean asks again.

"Why, Perry did, silly," his mother replies.

"When did Perry fall in a pond, Mum?"

"The day Edward took that," Cynthia says, nodding at the photo. "Don't you remember?"

Sean stares at the photo and struggles to recall the incident. But though he can locate a vague feeling of panic, a sense of urgency that seems to linger in the borders of the image, he's unable to remember the details. "Not really," he finally admits.

"After this one," his mother says quietly, tapping her finger on the photo. "Your father wanted one with both of you. That's when we realised he was missing."

"Right," Sean says, squinting. Perhaps he *does* remember something. Perhaps he remembers being cast aside urgently; perhaps he remembers watching his mother run away from him through the French windows, heading off to save his brother from the duck pond. Or has he just, this instant, manufactured those images to fit the story? It's difficult to say. Memory is such a strange thing.

"So, what about this one?" he asks, nervously sliding a square black and white photo from the pack. "Do you remember this one, Mum?"

He holds the photo out and studies his mother's face and prays for a sign of recognition. "The inseparables," she says. "It's what the French call lovebirds, you know. *Les Inséparables*."

Sean wide-eyes his mother. "Wow," he says. "You *are* with it, today. And this little girl. Do you remember *her* name?" He points at the little girl in the photo, hiding behind her hair. He wills his mother's lips to move. He wills them to say "Catherine."

Cynthia works her mouth as she thinks about this for a moment. Then a shadow crosses her features and her eyes start to water. "No," she says, feebly, "no I don't. It's all gone again."

Sean reaches out and rubs her back. "That's OK, Mum. You're doing really well today. And this was ages ago. Years and years ago."

"Was it?" Cynthia says, sounding confused, sounding frustrated. "It's so misty, that's all. Everything's misty and mixed up. It's all just... *wrong*."

Sean crosses the room and returns with a tissue which he hands to his mother. "That's normal, Mum," he says. "Don't worry."

"... so cold," Cynthia says, as she dabs at her eyes with the tissue.

"You're cold?" Sean asks, glancing over at the radiator which is on full blast. He can feel the heat from here.

"No, in *Cornwall*," Cynthia says, irritatedly. "It was summer, I think, but it was freezing the whole time."

"Gosh, you remember that, do you?" Sean says. "That's amazing."

"Silly little dresses," Cynthia says. "Silly, summer dresses. She was cold all the time, the poor thing."

"The little girl? My friend?"

Cynthia nods. "They were camping, too. With blankets. Not even sleeping bags. *We* had a villa, of course, but *they* were camping. She stayed with us the whole time, really. We dressed her and fed her. It was hardly surprising that she didn't want to go home."

Sean covers his mouth with one hand as he moves the photo closer with the other.

"Show me another one," Cynthia says. "We've done that one."

"OK," Sean replies. "But just... these dungarees she's wearing. In the photo. Were they mine?"

"Of course they were yours," Cynthia replies. "Whose do you think they were? They were too big for her. We had to roll up the bottoms but she still kept tripping over."

Sean chews his bottom lip as he tremblingly pulls another photo from the envelope. "Is this her, Mum?" he asks, putting a different photo of five-year-old Catherine before her eyes. "Is this the little girl?"

Cynthia frowns at the photo. "Well, how should I know?" she says.

"Please look, Mum," Sean pleads. "Just for a moment. Just for me. It's important."

Cynthia frowns at her son as if he's perhaps a little crazy, then returns her gaze briefly to the photo. "*I* don't know," she says, in a petulant tone of voice. "It might be her, it might not be her. Why are you asking me all these questions, anyway?"

Sean sighs and lowers the photo. He runs his hand across his face. "Right," he says, despondently. "Right, it doesn't matter."

"A terrible slattern, though. An awful woman. She was drunk most of the time."

Sean's eyebrows twitch skywards. "Who was?" he asks urgently, suddenly hopeful again. "The little girl's mother?"

Cynthia nods. "A very vulgar woman, she was. Always drinking beer and burping. And giving you money for chips all the time. We didn't want you eating chips. We wanted you to eat proper food."

"Chips?" Sean repeats, starting to smile.

"Yes, chips. There was a chip-shop near the campsite. A fish and chip shop, actually. But all they ever seemed to eat was chips. Your father wasn't happy."

"But we ate a lot of chips? Me and the little girl?"

"Yes. Oh, she was nice enough, I suppose, but the mother, Winnie or Wendy, I think. Yes, that's right. Wendy. *Windy Wendy* your father used to call her. She was a horrible, vulgar woman, always drinking and swearing and eating her horrid chips. Imagine growing up with a mother like that! Lord knows what happened to the little girl. The poor little sod."

• • •

Sean barely makes it to his car before he collapses into tears, before he allows himself to slump onto the steering wheel and weep.

He weeps, first, for his mother, who remembers a fish and chip shop from over forty-five years ago, but can't remember why she's in a nursing home today. He weeps for Catherine, who is gone, who he now knows he has loved since he was seven years old. And finally, he weeps the hottest, angriest tears of all for the fact that it's now too late to tell her that, for the fact that she'll never ever know the biggest miracle of their lives together.

He had known all along, he now sees. Not for the reasons he thought he knew, but yes, he had known all along. Finding the photo at Catherine's mother's house hadn't been the *origin* of the thought, he finally understands. It had been merely a convenient peg to hang the thought upon. Because deep down, yes, he had known. He had always known that they were fusional, that they were meant to be together and that their meeting in Dreamland had been somehow more than mere chance.

Once the tears have faded, he sits, feeling numb, and stares blankly at the misty windscreen.

The final riddle of his life with Catherine has been resolved and, perhaps only now can he truly say that he knew her. He's overcome by a momentary wave of gratitude for that simple, yet majestic privilege. He'd been right when he'd told Catherine that no one ever knew anyone else – not really. And she had heard him and saved that gift of knowing until the very end. And it's a huge gift, perhaps the biggest gift of all.

He's just drying his eyes on the car-cloth when his mobile, in the door-pocket, buzzes.

He sniffs as he glances at the screen for the first time today. "Missed calls: 8" it reads. "Incoming call: Ronan."

• • •

When Sean arrives at the hospital, the first person he sees is Maggie.

She's standing out in the cold sunshine sipping coffee from a plastic cup. "Sean!" she exclaims. "God, they finally got through to you, did they?"

"Yes," Sean says. "Bloody phone was on silent. And how did you manage to get here before me?"

Maggie shrugs. "*My* phone *wasn't* on silent," she says. "Go up and meet him. He's beautiful. I'll be up in a minute."

"He's here? It's all over?"

"Yes, all over bar the shouting," Maggie says. "He's got a good voice on him for shouting, too. You'll see. Go!"

Sean glances at the doorway before looking back at Maggie. "Where is it?"

"Third floor," Maggie says. "Then down the long corridor, turn right where it goes from green to blue, and then room twenty-nine. If you go up the stairs in the corner there, you won't have to pass by reception. She's not the fastest receptionist in the world..."

Sean crosses the lobby, pushes open the door, and then sprints up the staircase. By the time he reaches April's room, his heart is racing.

"Dad!" April exclaims, as he bursts through the door. "You made it!"

Ronan is lounging on the bed beside April, and in her arms, swaddled in a white blanket, is her tiny, newborn child.

Sean freezes at the threshold and stares, in shock, at the scene. Memories of lying next to Catherine on a similar hospital bed momentarily flood his mind.

"Well, come on," April says. "Come and meet Jake."

"I'm so sorry I missed all of this," Sean says, crossing the room. "I was visiting your gran down in Wiltshire."

"I know," April says. "Ronan told me. But it doesn't matter. You're here now."

"I did try to call you," Ronan says. "But there was never any answer."

"Sorry," Sean replies. "Bloody phone was on silent," then, addressing April, "Did you say, *Jake*? I thought it was going to be Jack."

"Oh, I know you're not keen, and we'll change it if you're really dead set against. But we both really like it, don't we?" She glances at Ronan who nods, shrugs and smiles simultaneously.

Sean crouches down at the bedside and reaches out to gently stroke the baby's tiny ear. "Jake's fine," he says softly. "I'll get over it. I already did, actually."

Baby Jake blows a bubble of spittle and half-cries, half-gurgles as he tries to reach for Sean's finger, but April moves him away. "Sorry Dad, but could you wash your hands, do you think? Because this baby sucks *everything*."

"Sure," Sean says. "Of course. I won't be a tick."

By the time Sean gets back from the bathroom, Maggie has returned. "Isn't he beautiful?" she says when Sean re-enters the room.

"He is," Sean agrees. "And he looks exactly like his mother did when she was born."

"Hopefully I wasn't *quite* as blotchy," April says.

"You were exactly as blotchy," Sean tells her. "But don't worry, it soon goes away."

"Thank God for that," April says. "So does he really look like me? Or is that just something everyone feels they have to say?"

"No, he really does," Sean tells her. "You had that same expression on your face. Like you were permanently surprised." He looks from the baby to April and their eyes meet for a moment too long. April sighs and bites her bottom lip and Sean's eyes begin to water, and he knows that they have had the same thought at the same moment – he can sense that they are both missing the same person at the same time. He can feel that they are standing side by side in that moment, peering together into the void of Catherine's absence. Sean swipes at his watery eyes and manages to force a smile and wink at his daughter.

"Have you held him, yet?" Maggie asks, breaking the tension.

Sean clears his throat. "No," he says. "No, I haven't."

Less than ten minutes later a nurse appears, to bustle them from the room. "Rules is rules," she says. "I don't know how you even got in. You can come back at visiting time, but right now, you need to be O.U.T. out!"

In the corridor, Sean lingers, momentarily unsure what to do for the next three hours.

"Coffee?" Maggie suggests. "There's a Costa opposite. And I could do with some food to tell the truth. I think I might faint otherwise."

"Sure," Sean says. "That's a great idea."

The second they are seated, Maggie sinks her teeth into her sandwich, groans with pleasure and then asks, through crumbs, "So how does it feel, Grandpa?"

Sean snorts. "Grandpa," he repeats. "It feels lovely. A bit sad, too, actually. A bit bitter-sweet, you know?"

"Without Catherine here to share it..." Maggie says, understandingly, "it's bound to be."

By way of reply, Sean simply blinks slowly and nods.

"Yes," Maggie says. "That must be hard. That must be *really* hard."

"But they're all fine," Sean says, forcing an up-beat tone. "That's the main thing. April, Ronan, Jake. They're their *own* little family now." He shakes his head as if he can hardly believe it's true.

"April said you didn't much like Jake. As a name, I mean."

Sean sighs and peers into Maggie's eyes. He wonders if she knows the reason why. But the regard that meets his own seems innocent enough. Innocent, naive, warm...

"Did you ever finish those tapes?" Maggie asks, as if she's been listening to his thoughts.

"Yes," Sean says. "Yes, I did, actually."

"Were there any more revelations?"

Sean laughs. "Yes," he says. "Yes, there were quite a few."

Maggie nods. She waits for a moment for Sean to continue, but then visibly realising that he isn't going to, she says, hesitantly, "Right. Well... good. That you finished them, I mean."

"You know..." Sean starts.

"Yes?"

"Oh, nothing," he says, wrinkling his nose. "It's just a silly thing Catherine said."

"No, go on."

Sean shakes his head. "Really!" he says. "Best not."

Maggie tuts and rolls her eyes. "You're such a tease. You always were."

"A tease?"

"Yes, a tease. You know it drives me insane when people start to tell me something and then change their minds. I'll now drive myself mad for weeks trying to guess what it was you were going to say."

"Really?"

"Really."

"OK, then," Sean says. "You asked for it. There was one revelation, as you call them, that involved you, actually."

357

"Me?" Maggie says. "Oh, you mean the supposed affair I had with you? You already told me about that."

"No, she changed her mind about that, actually. She didn't think we'd had an affair after all. Not in the end."

"Oh," Maggie says, softly. "Well, that's a relief. I hated the idea that she'd... you know... thought that the whole time."

"But she did think that you might be in love with me," Sean says, letting the words rush out before he can change his mind.

Maggie frowns at Sean deeply, then opens her mouth to reply before closing it again and glancing towards the door of the cafe instead. Finally, she looks back and says, in a very matter-of-fact tone of voice, "Well, it makes sense, I suppose. Seeing as she thought we had an affair and everything."

"Yes, but like I said, she changed her mind about that. She just thought it was some sort of unrequited love thing between us, I think. Something we'd never dared talk about. Or even thought about, even."

"Really?" Maggie says. She blushes and looks down at her cup and saucer for a moment. She fiddles with her teaspoon. "I'm... I'm not sure quite what to say to that."

"Nothing, I suppose," Sean says with fake disinterest. "I mean there's nothing *to* say, really, is there? Especially if it's not true. Especially if she got that wrong, I mean."

"No," Maggie says, averting her gaze by glancing back at the door again. A young woman is struggling her way through it with a pushchair. Maggie jumps up and crosses the café to help her.

"So!" she says, when she finally returns.

"So," Sean repeats.

Maggie looks at him coyly.

"*Did* Catherine get that wrong?" Sean asks.

"Um?" Maggie says. "Oh... Well, of course she did."

"Oh, OK," Sean says, flatly.

"Morphine," Maggie says, nodding knowingly. "That's what's on those tapes, Sean. I told you. Morphine."

"Right," Sean says, pulling a face. "Actually, don't... please. Don't, you know... reduce them to that."

"No," Maggie says. "No, I'm sorry."

"There was a lot of stuff on those tapes and some of it may have been a bit... a bit wide of the mark, perhaps. But there was also a great deal of truth on them. They were quite amazing, actually."

"I'm sure," Maggie says. "I didn't mean anything."

Sean shakes his head sadly and sighs.

"I didn't mean to upset you, Sean. It's just, well, that came out of left field, that's all."

"It's fine," Sean says. "Really. And it's not you. It's just... regret. You know, there were so many things we never said to each other. So many opportunities wasted. And by the time Catherine put everything out there in the open, well, it was too late, really."

"Too late for what?"

"Too late for us to say the things we *needed* to say, I suppose."

Maggie nods. She reaches across the table for Sean's wrist. "Right," she says. "Well, that's just human, isn't it? We all have lots of things we should have said or *could* have said. Life's all about what might have happened *if*, isn't it? Because there are so many possibilities, aren't there? So many different paths. But you only get to choose one."

Suddenly self-conscious, she pulls her hand sharply back. "That was me comforting you, by the way," she says, in a professorial tone of voice. "Not me being in love with you. Not that at all. Just to be clear."

"Just to be clear," Sean repeats, grinning.

From that point on, the conversation becomes stilted, so they quickly finish their drinks and pull their coats back on.

Outside in the street, they hug rigidly and head off in different directions, Maggie towards the railway station and Sean towards the hospital. He has decided to move the car from the outrageously expensive hospital car park and find a hotel room nearby. He suddenly feels *incredibly* tired. There's been too much emotion for one day, and all he wants to do is find the nearest bed and collapse in it.

As he reaches the car, he hunts for the car keys in his pocket but finds, instead, the lump of rose quartz April gave him. He caresses it fondly, releases it and then pulls his keys from the other pocket. On hearing the clip-clop of heels behind him, he pauses and turns.

"Sean!"

"Maggie," Sean says, smiling lopsidedly. "Sorry, did you want a lift somewhere, or...?"

"No," Maggie says, bending to put her hands on her knees and panting. "So unfit!" she says, then breathlessly, "No, I wanted to ask you something."

"You did?"

"Yes, what you asked me in the cafe," Maggie says, straightening.

"Yes?"

"Was there a reason?"

"I'm sorry? Was there a reason for what?"

"Oh, don't be obtuse, Sean. Was there a reason why you told me that? Of all the things that were on the tapes, that's the thing you chose to tell me. Why was that?"

"Oh," Sean says. "Right. Sorry. Um, I suppose it was just because it implicated you, really."

"It *implicated* me?" Maggie repeats.

"Well, yes. It was about you."

"OK. Right. So, I suppose the question is, did it *implicate* you, Sean?"

"I'm not sure I'm following you."

"Oh, forget it," Maggie says. "This is pointless."

She starts to walk away, but Sean calls her back.

"Maggie!" he says. "Wait." When she turns to face him again, he gestures with open palms and says, "What is all this? I don't understand."

Maggie laughs. "I don't either," she says. "Maybe it's just another one of those missed opportunities we were talking about."

"Missed opportunities?" Sean repeats.

"Perhaps. Look. God, this is so difficult... But, what the hell... The question is, I suppose, what would it change, Sean?"

"What would what change?"

"What would it change if I'd said 'yes' instead of 'no'?"

Sean's features shift to a mixture of confusion and embarrassment. 'Why?" he says. "Is that something you think you might have said?"

"Just... answer the question, Sean," Maggie says irritatedly. "What would it have changed if that were the case?"

"What, you mean, if... if you'd said you were, a bit..."

"Yes," Maggie interrupts. "Please stop making this so bloody difficult, would you? What would it change if, theoretically speaking, I'd admitted to... I don't know... to... perhaps... liking you, let's say, more than I should."

"More than you should?" Sean repeats.

"Yes."

"Theoretically?" Sean says, through laughter.

"Yes, *theoretically*. And don't *laugh* at me. This isn't easy, Sean."

"No," Sean says, forcing a circumspect expression. "No, not laughing at all, here, Mags. Um. Well, speaking theoretically," he continues, "I suppose…" He rolls his eyes skywards, desperately searching for inspiration, for clarity. "I mean, I'm not ready. I'm not ready for anything."

"Well, no, obviously you're not."

"But later, perhaps, somewhere down the line… If that were to be true, I mean, if you did like me, *more than you should*, then perhaps that *might* change things."

"Right."

"That might change quite a lot of things, I suppose."

Maggie narrows her eyes. "Do you mean in a good way. Or a bad way?"

Sean shrugs. "In a good way, I think. Yeah. I mean, like I say, I'm not ready, right now, for anything. But, potentially. Theoretically. In the long run. Yes, it *might* change things. It might change things in a very good way indeed."

THE END

The Other Son

A novel by Nick Alexander

Selected by Amazon as one of the best fiction titles of the year.

From Nick Alexander, the author of the #1 ebook hits, *The Photographer's Wife*, *The Half-Life of Hannah* and *The French House*.

Alice has been lying to herself for years, holding fast to the belief that the needs of her family far outweigh her own.

But her outwardly successful marriage hides dark secrets, and for much of her life, the children were the only reason she stuck around.

These days, though her successful banker son lives nearby, his young wife seems to do everything she can to keep Alice at bay. As for Alice's other son, he has always been something of a stranger and has been traveling for so long that Alice isn't even sure what continent he is on anymore.

Alice can't help but wonder if the effort she expends presenting a united front to the outside world is actually helping anyone and what would happen if she suddenly stopped pretending.

Could life, like the novels she devours, hold surprises in its closing chapters? And if she did shake everything up by admitting the truth about her marriage, would anyone be on her side? Has the time finally come for Alice to put her own needs first?

For the first time in years, her heart is racing. Can Alice really change her life?

Dare she even imagine such a thing?

The Photographer's Wife

A novel by Nick Alexander

A number #1 hit. Over 180,000 copies sold.

From the author of *The French House*, *The Half-Life of Hannah* and *The Case of The Missing Boyfriend*, Nick Alexander's #1 bestseller, *The Photographer's Wife*, is an epic tale set in two eras, a tale of the secrets one generation has, rightly or wrongly, chosen to hide from the next.

Barbara – a child of the Blitz – has more secrets than she cares to admit. She has protected her children from many of the harsh realities of life and told them little of the poverty of her childhood, nor of the darker side of her marriage to one of Britain's most famous photographers.

With such an incomplete picture of the past, her youngest, Sophie, has struggled to understand who her parents really are, and in turn, Barbara sometimes worries, to build her own identity.

When Sophie decides to organise a vast retrospective exhibition of her adored father's work, old photos are pulled from dusty boxes. But with them tumble stories from the past, stories and secrets that will challenge every aspect of how Sophie sees her parents.

Lightning Source UK Ltd.
Milton Keynes UK
UKOW04f0913131117
312658UK00001B/209/P